"You do not believe me," Alexander stated.

"I do not know how to do so," Lillis replied.

Fury surged through him—hot, deep, encompassing. He was the lord of Gyer. His word was sacred. It had *never* been questioned.

"You will learn it." Alexander seethed, beyond knowing what he spoke.

Lillis gazed at him as if he were some poor idiot, as if she pitied him.

"I shall see you at the evening meal," he said curtly, moving toward the door.

"I'll not come for the evening meal," she declared. "I will eat in my chamber. Let your cousin play lady for you."

"You will come down to table of your own free will," he said, "or I shall come and fetch you. Either way, you will sit in your place as Lady Gyer. Believe me, madam wife, you will...."

Dear Reader,

Susan Paul may be a newcomer to Harlequin Historicals, but her unforgettable medieval tale, *The Bride's Portion*, should have our readers asking for more from this talented author. Her hero is a knight who is forced to kidnap and marry the daughter of a neighboring lord in order to prevent the destruction of his own holdings. A course of action that puts him into the most serious of conflicts with the daughter, the heroine.

And from native Nebraskan Cheryl St.John, whose first book was published in our 1994 March Madness promotion, look for this month's *Land of Dreams*, a Western that has earned the author her third Gold 5 ★★★★★ from *Heartland Critiques* in as many books. Don't miss this heartwarming tale of hope and love.

And be sure to pick up our other two titles this month wherever Harlequin Historicals are sold: *Pearl Beyond Price*, the second book in Claire Delacroix's Unicorn Series about the descendants of the lost kings of France, and *The Heart's Wager*, a sequel to Gayle Wilson's first book, *The Heart's Desire*. We hope you enjoy them all.

Sincerely,

Tracy Farrell
Senior Editor

Please address questions and book requests to:
Harlequin Reader Service
U.S.: 3010 Walden Ave., P.O. Box 1325, Buffalo, NY 14269
Canadian: P.O. Box 609, Fort Erie, Ont. L2A 5X3

SUSAN PAUL

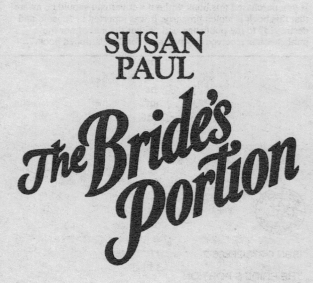

The Bride's Portion

Harlequin Books

TORONTO • NEW YORK • LONDON
AMSTERDAM • PARIS • SYDNEY • HAMBURG
STOCKHOLM • ATHENS • TOKYO • MILAN
MADRID • WARSAW • BUDAPEST • AUCKLAND

ISBN 0-373-28866-2

THE BRIDE'S PORTION

Copyright © 1995 by Mary Liming.

SUSAN PAUL

lives in Duarte, California, with her husband, two young daughters, two dogs and two cats. She started her first novel when she was in her early teens, but eventually put it aside, unfinished, in favor of more important interests...such as boys. Now happily married and—somewhat—settled down, she's returned to her love of the written word and finds it much easier to finish the books she starts.

Dedicated with love and thanks to
Margot Anne Hoyt. A lot of years have passed
since we were eleven, Margot, but during all of them
you've been a constant source of encouragement and
faith. I wouldn't be writing today if it weren't for
you. I'm so glad that out of all the people in this
world, I'm the one who's able to call you my
best friend.

Chapter One

England, early Fall—1405

The chamber was both cold and dark, save for one greasy candle that sat glowing on a small table, putting more smoke than light into the damp air.

"They might at least have lit the fireplace," Lillis said, rubbing her arms in a vain effort to warm herself. "Those wretched boys! Putting us in this filthy room as though we were criminals. I suppose they thought we might escape from someplace clean."

She paced the dark room, careful not to stub her toe on one of the many pieces of furniture there. It must have been a bedchamber once, for there was a large fireplace on one side of the room and a locked balcony and windows on the other. Now it appeared to be used as a storing place for unused furniture. Some of the pieces were covered to keep the dust off and some were left as they were. When Lillis and her maid had first been shoved inside, they had been horrified at the number of rats that ran to their hiding places and at the thick dust that pervaded the room. But they were grateful at least to have chairs to sit in and a table to rest their hands on. There was even an old, lumpy bed on which they could sleep if they needed to, though the rats had done a good job of removing a great many of the mattress feathers.

How many hours had they been locked in here, now? she wondered, rubbing her hands harder to keep from shivering. It had been early morn when those horrid twins had so suddenly leapt out of the woods at them, aiming readied crossbows at the heads of her two guards. Her first reaction had been to scold them as thoughtless rascals who should be greatly punished for playing such frightening tricks on innocent travelers, but when she'd seen that they were serious about what they were doing, the anger had died on her lips. She had been a little afraid of them then, for they certainly must have been demented to have done such a thing in earnest.

By the time they had dragged Lillis and her companion to the castle they were now imprisoned in, however, she had reverted to her original conclusion. The wretched creatures were far from insane. Oh, no, they were worse than that. They saw themselves as righteous crusaders who had captured an enemy. When Lillis made the mistake of informing them that they were being perfectly foolish, that she was Lillis of Wellewyn and that Wellewyn had no fight with them or anyone else, they had simply become happier about what they'd done.

Rotten little beasts.

The worst part of this nightmare was that she didn't even know where she was. It had been years since Lillis had been home, and she didn't recognize either the area they had ridden through or the castle she'd been taken to. The twins had refused to tell her and hadn't let her guards speak, so neither Lillis nor her companion had the slightest idea where they were, or how far away Wellewyn was.

And they'd not had a chance to see much of the castle to which they'd been brought, either. She and Edyth had barely dismounted before the twins had separated them from their guards and had dragged them through the castle and up several flights of stairs to an obviously unused portion of the household.

"You cannot mean to keep us in here!" she'd protested after they'd been shoved inside the filthy room. "I demand to see the lord of this castle!"

"Our brother isn't home," one of them stated with obvious satisfaction, "but you may be certain we'll tell him you're here as soon as he returns."

They had gone, oblivious to her pounding on the door and the furious threats she'd shouted at them. Many hours had passed and no one had come, not even to bring them water. Edyth, fortunately, had come across a few old tallow candles and a flint box. The room had been dark to begin with, though a little light made its way through the boarded windows before the sky darkened and it began to rain. By now the room would have been black as pitch were it not for the dim light of the candle, and Lillis tried to be as grateful for that as she could. But they were very cold and very hungry and very frightened. As the hours crawled by she began to wonder if the fiends hadn't forgotten all about them and gone on to their next amusement. Some months from now, when the lady of the castle needed extra chairs for company at Christmas, someone would come to this room and find two skeletons sitting companionably side by side around the table.

Lillis shuddered and tried to put *that* thought out of her mind. If someone didn't come by daybreak she and Edyth would simply have to do something drastic. What, she didn't know, but something. In the meantime she kept herself busy with thoughts of what she was going to say to the lord of this place when she finally got a chance to do so. Yes, indeed, she was going to enjoy giving him a few well thought out ideas she had concerning the respective futures of his two brothers.

She only hoped that, when the man returned from wherever he was, he would immediately put things to right. Surely he would! He was certain to be as horrified at what his brothers had done as she was, and he would be bound by duty to severely punish the beasts. She could almost feel sorry for the poor man, burdened with such troublesome pests. But that was his concern, not hers. What mattered to Lillis was getting out of this place and home to Wellewyn as quickly as possible.

Wellewyn! Lillis clasped and unclasped her hands with anxiety as she took another turn around the room. Her father would be sick with worry because she had not yet arrived. Already they were a day late in getting there, having been delayed by the bad weather, and now they would be even later. Father would be outraged when he learned of her treatment at the hands of a neighboring lord's siblings. She wouldn't be surprised if he did indeed go to King Henry and demand their heads.

"It must still be raining." Edyth broke into Lillis's thoughts with her soft, sad voice. She sat at the table, sniffling and pressing a tear-soaked handkerchief to her eyes.

Lillis looked at her companion with affection. Poor Edyth! What a terrible ordeal this had been for her. Lillis had spent the better part of the afternoon trying to comfort and reassure her weeping maid. The older woman had been with her for as long as Lillis could remember, and she well knew her to be a timid, easily frightened soul.

"Yes, I believe it must be," Lillis agreed, still rubbing her arms. "It makes the room very damp, does it not?" She crossed the room and put her hands reassuringly on Edyth's shoulders. "It will not be much longer, dear. Someone is sure to come and set us free."

"Do you really think so?" Edyth asked hopefully.

"Why, of course," Lillis assured her without much belief in her own words. "We haven't really been here that long. It only seems so because we've not had a way to tell the time." How long had they been there? she wondered.

"Did—did you see the way the people looked at us when we rode through the village?" Edyth asked in a quavering voice. They'd not yet spoken of what had happened to them that day, other than to comment on the unbelievable behavior of the two boys.

"Yes. It was most odd. It was as if they hated us, though God above knows there is no cause." She paused, then continued thoughtfully, "If only we knew where we were. What kind of place is this that they allow their children to roam free and bring home stray prisoners to lock in filthy rooms?"

Edyth turned to look up at her mistress. "It is strange, is it not? And yet the castle seemed well kept. Everything was so clean and fine."

Lillis nodded. "Yes, I saw that, too, though we hardly got a chance to notice much the way those two rushed us up here. But it would seem that the castle is well managed. I cannot, for the life of me, imagine why any kind of responsible people would allow something like this to happen. It is really quite...abnormal."

She could feel Edyth's shoulders stiffen beneath her hands. "Oh, Lillis! We never should have left the convent! We never should have gone traveling with only two men to guard us! What will happen to us now?"

Edyth broke into fresh wails and Lillis did what she could to calm her. She barely had time to quiet her companion before they heard footsteps approaching and saw a light shine beneath the door. Edyth's crying ceased only because she was too frightened to make any sound, and Lillis struggled to keep her own fears under control. She tightened her grip encouragingly on Edyth's shoulders and stood as tall and straight as she could.

"Courage, Edyth," she admonished as a key rattled and the door's lock turned. "Courage."

A demon walked through the door to greet them, or so it seemed. It was a large, dark man, girded about in armor, his face hidden in the shadows, who made the first steps into the room. He dripped with wetness, and the light coming in behind him caused him to look more unearthly. Lillis, already trembling with abject fear, watched him enter the room with real terror. He looked like a specter, and after the day she'd already spent she wouldn't have been surprised if he had announced that he was such.

Edyth wilted beneath her hands and Lillis shook her imperceptibly while the ghostly figure approached. She was thankful that it spoke first, since she had lost her own voice.

"Who are you, lady?"

Lillis trembled at the harshness of his words.

"Who are *you,* sir?" she asked shakily.

"I am the lord of this castle," the ghost responded, his image now fading into that of a man.

"Oh" was all Lillis could say for a moment. So! *This* was the man she had been waiting for. What a frightening phantom he made! "Sir," she said more steadily, "I am Lillis Ryon of Wellewyn, and this is my companion, Edyth Lielyn. I fear your brothers have made a serious mistake."

For the first time she saw that others had entered the room behind him. The man alone came closer, becoming more and more human in the light of the candle.

"Your father is Jaward, Lord of Wellewyn?" he asked, looking at her intently.

At this closer distance Lillis could see the haggard expression on the man's face, though she could not tell whether he was young or old.

"He is," she said, and lifted her chin.

It was difficult to tell what his reaction to this was. He stared at her quietly, looking directly into her eyes, and Lillis returned his stare and wished she could think of something to say. This wasn't how he was supposed to behave. He was supposed to be groveling at her feet and begging her forgiveness for the treatment she and Edyth had received in his home. He wasn't supposed to be standing there and staring at her as though trying to decide what kind of animal she was.

Those who had also entered the room gathered behind him, their faces eerily illuminated by the glow of torchlight. Lillis was surprised to see a matronly woman among them.

"My lord—" Lillis began, then stopped abruptly when she noticed that the twins were there, standing to the side of their brother, their arms folded across their chests, smiling at her with smug satisfaction.

"You two!" Lillis snapped, pointing at them. "You wretched, miserable fiends!" She looked back to the lord of the castle, who had ceased his thoughtful staring and now looked at her with some amazement. "My lord," Lillis spoke curtly, "these two misbegotten devils waylaid my companions and myself on the open road this morn and brought us to your castle by force. They have locked my maid and me in this filthy chamber all day and have not even had the human kindness to bring us food or water. I cannot begin to imagine what they've done with my two guards.''

"They're all right," one of the boys answered sourly. "Sir Alan has them under guard in the men's quarters."

"Then they've probably received better care than you have spared us," Lillis informed him hotly. "Did you not think at all about the two women whom you'd locked up all day? Did you not consider that we might be cold and hungry in this miserable place?'' She indicated the room with a sweep of one hand.

The twins made no reply, but the lord of the castle said quietly, "You speak truly, my lady. Your treatment at the hands of my brothers has been unforgivable. I promise you they shall be punished."

"But... Alex!" one of the twins protested.

"Quiet!" the lord commanded, his steely voice bringing utter silence to the chamber. He returned his attention to Lillis and spoke more evenly. "I beg your pardon, my lady, as well as the pardon of your maid." He nodded in Edyth's direction. "I have only just returned to the castle, else you would have been released sooner. My aunt—" he indicated the plump figure behind him "—had no knowledge that you were here, and learned of it only now, just as I, and the rest of my castlefolk, did. Had she known, my lady, you would have been well cared for, and never subjected to such as this. I pray you will believe me."

"We had wondered, my lord."

He inclined his head. "That is understandable, but all will be made well, I vow. You shall be taken to a suitable chamber to spend the night and all of your needs will be tended to immediately. In the morn we will see what is to be done."

"I thank you, my lord," Lillis replied, "but that is not necessary. If you will return my guards and our horses, we will leave this place at once."

He gazed at her unwaveringly.

"I am sorry," he said, "you cannot leave tonight. But do not fear for your guards. I will make certain that their comfort, as well as yours, is provided for."

"No," Lillis returned firmly. "That will not suffice. We will leave tonight. Please have our mounts made ready and our belongings returned to us."

The breath that came from him sounded like a sigh, and a weary one at that. "You cannot leave tonight, my lady," he repeated. "The wind howls outside like the Fiend himself, and the rain pours in rivers. I would be less than human were I to send any lady into such weather, especially in the darkness." His tone changed slightly, growing more persuasive. "Come, accept my hospitality and we will speak with one another in the morn."

Lillis tried to control her voice, to force it to speak with an obedient calm. "My lord, I am grateful for your consideration, but pray do not concern yourself with our welfare. The weather will indeed be an inconvenience, but I promise you that we would far rather face it than spend a night enjoying your kind hospitality. We have enjoyed enough of it already this day."

There was a gasp, followed by shrill words. "Alexander! Will you let her speak to you in such a manner? She is churlish and rude!"

"Silence, Aunt Leta," he commanded quietly, and the room fell still again. So still that Lillis thought she could hear the frantic pounding of her heart.

"My lady of Wellewyn," he spoke with unnerving softness, "let us have an understanding. I assure you that you will not leave here tonight."

Lillis felt Edyth trembling violently beneath her hands, and she licked her dry lips.

"We *will*," she insisted.

"You will not."

Lillis understood him, could hear in the tone of his voice exactly what he meant. They were prisoners. She wanted to give way to the fear that struck her so fiercely, but she wouldn't. She would *not*. Instead, she demanded, "What is your name, sir, and what place is this?"

He seemed surprised at her question, as though she should know where she was and to whom she spoke.

"This is Gyer, my lady, and I am Alexander Baldwin, the Lord of Gyer."

He spoke the words with such meaning and expectancy that Lillis felt even more unsettled. He was watching her for some kind of reaction and seemed dissatisfied that she had none.

"You do not know of Gyer," he stated.

"I have not been home for more than ten years, Alexander of Gyer, but I do have some small memory from my childhood of a place called Gyer. Is it not a neighboring fief to Wellewyn?"

He gave her no answer, but turned to address those behind him.

"They will stay in Mother's chamber. Aunt Leta, send servants with food and drink. Tell them to give these ladies whatever they require."

"Your mother's chamber, Alexander? It isn't right!"

"It will be as I say," he answered curtly. "Go now. Willem and I will escort the ladies to their chamber." He looked at the twins. "Wait for me below," he said in a voice that made them leave the room at once.

Lillis and Edyth found themselves alone with Alexander of Gyer and the man named Willem.

"You will come with us," the Lord of Gyer stated rather than asked.

Edyth shook her head and clutched Lillis's hands. "Oh, no, my lady!" she sobbed. "They are going to hurt us! They are going to kill us!"

Lillis bent to put her arms around her companion's trembling form. "Now, my dear, they're going to do no such thing. They shall take us to a very nice chamber—" she sent an angry glare at the Lord of Gyer, who nodded "—and we shall eat until we are full and then we will rest."

"I—I am very hungry," Edyth whimpered, shuffling toward the open door.

The man named Willem carried a torch to light their way, but when they reached the first stair Edyth stumbled. Lillis moved to hold her up, then was surprised to find that the Lord of Gyer had also reached out a steadying hand.

"Let me," he murmured, prepared to help the older woman down the stairs. But he had made a mistake. When Edyth realized, even in her weakened state, whose hand it was that grasped her arm, she shrank against her mistress in a state of full distress.

"Don't touch her!" Lillis warned, stopping on the step and enclosing Edyth in a strong embrace. Her trembling maid fell against her and wept.

Alexander of Gyer stared at her.

"Are you a knight, Alexander of Gyer?" Lillis asked angrily.

His face registered shock. "Yes."

"Then I hope you pray well to God tonight."

He understood her meaning, she saw, but said not a word, only nodded and turned to lead the way down the stairs.

It took some time to reach their destination, Lillis having to help Edyth every step of the way, but finally they stopped in front of a door that opened to a beautiful chamber, as clean and orderly as their previous chamber had been filthy and disorderly. Lillis guided Edyth inside, relieved to see that a fire was already burning in the fireplace and that candles had been set out for illumination.

"Someone will come to see to your needs," Alexander of Gyer said. Finally Lillis looked at him. He appeared different in the full light, bigger and more formidable. He was wet and obviously tired, and his heavy armor looked uncomfortable. He was younger than she had originally thought.

"We will speak in the morn, my lady. I will wish you a good eve until then."

Making a slight bow, he turned and left, the man named Willem trailing behind him. The door closed with a thud, and Lillis heard the unmistakable sound of the lock being turned.

Chapter Two

"Here you are," Willem said as he stuck his head through the door. "I should have known where you'd be when you didn't appear for the morning meal."

Alexander looked up from the table at which he sat and gave Willem a brief smile. "Come and keep me company." He nodded at a chair across from him. "I fear I slept ill last night and rose earlier than usual. Cook fed me some bread and cheese in the kitchen."

Frowning, Willem strolled across the room. "You do look tired, Alex. This matter with Wellewyn wears on you, and I imagine our...*guests* trouble you, as well. Have you decided what you'll do with them?"

Alexander shook his head and lifted one hand to rub his tired eyes. Slept ill last night? In truth, he'd not slept at all. Coming home to find Lillis of Wellewyn a captive in his home had left him in shock, and he had lain awake, staring into the darkness and wondering what he should do with her. He had several choices, and not a one of them ideal.

He could send Jaward a missive, letting him know that his daughter was being kept at Gyer, and could word it in such a way that no obvious threat would be implied, or he could come right out and tell Jaward to meet his terms else his only child would suffer. The problem with the latter was that Jaward would probably realize Alexander didn't possess the meanness to actually hurt a woman; the problem with the former was that Jaward would simply go to the king and petition his aid in having his daughter returned. Holding

Lillis of Wellewyn certainly seemed like a good way of getting what he wanted from the old man, but Alexander wasn't yet sure how to go about using her to his advantage.

"No," he answered at last, leaning back in his chair. "I've not yet decided what I'm going to do. I've instructed Aunt Leta to bring the lady to me after she and her companion have breakfasted. I thought I would see what she knows about her father's activities. Any information she can give us will be helpful. *If* she has any information that she's willing to give."

Willem was quiet for a moment, then said, "She's very beautiful, is she not?"

A glance at his younger brother showed that Willem was carefully inspecting his knees, his face having turned red, and the sight made Alexander grin. Willem was one of the bravest men Alexander had ever known, especially in battle, yet for all that he was painfully shy of women. Merely mentioning that he found a lady to be beautiful made him blush.

"Yes, she is," Alexander agreed. "Most beautiful. Not at all what I expected after seeing Jaward."

Not at all what he'd expected, regardless of Jaward. Alexander had walked into that chamber last night and found himself faced with a woman unlike any he had ever before seen. She was certainly the tallest woman he had ever met with, and she had the blondest hair he'd ever seen, as well. She had looked like a shining angel in the glow of the candlelight. Even her brows were blond, causing her blue eyes to stand out quite noticeably. Alexander had been able to see the light blueness of them right through the dark. Her features were fine, with high cheekbones and a full mouth complementing her pale, white skin. He remembered her hands—strong hands, beautiful, with long, shapely fingers that looked as though they could mete out a great deal of pain—or pleasure.

"Have you decided upon a punishment for the twins, at least?" Willem pressed. "They're already in the village crowing about their deed to any and all who will listen. Did you know that?"

Alexander gave a sigh, which sounded as tired as he felt. "I know, Willem. God alone knows how well I know. And no, I've not decided what I'll do with them, either. Most of the castlefolk and, I suspect, most of my people, believe I should give them a hero's reward for what they've done. If I punish them as they deserve I'll have a hundred and more unhappy voices ringing in my ears."

"And if you don't punish them," Willem returned, "you'll have Hugh and Hugo spending all of their days waylaying travelers on the main road and bringing them back to Gyer as prisoners."

"I know, I know," Alexander repeated, lifting one palm in the air in a gesture of helplessness. "But what can I do? Nothing seems to stop them. No punishment, no amount of deprivation, no efforts to make them see the error of their ways. The truth, Willem—" Alexander met his brother's eyes "—is that when Father spoiled those two, he did it for all eternity. Sometimes I wonder if we shouldn't all of us accept that fact and simply try to live with it as best we can."

"We could always foster them," Willem suggested. "At least we'd be rid of them for a couple of years."

Alexander made a smirk. "Willem," he chided, "you know as well as I that the twins will never make knighthood. Fostering them with a master who could train them for that purpose would be utterly foolish. Aside from that, I doubt anyone would take them."

"If you offered sufficient payment—"

"It wouldn't matter," Alexander cut him off. "I could probably offer every groat I possess and it wouldn't be enough. God knows no one could ever pay *me* enough to take those two on if I didn't already have to keep them out of familial responsibility. And," he added morosely, "you know full well that Father forbade me from ever causing Hugh and Hugo to do what they didn't wish, and although I deeply regret having made him that foolish promise, I must abide by it."

The door to the chamber was flung open so suddenly that it caused both men to start. Lillis of Wellewyn, breathtakingly lovely in a dress of light blue silk that matched the color of her eyes, strode into the room as if she had every right to do so without first being invited. Aunt Leta came puffing in behind her, unable to keep up with the taller woman. Both men quickly rose to their feet.

Lillis of Wellewyn, chin held high, stopped in front of Willem and Alexander and opened her mouth to speak, then, with a look of bewilderment, shut it again. She looked from one man to the other, then back again, with a frown. Finally she settled her searching gaze on Alexander and stared at him for a long, assessing moment. He held very still as her blue eyes moved over him, from his face all the way down to his booted feet. When she looked into his face once more her expression was resolved.

"My lord—" she began curtly, but was interrupted.

"I have never known such ill-mannered behavior in all my life!" Aunt Leta exclaimed with indignation. "She would not follow or even wait for me! She went storming down the hallways and I barely had time to tell her which direction to take. One would think she'd been raised as a heathen rather than as a lady!"

Lillis of Wellewyn did not turn her gaze from Alexander's, and he thought he saw a small, amused smile play on her lips. It vanished as soon as it came, unlike her defiant glare.

"Thank you, Aunt Leta," Alexander said dismissively.

Aunt Leta stamped her foot in displeasure, and Alexander glanced at her.

"Thank you, Aunt Leta," he repeated. His aunt angrily pursed her lips and left.

Not hearing a request from Willem to be excused, as he expected, Alexander looked and saw, with amusement, that his brother was gaping in stunned silence at the beautiful lady before them.

"My lady, I trust you passed a pleasant night?" Alexander inquired, turning his eyes to her again. She truly was quite stunning, he thought, even when she was angered. "May I make my brother known to you? This is Sir Willem Baldwin. I regret we had no moment for such courtesies last eve."

To his surprise, the lady lost her basilisk stare, turned to his brother, graced him with a pleasant smile, and said, "Oh, we did wonder who you were, sir, though we knew your name was Willem. I am pleased to meet you."

Willem turned bright red. His mouth opened and closed several times but no sound came out. Finally, painfully, he managed to sputter, "I am . . . *honored,* my l-lady."

"Thank you, Sir Willem," she rejoined politely, then turned to Alexander again and promptly regained her angry glare.

"I believe we have some few matters to discuss, Alexander of Gyer," she informed him, as though their meeting had been her idea and without a hint of the gentleness with which she'd just treated Willem.

"Yes, we do," Alexander agreed, suppressing the odd, vague jealousy that tickled the edge of his thoughts. With a hand, he indicated the chair Willem had vacated. "Please sit, my lady. Willem, will you do me the favor of seeing to any matters that the tenants might need settled this morn?"

Willem was still staring at the lady Lillis, but Alexander's words brought him back to life. "Of course—of course, Alex. Very glad to—to take care of that for you." He bent a clumsy bow in Lillis of Wellewyn's direction, then left the room at a near run.

Once his brother was gone, Alexander took a moment to gather his thoughts. He didn't cherish the position he found himself in. How did one go about telling another person that she was his prisoner?

"I hope you found your chamber comfortable, my lady?"

"Very," she replied coldly.

"And how is your maid this morn? Edyth is her name, I believe?"

"She is fine, thank you. Frightened and unsettled, but otherwise well."

Alexander nodded. So, now he was reduced to frightening frail, elderly women out of their wits. The foreign feeling disgusted him, and he wondered how he was going to be able to carry out any of this. He'd understood Lillis of Wellewyn only too well when she had asked whether he was a knight. He had taken a knightly vow to serve God, to defend his country, and to protect and cherish the fairer sex. He certainly was failing in the latter! And yet, he thought, keeping Gyer out of war was worth breaking every vow he had ever made.

"I'm sorry for that. I assure you that my intention is not to frighten or upset either your maid or yourself. Please believe that you will both be treated with respect and consideration while you are here."

"How very kind you are, my lord," she replied icily, "but as I told you last eve, we merely wish to take our leave of Gyer as soon as possible. We have enjoyed quite enough of your hospitality."

Alexander chose his next words carefully. "Again, my lady, I am sorry. It will be necessary for you to remain at Gyer for the time being."

He was prepared for a typically female reaction to this statement: crying, screaming, wailing. He was not prepared for Lillis of Wellewyn's reaction. She regarded him coolly, very little emotion showing on her face.

"You appear to be a reasonable man, Alexander of Gyer," she said, much of the chill gone from her tone. "I cannot be certain, of course, but I do not think you are either insane or inherently evil, so there must be good cause for what you are doing. I would appreciate it, my lord, if you will explain the matter to me."

Alexander was almost as shocked by her calm response as he'd been by the lady's looks. Any other female of his acquaintance would now be in a puddle of tears at his feet. But if Lillis of Wellewyn could behave calmly and reasonably, so much the better for all concerned.

"You said last night that you had not been home for many years. I think perhaps you may be unaware of your father's recent activities. Is this so?"

"My father?" she repeated with surprise. "No, I do not know what his activities are. Even had I been living at home I might not know, for he has ever been private about the management of the estate. Has he—has he done something wrong?"

Alexander regarded her for a moment, then said, "About six months ago your father built a dam on the Eel River, cutting off the main water supply to Gyer. I do not know why he did it, only that he did and that he will not negotiate with me regarding it. As you can imagine, my people have suffered a great deal because of this. Most of their crops have been ruined and now they are wondering how they will survive the coming winter, how they will put bread on their table. I am a wealthy man, my lady—" he shrugged "—and will not hesitate to make certain that my vassals and villeins are cared for, but that will not solve the problem of next year's crops, and of the years after that. One way or another, by truce or by war, the dam your father built must be torn down. The thought of war is not a happy one for me, but I can see no other course while your father remains so stubborn."

She had grown still while he spoke. Her eyes had widened and now she stared at him in utter shock. "I had no idea," she whispered. "I swear I did not." Her expression pleaded with him to believe her, and he did. "It is no wonder that the people of Gyer received us so angrily yesterday," she continued, as though speaking to herself. "They must have seen that our guards wore my father's colors and realized we were from Wellewyn. After what my father has done, I cannot blame them. But *why?* Why would he do it?"

"I don't know," he answered. "I had hoped you might be able to tell me, or give me some clue, but I see that you are as much in the dark as I. Your father has proved immeasurably stubborn in the matter. I've tried everything I know of, from offering money to making threats, but he'll not be swayed. Yesterday I rode to Wellewyn to make him a final offer and he practically threw me out of that rotting pigsty he dares to name castle."

She frowned at him, and Alexander belatedly realized what he'd said, how basely he'd insulted her home. "Forgive me, my lady. That was mean spirited of me."

"I understand, Alexander of Gyer. You are very upset and have every right to be. What my father has done is unforgivable." Still frowning, she looked away from him.

Alexander gazed at the penitently bowed head of his captive and knew an unbidden desire to comfort her. She seemed genuinely unhappy about what her father had done; it would have been cruel for him to turn his anger with Jaward upon that man's innocent daughter.

"You are not to blame for this, Lillis of Wellewyn. I believe you had no knowledge of your father's deeds."

She gazed at him fully, causing his heart to know a strange agitation. "I did not know," she promised, "but now that I do, I vow I shall do all I can to have the dam torn down. Have you not petitioned the king regarding it?"

He shook his head. "That is the beauty of your father's scheme. It is perfectly legal, the dam having been built on his land, or rather, on your land. If I ride into Wellewyn to tear it down, I am the one who will attract the king's wrath—for trespassing on another man's property."

She seemed confused. "Why do you call it my land? No part of Wellewyn is mine."

"But it shall be, my lady, when you wed next month. Your father took particular delight in informing me that, even if he wished to do so, he could not sell the land on which the dam is built because it is part of your bride's portion. The only man who will have power over that land will be your future husband, the Lord of Dunsted."

"Then I shall have the dam torn down when I am wed," she declared, though somewhat uneasily. She seemed to become more embarrassed with each new revelation, and Alexander wondered if she had ever been aware that she had a claim to the lands of Wellewyn.

"That would be ideal," Alexander admitted, "however, your father made it clear that he'd had the choice of the man you shall wed, and that he and Jason de Burgh have an excellent understanding between them. You do know that Dunsted is directly to the south of Gyer, do you not?"

Again she looked surprised. "No, I did not, though when my father wrote to tell me of my marriage, he said I should live close to Wellewyn. That is one of the reasons I agreed to it. Are you not . . . friendly with my future husband?''

A bitter laugh escaped him. ''Not the least bit friendly, though God knows I have tried time and again to come to terms with the man. There is a strip of land bordering Gyer and Dunsted that the people of both fiefs have disputed the ownership of for many years. The land belongs to Gyer, but Jason de Burgh and his are so stubborn over the matter that they refuse to give way. They insist on making pests of themselves by visiting raids on Gyer, while my people retaliate in kind, regardless of my efforts to stop them. I've tried to meet with de Burgh in an effort to come to some kind of settlement, but he persistently refuses to see me.'' He drew in a taut breath, then released it. ''I think your father has somehow convinced him that a war with Gyer would be profitable for them both, though God only knows what a madness that is.'' Alexander rubbed his eyes again and felt weary.

''But this is dreadful,'' she whispered, her lovely face gone pale.

''Yes, it is,'' Alexander agreed. ''With Wellewyn to the north and Dunsted to the south, I shall have quite a noose around my neck, shall I not? The worst part of the scheme is that I am the one who will be forced to declare war. I am the one who will be seen as the aggressor, who will have to face the wrath of the king. Your father could not have plotted a more perfect plan to bring me to ruin.''

Lillis of Wellewyn looked wretchedly miserable. ''I hardly know what to say to you, my Lord Gyer. I am so very sorry for what my father has done.''

''You have no need to apologize, my lady,'' Alexander assured her. ''I have already said that you are not to blame.''

''Still,'' she persisted, ''it is my father who is the source of your troubles, and I want you to know how deeply ashamed I am.''

''You do not find it hard to believe that your father would do such a thing, though, do you?'' he asked, considering her.

"Do not misunderstand, Alexander of Gyer. I love my father. He is all I have ever had and has always shown me great love and kindness. Yet I must admit," she said almost guiltily, "I have thought that he might be hard-hearted toward others."

Alexander almost snorted at such a gentle term being used for a devil like Jaward, but since the unhappy lady before him was the man's daughter, he kept silent.

"I understand, my lord, why you wish to keep me here, and I agree that war must be avoided at every cost, but I beg you to release my companions and myself. I swear to you that I will speak with both my father and my betrothed. I will make certain that the dam is torn down, even if I must tear it down with my own hands."

"No," he said softly. "I do not believe that either your father or Jason de Burgh will be stopped simply because you ask it of them."

She stood suddenly, and her hands fell to determined fists clenched at her sides. "But I give you my vow that I will have the dam destroyed! I will swear to honor this vow by all that is holy, by God himself. All I ask is that you trust me. You will not have reason to be sorry."

Alexander stood, as well, more out of a desire to be polite than anything else. He was struck again by her tallness; really, her height was a pleasant change from towering over other women.

"I believe you would do your best to carry out what you say, my lady, but I do not believe you would be successful. I have spent the past six months doing all in my power to persuade your father to tear down the dam only to have him laugh in my face. Yesterday he assured me that naught would change his mind."

"But he would listen to me!" she insisted. "I do not know why he has done what he has, but I do know that he has never denied me anything I have asked of him. I am his only child, and he loves me."

Alexander raised his eyebrows. "He loves you so much that he kept you from your home for more than ten years?"

Her expression became so suddenly stunned and pained that Alexander wished, powerfully, that he'd never spoken the careless words. She looked at him as if he'd slapped her.

"My lady—" he began in his sincerest, most apologetic tone.

"He did *not* send me away," she informed him shakily. "I was living at the convent in Tynedale and being taught how to read and write and work figures. He came to visit me several times, and he wrote to me constantly!"

Worse and worse, he thought. She sounded as if she were trying to convince herself more than him.

"My lady," he tried again, but she didn't seem to want his apology.

"I tell you he will listen to me!"

"He might," Alexander said, "but he might not. Indeed, it's most likely that he will not. You've already admitted that your father has never confided in you regarding the management of Wellewyn. If this is so, then there is little reason to believe he will suddenly listen to any request you might make regarding land that he's never seen fit to explain will one day be yours. You claim that he loves you, but what kind of man loves his child and sends her from his presence for ten years? Did he never once want you home, even for Christmastide?"

She flushed deeply. "That is no concern of yours, Alexander of Gyer! And it has naught to do with the matter at hand. I have given you my vow that I will see the dam torn down. My sacred, solemn vow. Will you or will you not let my companions and myself go free?"

"I have told you that I will not," Alexander replied, "and I have told you why."

She drew in a deep breath, pressed her lips together tightly and sat down with a thump. Alexander sat again, as well, wondering rather uncomfortably if he was now going to be treated to the screaming and wailing he had expected earlier.

"Will you at least let me write my father and ask him to fulfill your demands? He will be more inclined to comply if I do the writing."

Well, so much for screaming and wailing, he thought, picking up his ink quill in a careless gesture.

"I've not yet decided whether I'm going to write to your father. I shall have to consider what is best to be done."

She sat forward in her chair. "But you must write him! My father's not been well, and he's been expecting me these past two days already. He'll be terribly worried by now. You must at least let him know that I'm all right."

Alexander felt an unexpected surge of anger. "You will have to forgive me, my lady, if I don't care whether your father worries or not. He's given my people and myself no reason to love him."

His sudden anger caused her to sit back again, as though she wished to be as far away from him as possible, and he regretted having spoken so harshly.

"Forgive me," he apologized quietly, thinking that it was more than the third time he'd done so that morn. "I fear I am rather worn from dealing with your father of late. I have a great many vassals who have labored hard to save their crops, to no avail. The thought of having to tell them to prepare for war against both Wellewyn and Dunsted in the face of all they've already suffered sickens me."

She made no reply, and Alexander looked up and saw that her eyes were wide upon him, filled with a sympathy he'd never have expected from the daughter of his enemy.

"I understand what a terrible situation you're in, Alexander of Gyer," she said, "but what good will it do you to hold us here? If you don't let us go, there will most certainly be a war. My father will call on Jason de Burgh and you will have his men, however few they may be compared to your own, swarming around you, demanding our release."

"I know," Alexander admitted soberly. "That is why I must think carefully on what is to be done. I harbor no falsehoods about which side will win should a war erupt. Neither your father's nor your betrothed's men could possibly stand against the strength of my own army. Still, I have no desire to kill any man without need. But these are not matters to concern yourself with, my lady. I shall do my best to keep anyone from coming to harm." He offered her what he hoped was an encouraging smile. "Now that you are aware of why you are being held I will try to come to some kind of decision as soon as I can. Until then, please believe that you and your maid and guards will be treated as guests in my home, save you'll not be allowed the freedom of the castle without escort or be allowed to go outside the castle itself. Have you any requests to make of me regarding your comfort?"

She contemplated Alexander in silence, long enough for him to feel uncomfortable beneath her steady gaze, long enough for him to understand something about the pride behind the eyes that held his own so determinedly. "My maid and I will take all of our meals in our room," she answered at last, breaking the silence and bringing him relief. "As prisoners in your home, we would not feel comfortable partaking food with your family. We will wish to attend chapel in the mornings. I assume you have a chapel at Gyer?"

Her mocking tone made him smile in wry amusement. He was one of the wealthiest men in England, as she must have very well surmised from the size and richness of Castle Gyer. Of course there was a chapel, which she must know very well, too. "Yes, indeed, my lady," he answered with a hint of matching sarcasm. "It is just outside the inner bailey. I shall be happy to escort you and your Edyth there for the morning mass."

"You are kind, sir," she said without expression. "Our things were brought to us this morn and we now have our needlework to keep us occupied. However, the chamber we are in does not receive enough light during the day to make the work easy, and so we will require a place that is well lit in which to pass the day."

That was easily enough remedied. "The women of the household do their needlework in a certain corner of the great hall that receives full sunlight during most of the day," he said, "and that is near a fireplace for warmth. I'm sure that both my aunt and my betrothed will be glad to have your company there."

"Your betrothed?"

"The Lady Barbara Baldwin," he replied, noting her look of surprise. "You've not had a chance to meet the rest of my family yet. My betrothed is my cousin, distantly related, and lives under my protection. Both she and her brother reside at Gyer."

Lillis of Wellewyn seemed to struggle for a moment, then finally said with forced politeness, "Becoming acquainted with the rest of your family, my lord, is a pleasure that I fear I do not crave. Your brother, Willem, seems meet enough, but your aunt and twin brothers—"

"Yes, I know," he interrupted in an angry tone. "My younger brothers are wild, untamed fiends, as you know firsthand. Our mother died seven years ago when they were but eight years of age, and they've been out of hand ever since. Even before then they were my father's favorites, and spoiled beyond enduring. After my mother's death he kept them close to himself and gave them free rein. No one was allowed to reprimand them, and he certainly never did. He coddled them into just the sort of creatures whom you met yesterday, and since his death I've not had much luck in taming them."

"Then you are much to be pitied, my Lord Gyer."

Something about the tone of her voice made Alexander defensive. "I *have* tried to discipline them, my lady."

"I'm sure you have, my lord. Now, about my guards—"

He raised a hand to stop her. "I saw to them this morn. They have been moved to suitable quarters and are being kept under watch. I've made it clear that they're to be allowed as much freedom as possible with supervision. Their meals will be the same as those that you are given, so that you will know they are well fed."

She seemed satisfied with this and rose to leave. "That is well, then. I should like to return to the chamber you've given us, my lord, and inform my maid of our situation. We will devote the remainder of the morn praying for a resolution to the problem at hand, as it is now far too late to attend mass."

She sounded just like the nuns she'd once lived with, Alexander thought as he rose to escort her. "You must not worry, Lady Lillis, over your care while you remain at Gyer." He spoke the words without thought, as simple courtesy. "I swear by God's holy name that you and your companions shall be treated as though you were members of my own family."

She seemed to find his words quite amusing, for she smiled, then laughed, and looked and sounded so beautiful doing so that it nearly stole Alexander's breath away.

"My lord," she said, "I do hope you'll not take my words amiss, but I promise you that my companions and I would far rather be counted your prisoners than ever be considered members of the family Baldwin."

Chapter Three

Lillis hadn't slept well the night before, either. The chamber she and Edyth had been taken to was comfortable enough; indeed, more than comfortable. It was lavish compared to the spare, plain room they'd been used to at the convent. The furniture in the chamber was finely made, ornamented with delicate carvings and embroidered with intricately sewn needlework. Artful tapestries covered the walls, depicting scenes of romance and adventure, and in the center of the room sat a large bed, heavily curtained with rich, burgundy-colored velvet hung by gold rings. The feather down mattress in the bed was unimaginably soft, and both she and Edyth regarded it with some awe before allowing themselves to actually sit on it. Their beds at the convent had been about as comfortable as a cold stone floor.

Lillis had realized immediately that the chamber was meant for the lady of the castle, for there were many feminine touches declaring both its rank and occupancy. Silver brushes and an ivory comb sat on a silver tray in front of a highly polished steel mirror, perfume decanters offered the exotic scents of sandalwood and lilac, and a woman's jewelry chest made of fine cedarwood sat on a lady's dressing table next to a silver filigreed makeup box.

Servants came and went, bearing trays of food and drink and buckets filled with hot water with which they filled a large wooden tub set beside the fire. They went about their duties in a meaningful silence and left Lillis and Edyth alone in the chamber without speaking one word to either of them.

The food and wine that had been brought tasted better than anything Lillis had ever eaten, probably, she knew, because she was half starved and also because she was so used to the simple food that the nuns at Tynedale ate. She had no doubt that the food at Gyer was better than the viands that would nourish them at Wellewyn would be, if they ever got to Wellewyn, because her father was very poor and could not afford fine cooks and expensive fare.

"If we must be prisoners, at least we'll be well-fed prisoners," she jested with Edyth, who was in a trancelike state after taking a bite of pears cooked with wine and raisins.

After their meal they undressed and bathed in the still-warm bathwater. A bar of scented soap was included with the provided necessaries and the two women exclaimed over it. At the convent they'd been used to washing with rough soap that smelled like the sheeps' fat it was made from, but this soap was soft and soothing and smelled like lavender. They dug through their belongings and pulled on their nightclothes.

They'd gone to bed, both of them amazed anew at the softness of the mattress, and Lillis could tell by her steady breathing that Edyth had fallen to sleep almost immediately. Lillis herself, however, had spent much of the night awake, trying to sort out their situation, and now she was suffering for it.

She sat back in the comfortable chair she'd been sitting in for some hours and forced her eyes to stay open. The midday sun filtered through the many windows at the end of the great hall where she and Edyth were passing their time, and the light and warmth made Lillis feel sleepy. Just beyond the windows she could see glimpses of a beautiful garden. How she would love to explore that garden, to smell the fragrance of the flowers and feel the breeze on her face. Never before, until she'd been denied them, had she so missed the clean smell of fresh air, or the giving of the earth beneath her feet. There were two guards now, standing nearby, who would protest if she tried to enjoy such simple freedoms, for Alexander of Gyer had made it clear that she was not to be allowed outside the castle walls unless he was present.

"Careful, dear!" came Edyth's voice, startling Lillis.

She looked and saw that she'd dropped her needlework onto the rushes that covered the floor. The rushes were clean and looked as if they'd recently been placed down, but Lillis scooped her material up just in case. She took too much pride in her needlework to take any chances with it. Folding it on her lap, she glanced across the room. With some amusement she saw the women who were sitting at the other end of the hall quickly lower their interested eyes.

"He said they would be only too happy to receive us here," she remarked, more to herself than to Edyth.

"What was that, dear?" Edyth looked up from her needlework.

Lillis nodded in the direction of the group of women. "Them. The womenfolk of Castle Gyer. Alexander of Gyer assured me this morn that we would be well received by them, but it seems that the only thing those ladies well receive is the gossip Aunt Leta gives them. I can see from here that she says a few words, then looks our way, says a few words, then looks our way..." Lillis craned her neck to see the women better. There were seven sitting together in a group, bent over needlework and talking when they weren't staring at Edyth and herself. "I wonder which one is his betrothed?"

"Whose betrothed?" Edyth asked, then added, "Lillis, it is quite rude for you to stare at them so!"

"I know, Edyth, but if they're going to sit there and look at us as though we were oddities we can certainly return the favor."

Edyth sighed and looked back to her needlework. "Whose betrothed?" she repeated.

"The Lord of Gyer's. She was supposed to be one of the women who would be happy to welcome us here. She is also his cousin."

"My goodness, you certainly did learn a great deal during your meeting with him this morn."

She certainly had, Lillis thought with heartfelt sincerity.

The moment she'd seen the two men standing in that chamber she thought perhaps she'd walked through the wrong door by mistake. Neither of them looked like the man who had introduced himself to her the night before. One of them, the one nearest her whose face was a vivid red color, was much too tall to be Alexander of Gyer, and the other, who stood behind a table, looking rather expectant, was much too handsome. She had stared at both of them in turn until she'd finally realized that the handsome one *was* the Lord of Gyer.

The discovery had been a distressing one, for Lillis had little experience with men, even less with one so handsome. He'd stood before her, green eyed and dark haired, tall and muscular and much younger than she had realized. His features were purely aristocratic, with a straight nose, expressive eyebrows and a well-shaped mouth. As well, there had been about him a mild and utterly natural expression of superiority, which marked him as the nobleman he was.

It had taken only a moment before she'd determined that her best defense against such a man would be anger, and so she had steeled herself against him.

The conversation with her captor, once begun, had gone more smoothly than Lillis had expected. Alexander of Gyer was not the tyrant she had thought he must be; instead, she found him polite, well-spoken and intelligent. He had explained her situation with honest regret, and had listened to all that she'd had to say.

She'd suffered some shock when he told her of the things her father had done, but he was right when he said that she was not really surprised. Lillis loved her father deeply, for to her he had always been loving and kind, but she knew he was a vengeful man and could be quite cruel. She'd seen enough during her childhood of how he treated his servants and vassals to know these things about him. But she also knew he would listen to her if she only had a chance to speak with him, for he had never been able to deny her anything she'd asked of him. The fact that Alexander of Gyer didn't believe this was understandable, of course, but extremely frustrating.

"Are you quite sure that he'll not change his mind, my lady?" Edyth asked. "Your poor father must be terribly worried by now."

"Yes, I'm sure he is," Lillis agreed. "But, no, I do not think Alexander of Gyer will change his mind. I don't know what he will do or how he will use us, save I am reasonably certain we shall not be killed or beaten. Still, I do feel foolish sitting here and enjoying ourselves in the luxury of Castle Gyer while my father is probably worrying himself into illness. Too many more days and I promise that I will begin to think of ways to escape our benevolent prison." At these words Edyth looked absolutely panicked, so that Lillis quickly added, "But we'll not speak of such things yet. We shall wait a day or two and accept whatever hospitality Alexander of Gyer offers us, and pray that he finds a solution by then."

Edyth seemed comforted, and managed a slight smile. As Lillis returned the smile she chanced to look behind Edyth's chair and saw a movement in the shadows. She bent forward to look more closely and noticed that the shadows were actually two small figures; children who were hugging themselves tightly against the wall to keep from being seen.

"What now!" Lillis said lightly. "Who have we here? Come and let us see you. Come," she coaxed. "We'll not harm you."

Edyth turned to see who it was that Lillis addressed and, being closer to the children, was able to discern them more clearly. "Why, what precious little ones!" the older woman exclaimed, dropping her needlework. "What do you do there, hiding so? Will you not come and say hello?"

But the children seemed thoroughly frightened, if not of Edyth, certainly of Lillis.

"You're a witch!" accused a small, trembling voice.

"My goodness!" Lillis declared with surprise. "Whatever makes you say such a thing?"

"You look like a witch" came the reply. This time the voice belonged to a boy.

"Do I? How is it that I look like a witch? I've never seen one before, so you must tell me."

"You are all white. And you are a giant."

"Oh, I see," Lillis said, repressing the urge to laugh. "Well, I suppose I am all white, as you say, but I assure you that I was born this way and that being such doesn't make me a witch. As to being a giant, why, I'm not nearly as tall as the Lord of Gyer, am I?"

"No," said both voices.

"And is he a giant?"

"No."

"Then, if I am not as tall as he, and he is not a giant, I am not a giant. Does that not make sense?"

They were quiet, clearly thinking this through. Finally the boy spoke again. "Barbara said you are a witch. She said that you turn children into mice and drown them in wells. She said you can put a house to fire by pointing your finger at it."

"Barbara said you cast spells on people that makes them howl like dogs," the little girl added enthusiastically, "and that they grow hair all over their bodies and can never be the same again."

"Oh, my!" Edyth put one hand over her heart in distress. "What dreadful things to tell children!"

Lillis finally gave way to an amused chuckle. "So the lady Barbara told you I am a witch, did she? Well, she is quite wrong. I can do none of those things and I most assuredly am not a witch. Come now, I promise I shall not harm you."

The children did come, but warily. The closest child was a beautiful little girl, seven or eight years of age, with golden auburn curls atop her head and large hazel eyes full of curious expression. The other, a boy a couple of years older, was surprisingly lanky and thin. He had brown hair and deep brown eyes, and the most serious expression Lillis had ever seen on a child.

"What lovely children!" Edyth exclaimed, putting out a gentle hand to draw them closer. They willingly moved to the older woman but kept their distance from Lillis, whom they stared at with open distrust.

"What are your names, my dears?" Edyth asked them.

"Candis," whispered the little girl, never taking her eyes from Lillis.

"I am Justin," the boy said.

"It is a pleasure to meet you, Candis and Justin." Lillis nodded to them formally. "Do you belong to someone in the castle?"

They looked at her with confusion.

"How is it that you are here in the castle?" she clarified.

"We live here. Alex is our brother," Justin replied.

"Oh," Lillis said with disappointment. She had assumed that they belonged to the cook or one of the servants, and had been happy with the prospect of having children close by to spend time with. She sincerely doubted, however, that Alexander of Gyer or his family would appreciate her and Edyth even speaking to Candis and Justin. She looked to see whether the women across the room had any reaction to the children being with them and was relieved to find that Aunt Leta and the others had their heads bent in conversation.

"Why are you not doing your lessons now, children?" she asked. "It is not yet time for the midday meal, is it? Do you not have a tutor?"

The boy shrugged. "We do what we want. We did have a tutor last week, but Hugh and Hugo put a snake in his bed and he left. Alex hasn't found a new one yet, but it won't matter when he does. Hugh and Hugo always get rid of them in a few days."

"Once they put salt in the tutor's wineglass!" Candis said with a giggle. "It was so funny to see him try to drink it without choking! He was too afraid to tell Alex that the wine was bad!"

"How horrid!" Lillis said, surprised at the anger in her voice. "Are your brothers not punished after they do such things?"

"Ye-e-es," Justin replied haltingly, sounding somewhat uncertain.

Amazed, Lillis shook her head. "That's too bad for the both of you, is it not? You are deprived of an education because of your brothers' behavior. Where are your nurses? Who looks after you during the day?"

"We only have one nurse," Justin supplied. "Her name is Molly and she sleeps a lot."

Candis giggled again. "She keeps wine hidden in her room and drinks it during the day. We wait until she's snoring and then we sneak out. But it was hard to wait today, because we wanted to see the witch."

"Well," Lillis said with some disgust, "I've already told you that I'm not a witch. As to your nurse—" She was so angry she couldn't continue.

"Does the lord of the castle not care that your nurse is so *sleepy* all the time?" Edyth asked.

"He's very busy," Justin replied, as though that should explain.

"I see," Edyth said feebly, and exchanged wondering glances with Lillis.

"What of your Aunt Leta?" Lillis asked. "She manages the household for your brother. Does she not care about your lack of supervision?"

The children cast glances at each other, then looked at Lillis.

"Aunt Leta doesn't mind us as long as we're quiet. And Barbara says it would be mean to make us do what we don't want to, because we don't have parents."

"Oh, my!" Edyth cried, unable to contain herself any longer. "What kind of place is this? Even the children in the orphanage had better care!"

"It's none of our concern, Edyth," Lillis warned. "We'll not be here long enough to make any difference in the lives of these children, so just get those thoughts right out of your head."

Edyth looked at her very pleadingly. "But, my dear, they're just babies—"

"It would be unwise for us to become involved with these two," Lillis said firmly, then looked at Candis and Justin. "Although I suppose it would be all right to see if they like to play games. Do you?"

"What kind of games?" Candis asked, wide-eyed.

"Why, all kinds. Edyth and I know almost any game you'd care to name. And stories, too. I know a wonderful story I can tell you this very minute, if you wish it."

They did wish it, and both came closer. Edyth set one child on each knee and Lillis began her tale.

"The knight took up his lance," Lillis said toward the end of the story, standing and using her arms to demonstrate just how it had been done, "and he took one step, two steps, three steps closer to where the evil man lay. Slowly he lifted his lance, aimed it at the man before him, and—"

A shriek from across the great hall surprised the little group. The children clung to Edyth, and Lillis dropped her hands; all of them looked to where the scream had sounded from.

It seemed to have come from one of the ladies who sat sewing at the other end of the hall, though from which one it was impossible to tell, as they were all now standing and looking with distress at Lillis and Edyth. Two of the ladies, Aunt Leta and a stunningly beautiful redheaded lady, came flying across the room.

"Hold them!" Aunt Leta shouted to the guards behind Edyth and Lillis. "Hold them!"

Looking rather uncertain, the guards moved to do as they were bid, and in a moment Lillis and Edyth found themselves dragged into the firm grasps of the two men. Justin and Candis still clung to Edyth's skirt in an effort to protect themselves from whatever it was that threatened them.

"How could you threaten such innocent children?!" the redheaded lady cried as she came upon them. Lillis stared at her in surprise.

"I—"

The redheaded woman, or rather girl, for she was certainly younger than Lillis, grabbed Candis and pulled her away from Edyth, scaring her so badly that the child began to cry. Aunt Leta came huffing and puffing behind her and did the same to a bewildered Justin.

"What were you doing to these children?" she demanded.

"I—we—" Lillis sputtered in wonder. What did they think they had been doing to them?

"She was telling them a very interesting story," came a voice from the shadows of the nearby stairwell. "I should think that would have been obvious, Aunt Leta."

Alexander of Gyer strolled slowly into the light.

"Release them," he instructed the guards, and received immediate compliance. "Do not lay hands on these ladies again unless your instructions come directly from me. And I mean directly. Do you understand?" he asked. They nodded.

"Alex!" The redheaded lady stamped her foot angrily. "That woman was getting ready to strike one of the children! I saw it with my own two eyes. You should have the both of them locked in chains in the cellar. Who knows what a daughter of Wellewyn is capable of doing? She's already caused poor Hugh and Hugo to be punished quite horribly."

"Barbara." Alexander of Gyer sounded surprised, and Lillis couldn't keep herself from looking at him. His expression was pained as he gazed at the redheaded girl, and she suddenly realized that the tiny creature before her was his betrothed. Barbara. She looked back at the girl and felt a familiar twinge of jealousy. Here was everything that Lillis, herself, was not, yet had always wished to be. The lady Barbara was as delicate as a butterfly, her features were lovely and feminine; her hands, her feet, everything about her was dainty and frail looking, as though she could easily be broken. And she was beautiful. Very beautiful.

"It's true, Alex," Barbara returned petulantly, "and I'm disappointed that you would take the word of this—" she looked at Lillis with contempt "—*lady* over your own brothers. And after they did you such a favor by capturing her. You should be praising instead of punishing them."

How did she do it? Lillis wondered. How could she speak so angrily and yet still seem so sweet and merely a little silly? If anything, her childish speech would melt a man's heart rather than enrage him. Lillis looked to see what effect it had on Alexander of Gyer.

"No, Barbara, I'm the one who is disappointed," he chided gently, coming closer and looking impossibly handsome. "I assured our guests that you would be ready to welcome them in the hall this afternoon, but when I came to see how things fared I found they had been kept separate from the other women. I expected better of you, and certainly better of you, Aunt Leta." He gave that lady a more pointed look.

The dainty creature's big green eyes welled with sudden tears. "You—you cannot be so cruel as to expect me to entertain them! *Prisoners,* my lord?"

"While they are here," he said curtly, "these ladies will be treated as honored guests. Now take the children to their nurse. We shall discuss this matter later."

His tone did not invite discussion, though both Aunt Leta and Lady Barbara looked as though they had more to say. However, they kept silent and dutifully led Justin and Candis toward the stairs. A gentle hand grasped Lillis's elbow.

"I beg your pardon, my lady," Alexander of Gyer apologized sincerely. "You must forgive my aunt and cousin. They tend to think the worst of anyone from Wellewyn, I fear."

"Do they?" Lillis wrenched her elbow free. "Do you know that your betrothed has been telling your brother and sister that I am a witch who turns children into mice and sets houses afire?"

He stiffened, yet his expression remained polite. "If that is what Candis and Justin told you, then either you misunderstood them or they are mistaken. I know they have some childish idea about you being a witch, but Barbara would never tell them such ridiculous tales. They heard them from Hugh and Hugo, more like, or from one of the villagers."

"I did not misunderstand them, my lord, but that is neither here nor there. She is your betrothed, not mine, and you may believe what you wish of her. She is none of my concern."

He seemed amazed that she would dare speak to him so. "That is true, my lady, and you will do well to remember it.

My cousin is my concern alone, and I'll not discuss her with you. Do not speak of her again."

Lillis uttered a laugh. "As a matter of course, my lord, it would please me greatly to neither speak of nor see her again. My companion and I have enough to worry over without having to endure the distinct pleasure of Lady Barbara's company."

Alexander of Gyer's face flushed, but still his voice was calm. "I had thought, my lady, to give you as much access to my household as possible as a way of making your stay more pleasant, but I begin to think I was wrong. Mayhap I should keep you and your Edyth locked in your chamber. Then you'd need not worry about having anyone's company but your own."

His rigid self-control and polite manner of threatening were unnerving, but Lillis wouldn't let herself be intimidated.

"Perhaps you should," she agreed. "But why stop there, my lord? Why not do as your Barbara suggests and shackle us in chains? It would be most gratifying to know that your brothers had come by their inhuman natures honestly."

His eyebrows rose in further amazement, indicating the success of this strike; nonetheless, his tone remained maddeningly calm.

"Perhaps I should," he softly repeated her own words back to her. "Perhaps, depending upon your father's future behavior, I shall. For now, however, I have promised that you shall be treated as guests, and will be content to escort you to your chamber so that you may enjoy the afternoon meal in the privacy you requested of me this morn."

Lillis measured his polite words and expression and understood that he'd ceded the battle to her. He'd not argue the matter with her further, which was a relief, though Lillis wasn't certain if he'd given way because she was too unimportant to waste his time on, or because he'd known that she, herself, would not give way. She would, however, gracefully acknowledge his peace offering by extending one of her own.

"You have not yet been properly introduced to my maid," she told him, reaching out a hand to draw her timid companion forward. "Alexander of Gyer, I make known to you Edyth Lielyn, daughter of Sir Edward Lielyn of Cantfield."

He looked appropriately surprised to discover that Edyth was a lady by birth, and immediately bent to take Edyth's hand.

"I am honored to make your acquaintance, Edyth of Cantfield. The circumstances of our meeting are somewhat unusual but I hope you will believe that I am very pleased, nevertheless. And I hope you will accept my apologies regarding the behavior of my aunt and cousin—" he glanced at Lillis "—as I hope your mistress will accept them."

Edyth shyly stammered something appropriate while Lillis met Alexander of Gyer's frank gaze steadily.

"Let us speak of it no more, Alexander of Gyer." She offered the truce gracefully.

The Lord of Gyer nodded and extended an arm to Edyth. "Will you allow me the honor of escorting you to your chamber, Lady Edyth?"

Edyth blushed vividly but placed her hand upon his arm, allowing herself to be led forward. Lillis and their guards followed behind as they made their way up the staircase and to the chamber that was their jail. Not for the first time Lillis regretted that she and Alexander of Gyer were destined to be enemies. Despite their short-lived battle of wills, she liked him, and liked him very much. He seemed to be a fair man, one who possessed both strength and gentleness, and she could not help but admire his willingness to give way in a dispute. She knew little of men, but this, it seemed to her, was a fine and rare quality in them. It had been mean spirited to suggest that he shared his twin brothers' mischievous natures, especially in the face of his kindness to Edyth. She could not remember when, if ever, Edyth had been treated with the respect she deserved. Lillis herself did not even do so.

"Can you tell us, my lord," she asked conversationally, "what the door in our room is? Not the main door, but the door that is in the middle of one of the walls?" She wasn't going to admit to him that she and Edyth had already unbolted the door and tried, without success, to open it.

He was thoughtful, then, remembering, said, "Ah, yes. It's been so long since I've used that door that I've almost forgotten its existence. It's an unusual feature, I suppose, but was designed that way apurpose by my father. The chamber you're staying in was my mother's, the chamber next to it was my father's and now is mine. The door you speak of joins the rooms together." He glanced over his shoulder and smiled at Lillis. "My father felt that the device made his life much easier, as my mother wished to have a private place of her own. She spent a great deal of time there, and I think the door must have been useful when she and my father were arguing."

They had reached the hallway of the floor that was their destination by the time he finished speaking, yet both women stopped and gaped at him. Lillis, in fact, drew to such a sudden halt that the guards nearly stumbled into her, and Edyth removed her hand from Alexander of Gyer's arm and stepped away from him. The look on her face was as horrified as Lillis knew her own must be.

The Lord of Gyer looked at them first with concern, and then with curiosity. "Is something amiss?"

"Amiss!" Lillis heard herself saying. *"Amiss!"* she repeated, unable to think of anything else to say.

He looked at her strangely, and then at Edyth, who took a step farther away.

"Good day," a pleasant voice broke in, and Willem appeared, strolling toward them from the other end of the hall with a shy smile. He stopped beside his brother and surveyed the two unhappy women with interest.

"We—we cannot stay in that chamber any longer," Lillis said. "You must lodge us elsewhere."

Alexander of Gyer's face held honest surprise. "Because of the door? Why?"

"Why!" she half shouted in disbelief. "How could— how—how *could* you put us in a place where almost anyone could walk in at any moment and—and—well!" She clamped her jaw shut tightly and didn't notice that she had dropped everything she'd been holding. Fine silk thread and cloth fluttered noiselessly to the floor.

"Anyone?" Alexander of Gyer repeated, his voice deepening with anger. "You mean *me*, do you not, my lady? You think that I would come into your chamber unannounced simply because our rooms are joined?" He was clearly insulted, and for a brief moment Lillis feared him. He was a big man, and seemed bigger in his fury. "If you've not noticed," he continued curtly, "there is a bolt on your side to keep you safe from any such intrusion. And there is one on my side to keep me safe, as well. And, Lillis of Wellewyn—" he bent, speaking close to her face "—I will have you know that *I* am the lord of this castle. If ever I want to come into your chamber unannounced I will do it! *Without* your permission. Not—" he leaned even closer "—that I would ever want to enter your chamber, for *any* reason, in the first place."

Lillis could have done without his last sentence and its most obvious meaning. She knew full well that she was odd looking and unattractive. She didn't need Alexander of Gyer to tell her that. The nuns at Tynedale had spent ten long years making certain she understood it. And yet it hurt deeply, hearing the truth from the mouth of such a man, and Lillis felt young and angry all over again, as if she'd never left Tynedale at all.

"What a good thing it is, Alexander of Gyer, that you'd never have reason to do such a thing," she said between clenched teeth, praying that she wouldn't start crying and make a perfect fool of herself in front of him. "If I ever thought you'd come to my room with that intent, I would most certainly be ill!"

But this only enraged him more, and the expression that contorted his handsome features made Lillis's hands clench in quick fear.

"Have no fear, my lady," he assured her, "you shall never be subject to such an incident. But even if there were any danger of that event taking place, I would not move you to another chamber. I feel much safer at night knowing that you are so close by. I am a light sleeper, you see, and would know of it instantly were you to attempt an escape. You'd not get past the hallway before I caught you again.''

Lillis laughed at him contemptuously. "Of course you would. The guards outside our door would alert you. Do you think us complete idiots, my lord?''

How long this exchange might have continued, no one would ever know. Willem had been standing by, horrified, watching his brother speak to a lady in a manner he'd never before heard him speak to anyone.

"Alex," he said, stepping between his brother and Lillis of Wellewyn, "I should be most pleased to offer my chamber to these ladies, if they are unhappy with Mother's chamber."

Alexander frowned at him. "I have said they will stay where they are. There is no need to make such an offer."

"This is so," Willem agreed diplomatically, "but perhaps it would be best to consider the idea. Lady Lillis and her companion are already being kept at Gyer under unhappy circumstances. It seems a small thing to make them as comfortable as possible."

Driven by a demon that she, herself, didn't approve of, Lillis said oversweetly, "Thank you kindly, Sir Willem. You are truly a noble and chivalrous man. It is certain that you've taken your vows to God quite seriously."

Alexander of Gyer's eyes narrowed. "And I have not? That is what you mean. I have done all that I can to make your confinement at Gyer pleasant, yet you would make me a villain who has no right to call himself knight. I was fool enough to think this morn that perhaps you sympathized with the difficulty of my situation, but I now see that you are as stubborn and thickheaded as your father. I never should have supposed otherwise, Lillis of Wellewyn."

"Alex!" Willem gripped his brother's tensed arm. "You know not what you say! Please forgive him, my lady."

Willem's words fell on deaf ears, though his standing between Lillis and the Lord of Gyer was the only thing preventing her from slapping Alexander.

"How *dare* you expect sympathy from those whom you hold against their will!" she cried furiously. "There is naught you could do to make our captivity pleasant, save to let us go free, and well you know it! As to your knighthood, *Sir* Alexander, you may examine for yourself how well you have kept your vows. *I* will not be made to feel guilty for *your* failings."

He stared at her for a silent moment, then shook off Willem's hand. "Take them to their chamber. Mother's chamber. That is where they will continue to stay, and I'll not argue the matter further." He gave Lillis an especially aggravated look. "Make certain to lock them up well. It is clear—quite clear—that one cannot trust a daughter of Wellewyn."

"Oh!" Lillis shouted after him as he strode toward the stairs. "I would rather be the devil's daughter than have anything to do with Gyer!"

But he neither stopped nor made any reply. In a moment he had made his way out of their view.

Chapter Four

"**D**amn!"

Alexander slammed his way into his private chamber.

What in God's holy name had just happened? He could barely remember, though he'd walked away from Lillis of Wellewyn only moments before. He didn't even know what he'd said to her, exactly. All he knew for certain was that he'd been unforgivably rude, that he'd behaved like a common, ill-mannered lout. What was he about to be speaking to anyone in such a way, let alone to a lady? Especially to Lillis of Wellewyn. Was he not already using her badly enough without hurling insults of the worst kind at her, as well?

"Oh, God!" he beseeched the ceiling and the Being Above. "Tell me I didn't say the things I think I did. Make it all a terrible mistake of my memory."

Why had he done it? He paced the room angrily. The very room where that morning they had talked so reasonably with each other. Where he had felt so much admiration for her. And attraction. And desire. God's mercy! What was happening to him? He was a betrothed man. He had no right feeling such things for anyone but Barbara, no matter how fair Lillis of Wellewyn might be. She was nothing more than his prisoner, and nothing less than his enemy's daughter. These facts he must not lose sight of. Ever.

Turning sharply, his eyes sought the banner of Gyer, which hung above the mantel. There—the red and the white. The red and the white. Looking at it, Alexander could al-

most feel his father's hand closing about the neck of his tunic and dragging him up from the muddy practice field; he
could see again the rage on his father's face, and hear the
words, as he'd heard them over and over in his dreams and
nightmares.

"Weakling! Stupid, *foolish* weakling!"

The faces of his father's men, noble, fighting men whom
Alexander revered, were there in his memory, too, some
grinning in amusement, some watching in silent sympathy.
It had been humiliating, being felled so quickly on his first
day of battle training; more humiliating when the tiny blow
he'd received had drawn blood; utterly humiliating when the
sight of the blood had made him physically ill, right there in
front of them all. In front of his father.

Alexander could still see the silk banner his father had
snatched from his steed, could remember just how the colors had looked, thrust before his face, mangled in his father's fist.

"The red is for courage, Alexander!" his father had
shouted at him. "The white is for honor! *Red* for *courage!*
White for *honor!*"

The colors had blended before his eyes, the silk had felt
cold when his father roughly scrubbed Alexander's face with
it.

"Red for *courage! White* for *honor!"*

His father had tossed him down, then, and he remembered the damp chill of the earth, and lying there as the men
moved away. His father had been the last to go.

"God, but you sicken me," his father had said. "I'm
ashamed to have such a weakling for a son. What honor will
you ever bring Gyer?"

Running one hand through his hair, Alexander let out a
long, taut breath. It was good to remember that day. Always good. When he thought of that day, he remembered
anew the vow he'd made himself, and remembered, as well,
that he'd kept that vow. Gyer was his now. *His.* It was
wealthy and strong and secure, as it had never been under
his father's hand, and Alexander himself was one of the
most powerful men in England. Nothing was going to

threaten that—not memories of his father, not Jaward of Wellewyn, not Lillis of Wellewyn.

Lillis of Wellewyn.

He would apologize to her. God knew he'd done it plenty of times already since he'd met her, once more would make little difference. She would understand. He would explain that he was under a great deal of stress and worry. She would accept his apology. Really, aside from her beauty, she was a most intelligent woman. And quite a worthy adversary. Barbara would have cried and whimpered if he'd spoken to her the way he had to Lillis of Wellewyn this day.

He strolled to one of the several windows in the room and looked at the garden in the bailey below. It was almost time for the midday meal. He wondered if Lillis of Wellewyn and her maid had eaten yet, and he hoped, if they had, that the food had met with their approval.

His prisoners.

What was he going to do with them? He'd been avoiding the question most of the day since his interview with Lillis of Wellewyn had ended.

A knock at the door interrupted his thoughts, and a castle page entered bearing a tankard.

"There is new ale just opened, my lord. Lady Baldwin bade me bring you some."

Alexander gave the boy a curt nod. "Put it on the table, then."

"Yes, my Lord Gyer."

"Thank you, Cedric. I'll be out for the meal in a few minutes. Tell the others to begin. Sir Willem may give the blessing if he is there, and Sir Alan if he is not."

When Cedric had gone, Alexander returned his gaze to the garden below, considering the choices from among which he must soon choose.

"Alex!"

He smiled before turning to look at Barbara, who stood against his chamber door. How she had gotten in so quietly and why she had closed the door didn't matter. He was glad to see her there. She would keep his mind from his troubles. Momentarily, at least.

"Hello, sweet," he greeted softly, and held out a hand to her. She was across the room and throwing herself into his arms in only moments.

"You're not angry with me, Alex?" she asked shyly, burrowing her head against his shoulder.

She felt good to hold. Comforting. "Why should I be, sweeting?"

"Because of that woman from Wellewyn," she replied petulantly. "I thought you were angry with me because of her. You spoke so sharply to me."

He laughed at her innocence. She sounded like a little girl who needed a parent's reassurance. "Of course I'm not angry with you, dearest." He gave her a gentle squeeze. "It must be very hard to have a stranger in the household and staying in the chamber that will one day be yours. I'm sorry to put you through so much."

He felt her smile against his shoulder. "Oh, Alex! You are always so kind!" She lifted her pretty little face and gazed at him adoringly with her green eyes. "Kiss me before Aunt Leta comes to find us. I've missed you so much all day!"

Alexander could not resist the rosebud lips she offered him, puckered together to receive his kiss. He lowered his head and felt her soft arms sliding around his neck to hug him closer. He let himself draw comfort from her mouth, which opened under his and allowed his tongue to explore. He let himself forget his worries and lose himself in her tenderness. When she pressed her slender body against him provocatively, what little control he had slipped away. One hand tightened around her waist while the other began to roam. Just as he was ready to give way to passion, he felt himself being pushed away.

"Oh Alex," she said with a sigh. "When will we be married?"

He groaned and tried to capture her elusive lips again.

"When, Alex?" she persisted, her delicate hands pushing at his shoulders.

Alexander drew in a steadying breath and straightened up and away from her.

"I don't know," he said, wondering why this subject seemed to come up every time he kissed her. "You know I can make no promises."

She stiffened beneath his hands. Her eyes were sharp and clear; there was nothing in her to evidence the passion that he was feeling.

"I don't know why you make us wait!" she declared, pushing at him in earnest until he let her go. "It's the fault of that woman from Wellewyn! If it weren't for her wretched father we should have already been married!"

"Barbara," Alexander said shortly, "we have discussed many times the reasons as to why we are not yet wed." He went to where Cedric had left the ale, and picked up the tankard. "I'm in no mood to discuss them again. You shall have to be patient." He took a long drink.

He heard her sharp intake of breath, and could almost envision the expression on her face.

"You want her!" Barbara accused, her voice full of hurt. "You find her beautiful!"

"Her?" Alexander repeated with bewilderment. "Who is it you speak of?"

"Lillis of Wellewyn! You won't marry me because of her!"

"That," Alexander said, setting the tankard down and moving to pull her into his arms, "is the most foolish thing I've ever heard, and you well know it. It is you I want, and none other." He hugged her more tightly. "You have been dear to me since I can remember. Since I was a boy and even before. Say anything you want to me, but tease me not about about such feelings."

"Alex." She sounded as though she might cry. Her arms were clasped firmly around his neck, squeezing him very hard. "I don't mean to be so childish, my lord, but I cannot help myself. Lillis of Wellewyn is very beautiful, and I hate you having anything to do with her. But I know you'd not be unfaithful to me, for you have ever been kind and honest in your dealings with John and me. It was foolish of me to accuse you of such a thing."

"It's all right," he said with some relief. "We're both under a great deal of tension, of late. We'll be married soon, dearest." He smiled at her, and kissed her quickly. "As soon as possible, I promise. Can you be patient a little longer?"

She returned the smile brilliantly. "Forever, if I must, Alex," she promised. "Let us speak of it no more. Come and eat, before Aunt Leta starts pounding on the door. You must be starved by now."

Willingly Alexander gave her his hand, and let her lead him out the door.

From one of the windows in her chamber, Lillis could see more clearly the garden she had wanted to explore earlier that afternoon. She sat on the wide ledge of the window's arch and surveyed the inner bailey of the castle, its gardens, the village beyond, and the open land after that as far as she could. It was such a beautiful land, so well kept and settled, so very different from Wellewyn. The sun was beginning to go down, though the rays that fell upon her were still warm and bright. What a different day from the one before with all its rain and misery.

A brief glance toward the bed showed that Edyth was still soundly napping. They had eaten and enjoyed the sumptuous meal that had been brought to their chamber earlier, and had even drunk the wine that had been brought with it. They had not been used to drinking much wine at the convent, except for communion and on the Sabbath and holidays. Not that drinking wine was considered a sin; on the contrary, the sisters at Tynedale fermented and bottled quite a bit of wine each year for their own use. It was, however, less costly to drink well water or goats' milk with the daily meals, and the wine was used sparingly. In truth, neither Edyth nor she had ever before consumed so much wine as they had that afternoon, and it made both of them feel tired and pleasant.

As soon as they had finished eating, Edyth had stretched and yawned and announced that she would like to nap. With very little encouragement she lay down on the bed and was soon soundly asleep. Lillis smiled with affection at her companion; Edyth always slept the sleep of the innocent. There was never the tossing and turning that Lillis suffered, or the slumberless hours of staring into nothing while trying to blank her mind and go to sleep. Edyth's was a pure soul and a pure mind. She was content to live a simple and unassuming life. Even her ability to sleep reflected it. Lillis sighed and looked back out the window. If only she were more like Edyth. If only she weren't so restless, so wanting.

It came from living so many years in the convent, she thought. It had been a quiet and spare life, one filled with daily hard work and sacrifice. During the ten years that she had lived and worked and studied at Tynedale, Lillis had come to respect and appreciate the women who had dedicated their lives to the Lord's service, for really they had nothing for themselves save the satisfaction of doing what they felt God wanted of them. She herself could not have made a life of such sacrifice. Ten years had been quite long enough.

They had been hard years and sometimes lonely, though she was one of several girls who had lived at the convent. She had studied in the mornings and worked with the orphans or with the nuns during the afternoons. In the evenings there was cooking and cleaning to be done, and from season to season there were always the gardens and livestock to tend. All during the day, at different times, there were masses, prayers and devotions in the chapel, and all were required to attend. At other very specific times during the day, plain meals of bread and cheese, vegetables, a stew or soup, and occasionally a chicken or loin of beef were served. The entire day was spoken for by routine from the moment one rose to the moment one returned to rest, and Lillis had dreamed of and longed for the time when she would be able to spend her days as she pleased.

She'd learned many things at the convent and from the nuns. Truly, if she could go back and have the choice of either staying at home with a tutor or going to the convent, she supposed she would have chosen the latter all over again. In truth, the time she'd spent in Tynedale had been invaluable. The nuns had given her the charge of many responsibilities, including the overseeing of the schoolgirls when she was fifteen and the management of the orphanage at seventeen, and those duties had trained her to be disciplined, strong and very capable.

The thought of one day managing a large household didn't frighten Lillis in the least—it couldn't possibly be any worse than managing an orphanage of over one hundred children—and the idea of someday having to live on a very tight budget wasn't at all daunting. She could cook, clean, garden, make soap and candles, dye and weave cloth, and sew quite beautifully. Indeed, her greatest pleasure at the convent had been her sewing, when she had had a spare moment or two to do it.

She'd made beautiful clothing for herself, for the future, when she would return to her life as a lady, much to the chagrin of the sisters who felt that indulging in any type of outward finery was self-serving and vain. But Lillis refused to feel guilty for trying to make herself more presentable. Goodness only knows that a woman such as she, large and mannish, needed every help she could find, and, too, she'd grown weary to tears with wearing the scratchy white undergarments and plain brown surcoat that all the girls at the convent wore, and of covering her hair with brown wool cloth every minute of the day. She had made herself a promise to keep her head uncovered for as long as she could once she left the convent. The nuns, she knew, would have been horrified.

Edyth had thrived on convent life, but Lillis was ready for something altogether different. She wanted to live and be free to do as she pleased, to marry and have children of her own, to be in love with a man and to be loved in turn. These were the dreams that had sustained her through ten long years.

She had never met her betrothed, Jason de Burgh, or if she had she'd forgotten him. Her father had arranged the marriage and assured her that de Burgh would make a fine husband and a good father, regardless that he was nearly as poor as her father. Perhaps when they were wed, she could help him to make the most of the estates he had, and perhaps she might even come to love him one day. She did hope so. Yes, she hoped so very much. To love the man she married would be the most wonderful thing in the world.

She'd not believed Alexander of Gyer when he said that her father was simply trying to achieve an alliance with de Burgh through her marriage to him. Oh, she could believe that her father would be happy for the circumstance of an alliance with Dunsted, but he wouldn't have considered de Burgh for her if that man hadn't met his rigid requirements. Lillis smiled. Alexander of Gyer was, indeed, foolish if he thought her father would marry her away like so much cattle. But perhaps he wouldn't understand that. He had only ever seen the side of her father that Lillis, herself, tried to ignore. The harsh side, the angry side.

Her father had been that way since her mother had died, when Lillis was four years old. Her memories of her mother were vague at best, but she remembered how passionately her father had loved her. After her death, though, he'd become a miserable, hateful man. The only love he spared was for Lillis. For everyone else he had only impatience and irritation. His servants, vassals and villagers all lived in dread of Jaward of Wellewyn. Lillis had long since determined that she must do what she could to soften him. Once she was married to Jason de Burgh, and living so much closer to Wellewyn, she would devote herself to finding the key to her father's misery, to solving the reasons for his cruelty.

If she ever got out of Gyer, that was. If Alexander of Gyer ever decided what he was going to do with her.

Chapter Five

"Has Alexander of Gyer come to a decision yet?" Lillis asked as she followed Aunt Leta, making a conscious effort to stay behind her this time rather than in front.

Aunt Leta snorted disdainfully. "You've no manners whatsoever to ask such a thing," she stated. "The training you received at that convent certainly wasn't as it should have been."

"I do plead your forgiveness, my lady," Lillis replied in the wilting tone of repentance she'd been taught at Tynedale, but Aunt Leta only made another sound of disgust.

She waited demurely while Aunt Leta knocked on the door of the same chamber she'd been directed to that morn. Alexander of Gyer called for them to enter and the older woman escorted Lillis in, then left, surprisingly, without being asked to.

He was standing by one of the many long windows in the room, looking out at the setting sun, his hands clasped behind his back. The light, soft and yellow at this time of day, highlighted the multitude of red-gold strands in his dark hair and showed fully the strong features of his handsome face. He did not turn to greet her, and Lillis stayed where she was, waiting.

He was silent a while, then said quietly, "I seem to be forever apologizing to you, my lady. I would ask your forgiveness for my behavior of this afternoon. My words to you were rude and uncalled-for, more so because they were made in the presence of others." His gaze fell to the floor. "I am sincerely, deeply ashamed, and I can only hope that you will be kind enough to forgive me. You had every right to speak as you did about my lack of chivalry.''

He completed this speech and looked out the window again. The muscles of his face were taut and his hands were clasped so firmly that the knuckles turned white. Lillis cleared her throat and held her own hands together in front of herself.

''I believe, my lord, that I am the one who should apologize. I should not have made the accusations about your honor that I did, and I am fully ashamed of myself. I fear I am possessed of a terrible temper. The nuns at Tynedale used to be hard put to know what to do with me, sometimes.'' She offered him a smile but saw that his frowning gaze remained out the window. ''But that is no excuse,'' she continued, chagrined. ''There is never any excuse for a lady to behave so badly. Please forgive me.''

His hands unclasped, and the one side of his face that she could see displayed relief. He ran one hand through his hair, released a full breath, then finally turned to look at her. ''It seems we have a truce, then, Lillis of Wellewyn,'' he said, smiling with a charming uncertainty that made her knees feel weak. ''Perhaps, considering our situation, we are allowed some few shortcomings. You had good cause to vent your anger on me, my lady, while I'd none to countenance my behavior. But I am grateful to you for being so kind as to try to take some of my blame. Come. Let us accept each other's apology and be done with it.'' He walked toward her with one arm outstretched. Lillis put her hand out, not thinking of what she did.

His grasp was warm and strong, and he gently squeezed her hand and arm and smiled into her eyes. Lillis smiled at him, too, yet had no conscious thought of doing so. She was only aware of the strange sensation of being so close to a man, of holding his arm, of being alone in a room with him. Except for that morning, she had never before been alone with any man other than her father. The very thought made her heart beat faster.

She did not know how long they stood thus, clasping arms and staring into each other's eyes, but it seemed a long time. Slowly Alexander of Gyer slid his hand to hers, taking hold of it and turning it. His eyes moved to gaze at her palm, then, very purposefully, he drew her upturned fingers to his lips and gently kissed them. He looked back into her eyes as his lips pressed against her skin, and Lillis felt herself trembling. He must have realized it, for he immediately lowered her hand and released it.

"Come and share a cup of wine with me, Lillis of Wellewyn," he invited, turning from her.

Lillis stood where she was and tried to keep her body from shaking. Nothing like this had ever happened to her before and she didn't like it. The way his mouth had felt on her—no, she didn't like it at all.

"Thank you," she replied out of habit, her trembling voice causing her to wince self-consciously.

"Come and sit, will you?" he said, pouring the wine and setting a goblet for her on his desk, in front of the chair she'd sat in that morn. Lillis sank into the chair gratefully, wondering how much longer she would have been able to stand with her knees shaking so badly.

"Have—have you come to a decision yet?"

Alexander of Gyer didn't sit across the table from her as he had that morning; instead, he pulled another chair close to hers and settled into it.

"Not yet," he answered. "I thought perhaps we might discuss the matter further." He cast her a teasing grin. "If we can keep from fighting each other, that is."

Unable to help herself, Lillis smiled in turn and wondered, as she did, whether a man more handsome than this existed on God's earth. He had the greenest eyes she'd ever seen.

"I know it is strange," he continued, "to want to speak with you about such matters. You'll be thinking me crazed, I suppose. The truth, my lady, is that you're a most sensible captive."

"Oh?" Lillis lifted her eyebrows in mock amazement. "There are others to compare me with, then? You make a habit of holding people in your home against their will?"

He laughed aloud. "No, no," he assured her. "You and your companions are the only ones. I should have said, I think, that you are the most sensible woman I have ever known, instead."

Lillis forced a smile even though she again felt that twinge of jealous pain. She was a sensible female, never an attractive one.

"Thank you," she murmured, and with a steadier hand lifted the goblet and took a sip of the somewhat bitter red wine.

He studied her curiously. "Do you know, I find it impossible that Jaward of Wellewyn is your father. There is naught of him in you whatsoever."

"I take after my mother," she said. "Did you ever meet her? I'm sure I never met either of your parents, or any of your family, when I was a child."

He shook his head. "I cannot remember ever meeting your mother, and I didn't even know you existed until yesterday, when your father informed me of your impending marriage to Jason de Burgh."

"It is rather strange, is it not," she said thoughtfully, "for neighboring families to not know one another? Even in Tynedale we knew most of the people for miles around. I wonder how it is that we lived so close to each other and yet never met."

"I don't know, though I agree it is unusual. But your father has ever been something of a recluse, and my father and he hated each other, so they had no reason to go visiting."

"Did they?" Lillis asked with real surprise. "I didn't know that. Why did they hate each other?"

Alexander of Gyer gave a weary sigh. "I don't know. I was hoping you might be able to tell me, but it sounds as though you know less about it than I. I'm convinced that whatever was between Jaward and my father is the reason for Jaward's building the dam. He's set on revenge, and I don't even know why. I've asked him but he refuses to tell me."

Lillis frowned into her goblet, watching the red liquid wave back and forth in the cup. She wondered if what Alexander of Gyer said was true. Her father never discussed such matters with her, just as he never told her about the dam or about the tense circumstances with Gyer. It occurred to her that perhaps she didn't realize the full extent of her father's vengeful nature.

"I could find out, if you would let me," she offered.

"No." The word was final.

"Well—" she smiled at him briefly before returning her gaze to her cup "—it was worth a try."

They were quiet, then. Lillis could feel Alexander of Gyer's gaze upon her and somehow could not bring her own to meet it.

"I wish there was something I could do to help," she finally said. Anything to break the uncomfortable silence, though she sincerely meant the words.

"I know you do," he murmured, "and I appreciate it more than I can say. You and I share the matter of this problem so closely. Our fathers created this situation, and we are the ones who must set it to rights."

"This is true, Alexander of Gyer," Lillis agreed, standing and putting the goblet on the table. She walked to the window where Alexander had stood earlier and gazed out at the growing twilight. "But I have already told you my solution for the matter and you have decided against it. What more can I do? Other than be a complacent prisoner?"

He rose and joined her beside the window, looking at her intently. "Believe me, my lady, it is not you I distrust. It is your father. I have already told you why I dare not take the chance of letting you go to him in the hopes of turning him. He will quickly refuse to do anything that you ask, and I'll have lost the only power I have over him. It's too much of a risk."

"Then let me write to him!" she pleaded, holding out an entreating hand.

He shook his head. "He'll go to the king the moment he knows you're here. Impossible."

With a sound of exasperation, she turned her head to look out the window again. "We are still at odds, then."

"What about de Burgh?" Alexander of Gyer asked. "What do you know of him?"

"Little, my lord," she said with a slight shrug. "I've not even met him, I don't think, unless it was as a child. I don't remember him, if I did. But I thought you had already decided he is plotting with my father. Do you think he might somehow be useful?"

"I don't know," he answered thoughtfully. "We've never gotten along, as I told you, but even so, I've never thought that de Burgh wished to actually war with Gyer. He *is* an unreasonable, stubborn-headed dog, true enough, but is that reason to make him send his people to their certain demise?"

Lillis ignored this insulting slight to her betrothed and instead offered up a new idea. "I know! I shall make having the dam torn down a contingency of my marriage. If my father wishes me to wed de Burgh he'll have to tear the dam down first. What could be simpler? I don't know why we didn't think of it earlier." Her voice was filled with excitement.

He thought this over briefly, then frowned. "I cannot think your father will tear the dam down for such a reason. He'll probably threaten to keep you a maiden at Wellewyn your whole life long rather than lose his power over Gyer. You'd have done better to stay at the convent and take up the veil."

Lillis was undaunted. "Perhaps I could make certain that the marriage contract is written so that I will keep control and ownership of the land after my marriage. I'll demand that it be made a part of my dower. Would that not settle matters?"

"I should like to see you do it!" he replied with a bitter laugh. "Do you truly think either your betrothed or your father would agree to such a demand after all their careful planning? I doubt it very much."

"Oh!" Lillis snapped. "I give way! Nothing is acceptable to you. I'll grow old in this place while you try to make a decision."

Alexander gazed at her sympathetically. "I'm sorry. I know this is as unpleasant for you as it is for me. More so, as I have my freedom." He sighed and raised one arm to lean against the side of the window opening. "What a troublesome knot we must untie!"

Lillis was about to agree when the door to the room flew open. They both turned to find Willem standing there, breathless and tense.

"Alex! There's a fire in one of the tenants' villages."

"Damn!" Alexander pushed from the window, his face pale. "Where?"

"The northern fields." Willem's expression was grim. "It's bad, Alex."

The Lord of Gyer was already on his way to the door. "Take Lady Lillis back to her room," he barked, "and meet me at the stables. I'll gather the men."

Lillis didn't need to be told. She obediently went with Willem.

"No one will be harmed, do you think?" she asked anxiously as they made their way up the stairs.

"I hope not," he replied. "We can only pray that the rains of yesterday will slow the fire and keep it from spreading."

"Does anyone know how it was started?"

"No," he said, then added tersely, "Dunsted probably." She could hear the anger in his voice, and cringed.

Surely Jason de Burgh would never countenance his people doing such a horrible thing! No, the fire must have been started by accident, from a fallen candle or a smoking fire pit. These things often happened; it would make more sense than suspecting someone of deliberately setting it. Lillis hoped this was so. She knew only too well who would be blamed if Dunsted was responsible for the fire.

They reached the chamber door and Willem fumbled with the keys.

"I'm sorry to be so unmannerly, my lady, but you must understand." He opened the door and fairly shoved her in.

"Of course, of course," she reassured him. "Please be careful, Sir Willem. I hope you get there in time."

He nodded his gratitude, then closed and locked the door, leaving her staring at it.

"What is it, dear?" Edyth said, and came up behind her. "What's happened? How did your meeting with the Lord of Gyer fare?"

"Edyth," Lillis said, taking her companion's hand and squeezing it, "I have a dreadful anticipation that we are about to be in more trouble than we presently are. I do believe it might be well if we spent much of this night on our knees."

Chapter Six

‌The trip to the Lord of Gyer's private chamber was becoming a regular journey, Lillis thought the next day as she dutifully followed the servant who had come to escort her. She and Edyth had been woken at an unusually early hour that morn by Aunt Leta, who, in an agitated manner, had told them to rise and prepare themselves, though for what she didn't explain.

Lillis hadn't been able to get a word of information out of anyone about the outcome of the fire, though she'd sensed tension and trepidation in every servant who had come and gone in the hours that lapsed between their rising and the summons that finally came from the Lord of Gyer.

The servant and she reached the bottom of the stairs, and Lillis glanced out across the great hall. The sight that greeted her there was totally unexpected. The entire Baldwin family, including the children and the twins, along with what seemed to be the rest of the castlefolk and several villagers, were assembled there. With shock she realized they were all staring at her. Every single one of them. Their expressions were openly curious, as well as condemning, and with a jolt of fright Lillis turned her head and continued on her way after the servant.

Loud, argumentative voices could be heard as they neared the closed doors of Alexander of Gyer's private chamber, and the servant signaled her to halt. They stood there for some time, listening to the muffled voices that were sometimes pleading, sometimes crying, sometimes yelling, until the doors flew open and Barbara ran out into the hall. Her delicate hands were pressed against her face, so that she did not see where she went, and she stumbled against the wall. She was so distraught and blinded, totally unable to help herself, that Lillis instinctively moved toward her, putting one hand out to support and guide her.

"Lady Barbara, are you well?" she asked with concern, steadying the girl.

Barbara lowered her hands. She swayed momentarily, her wet face a picture of misery, until she realized who it was that helped her.

"You!" she screamed, drawing back and slapping Lillis so hard and suddenly that Lillis was temporarily stunned. She barely had time to realize what had happened before the hysterical creature hit her again, screaming and crying words that Lillis couldn't understand. Barbara lunged at her with both hands held out, as though to strangle her, but just as suddenly was snatched aside.

"Stop it, Barbara! Stop it!" It was Willem who held the struggling girl, shaking her by the shoulders in an effort to calm her. "Barbara," he said firmly, "remember yourself."

Lillis stood dumbly, staring openmouthed at her attacker. Barbara stared back with venom.

"I hate you!" she shouted like an angry child, then ruined the effect with a pitiful sob. "I'll not let you take what's mine! I would rather see you dead first!"

This earned her a couple more shakes from Willem. "Be quiet! You don't know what you say. Take the lady Lillis in," he instructed the servant who stood close by. "I'll take care of Lady Barbara." He dragged the girl away, leaving Lillis staring after them in shock.

"My lady?" the servant asked tersely, causing Lillis to look at him. He eyed her with hostility, as though she'd been the one who'd done the attacking, and motioned her forward with his hand.

Lillis looked at the chamber doors, then squared her shoulders, took a deep breath, crossed herself twice and walked in. The servant shut them behind her.

Alexander of Gyer looked terrible. Once again he stood gazing out one of the long windows, but unlike the day before, his clothes were covered with soot, as were his face and hands. His handsome chin showed evidence of unshaven stubble, and his dark hair was in a state of disorder. He looked as if he hadn't slept all night, indeed, it was obvious that he'd only just returned to the castle.

"My lord, what has happened?" she asked softly, amazed at the timid sound of her own voice.

He turned to look at her, and Lillis shivered. He was furiously angry, she could see it in his face and in his eyes. He looked ready to do violence.

"Four dwellings were completely destroyed," he answered with equal quietness. "Several others were damaged. It took most of the night to put the fire out."

"Was anyone—?" She squeezed her hands together until they hurt.

"Killed?" he finished for her in a menacing tone. "No. Thank God! We thought one of the children had been lost, but she was found safe this morn. Aside from the tragedy it would have been, I hate to think what the people of Gyer would have demanded of me if she had died." His meaning was very clear. Afraid, Lillis lowered her gaze.

"How did it start?"

"Not Dunsted," he informed her, taking a few slow steps closer, standing in front of her.

Lillis forced herself to meet his intense glare steadily.

"Are you relieved? You have no reason to be. Did you think that was the reason for the tension you feel about you today? For the angered looks from the people of Gyer? You are wrong, Lillis of Wellewyn. I will tell you why my people want me to hand you over to them so that they can deal out justice as they see fit." His teeth were clenched and his words seethed out. "The fire was started quite accidentally," he said, "by a smoking fire. Can you imagine? It should have been a simple matter to put it out with only a few buckets of water. Especially after the rains of the night before. And especially because the Eel River ran practically right outside the door of the dwelling involved. Save that it does not run anymore, does it? Thanks to your loving father, the people who lived in that village had to stand by and watch their homes burn to the ground because they didn't have sufficient water to put out a small, smoking fire.''

Lillis gazed at him, fighting back tears of both horror and panic. Alexander of Gyer stared at her with growing anger. He grabbed her by both arms and shook her, his voice rising with his fury.

"Don't you dare to look at me like that!" Each word was punctuated with a shake. "I don't want your damned sympathy! I have people who no longer have a roof over their heads and winter coming fast on their heels! I've just spent an entire night listening to their children wailing and to them worrying and wondering what they will do to survive. And all because of your father. Your beloved father." He spat the words at her. "So don't dare to stand there and have tears in yours eyes, Lillis of Wellewyn. I've not an ounce of pity left to spare you."

She tried to shake free, but to no avail. Alexander of Gyer held her fast. "I don't want your pity!" she cried. "Can't I feel badly about what happened? I'm not the one who dammed the river!"

"No, you're not," he agreed bluntly, releasing her, "but your father did, and you and I are the ones who'll pay for his sins."

There was something very final about his words, about the way he looked at her, and Lillis felt a shiver of apprehension.

"What—what do you mean?"

"I mean that I've come to a decision, Lillis of Wellewyn, about what I'm going to do with you."

That stunned her. He certainly seemed angry enough to hand her over to a violent crowd. The thought terrified her, for she knew very well the painful death she'd suffer. Perhaps she had learned how to be brave in the face of a hundred unruly children, but that was the extent of her courage.

"Have you?" she managed to say in a shaking whisper.

"I have," he said, looking at her directly. "We are going to wed, you and I. The only way that I can get rid of that

dam is to have control of the land on which it is built, and
the only man who will have control of that land is the man
who is your husband. But that man will not be Jason de
Burgh, as your father has planned.'' He moved closer.
''That man will be me.''

Alexander knew he shouldn't be seeing her now. He was
angry, upset and very, very tired. His emotions had frozen
like ice, leaving him with nothing but raw anger. Enraged as
he was, he couldn't be anything but unpleasant to her. But
he'd ridden all the way to Castle Gyer, after spending the
whole night and some of that morning fighting a fire that
wouldn't stop until it had done its damage, thinking of
naught but the decision he'd come to.

They would marry. He and Lillis of Wellewyn. He didn't
know why he hadn't thought of it before. It was the perfect
solution. They would marry and he would gain control of
the lands that came to her through her marriage. He would
tear the dam down, settle matters with Jaward and de
Burgh, and then let her go. She could go back to Wellewyn,
afterward, if she wished. She could go wherever she pleased.

He'd frightened her that morning, though he hadn't
meant to. He had seen immediately when she'd walked into
the room that she was anxious, her face pale and drawn, her
eyes circled with the exhaustion of a sleepless night.

It had been wrong to see her after having told Barbara of
his decision—a task that had been most unpleasant—so that
he'd greeted Lillis of Wellewyn with doubled anger. Now,
watching her lovely face contort with shock, he was deeply
sorry for it.

''You cannot mean that!'' she whispered in disbelief.

''I do. We are going to be married. Tomorrow. There is
no other way.''

''No,'' she said, shaking her head, staring at him from
wide, panicked eyes, ''I will not do it.''

''You will,'' he assured her without malice, turning and
walking toward his working table.

''I'll *not!*'' she cried from behind him.

He turned, leaned against the table and folded his arms across his chest. "You will. If you do not, I will ride against Wellewyn with my entire army and utterly destroy it. I will kill every man, woman and child who crosses my path and I will let my men do whatever they wish with whoever survives. Do you understand what it is that I say?"

She did, he saw. Her eyes widened with horror.

"I don't believe you," she murmured. "You are a man of peace. You could not do such a thing!"

Alexander was amazed at how cold he was. It was as though he'd died and someone else now lived in his body, someone filled with anger and weariness. "Yesterday I would have agreed with you, my lady, but today I can think of nothing I would enjoy doing more. You may believe what you will about me, but if you do not believe that I shall do as I've said then you condemn the people of Wellewyn to their deaths. This I vow before God."

"But it—it will not be legal," she said. He didn't miss the hopeful note in her voice. She looked at him again, a light in her eyes. "It will not be legal!" she repeated triumphantly. "There is no marriage contract. Without a marriage contract approved by both my father and the king, it will not be legal. The land will not be yours."

"I have arranged with Father Bartholomew at the monastery for the writing of the marriage contract," he said. "It will be completed this afternoon, and both you and I shall sign it before witnesses. Tomorrow morn we will have a large wedding and mass, attended by the entire village. You will behave like any other happy bride. You will walk to the altar with me willingly. You will repeat your vows willingly. There will be a celebration feast afterward with music and dancing, and you and I will attend and enjoy ourselves for all to see. The marriage will be consummated on our wedding night. The following day your Edyth will take the evidence of the sheet to Wellewyn, along with the marriage contract, to show Jaward. I should like to see him refuse to recognize the legality of our marriage then."

He stopped and smiled at the thought of Jaward's reaction. How he would love to be there to see the old man's face when he saw the sheet and read the letter that Alexander would send with it. His beloved daughter ruined and forced into a loveless marriage, his plans for destroying Gyer turned back on him. All in one master stroke. It would be worth any price to be able to see it.

"I will also send a copy of the marriage contract to the king requesting his approval," Alexander continued. "I shall have to supply an appropriate excuse for our breach of the law, of course. Perhaps I will tell him that we had to rush the marriage along so that our future child would not be born less than nine months from the wedding date. Would that suit, do you think?"

If it was possible, Lillis of Wellewyn's face grew even paler. Her hands trembled noticeably and she stumbled to the nearest chair and dropped into it.

"You are very angry now," she whispered. "You're not thinking clearly. In a day or two you will be able to consider what you're doing, and see how wrong it is. I beg you, Alexander of Gyer, do not do this thing."

He hoped she was right. He hoped he would be able to feel again soon, to think clearly, to regret what he was doing. She was a beautiful, admirable woman. The very least he owed her was sincere remorse.

"I'm sorry," he muttered, looking away. "I know the situation is—unpleasant."

"Unpleasant?" she repeated shakily, rising from the chair. "*Unpleasant!* I've spent most of my life in a convent, dreaming of the day when I would be free to marry, to have children and a home of my own. Now you say you will force me into an alliance of convenience for the sake of tearing down a dam that I have already sworn I would tear down myself if you would only trust me!" Her voice broke, causing Alexander's heart to lurch painfully. He could not bring his eyes up to face her. "I know that you love your Barbara," she continued when she could. "How could you do this to her, as well as to me?"

"You know nothing of my feelings for my cousin," he returned coldly. "Barbara is young, I will make certain that she is suitably married. It is you and I who will pay the price for our parents' misdeeds. I will give up the woman I intended to wed and you will give up your dreams. But you need not fear suffering my advances. I'll not demand my rights as your husband, and I'll not force you to remain at Gyer and live a lie. Once the land is legally in my hands you will be free to leave, to return to Wellewyn if you wish, though you must remain my wife. You may live as you please, where you please. You will be made an allowance so that you will never lack for money.''

"You are generous, Alexander of Gyer!" she informed him heatedly. "But if you do this thing, you will be making me your lifelong prisoner, complete, will you not? I may be free to live where I please, but I will still be your prisoner as surely as if I were locked away in that filthy room above stairs. I might as well have stayed at the convent! At least it would have been my choice.''

Alexander made an impatient, irate gesture with his hand. "It is too late to speak of what might have been. We have little choice, either of us, but to accept what is going to be and try to make the best of it. You should be grateful that I'm willing to allow you such freedoms. By all rights, once we are wed, you should be made to live at Gyer, or wherever I please to put you.''

She threw him an angry glare and walked to one of the open windows. "Your kindness overwhelms me, my lord. It is easy for you to speak of what will be. Your life will not change overmuch. You will still have your family, your people. You've had a whole lifetime of freedom, already. All I have ever done is dream of it.'' Her voice filled with longing. "Now I shall never know it.''

Alexander began to thaw. The sadness in her voice called forth an unwilling response of sympathy in him. He wanted to take her in his arms, comfort her, reassure her that it would not be so bad. He wanted to tell her that he understood how she felt, that he was sorry, that he would take care of her and be gentle with her in every way until she left Gyer. He didn't seem to be able to find a voice to express these thoughts, however, so he watched in silence as she dropped her head and again fought back tears.

It was a futile struggle and she cried quietly for a minute or two, her shoulders shaking slightly, her hands moving to wipe at her cheeks. And the anger in him continued to melt.

"Lillis—"

"Don't." She stopped him. "You have said quite enough, my lord. I thank you. I do not wish to hear more. I understand my circumstances perfectly." She drew in a shaky breath. "I am a great believer in accepting one's fate, you know. You could not have picked a better victim for your plan. I'll not treat you to a fit of hysterics."

"I will respect your feelings, Lillis of Wellewyn, and I will respect your person. You need have no fear of me. I shall do all that I can to make you comfortable as my wife."

She nodded mutely.

Alexander felt weary. All the anger had drained out of him. All the coldness had been melted by the gentleness of her. But he felt no regrets. He was the Lord of Gyer. He'd made the right decision.

"Come." He held out a hand to her. "We shall go and tell those who are in the hall. My people will be glad when they hear the news, and they will cease talk of sharpening the ax. You'll be well loved, you know, once the dam is torn down."

Her face held no expression as she walked toward him and placed her hand on his. She stood wooden before him, as if she had no life in her. Alexander didn't even know he'd lifted his other hand until he saw his fingers stroke her cheek in a gentle caress.

"All will be well, Lillis," he promised quietly. "All will be well."

She neither moved nor answered, but only stared at him, her pale face blank of everything save exhaustion. It was a state he was familiar with. As soon as the announcement was made, he thought, leading her toward the great hall, he was going to sleep like a dead man.

Chapter Seven

"I'm weary, Willem. Can this not wait till later?"

Willem followed his brother closely up the stairs.

"No, Alex, please let me talk to you. It won't take long."

Alexander pushed open his bedchamber door. "Talk, then," he invited grudgingly, sitting on his bed and pulling off his boots. "But make it quick."

"Alex," Willem began carefully, "I have a suggestion that I think might be helpful."

"Do you?" Alexander raised an eyebrow at him. After all the screaming and yelling he'd just encountered from his relatives about his plans to marry Lillis of Wellewyn, he could only wonder at what kind of idea his brother might have.

Willem nodded and, to Alexander's surprise, blushed.

"I would like to offer to marry Lillis of Wellewyn myself," he said. "There is no reason that you should be the one to make the sacrifice. You and Barbara have been betrothed since you were both children, while I've no previous attachments to hold me back. The land will come to Gyer no matter which one of us marries Lady Lillis, and it would be better for me to be the one, I think."

For some reason that he couldn't understand, Alexander felt like punching Willem squarely on the jaw, regardless of the fact that he knew his brother was only trying to be helpful.

"No," he said firmly. "I'll not have you make a sacrifice of yourself for my sake. I'm the one who'll do the marrying. I am the Lord of Gyer and it is right that I be the one to take the responsibility for my decision in this matter."

Willem shifted from one foot to the other and studied the floor.

"It wouldn't exactly be a sacrifice," he said quietly.

"What?" Alexander was certain he hadn't heard his brother correctly. His boots dropped to the floor with a loud thunk.

"I said—" Willem looked at him "—it wouldn't exactly be a sacrifice were I to marry the lady Lillis. I—I find her very attractive and, though I've only known her a short time, I think she is a rather admirable female."

Alexander was so stunned that momentarily he could not think of a single thing to say. Something inside him longed to tell his brother that Lillis of Wellewyn belonged to *him*, and that if Willem wished to keep his head on his shoulders he'd best keep his distance from her.

"Willem," he said as calmly as he could, "this is going to be a marriage of requirement between Lillis of Wellewyn and myself, not one of truth. I've promised her that she may go free once the land has been put legally under my control. Attraction and admiration have nothing do to with the union."

Willem blushed painfully under his brother's stern gaze. "I realize that is what you have to offer her, Alex, but I believe I could offer her something more. You know that I am not very...comfortable...with women, but I think she and I could be comfortable together. At least she would have someone to share her life with, instead of having to be alone. I know we don't love each other. How could we, having so recently met? But I have reason to believe that she might not be adverse to the idea."

"Is that so?" Alexander demanded angrily, standing full height. "And what gives you the idea that Lady Lillis might possibly feel that way? Has she said as much to you? Has she?"

"No, Alex, we've hardly spoken to each other," Willem assured him quickly, taking a few prudent steps backward. "We've never been alone long enough to be able to do so."

The words came tumbling out. "But she has been pleasant to me, nonetheless, and I'm not nervous with her as I am with other women. I simply think we might suit. Don't you want to be able to marry Barbara?" he asked with confusion.

Alexander quickly turned away. Barbara! His enchanting little cousin. Wouldn't he give everything to be able to marry her? Wouldn't he? All of his life he'd expected to wed her, had grown used to her, and feelings such as that didn't die easily. Perhaps he didn't love her as a man should love a wife, but he did care for her, and he certainly found her to be everything a man could want in a wife. Yet a remembrance of her unpleasant behavior that morn flashed through his mind—how expectant he'd been of just such a reaction. Just as quickly he had a vision of Lillis of Wellewyn softly crying and accepting her fate. If the truth were known, he'd wanted to send Barbara away so he wouldn't have to listen to her wailing, but he'd wanted to hold Lillis of Wellewyn, to comfort her, to let her comfort him in return.

"I'm going to marry Lillis of Wellewyn tomorrow, Willem. I'm sorry if you possess some kind of affection for her, but my decision stands. Now, if you will, I'm very tired."

Willem was quiet behind him, neither speaking nor moving. A loud, furious knock came at the door, and John Baldwin stormed in without waiting for Alexander's admittance.

"So!" John shouted furiously, slamming the door behind him. "I've come to give justice, Cousin!"

Without warning, the redheaded man launched himself at Alexander, catching him hard across the left cheek with his fist. The blow knocked Alexander back a step or two but did not fell him. Alexander made no move to return the insult, but only fingered his face where the blow had fallen.

"Hello, John," he greeted, grimacing from the pain. He had to give his cousin his due. For such a small man he had delivered a stinging blow. "I've been expecting something like that from you."

"She's in her room, crying," John Baldwin informed him hotly, both fists clenched at his side. "It would have been kinder if you'd simply killed her."

Alexander had no time for such foolishness. "I'm sorry, John," he said curtly. "You know I'd never have hurt Barbara could I have avoided doing so. I care for her greatly."

"You care for her!" John Baldwin was incredulous. "Bastard! You put her aside so that you can marry that whore from Wellewyn, yet still you say you care for her?"

He threw himself at Alexander again, but Alexander deftly caught his two clenched fists and held him back. Willem came from behind to pin John's arms down. Thus contained, John was forced to give up the assault. He struggled only a moment longer, then wrenched his arms free and glared at Alexander.

"Go on!" Alexander muttered. "I'll not speak with you when you're so overset."

"You don't care anything about my sister," John insisted. "She's devoted most of her life to loving you, yet you destroy her for a piece of land. Well, you may have your land and Lillis of Wellewyn—and welcome to them. Only keep away from Barbara. I mean it." He left as he had come, and slammed the door behind him just as loudly.

Willem turned wide eyes on his brother. "If you change your mind about my offer, Alex, I'll be ready. Even to the last minute."

Alexander shook his head. "I'll not change my mind. Don't waste your time waiting."

Willem left and Alexander finished undressing. He wanted to sleep, to blank his mind from the thoughts that stirred inside him. Instead, he sat on the edge of his bed, naked, and stared at the adjoining door.

She was on the other side. She and her Edyth. He wondered if she was all right, if she was able to rest any more than he. There was a way for him to use that door that she didn't know about; a pin he could push that would allow him to unlock both bolts from his side. His father had designed it that way so that his mother could never effectively lock herself away, so that he would always have a way to get into her room. Alexander himself would use it if the need ever arose, if Lillis of Wellewyn ever defied him entrance to her chamber once she had become his wife.

Alexander stared at the door a few moments longer, and then he put himself to bed. He was exhausted beyond belief, his thoughts already wandering into dreams the moment he lay down on the soft feather bed. He slept, restlessly, until a servant came to tell him that Father Bartholomew had arrived with the marriage contract.

Time didn't have much substance for Lillis after her talk with Alexander of Gyer ended. She had done her best to change his mind, and in the end had been forced to accept the inevitable.

As soon as she accepted her fate she fell into a state of deep despair. She was aware that things were happening, that people were talking, that she herself was moving and living and breathing, but she had no real involvement in any of it.

He had led her into the great hall. Every eye in the room had been upon them. He had made the announcement and those present had reacted. There had been relief on the part of the village leaders, who had originally come to demand her head, Candis and Justin had cheered loudly, the twins had stared openmouthed, Willem had looked unspeakably shocked, Barbara had cried while a man whom Lillis assumed was her brother tried to calm her, and Aunt Leta had fainted dead away.

It was Willem who'd taken her to her room, finally, and she had sensed a great deal of sympathy in him. He had squeezed her hand and kissed her cheek, the first time a man other than her father had kissed her at all, and he'd reassured her that everything would be all right. Once she had gone into her bedchamber Edyth had taken charge, caring for her while she was unable to take care of herself.

Somehow she'd found a way to tell Edyth what had happened, and the two of them spent the rest of the day sitting side by side. Edyth had cried and cried. Lillis couldn't really remember what she had done, other than sit. Alexander of Gyer came later with a priest, and she had mutely signed the marriage contract that was placed in front of her. They had left immediately after.

Had she eaten that day? Or slept that night? She didn't know. When had the afternoon passed into the night? And when had the night passed into the next day? Before she knew it she was besieged by servants—servants and a subdued Aunt Leta, who had come to prepare her for the wedding.

She had only a vague memory of what preparations took place. She was bathed in water that smelled like lilacs, then dried and perfumed. She was dressed in underclothes of the finest white silk, so different from the plain, rough underclothing she was used to. A surcoat of gold-embroidered purple damask was fitted over these and belted with a gold chain ornamented with rubies and diamonds. Her hair was braided and fashioned atop her head, then covered with white silk. A circlet of gold and rubies was carefully arranged on top.

Edyth cried throughout the whole of it, sitting on the bed and sniffing into her handkerchief.

Sometime later someone came to get them, and Lillis was led down the stairs, into the great hall, and out of the castle to the inner bailey. Who led her, she did not know, though she thought later it might have been Willem. She remembered being greeted outside the chapel by a great throng of people who cheered loudly at her. Inside she remembered seeing only him, Alexander of Gyer, waiting at the start of the long aisle to lead her to the altar.

She repeated her vows dumbly, never able to recall later what she had promised to do and not do. He spoke, as well, looking at her with his beautiful green eyes. He was more handsome than she had remembered, his dark hair brushed smooth, his face cleanly shaven. He clasped her hand tightly throughout the ceremony, as though afraid to let go of her. Afterward, having received the kiss of peace from the priest, he kissed her gently on the lips, the second kiss she had ever received from a man, though the first on her lips. From somewhere close by she heard Barbara wailing loudly, while directly in back of her, Edyth began sniffing again. A slight tremor passed over Alexander's features when he heard the women crying, and Lillis thought dimly that he mourned the loss of his Barbara. He led her outside then, one arm strong about her waist. The crowd cheered and cheered, and he took her into the castle.

A great feast followed. Her husband escorted her to the long table, set upon a dais at the front of the great hall, seated her in the place of honor and then sat beside her. There was music and feasting; people danced and laughed and ate for many hours. Lillis didn't recall what she ate, or whether she drank any wine; she was only aware that he held her hand throughout the celebration, sometimes stroking her fingers and sometimes squeezing them. They did not speak to each other at all.

At last Aunt Leta came and, with some of her ladies, took her away from the table and led her upstairs to her chamber.

Edyth was there, pale and still tearful, and rushed to take Lillis's hands.

"Oh, my dear!"

"Please don't cry any longer, Edyth," Lillis murmured, feeling very weary. "It's all over now."

"Not yet," Aunt Leta disagreed, though not unkindly. "There is still the matter of the consummation, and then it shall be over. Come, now—" she waved the four ladies who'd accompanied them toward Lillis "—the Lord of Gyer will be here shortly, and she must be made ready."

"But—" Lillis felt utterly bewildered as the women began to undress her.

"Hush!" Aunt Leta admonished, removing Lillis's chain girdle with care. "We've no time for talk. Hurry, Jehanne, and unbraid her hair. It must be brushed before we put her to bed."

"Edyth?" Lillis looked for her maid and found her standing in the shadows, tears pouring out of her eyes as she shook her head with misery.

"Oh, my dear," Edyth cried. "My poor, sweet lady."

Aunt Leta made a sound of impatience. "Poor, indeed! Do you suppose my nephew's going to do anything to her that men haven't done to their wives since God made Adam?"

The words caused Lillis's frozen rage to uncoil, and she came to life all at once. With nothing to cover her nakedness but her thin chemise, she pushed the women away.

"No more!" she demanded furiously. "I'll not be treated in such a manner, as if I were naught but chattel!" With a shaking finger, she pointed to the door. "Leave me at once. All of you, save Edyth."

"Don't be a fool!" Aunt Leta snapped. "We'll not leave until the consummation of the marriage has been witnessed. Are you so ignorant, my girl, that you don't know this?"

Lillis felt as if the breath had been sucked right out of her and, trembling, backed away from the women until she came up against a wall.

"No," she whispered in horror. "No, I don't know... Witness the—?"

"Witness the consummation," Aunt Leta repeated firmly. "How else is Alexander to gain that land unless the marriage has been legally consummated? And how can he prove it's been legally consummated unless there are witnesses? Without witnesses your father will have this marriage annulled as quick as this." She snapped her fingers. "Now, cease this childish behavior and let us put you into the bed, else your lord and his men will find you without, as you are."

Alexander watched Lillis go as Aunt Leta and the other women led her toward the stairs. She went with them in the same dazed state she'd been in all day, not really knowing where she was or what she was doing. He was rather stunned, too, by the speed and the reality with which events had passed. It would be understandable for Lillis to be more so. She'd not spoken a word to him during the day, other than her vows, and he wasn't altogether sure that she remembered saying those. Indeed, he'd had a suspicion during the ceremony that if he didn't tightly hold her hand she would collapse into a stupefied heap on the chapel floor.

The wedding feast had been like a waking nightmare for him; a host of conflicting sounds and faces. The villagers and castlefolk who crowded the great hall laughed and danced and lost no opportunity to express their well-wishes to their lord and new lady; Barbara cried incessantly and miserably at one end of the long table; Willem looked as if he'd lost his best friend; and his bride sat silent beside him, staring at nothing. He'd been relieved when Aunt Leta had finally come to take her away to prepare her for the wedding night. Once the marriage was consummated, the ordeal would be over, for Lillis, at least. For him it would continue until every last stone of the dam that stopped the Eel River was torn down.

Alexander wasn't looking forward to what he must do this night. It certainly wasn't going to be the joyful consummation he'd always imagined he'd share with Barbara; indeed, his coupling with Lillis of Wellewyn—no, Lillis of Gyer, now, he must remember that—promised to be nothing short of wretched for them both. When it was over...when it was all over, he would find a way to make up to her the humiliation he was certain she would suffer, and he would repay her a hundredfold during their marriage what the loss of her land and freedom were worth.

He let one quarter of an hour pass, then rose, nodding to the men he'd chosen as witnesses: his chamberlain and marshal, one of his most trusted barons and Father Bartholomew, the priest who'd married them. With understanding, the men rose, and at the same time the crowd in the hall came to life, seeing that their lord was about to make his way up to his bride. A man was sometimes carried to his marriage bed by a group of revelers, but none who knew Alexander of Gyer would ever dare such a thing. Even the most drunken among those at the celebration gave their lord plenty of freedom to pass by unmolested.

The five men traversed the stairway in solemn silence, but as they neared the chamber that was their destination, the sound of women's voices made them pause.

"I'll not be handled like a brood mare! I'm perfectly able to care for myself!"

"Oh! I should have known that Lillis of Wellewyn would have the manners of a stubborn ass! God only knows your father was ever thus!"

"My father! Look to your own nephew if you want a lesson in crudeness! Any man who would forcibly wed a woman for the sake of a strip of land is naught but a—"

Alexander pushed the chamber door wide, and the room fell utterly silent. Walking inside, he encountered the surprised expressions of several of his aunt's ladies-in-waiting, the doleful face of Edyth of Cantfield, and the equally furious faces of his aunt and bride. His own questioning gaze fell upon Lillis, who, at the moment, looked more beautiful than any woman he'd ever seen before. She was nearly nude, covered only by the thin garment that she held protectively against herself, with her pure white hair flowing free to her hips and her light blue eyes glaring at him with all the fire of some mythical Amazon, ready to do battle. He found it amusingly ironic that any bride should greet her groom thusly, so totally unwelcoming, and had it not been for the fact that Jaward of Wellewyn would use his daughter's unwillingness at the moment of consummation as an argument against the legality of the union, should he ever hear of it, Alexander would have laughed.

Instead, angered at the possibility of losing what he'd given up so much to gain, he frowned darkly at his bride. Without a word he stalked toward her, saw the defiance in her face and gripped her shoulders with both hands.

"My lady," he greeted quietly, hearing, irately, the maid Edyth sniffling dramatically nearby.

In response, his lovely wife made a face at him, which was as close to snarling as anything he'd ever seen a human do before.

Alexander pressed his fingers into her soft flesh more tightly, and saw, with satisfaction, that she understood at once.

He leaned very close and whispered, "You will do this willingly, madam, without complaint, exactly as I want you to, else I will do as I've promised and destroy Wellewyn. I will do it this night, as a wedding present to you, my sweet. I swear this by my own mother's soul. I shall mount up every man I possess and ride within the hour. Your father shall be dead, by my hand, before the sun rises in tomorrow's sky." He met her angry glare steadily. "Do you give way?"

"You are a *swine*," she said between clenched teeth, so that no one but he could hear.

"Perhaps," he admitted, "but do you give way?"

Her chest rose and fell with harsh, unsteady breaths, and her mouth was set in a grim line of rage.

"Do you?" he said.

"You know full well I do."

"Good." His hands on her shoulders kept her pinned to the wall, but he turned his head and spoke to the others in the chamber. "Witness the purity of the bed," he demanded, and the four men and four ladies-in-waiting moved to do his bidding. The blankets and coverlet were pulled back and examined, as were the pillows and the bed curtains, and the mattress was felt and manipulated by eight pairs of hands.

"It is unassailable, my lord," the marshal of Gyer stated when they had finished.

Alexander looked at Lillis once more. "Hear the willingness of the bride. Father Bartholomew?"

Father Bartholomew cleared his throat uncomfortably, then queried, "Do you submit to the possession of your lord husband, my lady? Freely and willingly?"

Alexander didn't think anyone had ever looked at him with quite so much loathing as his bride did at that moment. Staring at him, she silently mouthed the words, "You have made me a liar," before answering loudly, "I submit, freely and willingly."

Having said the words, her chin rose defiantly, and Alexander knew, in that moment, that he would never again know such a woman as this. An odd feeling of pride possessed him, because she would soon be his wife, and his alone, and made him regret even more the humiliation he must next visit upon her.

With one hand, he ripped away the chemise she clutched and tossed it aside, leaving her utterly exposed; then, ignoring her gasp of outrage, he bent and scooped her into his arms, carrying her to the bed.

"Affirm the purity of the bride," he said harshly, dropping her onto the mattress and tossing a coverlet over her so quickly that none but he had a chance to see her nakedness. Heads craned to look over Alexander's broad shoulders, but dropped back when he turned to face them. Cursing his own foolishness for forging a weak link in his plans, he demanded, "Do you so affirm?"

Eight silent heads nodded, and Edyth, standing with Aunt Leta, broke into even louder wails.

With a shake of his head, Alexander turned and met Lillis's eyes once more. She lay in the bed, dearly clutching the coverlet with both hands, gazing at him with apprehension. It seemed strange to him that, in the midst of this, with an angry bride and a roomful of onlookers, he should be so completely aroused and wanting her. But she was so lovely—more perfectly formed than any other woman he'd seen unclothed—and she was *his*. Yet she was embarrassed, as well as frightened—he could see these things in her eyes, along with her hatred of him—but she'd not be alone in this. He would share the humiliation of what they were about to do in front of witnesses, though perhaps his experience would be more complete, as his body had already reacted to the sight of her. But she would know, beginning tonight, this very moment, that Alexander of Gyer would never ask more of her than he would of himself. With this in mind, he began to undress.

When it was done he made a slow turn before those in the chamber, holding his arms aloft.

"Affirm the state of the groom," he said, ignoring the flushed countenances of the ladies present and the shocked weeping of Edyth of Cantfield who, along with Aunt Leta, kept her head turned.

"We so affirm, my lord," replied the marshal.

Without another word Alexander stepped into the bed and drew the curtains shut, until he and his bride were left in near complete darkness. Moving right for her, feeling her trembling nakedness, he set a hand over her mouth, and set his own mouth to her ear.

"Be silent, and trust me, and I shall have this misery done with as quick as possible."

Tears wet the hand that touched her, but she nodded her agreement and Alexander, blanking every thought, moved above her. Her body shook badly beneath him, yet she complied as he whispered his instructions, as he made her his wife, and she made no sound, save when he tore her maidenhead, and then she only gasped and shuddered while he held her tight and completed the act. Never had he received such little satisfaction from giving a woman his seed, and he sent God a fervent prayer, in the moment of his release, that she would not conceive his child from this so unjoyful union.

She cried when it was done, pitifully, so that Alexander's heart ached.

"It's over, Lillis," he whispered soothingly, moving away from her, taking her with him and holding her. "You are my wife, now. There's only a little more, and then I shall make everything right."

Her body was warm and needy against his own. She pushed her face into the place between his neck and shoulder where a wife should be able to seek comfort of her husband, and Alexander held her, giving what he could in reply to her misery, loath to push her away as he knew he must. When he finally sat he did it quickly, giving her but a moment to understand what was coming. He shoved the curtains aside, and, wrapping her firmly in the coverlets, took her up in his arms and stepped from the bed, on the side away from the witnesses.

Eight pale faces met his gaze, then fell as one to the stained sheet on the bed.

"Bring the Lady Edyth forward," Alexander commanded.

Lillis wept against his shoulder, begging, "No—no—"

When Edyth was forcibly dragged to the foot of the bed by Aunt Leta, Alexander demanded, of all those present, "Witness the bed. Affirm the loss of Lady Lillis's maidenhead."

Weeping wildly, Lillis lifted a hand and struck him aimlessly, and Alexander, suffering the blow as his due, held her that much more tightly.

"We so affirm it, my lord," the chamberlain replied.

"Affirm, my wife," he demanded of Lillis, "that this is the blood of your innocence, that there has been no trickery between us in this matter."

She nodded and, with what Alexander felt was a valiant effort, murmured, "Yes."

"Swear, then, all of you, that the Lady Lillis has become my wife in truth, by her own will, and that any who question you will receive such a reply, that Lillis of Wellewyn has been made the wife of Alexander of Gyer in truth and in whole, that our marriage is complete and unassailable."

All present, save Edyth, so swore.

"Take the sheet," Alexander instructed his aunt, "and keep it safe. Take Lady Edyth to the chamber prepared for her, and in the morn bring her to me so that I may send her to Jaward of Wellewyn with this proof of his daughter's marriage. The rest of you may go."

With these words Alexander strode to the door that adjoined his own chamber, and took his wife into it. Everything there was just as he'd commanded it should be, and, satisified, he took Lillis to the bed and gently set her upon it.

The bed was soft and clean, and the room was warm from the fire that blazed in its place. Alexander of Gyer unwrapped the coverings that imprisoned her and tossed them aside, leaving Lillis wholly exposed. The bed was cool against her skin, compared to the fire, and she tried to relax, willing the ache that throbbed deep inside her, in that place where he'd hurt her, to go away.

All her life, she'd expected that moment to hurt. Did not every girl child know, from the moment she was able to understand, that this one moment in her life would hurt, and that the pain would be a sacrifice that would prove her purity? That it would be a glorious thing, the sign that she would be a godly wife to her husband and a godly mother to her children? That was what it was supposed to mean, wasn't it?

"Lillis." His voice moved over the tension in her body, making her aware of how tightly her hands were fisted. "Now it's done." His deep voice was soothing, reassuring. She felt his hand on her hip, turning her toward him, to lie flat. "Let me care for you, now. Just for tonight."

She jumped when he put the warm, wet cloth between her legs, but he said, "It's all right, sweet. It's all right," and Lillis lay still, very tired, wanting to sleep.

She did sleep, though she was aware that he bathed and dressed her and, afterward, held her.

"Please," she whispered, her last conscious thought, not able to say more of what she wished.

"Sleep," he said, stroking her hair, understanding what she wanted without hearing the words. "My beautiful wife," he said, after she'd passed into slumber. "Sleep."

Chapter Eight

"I'm sorry, my lord, but she has refused her food again."

The servant shuffled nervously, looking as though he were somehow to blame for what had happened. Alexander frowned at the man's bowed head.

"She's made no requests whatsoever?"

"No, my lord," the man answered meekly. "She says very little and then only when she is first spoken to. She sends the maidservants away when they try to bathe and dress her. She'll not even sleep in the bed, my lord, but sits in the same chair both day and night, wearing only her nightshift. One of the servants found her asleep in the chair last night when she had gone in to take her some food, but when she tried to put Lady Gyer to bed she would not go."

"Very well," Alexander muttered. He waved the man away. "Leave me."

It had been three days since the wedding and Alexander was at the end of his patience. In those three days Lillis had neither come out of her chamber nor eaten any food. She refused to see him or anyone else. The servants reported the same thing day after day. On the morn following her wedding night, Lady Gyer had returned to her chamber and pulled a large chair close to an open window, then had seated herself there almost permanently, rising only occasionally to use the chamber pot or to drink a little water. Always she returned to the chair. She even slept in it.

Wearily Alexander leaned back in his chair, closing his eyes. Perhaps he should have stayed that first morn after their wedding night, instead of leaving her there to waken in a strange chamber all alone. He'd thought, at the time, that she would prefer it that way, especially after all she'd suffered at his hands the night before, but now he wondered if his attempt to please her hadn't only angered her the more. Perhaps she'd taken his absence as a personal slight—a thoughtless act of discourtesy from the man who'd forced her into marriage. She must have thought so, Alexander told himself. She must have, else she'd have accepted the wedding gift he'd left on her pillow and not used the valuable brooch to rend his pillow to shreds with, instead. And she certainly never would have locked herself away as she had, behaving exactly like a spoiled child rather than the sensible woman he knew her to be. Indeed, this was the sort of sulking he expected out of the twins, never from the woman he'd taken to wife.

He'd thought it strange that first day when she made no appearance to partake of the morning meal. He'd been disgruntled, as well, because those few wedding guests who'd spent the night at Gyer could not help but notice that the new Lady of Gyer was absent, but he'd made excuses for her, saying she was weary from the activities of the day before, and had borne the teasing that came his way after. In truth, he'd been more concerned about Barbara's absence than Lillis's, for his wife might truly be weary or even feeling shy, while Barbara's only reason for staying away was her unhappiness, a thought that made Alexander's guilt weigh heavier than before.

He'd left the table and gone to his private chamber as quickly as he could. Shortly after, responding to his summons, Aunt Leta arrived with the marriage sheet, which had already been folded and wrapped in a neat package.

Throwing the package on his table, Aunt Leta announced, "Lady Gyer refuses to either dress or eat. I told her I was certain she would at least wish to bathe and she threw me out of the room."

The words, so unexpected, had thoroughly surprised Alexander. *"What?"*

Aunt Leta happily repeated herself, and by the time she'd finished answering all his questions, Alexander had been furious.

"Leave her be," he'd instructed. "If she wants to behave as a child, then let her do as she pleases. Perhaps a day without food and company is just what she needs to bring her to reason."

That first day, being so busy in making preparations to take over the lands that were now his by marriage, Alexander barely had a moment's time to think of his wife, sitting alone in her chamber. When he did think of her it was to convince himself that she would be all right—one day without food had never harmed anyone.

It was late when he finally made his way to his chamber that night and, worn to the bone from the long day's work, he put himself to bed immediately, not letting his gaze even fall upon the adjoining door. Lillis had refused food and company the entire day, Aunt Leta had informed him at the evening meal. Alexander had shrugged at this news and firmly put all thoughts of his wife from his mind, turning his attention instead to Barbara, who'd finally come to sit at the table with the rest of the family. Lillis would tire of her self-imposed exile shortly, and would come out in the morn. He was certain of it.

The following day Alexander kept himself busy dealing with the many tenant problems he'd not had time to take care of in the past month. He made arrangements for the rebuilding of the village that had been destroyed in the recent fire, and made certain that the families had sufficient dwellings and supplies to keep them until their homes could be repaired.

As busy as he was, however, and as much time as he tried to spend with Barbara in an effort to bring a smile back to her face, he grew more constantly aware of the fact that Lillis still had neither eaten nor come out of her room. The reports from Aunt Leta were the same throughout the day, and by the time the evening meal had come and gone Alexander was thoroughly irate. He'd given Lillis more than enough time to come to terms with what had transpired between them, and every indulgence had its limits.

That night, as he lay in his bed, straining to hear any sounds that might come from her chamber, he finally decided enough was enough. She'd been in there for two entire days. Something was wrong. If she was angry then she should rail at him; if she was unhappy she should let him offer comfort, but whatever her ailment was, Alexander would no longer let her starve herself into illness. Determined to put an end to her foolishness, he rose and went to the adjoining door. The pin pushed in and the bolt slid open, but when he pushed at the door he found it wouldn't budge.

"Lillis!" he called through the wood, making another ineffectual shove against it. Nothing. Damn! She must have put something on the other side to keep it closed. He pushed again to no avail. Damn!

"Lillis!" he repeated more loudly. "Answer me!"

He knew that she heard him; not even a deaf person could have slept through all the noise he'd just made, yet no sound came from the other side. She wasn't going to speak to him, and that knowledge, for some reason his normally logical, controlled self couldn't understand, enraged him all the more.

"I will let this pass for now," he shouted at the door, "but tomorrow night I'll use the outside door if I must. There will be no barriers between us, Lillis Baldwin. I am the lord of this castle, and I'll not be kept out of any room in which I wish to go."

She neither answered nor made any sound, and Alexander finally went back to bed. Eventually he fell into a restless sleep, waking on and off throughout the night with unbidden dreams that left him confused. Dreams of smoothing his hands through soft, white blond hair and of a warm, shapely body pressed against his own. By the time dawn arrived, he gave up the battle and rose for the day.

Now the third day had passed and she still had not eaten or come out of her room. What a thoroughly aggravating woman to behave in such a manner! If she didn't come down soon, he would fulfill his promise of the night before. Nothing would keep him from getting into that chamber. Nothing. He only regretted that he'd promised to wait until evening time, else Lillis of Gyer would already know who her lord and master was, and what kind of behavior he would accept from her in future.

There wasn't much longer to wait, however, for it was time for the evening meal. He'd give her one hour, once the meal was over, just one hour to make an appearance, and if she didn't then he would go and fetch her. That would be the end of it.

The sun was beautiful at this time of day, sinking into the land and glowing orange and gold. Lillis gazed out the window and wondered if her father might be looking at this same beautiful sight—a fall sunset, with such lovely colors in it, and the breeze soft on his skin, just beginning to chill as night came.

She'd thought of her father a great deal since she'd woken after her wedding night to find herself lying alone in Alexander of Gyer's bed. She'd thought of her father, and of many other people and things, though she'd dwelled mostly on her years at the convent.

She remembered the many travelers who'd stayed at Tynedale on their way to more interesting places, and how excited she and the other girls would become at the prospect of hearing about those places, about London and Shrewsbury and even of France. The knights who came were the most exciting of all; Lillis recalled how fiercely she and the others would fight for the honor of serving them at table in the hopes of hearing stories of the battle at Shrewsbury, and of the bravery of King Henry and his son, the Prince of Wales.

When she'd grown older, the arrival of knights and fighting men at Tynedale had signaled trouble for Lillis. Being in charge of the other girls at the convent, she'd necessarily spent many a night on guard, a heavy candlestick at the ready, to discourage any secret trysts after the nuns had sought their beds. She'd been quite good at scaring off those few amorous fellows who did make an attempt. She was as tall as many men and taller than some, quite strong, and her faithful candlestick was sufficiently heavy to give even the most insistent lover pause for thought. As far as Lillis knew, not a one of the girls in her charge ever lost her virtue during the years they were under her care. She, of course, had never been in danger of such a thing—none of the men who'd passed through Tynedale had ever shown an interest in her—in a mannish female whose height and odd coloring made children think her a witch.

What would the sisters think of her predicament? Lillis wondered. They'd all been so glad when they'd learned of her betrothal to Jason de Burgh and had made a celebration of her impending marriage on the day before she left Tynedale. What would they think now to know she'd let herself be wed to a man who wasn't her betrothed, for the sake of a piece of land?

Sister Agatha, she knew, would tell her as severely as possible to stop feeling sorry for herself and to make the best of a bad situation. Lillis could almost hear the elderly woman's grating voice assuring her that every circumstance in life is brought about with God's greater purpose in mind, and that she should be thankful for whatever came her way. That was exactly what Sister Agatha would say. And perhaps, Lillis thought, Sister Agatha was right.

A chill breeze caused her to shiver, and drew Lillis's gaze to the open window once more.

It was mid-September. Michaelmas would be celebrated soon in honor of the harvest. The people of Gyer would have little reason to celebrate, since their harvests had been mostly ruined by her father's damming of the Eel River, but perhaps the river would be running again soon and the field workers could begin planning next year's planting. Perhaps next year's crops would more than make up for all that had been lost this year. With all her heart, Lillis hoped it would be so. Everything she had gone through would be worth it, even her false marriage, if only the people of Gyer could regain what they'd lost because of her father.

Lillis would not be there to see it, if they did. She would be in Wellewyn when next year's crops were planted. She'd not watch them grow or see how they progressed or how the harvest turned out. What would she be doing? Probably sitting in the crumbling keep at Wellewyn, spending her days caring for her father and trying to keep their home from falling down about their ears.

And she would be alone, or rather, lonely. She would probably not see him again—her husband—once she left Gyer. When she left, he would have no reason to visit her. He would be glad to be rid of her, most like. He'd be able to get on with his life. He and his precious, weeping Barbara. He and the land that had once belonged to Wellewyn.

Stiffly Lillis rose from the chair. It was growing colder now, the open window inviting every breeze to chill her. Lighting a candle against the coming dark, she found the water pitcher. After a long, refreshing drink, she washed her face and hands, then searched out a bar of soap and a fresh bathing cloth.

Regardless of what had happened, of what his motives were, Lillis could not make herself hate Alexander of Gyer, though finding that insulting brooch on the morning after her wedding had certainly made her think she could, at least for the five minutes it had taken to vent her fury at being paid off like the veriest whore on his pillow. Other than that, he had dealt well with her. She could not forget how kind he'd been after the consummation of their marriage. His care had been the most gentle thing she'd ever known; she could not forget, ever, the painstakingly careful touch of his hands, the soothing of his deep voice, or the comforting heat of his arms and body during the following night. And even before that, he'd not purposefully tried to humiliate her in front of those who'd witnessed the act. In spite of her anger and shame in that moment, she'd known this. He'd done the best he could in the face of an unpleasant situation, and now she must do the same.

The evening meal had already begun by the time Lillis descended the stairs. She hadn't meant to be late, but she hadn't had enough time to bathe and dress and still arrive on time. All of the castlefolk, save the servers, were already seated, and a trio of musicians stood to one side, playing soft music to accompany the meal. She saw Alexander of Gyer sitting in the place of honor at the long table, but he did not notice that she'd entered the hall. Somewhat embarrassed, unsure of what to do but too hungry to turn back, Lillis made a slow, careful approach to the dais on which the long table sat. She had no practice with such matters, but she was fairly certain that she should be seated there, beside her husband.

As she neared the table, however, she saw that the chair next to Alexander's, the chair meant for the Lady of Gyer, was already occupied. By Barbara. Not only that, her husband was in the process of taking Barbara's hand in his, at the same time both smiling and leaning toward that lady with open affection in his eyes. Lillis stopped directly in front of him, struggling to control the confusion she felt, and the pain.

Finally he noticed her, but only because everyone else in the hall had stopped talking. He gazed at her with an odd expression, then stood, but he did nothing else, and said nothing. Lillis waited for him to speak, to welcome her at the table or simply to tell her to sit down somewhere, but he only stood and looked at her as though she were some kind of specter. It became clear after a silent moment that he wasn't going to ask Barbara to move down. He wasn't going to say or do anything.

Not knowing what else to do, and not willing to stand there a moment longer making such a fool of herself, Lillis turned from her husband's gaze and looked for a place to sit. There was only one table where places were still empty, and with as much grace as she could manage, Lillis lifted her skirt and made her way toward it, wishing with every step she took that those in the room would turn their attention back to their food. The fact that she had no cause as the Lady of Gyer in sitting with the servants didn't particularly bother her. At the convent the table was a place for eating, not for arrangements of social status.

Seating herself, ignoring the silence, she selected a round of bread from a platter on the table and began to cover it with the different offerings of meats and fish and vegetables. And then the fracas began. With an angry oath directed at his elder brother, Sir Willem left the table in disgust. A moment later Alexander whispered something to the lady Barbara that caused her to burst into tears, which enraged her brother, John, who stood and said something that in turn enraged Alexander, who delivered a blow so stunning to his cousin that Lillis thought the poor man might not waken for a week. It seemed that everyone in the great hall, other than herself, watched this spectacle with great interest. But Lillis continued to eat. She was very hungry, and really didn't care how or why the family of Gyer went about destroying themselves. They were quite the strangest people she'd ever known, and best left alone.

But she was only allowed the bliss of a few mouthfuls of food before her husband came striding purposefully toward her.

"I want to speak with you," he said, grabbing her arm the moment he reached her.

"I'm eating," she informed him stiffly, yanking her arm free, "and I'm hungry."

"If you are, then it's your own fault." He pulled her physically out of her seat and dragged her from the table. Lillis had no choice but to go with him.

They didn't get very far, however, before Alexander sensed that every eye in the room was still upon them. He stopped long enough to turn his angry glare at the stunned castlefolk.

"Eat!" he thundered at them in general. "And you!" he shouted at the musicians. "Play!"

Everyone complied at once.

Satisfied with this response, Alexander escorted Lillis from the room. They didn't go to his private chamber, as she'd assumed they would, but instead passed the doors to that room and continued down the hall, stopping in front of another set of double doors. These Alexander pushed open, then drew Lillis into a chamber already well lit with candles. His rough handling caused her to stumble, but she quickly regained her composure, straightened and looked about her. It was a solar of some kind, decorated with a more feminine hand than Alexander's working chamber was and with long windows that opened out onto what appeared in the darkness to be a garden terrace.

They were alone for the first time since their wedding night. She heard him bolting the doors behind her. For some reason her hands trembled, and her heart pounded in her chest. She drew in a breath, folded her hands together in front of herself and waited for him to speak.

Alexander fought his own battle, standing against the door and staring at Lillis's turned back. For a woman who'd spent the past three days starving herself, she looked damned good, especially dressed as she was in the blue surcoat he'd seen her in before and with her white hair arranged in one thick braid that traveled the path of her femininely curved back. The shock that had rendered him speechless when he'd first seen her, so suddenly, so unexpectedly standing before him in the great hall, looking more beautiful than he had remembered, now seemed magnified a hundredfold. He had the oddest desire to pull her into his arms and kiss her, an idea so utterly foolish that he had to wonder at how he could possibly even think it.

"You will explain yourself, madam." His voice sounded hard, even to his own ears.

Lillis stiffened at his angry tone. "My lord?"

"I want to know what you mean by your behavior of the past three days," he clarified curtly. "I assume you have some reasonable explanation for locking yourself away and denying yourself all manner of human comfort?"

"I do, but I cannot think why you should want to know it, sir." How strange it was, Lillis thought, to suddenly have a husband to call *sir,* to have a husband calling her *madam,* in the way that married people did.

He made an irate sound. "You are my *wife.* I am your *husband.*" He sounded as if he were explaining elementary knowledge to a naive child. "Everything about you concerns me."

Her expression was faintly amused as she turned to look at him. "You have little reason for concern, my lord. The land is yours regardless what happens to me."

Alexander's eyes narrowed, and he gazed at her with a displeased frown. "You do not know me well, Lillis Baldwin," he said quietly, "nor yet do I know you, but you had best learn not to speak to me in a manner such as that. My sufferance is long, but not without limit."

Chagrined, Lillis looked away from him again. He spoke the truth. As her husband, lord and master, Alexander of Gyer could do whatever he wished to her if she proved disobedient. And, in truth, did she want the man to think her a shrew? A woman without gentility and honor?

"I was fasting," she murmured contritely.

Alexander was sure he hadn't heard right. "Fasting?" he repeated with disbelief.

Eyes lowered, she nodded. "Yes. It is a very good way to settle one's thoughts when one is—unsettled." A faint blush crept to her cheeks, and she rushed on in explanation. "Fasting is a practice used often by the sisters at Tynedale, sometimes as a method of punishment or penance, but more often as an expression of faith. It truly can be most—spiritually cleansing."

Looking at her, seeing the slight paleness of her skin, the thinness of her face, Alexander said, "I have no wish to deny you a practice of faith, madam, but in future you will express your intentions *before* you commence starvation. Otherwise I will assume that your behavior is childish and willful, and shall have no choice but to punish you."

"In future, my lord, I shall not be at Gyer to subject you to such an activity," she informed him matter-of-factly, then, when she looked up to see the anger on his face, added, "and, in truth, my fast was not an entirely honest one. Each day the maids brought trays of food, and each day I took some bread and fruit and ate them. It wasn't much—not enough to be missed—" she made a guilty, childlike face that gave Alexander's heart a strange twinge "—but I was terribly hungry, and I've never truly been good at the practice." Then, to make her confession complete, she admitted ruefully, "At Tynedale, whenever the nuns would cause me to fast, I'd sneak food beneath my surcoat and eat it in my bed at night." She glanced at him for understanding. "I've never been very good at it," she said once more.

No one had ever spoken to him in such an open, honest manner before. At least, no one to whom he was not related. Her simple words moved over Alexander like some unseen force, giving rise to an unwanted feeling inside him. He didn't even really know this woman, he told himself insistently, or anything about her, save that she was his enemy's daughter, yet, looking at her, he couldn't keep himself from imagining Lillis as a young girl, a smaller, younger version of the beautiful Amazon she was, getting into all manner of trouble and mischief, and sneaking bread and sweets into her bed at night to keep from being hungry.

The desire to kiss her kindled into something fierce and, worse, unsettling, for Alexander was nothing if not controlled, logical, clearheaded—these were the qualities, *his* qualities, which had made Gyer what it was. But at the moment those things had traitorously fled him, leaving him staring at her, at his lovely wife, who hated him, and wondering, like some lust-sodden idiot, what it might be like to make love to her slowly and thoroughly, as he'd been unable to do on their wedding night.

Their wedding night! He remembered it vividly, remembered every moment. The misery of it—and the wonder of it, to find himself possessed of such a woman. Her full, rounded body, her soft, white skin—that hair, tickling his arms and back—and being inside her—his wife—

"What has happened to my maid? Have you sent her to Wellewyn?"

He stared at her.

"My lord?"

"What?"

"My maid. Edyth. I've not seen her these past three days."

Giving a shake of his head, Alexander made himself think more clearly. His body, aroused and hard beneath his tunic, he had little control over, but his mind, at least, he might force to his will.

"Yes, she's at Wellewyn," he replied as easily as he could, strolling toward the fire. "I sent her the morn after our wedding, and have had word back that she arrived safe and in good time." He set one hand on the mantel, and stared into the flames. "She took with her the sheet and a copy of the marriage contract, along with a letter from myself."

"But there's been no word, yet? From my father?"

She sounded so anxious that Alexander glanced at her briefly. "No, nothing from Jaward of Wellewyn yet. I admit, I did expect a reply by now, but he may be trying to find a way out."

"Or he might be ill," Lillis suggested.

Alexander made a snorting sound. "He's trying to find a way around what's been done, but he'll not be able to. He'll not, and when he's understood that there is no escape he'll send me word."

"Yes," Lillis agreed quietly, looking at her husband's broad back, thinking what a big man he was, and how heavy, and how that big, heavy body had felt pressed into her own. "And when he has, will I then be free to leave?"

"We'll speak of that when I've had his reply."

"But—"

"Why did you rend my pillow?"

"My lord—"

"Answer me." His tone held no room for argument, and Lillis tamped down the need to have her freedom made sure.

Drawing herself to full height, gazing at his turned eyes, she said simply, "If you must ask that question, sir, then I can only think you know little of women. Or that perhaps your nature is cruel, or your humor odd. I believe I am the one who should ask instead what you meant by leaving me such an insult. I was not aware I had done anything to warrant it, but if I have I beg you tell me, so that I'll not do it again. I should not like to be treated to such as that in future."

"Your tongue," Alexander said with a shake of his head, "certainly needs no sharpening, my Lady Gyer." He turned back to the fire and murmured, "If we must speak of odd humor, let us speak of God's, to put such a tongue against the body and face of an angel."

Lillis blinked. *"What?"*

"Nothing." This came out on a weary sigh. "It was no insult, the brooch. You took it as a kind of payment, did you not?" He glanced at her once more, saw her set face and said, "You did. The worst kind of insult, being paid for your land, for your maidenhead. I will admit guilt so far as that I did think your sensibilities might be soothed, but in truth, it was meant as a wedding gift. The piece belonged to my mother, and is meant to be the Lady of Gyer's, along with a full chest of other jewels. They are yours now, as you are the Lady of Gyer, and shall in turn be inherited by our eldest son's wife, or, should you only give me daughters, to the one who inherits my lands and title."

Utterly shocked, Lillis sputtered, "S-s-sons!" and was just barely able to get the word out of her mouth.

"Mmm," Alexander sounded out indifferently. "Or daughters."

"But—! But you said—you *promised* me that you'd not—not—" She wasn't entirely sure how to go on, but at least Alexander of Gyer had given her his full attention.

"Not what?" he asked with a slight frown.

"Do you not remember, my lord? When you told me of your decision that we wed, you said you would never demand your husbandly rights."

"Yes, and so I did," he admitted readily, seeing no problem with this. "I've no intention of forcing myself upon you more often than is necessary for the begetting of heirs, and not at all once you've given me a sufficient number of children. I am a man of my word."

Lillis's mind whirled; she wondered if perhaps the combination of her hunger and the shock of his words might actually cause her to faint.

Alexander was at her side in a moment, his hands on her arms, his face filled with concern. "You look unwell, Lillis. Come and sit by the fire and let me pour you a cup of wine." Setting her in a chair, he turned to fetch the drink.

"It's that damned fasting," he stated angrily, pushing the goblet into her shaking hands. "I will never again allow you to behave so foolishly for so long. One day of it is as much as I'll countenance in the future, and none at all when you're with child."

Lillis gratefully drank the wine while Alexander, muttering about the idiocy of certain religious rites, leaned against the mantel and watched her. She felt much calmer when she was finished.

"My lord," she said as she set the empty goblet aside, "please let us have an understanding of this. You assured me before we wed that once my father's land was legally yours I should be able to leave Gyer and do as I please, live as I please—"

"So I did."

"But you never spoke of children, you did not say that you would require heirs of me, and I'm afraid I assumed that once our marriage was consummated I should not have to receive you in my bed again. Ever."

The muscles in his face tightened. "Are you trying to tell me, madam, that you mean to refuse your duty to provide me heirs?"

"Of course not! I simply mean to remind you of your promises, sir. If you required children of me, why did you not tell me beforehand?"

He gave her a look that said her words were utterly foolish. "Would you have me speak what should be obvious? Shall I tell you that this fire is hot?" He swept a hand at the flames. "That the sky is blue? That snow is cold?"

"That makes no sense whatsoever," she returned hotly. "The two matters have nothing in common. What was obvious to me at that time was that you'd not demand your husbandly rights—your own words, my lord—and I certainly cannot conceive children on my own. What else was I to think?"

"Perhaps your conclusion was obvious to you," he said, "but what is obvious to me is that convent life has left you sorely lacking in common knowledge. I should have made the matter more clear before we wed," he admitted, "but even you will admit that the day was a poor one, and neither of us were fit for any kind of lengthy discussion. And, too, I assumed you would know that Gyer must have heirs. Such a thing must be plain to anyone who will only think the matter over. Even to you, my lady."

"You wed me only to gain land," she said pointedly. "That was, and is, all I understood."

"So I now realize. When I spoke to you of not pressing my rights upon you, I spoke of the normal conjugal relationship shared between a man and his wife. If I were not a man of honor, and if it pleased me to do so, I could demand those rights of you at any time, at any place. Even here." He looked at her intently. "Even now, if I so desired it."

"Oh," she said, hot color rising in her cheeks.

"And you did say you wished to have children, did you not?" he asked.

Lillis's blush deepened and she answered, embarrassed, "Yes. I have always wished for children. I should, in truth, be happy to have them."

Alexander was inexplicably relieved. Their conversation, for the past several minutes, had grown somewhat distasteful to him. He'd begun to wonder if she truly would refuse to accept him in her bed, no matter how perfunctory their couplings might be.

"Good," he said. "You are a kind and sensible lady."

"I should like some time to become accustomed to the idea, however."

Alexander inclined his head, not surprised at this. She must believe that the physical joining of a man and woman would always be what she'd experienced on their wedding night. There would be no difficulty in allowing her enough time to let that memory dim.

"You shall have as much time as you require, madam. Within reason, of course."

"But still I am confused, my lord," Lillis said. "You promised me the freedom to leave Gyer, to live where I please. I know little of such matters, but how am I to conceive if I live elsewhere?"

Alexander gave a slight shrug. "That shall prove of little trouble, I assure you. You shall come to Gyer once a year, or perhaps I shall come to where you are. Provided it is not Wellewyn," he added firmly. "I should not be able to share a roof with your father for even one hour, let alone the amount of time it will require to create a child. We shall work the matter out between us, and I think you'll find, my lady, that I am not a difficult man to make terms with."

"I had not realized—I had not realized we should ever even see one another again, once I left," she murmured. "I thought I should not even hear from you."

"Your ignorance is proved again," he said with some disdain. "As my wife, as the Lady of Gyer, your life and mine are now inextricably twined. We shall deal with one another for the rest of our days, regardless of where you decide to live. I should prefer it if you would remain in England though if you must live in Spain or France or Italy I'll not keep you from doing so."

"Oh, no, I shall not go so far. Only to Wellewyn. Nowhere else."

He folded his arms across his chest. "You are certain of this?"

"Yes, my lord. Quite certain. My father needs me."

"Your father is an old man. Will you remain at Wellewyn once he has died?"

She frowned slightly and looked thoughtful. "Perhaps. I don't know." She lifted her eyes to his. "You will be the Lord of Wellewyn when he is gone, will you not? Would you allow me to remain there?"

"Yes, if you wished it. You may do as you please, just as I told you. You may come to Gyer and take your rightful place as its lady. I should prefer that, in all truth, though I'll not force you to it."

Lillis was sincerely surprised. "You'd have me stay at Gyer?" Looking at her husband, so handsome in the firelight, thinking of being his wife in truth made her heart beat painfully.

Another shrug. "If you wished it. It's your right to be lady here, though my cousin can continue to serve in that position, and will in your absence until she, herself, has married. Once she has gone my aunt shall have the honor.''

''I see,'' Lillis replied, feeling both foolish and disappointed.

''Be assured, however, that when you are at Gyer you shall be treated with the courtesy and respect you deserve as my wife. This eve was a regrettable mistake, and one that will not happen again. I have already spoken with my cousin, and have made it clear that she is not to take your place when you are in residence here.''

Worse and worse. Married for her land. Married without love. Married to a man who had no use for her, save that of having children. She might play at being the Lady of Gyer whenever she wished it and not be missed at all when she didn't. Lillis felt a sorrow that moved all the way through to her bones. ''Thank you,'' she murmured. ''You are kind, my lord.''

''Would you wish to live here?'' he asked. ''Even to be near your children, if nothing else?''

Lillis looked at him sharply. ''To be near my children? What does that mean, sir? I shall always be with my children. Always.''

Alexander smiled, looking oddly triumphant. ''Then you will live here.''

She felt her patience slipping away. ''My lord, you just a moment ago said I might live where I pleased.''

''And so you may. You may live wherever you wish, Lillis Baldwin, but my children, all of them, will live at Gyer. With or without their mother.''

Chapter Nine

"If I don't go outside soon I shall shortly lose my mind!"

Lillis paced back and forth in front of one of the long windows in a partitioned section of the great hall. The midday sun spilled warmly through the window and onto the floor. Her skirts twirled up and around at each turn she made, then settled as she began another course through the sunlight until she reached the point of her next turn.

"It is already midday!" She stopped long enough to eye the two guards who stood to one side, dispassionately watching and listening to her. "It will soon be too late to enjoy the day, and there will not be many such days in the coming months." The guards said nothing, had no expressions, and Lillis felt like a child on the verge of a tantrum. "Oh!" She began to pace again. "He is only doing this to annoy me."

She had tried to go out into the garden earlier in the day but had been stopped by her guards. They had been polite but firm. They had their orders, and only when the Lord of Gyer gave them approval would they let her leave the castle without his escort.

Alexander of Gyer's escort! Ha! As if she should ever wish to spend any more time with that wretched, miserable beast than she already did. The man was utterly without feelings. A great block of ice was Alexander of Gyer. Three days had passed since their talk in the solar, yet her fury with him hadn't diminished at all.

Oh, yes, she'd flown into a fine rage after his pronouncement of keeping her children at Gyer, regardless of whether she, herself, decided to stay and live with a man who didn't want her, didn't trust her and certainly didn't love her. Even now, when she remembered the words that had passed between them, she felt her blood boiling anew.

"I'll take a lover," she'd lied, knowing the threat sounded as weak as it was. "You'll never know if the children are yours or not."

The look he'd given her had expressed his disbelief. He'd been supremely unimpressed. "That might be a happy answer for both of us, then," he'd replied mockingly. "I'll claim those that resemble me—Baldwins inherit very strong family features—and you may keep your bastards for company and comfort."

The man was a perfect swine. Truly. She didn't care how kind he'd been to her since that night, or how deferentially he treated her as the Lady of Gyer, always seating her beside him at table and making certain she was given the respect and honor due her newly attained station, no small task in the face of the daily antagonism she received from most of the castlefolk, who blamed her for Barbara Baldwin's unhappiness. But none of that mattered, really. Not when Alexander of Gyer was nothing more than her jailer, too powerful to escape and too knowledgeable to outwit. Lillis deeply felt her lack of worldly experience when she was with him. Indeed, he made her feel as if she were little more than a foolish, willful child.

He took his cousin walking in the gardens every afternoon. Lillis had seen them from out of one of the windows. She'd watched as they'd strolled together so slowly, talking and laughing and gazing into each other's faces. Barbara would set her hand on Alexander's arm, and he would cover that hand with his own, caressing the tiny fingers with his large, masculine ones, gently rubbing his thumb over her little pink nails in a particular way that told Lillis the action was one of long habit, done but not consciously thought of.

It was this, seeing this, that made Lillis long to go out of doors. How unfair it seemed to her that she should be made to stay inside this great tomb of a castle when they and everyone else could walk free and feel the sun and fresh air on their faces.

Today, after her guards had stopped her, Lillis had huffed and threatened and finally gone in search of her husband. She'd found him at the long table in the great hall, the meal they had enjoyed in almost total silence that afternoon having been cleared away. He was surrounded by several of his men: his chamberlain, his bailiff, his marshal and Willem, who served as his castellan, as well as by many of his knights and some men who she guessed were barons who'd pledged him their allegiance, and who therefore represented certain portions of his villeins and vassals. They had obviously been in the midst of discussing something important, and Lillis understood, somewhat guiltily, that she should not have intruded.

She approached the table and stopped directly in front of her husband, fixing him with what she hoped was an appropriate glare, and waited for his anger to fall upon her head. He had every right to be upset, she knew, for ladies weren't supposed to bother their lords when they were busy with their men. Of course, it would have been impossible to do otherwise, for Alexander of Gyer was *always* busy with the managing of his estates. She'd been surprised, then, to see that his initial expression was one of glad welcome.

"My Lady Gyer," he greeted with a nod.

Lillis returned politely, "My lord. Please forgive my interruption."

He made a small gesture with his hand, as if waving her words away. "You are welcome here, my lady, and your beauty is a far better feast than what we've fed upon this past hour. Indeed, we must thank you for gifting us with it." The men at the table murmured their approval of his words, causing Lillis to blush up to the roots of her white hair. "What may I do for you, good lady wife?" he asked.

Her anger thus fully assuaged, Lillis looked at him penitently, then at the other men at the table, all of whom stared at her most openly, worsening her discomfort.

"Please forgive me," she said again. "I only wish to go outside into the garden and enjoy the day, but your guards say you will not allow it."

"This is so," he admitted.

Her anger lit up again. "Do you mean that I may never go outside, save to traverse the short walk between the castle and the chapel? Must I breathe all of my fresh air in those few seconds?"

Alexander set down the parchment he'd been holding and regarded her calmly. "I did not say you could never go outside, my lady, only that I must be present to escort you. If you wish to go into the gardens I shall be happy to take you there as soon as I am finished here. We will not be much longer."

A swift vision of him walking with his cousin in those same gardens swam through her mind. "No, thank you, my lord," she replied stiffly. "If that is my only choice, I would rather stay inside."

He shrugged and picked the document up again. "As you wish."

Having so clearly been dismissed, Lillis turned to leave just as Willem spoke. "You don't need me here any longer, Alex. I should be happy to escort you through the gardens, Lady Lillis."

Lillis smiled at him broadly, filled with gratitude for this happy compromise. "That would be most kind of you, Sir Willem."

Willem's face lit with a returning smile, and he'd begun to stand, only to be held down by his older brother's large and heavy hand.

When Alexander spoke, it was tightly, with anger. "I said, my lady, that I shall escort you later. You will either wait until I am able to take you or you will not go at all."

Willem, allowing himself to be pushed back into his chair, gave Lillis an apologetic look.

"Not at all, then, my lord," Lillis said, turning toward Willem and adding sweetly, "I do thank you, Sir Willem, for being such a chivalrous and gentle man. You are a credit to your knighthood, sir."

Satisfied with Alexander's narrowing eyes, Lillis turned and walked away.

That had been an hour ago, and now Lillis was regretting the rage that had caused her to speak so rashly. Perhaps, if she had only remained calm, she might have been able to persuade him to let her go outside. Instead she had only made him angry; now she would have to humble herself and ask him to escort her through the gardens. It would be humiliating, but unless she found a way to get outside without her guards seeing her, she would be stuck inside the castle until the day she was able to go free. And God alone knew how long that would be.

She made another turn and paced through the sunlight again. She wondered if she should go in search of him. He must be finished with his meeting by now. Perhaps, if she—

"What are you doing?" a small voice interrupted her thoughts, and Lillis looked to see both Candis and Justin standing in the shadows, watching her. How long they had been there she didn't know. They certainly had a talent for moving about unnoticed.

She smiled at them. In the past three days, Candis and Justin had been her greatest source of comfort, and Alexander didn't seem to mind that she spent so much time with them. "I'm trying to keep myself from being bored to death, that's what I am doing. What are the two of you doing?"

"Playing," Justin said. "Why do you never go with the other ladies?"

He meant the other women of the castle, Lillis knew, who with Barbara had closeted themselves with their needlework in the solar where Alexander and she had had their argument. Lillis had realized at once that they were trying to stay away from her, and she had respected their feelings and let them be. The silences she had to bear during meals were bad enough; she didn't think she could put up with a whole day of it.

Her own needlework provided her some comfort during several hours of the day, especially when the children were busy with the new tutor Alexander had hired, and yet she couldn't deny that she felt lonely much of the time. Edyth was not there to lend her company, her guards rarely made an effort to speak to her, and the rest of the castlefolk treated her as a leper. Willem was always kind to seek her out during the long afternoons, and would sit with her for the space of an hour or more, conversing casually about all sorts of different things, and Alexander even made an effort to speak to her several times during the day, coming out of his working chamber specifically to ask how she fared. He didn't spend more than a minute or two with her during these visits; never longer than it took to ask his question, receive a reply and make a polite goodbye.

Lillis had asked Aunt Leta if she could help in managing the household as a way of passing the day, but the older woman had received this request with an air of insult, as if Lillis had ridiculed her abilities at running so large a castle. She informed Lillis that she'd single-handedly managed the household of Gyer for more than thirty years and had never had a complaint. Yet, in spite of the brittle tone in her words, Lillis sensed some small amount of approval from the older woman and pressed on, assuring Aunt Leta as humbly as she could that Gyer was indeed impressively maintained, and that she would be honored to be tutored in the management of a large household by one as experienced and talented as Leta Baldwin.

The words had done the trick, and Aunt Leta had huffily stated that that was a very proper attitude for the new Lady of Gyer to have, and that she would do her best to make certain Alexander's wife learned the proper way to manage her husband's home and be a credit to him. Goodness only knew that Barbara had never been interested in learning such necessary skills. Today, however, she already had plans to visit some of the villagers, and as Lillis could not leave the castle, there was very little she could do to help. Tomorrow, she promised, she would take Lillis on a tour of the castle and introduce her to all of the servants.

Tomorrow, Lillis thought, she would truly begin to feel like the Lady of Gyer, instead of Alexander of Gyer's prisoner. Tomorrow was a day she was looking forward to.

"Well, I didn't wish to sit with the other ladies because I was hoping to go outside today, into the gardens," Lillis explained to the children. "But I cannot, so I am standing here at the window and looking out instead. Now, why aren't the two of you with your new tutor?"

"He left this morn," Justin replied, "and swore he'd never come back."

Lillis's heart sank. "What did the twins do this time?"

"Snakes in his boots," Justin said.

"Snakes!"

He gave a disinterested shrug. "They weren't very poisonous. They wouldn't have killed him."

Candis tilted her head at Lillis questioningly. "Why can't you go outside? We can."

"Can you?" Lillis was grateful for a change of topic. "How delightful for you. Is it a nice garden? It looks very pretty."

"It has flowers," the little girl replied, "and trees. There is even a pond with fish, but we are not allowed to go near it. Justin fell in once and almost drowned and Alex said he would beat us if we ever went near it again."

"Oh, my!"

The children nodded their agreement of this sentiment. Candis continued, "The flowers smell nice in the garden, but they'll go away soon. They always do."

"Yes, they will," Lillis agreed, "but they'll come back in the spring. Will they not? And then they shall be twice as pretty."

"Yes, I suppose so," she admitted, then said more brightly, "Will you tell us a story?"

Lillis was about to say that she would when Justin shook his head. "We're going to go see Hugh and Hugo now. Candis forgot already."

Candis frowned at him. "I didn't forget," she insisted.

Lillis looked from one child to the other. "Where are Hugh and Hugo? Perhaps I can come, too."

Justin eyed her suspiciously. "Are you our sister now?" he asked.

Surprised, she gave a little laugh. "I suppose I am, in a way. Is that all right?"

Justin looked her over, obviously considering whether it was or not. Finally he nodded. "I guess so. You can come with us."

With one child holding each of her hands, Lillis was led up the stairs, past the floor that the bedchambers were located on and even past the floor that she had been jailed on. The guards followed steadfastly behind, causing Justin to turn and look back at them as they neared their destination.

"Why do they always follow you around?"

"They like me, I suppose."

"Oh."

The circular stairway went on and on and up and up until Lillis began to wonder whether they were ever going to come to an end, but Justin and Candis and even her guards seemed unconcerned about the never-ending ascent, and Lillis allowed herself to be led on. At the very top of the stairs was a small landing with two doors on either side. One door led to the roof and parapets outside and was heavily locked and barred against either entry or exit. The children led her through the other door.

It opened to an airy, partly enclosed room, which was roofed and protected yet had no wall to shut out the view from the parapet wall. The first thing Lillis noticed, other than the delightful breeze of fresh air that hit her face, were the several crates and boxes neatly stacked against the farthest wall. Looking closer, she saw that these contained a variety of birds, including pigeons, hawks and falcons. Bent over one of these cages, intent on what they were doing, were Hugh and Hugo.

They looked up as their guests walked through the door, and then gave Justin and Candis looks of disgust.

"What did you bring *her* for?" one of them asked angrily.

"And them." The other one nodded with annoyance at the guards who stood just outside the door.

Lillis wasn't surprised at this sour greeting—she and the twins had kept a purposeful distance from one another since the day after they'd brought her to Gyer.

Candis looked questioningly at Lillis, but Justin merely shrugged. "She's our sister now," he explained, walking over to see what the twins were doing.

"Thanks to you two," Lillis added, smiling at the twins, following Justin and dragging Candis along. "What are you two fiends up to now that you've expended the joy of scaring off yet another tutor?"

The twins glanced at each other with knowing smiles, then returned their attention to the bird whose talons they were carefully trimming. When they finished they held the creature up for inspection, revealing a beautiful brown-and-black falcon.

"Oh! What a lovely bird!" Lillis exclaimed with admiration. "Are all of these yours?" She looked again at the cages around her. The birds were well cared for, she saw, and the cages were large and spacious.

The twins were fully prepared to hate Lillis of Wellewyn for as long as she was going to be at Gyer, but anyone who was able to appreciate either their birds or their dogs couldn't be all bad.

"Yes," Hugh answered with pride. "And we caught or bred every single one ourselves."

"Every single one," Hugo echoed. "And we've trained them, too."

Lillis was truly impressed. She knew without a doubt that the twins were nothing but the worst kind of trouble, yet falconry was an admirable skill, indeed.

"A fine accomplishment," she told them approvingly. "And what a lovely place to keep your birds," she added, walking toward the ledge and leaning her arms on the parapet. "What a wonderful view." She strained to see if there was any sight of Wellewyn from there, but realized that she didn't even know in which direction Wellewyn was. Candis and Justin joined her and stood on their toes to peer over the top.

"This is our private place," one of the twins said from where they still sat with the bird. "Alex gave it to us a long time ago."

"He said we could have it if we'd keep out of his way," the other said with a laugh.

"I don't blame him," Lillis replied. "You are both rotten, ill-mannered beasts. I'm not sure whether I feel sorrier for him, being stuck with you, or for all the tutors you've scared away."

She heard them snickering behind her.

"I'd not laugh, were I you. One day you'll regret what you've done. Only think of the disservice you are doing to Justin and Candis. If you must keep yourselves ignorant, can you not at least allow them the opportunity to learn?"

"Oh, they're all right," said Hugh, putting the falcon back in his cage. "They don't want to be stuck with that boring stuff all day, anyway."

"They're just children," Hugo added, pulling a pigeon out of its enclosure and examining its feet. "They have lots of time to learn things."

Lillis turned, rested her back against the wall and folded her arms beneath her breasts. "I see. You believe you are doing them a favor, then, by chasing their tutors away. It is some form of brotherly love, I suppose. But what of the two of you? You are no longer children. What kinds of things have you learned?"

They both shrugged and continued to examine their birds.

"Can you read?"

"Some."

"Can you write?"

"Some."

"Can you work numbers?"

"No."

"What about preparing for knighthood? Have you done even the smallest amount of squiring? Have you learned how to use weaponry?"

"Enough to get by."

"Well, then, what *can* you do?" she asked with exasperation. "Other than get into trouble, I mean, and raise birds and dogs."

Justin was more upset than the twins by the insinuation in Lillis's voice. "They know how to do lots of things!" he informed her hotly, giving her his back, and Candis, taking Lillis's hand and pressing it against her cheek, asked, "Why are you so mean to Hugh and Hugo?"

"Dear Lord," Lillis muttered, growing more aggravated at the smug looks the twins gave her. "You've certainly charmed the children," she told them dryly. The twins laughed, delighted with themselves, and Lillis couldn't hold on to her fury. The little fiends *were* charming, at least when they wished to be. And they were more than a little handsome, as well, being possessed of the same green eyes and dark hair that their eldest brother had. She could just envision the trouble they'd cause when they were older—the innumerable female hearts they'd break.

"Justin." She set a hand upon his angrily stiff shoulder. "I'm sorry. I shouldn't have spoken as I did about your brothers, especially not in front of you and Candis. Do you forgive me?"

He did, readily, and Lillis once more turned her attention to the view beyond the wall. "Can one see Wellewyn from here?" she asked.

"No, not Wellewyn," Hugh admitted, coming up alongside her, "but look, over that way—"

For the next half hour Lillis stood pressed against the wall, squeezed between the children and the twins, while the twins happily pointed out every sight to be seen from that particular vantage point.

Hugh and Hugo, Lillis discovered, were possessed of excessive senses of humor. They laughed at everything, whether it was funny or not, and somehow caused her and the other children to laugh along with them.

"That bend in the road there is where we caught you and your companions." Hugh leaned over and pointed.

"We hid in those bushes on the right," Hugo broke in, "and waited until you had just made your turn. Then we jumped out at you!" He laughed.

"Did we ever surprise you, too!" Hugh added, laughing as if it were the funniest thing he'd ever known. "You should have seen the look on your face when we told you we were taking you to Gyer! It was wonderful beyond anything!"

"Well, it wasn't wonderful beyond anything for me," Lillis said. "Beastly children. If I were your brother I'd pack the two of you off to a distant monastery and commit you to six years' servitude." She pushed from the wall and brushed bits of gravel off her surcoat. "I do thank you for the grand tour, good sirs," she addressed the twins in a mockingly formal manner that amused them, "but I think I must take the children back down now. If your Aunt Leta has returned from the village she may be worried about them. Come along Justin, Candis." She took their hands.

"Hugh, look!" Hugo suddenly pointed to the courtyard below. "God's teeth, what's amiss?"

They all looked, and what Lillis saw almost made her heart stop. "Merciful God," she murmured, gazing with shock at what looked like dozens and dozens of armed men and their horses assembling in the courtyard in a wild rush. "Sweet merciful God—he must be thinking to march on Wellewyn!"

She reacted without rational thought and, still holding the children, turned, pushed her way past her surprised guards and raced down the dark stairway.

"Lillis! Wait!" It was the twins she heard, running close behind her. "Lillis!"

Careful of the children, she continued her descent, as fast as she could without letting them stumble, and her heart, every step, pounded violently in her body.

They made such a frantic, attention-getting entrance to the great hall that all activity came to a halt, and every eye turned their way. Willem, who stood nearby giving instructions to a group of men, gaped at her.

"Where have you been?" he demanded.

"What?" she replied stupidly. "I—I have been with the children. Sir Willem, what is happening? Has my father's reply been for war?"

Willem grabbed her hand, disentangling the children without care. "I think I'd best take you to your chamber, my lady. *Now.*" He began shoving her back toward the stairs.

"But I want to know what's going on! Where is my husband?"

Willem didn't have a chance to answer, nor did he have a chance to get her any farther. Her husband's booming voice took precedence over the entire room.

"Where—in—God's—holy—name—have—you—*been?*"

He shouted each word furiously from somewhere behind her. Lillis and Willem both cringed, then slowly turned. Alexander stood in the middle of the hall, staring at Lillis with an expression that made her knees start shaking.

He was addressing her, Lillis realized with some surprise. She hardly knew how to answer him. "I—" she began, but was cut off by the twins.

"She was with us, Alex," Hugh said quickly, stepping between them.

Hugo moved to stand next to his brother. "Yes, Alex, she was with us."

"And with us, too, Alex," Justin added, dragging Candis to where the twins were.

Only at that moment did Lillis realize what had been going on. Her husband hadn't been preparing to go to war against Wellewyn or anyone else. He had been preparing to go in search of *her.*

Alexander's face didn't soften as he gazed at his siblings. "Go to your chambers," he ordered quietly, then looked behind them to Willem. "Relieve the men. Tell them they may return to their quarters."

"Alex—" Hugh attempted.

"I said go to your chambers!" Alexander thundered. "*Now!*"

"Why do you shout at them?" Lillis demanded, moving from the protectiveness of Willem's side and approaching her husband. "They've done nothing wrong. Must you take your anger out on innocent children?"

She stood directly in front of him and met his furious gaze. His green eyes searched her face.

"I suppose I should not," he said with menacing softness, "since you are the one I am angry with." He extended an arm toward her. "You will come with me."

Lillis looked at him with sudden fright, then cast a helpless glance at the twins and Willem. The twins, especially, gave her looks of caution. She didn't have a chance to make a decision about what she would do, however, for Alexander impatiently took her hand and pressed it upon his arm.

"I am not going to kill you, wife," he promised, leading her in the direction of the garden. "Yet."

Chapter Ten

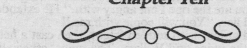

They walked in silence, Alexander tightly holding Lillis's hand and Lillis stumbling along, trying to keep up with his long, purposeful strides.

She was worried, Alexander knew, that he was going to vent his anger on her, but she was wrong. He was too relieved to have found her still safely at Gyer to be angry with her. In truth, it was himself he was angry with. He hadn't liked the way he'd felt when he'd been unable to find her anywhere in the castle. He hadn't liked it at all. But she hadn't escaped. She was still there; in fact, she was right beside him. Her strong, beautiful fingers—so different from Barbara's tiny ones—lay tensely in his grasp. There was nothing to be upset about. She was there. Alexander forced himself to calm, and slowed his pace.

The day was warm and beautiful; there wouldn't be too many more like this. The sun was beginning to settle into a red glow in the sky and the warm breeze caressed his face. He always enjoyed walking in the gardens with Barbara; there wasn't any reason why he shouldn't enjoy walking with his wife just as much. He'd felt an unpleasant surge of guilt when she'd appeared before him earlier in the day, asking if she might go out of doors. He should have thought of that before—should have known that she would desire such a thing, just as any human being would. But his thoughts these past days since his wedding were rarely what he wanted them to be.

"I said that I would take you walking in the gardens when I had a chance, did I not?" He brought their pace to an easy stroll and lightened his grip on her hand.

Lillis looked at him. "And I told you that I did not wish to see them under your escort."

"It seems you haven't a choice, madam. They're lovely, are they not? They were my mother's pride and joy. She planted nearly all of the roses herself."

Lillis pulled her hand away and stopped. Alexander stopped, as well, and looked at her.

"Are you not going to rail at me?" she asked.

Alexander drew in a deep breath. No, he wasn't going to rail at her. She looked so beautiful. Never had he seen such a woman. Her long white hair was braided tightly atop her head, but several strands had broken loose and were fluttering across her face in the breeze. Slowly he lifted one hand and tucked them behind her ear. His fingers grazed her cheek as he did so and the soft warmth of her skin unnerved him. Although she shivered when he touched her, Lillis continued to gaze at him solemnly, somewhat warily from her blue eyes.

"Do you want me to be angry with you?" he asked. "I certainly have every reason to be, I admit. I thought you had escaped, Lillis. I don't know how, but I thought you had done it."

"With such capable guards watching over me night and day?" she countered with disbelief. "I think they would rather die than let me out of their sight."

He frowned. "I couldn't find you anywhere. Your guards need changing if they allow you to hide yourself so well."

Color rose in her face, an occurrence that Alexander found disturbingly attractive.

"There is no need to change them," she said. "It was not their fault that I couldn't be found. In fact, I shall be quite angry if you do change them. I've grown used to those two silent statues following me everywhere."

"I'll not change them, then," he allowed, capturing one of her hands again. He led her toward a nearby bench. "It is a beautiful afternoon, is it not?"

Lillis sat where he indicated, and tugged her hand free. "My Lord Gyer, if you are going to be angry with me you had best do it now. I'll not pretend to exchange pleasantries with you until then."

Alexander shook his head ruefully. "I begin to think you've unnatural tendencies, my lady, to request punishment when none has been offered. I was angry when I thought you'd escaped me and, indeed, you would have been sorry to have met me if you'd tried such a thing, for I would have found you before you went far. But you are here and all is well."

Her expression tightened. "Of course, my lord. I understand. You thought your precious land was slipping through your fingers. You thought perhaps you had married me for naught. But I am here and all is well, as you say."

"Think of it how you will, my lady," he invited, settling himself on the bench beside her. "Whether it is true or no changes nothing. I've told you that you may not leave Gyer until the land is in my hands, and that holds fast."

She folded her hands in her lap. "Yes, I know that. And once you have the land you will be glad to see me go."

Alexander frowned at the words. Why did she speak so, when he had told her she might stay at Gyer and be welcome?

"I am curious to know where you were," he said, pushing the troubling thoughts aside. "I had the castle thoroughly searched before calling my men to readiness." She finally looked at him, with a little half smile that made his heart do strange flops in his chest.

"Candis and Justin took me to the twins' private place on the roof. My guards came, of course," she added quickly, seeing his look of concern. "It was very pleasant and I fear time flew from us. Did you not think to look for me there?"

"I've completely forgotten about that makeshift chamber until you spoke of it just now," he admitted. "I think I had it built some years ago in an effort to keep the twins occupied. They keep their birds there, do they not?" He spoke these words lightly and easily, but her reaction to them was one of quick anger.

"Yes, they keep their birds there! You don't even know! You don't care how your brothers and sister occupy themselves all day long?"

Now that, Alexander thought, rather stunned by her assault, was both ridiculous and unfair. He took excellent care of his brothers and Candis.

"Of course I care how they occupy themselves. I wouldn't have built that rooftop chamber for them, otherwise."

She stood up and away from him, fixing him with a look of disdain. "Why have your brothers not been trained for knighthood?" she demanded.

Alexander stood, as well. "They have no interest in pursuing that ordination. Would you have me force unwilling subjects into a holy order?"

"What about Candis and Justin?"

"Justin is too young for knighthood, madam. I'll not even comment on Candis."

"That isn't what I meant!" she cried, thoroughly upset. She moved farther away from him and Alexander couldn't help but follow. He had the oddest desire to pull her into his arms and soothe her.

"They have their tutor, and their nurse. What more would you have me do for them?"

Her mouth gaped wide and she stared at him with amazement. When he tried to come near she pushed him away.

"You don't even know!" she accused furiously, slapping at his consoling hands. "You don't know that the twins scared off the latest tutor only this morn! You don't know that the nurse you have entrusted Justin and Candis to is a drunkard, fit only for the village tavern! She sleeps away her drunkeness all day and leaves the children to care for themselves. What—what kind of brother are you?" She kept moving away, putting a distance between them.

All of this was news to Alexander. He'd always left the running of household matters to Aunt Leta and Barbara, being so busy with managing his estates. He never considered whether the twins and the children were being looked after or not; he always assumed that they were.

"I'm a concerned brother," he answered angrily, finally capturing her. "A caring brother." He put his arms around her and pulled her close. "If what you say is true, I will put it to rights. It has never been easy to keep a tutor at Gyer with the twins here."

"That is no excuse. . . ." She let her voice trail off, finding herself pressed tightly against his hard body. Her eyes widened and locked with his, her face flushed hotly. For all of five seconds they stayed thus, and Alexander knew that he was going to kiss her. Truly kiss her and not the ceremonial way he'd done at their marriage. He was going to kiss her. He was—

She jerked free, just as his lips touched hers.

"Have—have you heard from my father yet?" she asked shakily, turning her gaze to a nearby rosebush and pressing both hands to her temples in what looked like an agitated effort to keep her brain in her head.

Disappointment surged through Alexander. She'd felt good in his arms, pressed up against him, so different from the fragile delicateness of Barbara. The desire to taste her mouth—just once—was merciless, though he knew he had no right forcing himself on her when she did not wish it. God's feet! He'd brought her here to enjoy the gardens, not to ravish her.

"No, I've not." He felt unaccountably angry, and childishly deprived. "I have received an interesting missive from one of the king's deputies in response to my missive regarding our marriage."

"Oh?" She looked at him with sudden interest. "Has King Henry approved our marriage, then?"

"He'll not even consider the matter until he's had concurrence from your father that he approves of the marriage and the contract. Then we'll know. But that was not what made the missive interesting. It was that the deputy who sent the missive, Sir Malvin Giraut, claims acquaintance with you, from Tynedale, and sends his regards and congratulations."

Lillis's face lit with a smile. "Sir Malvin! Yes, I know him well, and also his brother, Sir Ywain. They and their men often stayed the night at Tynedale on their way to and from the battle at Shrewsbury. It was a great honor to be allowed to serve them, and I was often thus honored. How kind of him to remember me.''

"He did more than remember you, madam. He recalled how thoroughly besotted he and his brother were with you, of how they often argued between themselves which of them should be allowed to seek your favors.''

"What!'' Lillis cried with disbelief, then uttered a laugh. "But how foolish, my lord. Why ever did he write you such nonsense, I wonder? Sir Malvin and his brother were always most kind, but neither of them would have noticed such a plain girl as I. Surely he wrote you in jest. You know he must.''

"It did not seem so,'' Alexander said truthfully, bemused at the way she belittled herself. It was the way of beautiful women to draw out compliments by making less of their beauty, yet he'd never thought Lillis would sink so low. He felt vaguely disappointed in her.

"You may see the missive yourself, if you so desire. Sir Malvin recounted that Ywain was so much in love with the beautiful Lillis Ryon that he dared to sneak into her chamber one night, intending to declare his lifelong devotion, when the lady in question hit him on the head with a candlestick, robbing him of his senses. Sir Malvin believed his unfortunate sibling was only saved further wounds by the arrival of his squire, who made apologies to the outraged young lady and dragged his insensible master away.'' He chuckled at her look of amazement. "Poor Ywain never dared look at you again, so thoroughly discouraged and heartsick he was. Sir Malvin wrote that he pined over you for weeks afterward.'' He laughed again.

Lillis wasn't sure whether to scoff or join him in his laughter. The whole tale was utterly ridiculous. "My lord,'' she said, unable to stop the smile that tugged at her lips, "that is truly the silliest tale I've ever heard. Ywain Giraut happens to be a very handsome man—''

"I know well how Ywain Giraut looks," Alexander interrupted her with sudden curtness, losing his smile. "I fought beside him and Sir Malvin at Shrewsbury."

"Then you know full well how foolish Sir Malvin's words are," she said with what sounded like relief. "Every girl in the convent was madly in love with Sir Ywain, and each of them far lovelier than I. I admit that he tried to steal into our sleeping chamber one night, but it was to meet another that he did so. I was in charge of the girls, and simply discouraged him in his effort. That's all there was to it, I promise you."

Alexander didn't believe that for a moment, and his expression clearly said so. "Come, now, madam, and cease these protestations. This false modesty in you is clearly meant to beget compliments, for I think it impossible that you do not know your own beauty. No, no, my lady." He ignored her quick, sputtering attempt at denial and continued. "I shall tell you how I see it. In the ten years you lived at Tynedale, you enslaved every man who set eyes upon you, intentionally or no, with your loveliness, yet rightfully honored and protected your virtue as best you could. You behaved most admirably, madam wife."

His words came out half teasing, half serious, but certainly with no intent to harm. He meant what he said about her beauty, and he meant what he said about her not being so foolish as to sacrifice her maidenhead to any of the romantic, wandering knights who'd come her way during her years at the convent. The good Lord only knew how often young girls fell prey to such men, yet his wife had kept herself a maiden, perfect and whole.

But Lillis's expression grew hurt, as if he'd insulted her, and her beautiful eyes welled with tears.

"You are a hard man, Alexander of Gyer," she whispered, "yet I never believed you could be so cruel. You take delight in making jest of me, but I have not deserved that. I shall thank God when I can be free of you."

And she pushed past his shocked self, only managing a few steps before Alexander stopped her, locking his hands around her shoulders.

"Lillis! What does this mean? I gave you no insult!"

She turned teary eyes on him. "You called me beautiful!" she accused, and promptly burst into sobs, so that he pulled her into his arms and held her close.

"Oh, God's toes, Lillis," he said with a groan, "never tell me you do not know how lovely you are. Never tell me you are so blind, my Lady Gyer." But she was crying, and he knew she was too proud a woman to cry easily, especially in front of others—especially in front of him.

She was crying so hard that she couldn't even answer, and Alexander thought that she must be crying for all the days she'd been with him, ridding herself of all misery and unhappiness. He held her and let her cry, and knew without guilt that she felt good to him, just as a woman should feel. She felt right and perfect, and he held her and comforted her and enjoyed every moment of it.

"Lillis... Lillis," he crooned in a gentle voice. "Sweet wife."

"I'm not beautiful!" she sobbed unhappily.

"Ah, you are," he said, stroking her hair. "So very beautiful, my wife."

"No!" she insisted. "No!"

"Yes. Oh, yes, you are. Beautiful as none other is. Your hair is the color of the stars, Lillis. White and pure as they are. And your skin is smooth and—rabbit's fur—that's just what it is. White and smooth, soft, like a white rabbit's fur. And your eyes, madam—" he set his fingers beneath her chin and lured her wet eyes upward "—your eyes are the loveliest shade of blue I have ever seen. Very light and clear." He tilted his head consideringly, looking into her disbelieving face. "Not like the sky, exactly. Not the pale blue of water, either. Perhaps a combination of both. There is a light blue stone I've seen which, when polished, reminds me of your eyes." He tilted his head the other direction, still considering her. "I cannot believe you do not know these things. Were there no mirrors at Tynedale? Did no one ever tell you the truth?"

Lillis lifted a hand and wiped her cheeks, sniffling, blinking. "The sisters told me how I looked. They told me my coloring was odd, that I was mannish and unladylike and would be fortunate to find a husband who was as tall as I. And this is true," she insisted when Alexander made a face. "You cannot deny that I am tall and ungainly."

"I do not deny that you are tall," he agreed, "but you have never appeared ungainly, my lady. Perhaps, when you were growing you were given to some amount of clumsiness. That is common enough in all growing creatures." He had a fleet vision of her childish awkwardness being like that of a young deer trying to gain its feet—a sight both fascinating and lovely to watch.

"I am not beautiful," she said once more. "No one has ever said so before. None of the other girls—no one. It cannot be true."

Alexander smiled and lifted a hand to stroke her cheek. "You are a victim of ignorance, my dear. No female, vain of her own beauty, will admit that another is lovelier than she, especially not when the other is so very much lovelier. The sisters of Tynedale, I can only think, must have wanted to keep you from growing too great in your own estimation, and thus never spoke of your beauty to you. The men who passed through Tynedale were probably too stricken to speak to you, afraid that such a fair maid would spurn them outright. Indeed, Ywain Giraut received a strike on the head for his pains. You never encouraged any of them, did you, Lillis? You assumed they found you unattractive."

Silently she nodded. "I am not beautiful. Not beautiful as Lady Barbara is."

"My cousin is indeed lovely," he admitted, "but her beauty is very different from yours. Your beauty, my lady, is unique, like none I've ever before seen."

Her tears had stopped, and Lillis set both hands on Alexander's shoulders and pushed from his embrace.

"You are fanciful, my lord," she told him, "but sometimes kind. Sometimes. I am sorry that I called you cruel."

Alexander felt bereft when she left his arms, and cold from the lack of her warmth. Yet he held his expression blank and replied, "If you think me fanciful, madam, then you know nothing of me." It was no more than the truth.

He was no romantic, but a practical man with a practical mind. Alexander realized, with something of a jolt, that if circumstances had fallen differently, if he'd had to court Lillis of Wellewyn in order to make her his bride, he wouldn't have had the least idea of how to go about doing so. Which was certainly one reason why he'd been so grateful for Barbara, whom he'd never had to bother courting at all. "And if I have sometimes been unkind to you, it was not intentional."

She had returned to the bench, and sat wearily upon it. "Any man who tells his wife that he is going to take her children away from her is certainly not intentionally kind."

"I never said I would take your children from you," Alexander replied tautly, his former gentleness gone. "I merely stated that they would be raised at Gyer, as they should be. And I have told you that you may live here, as well, if it pleases you to do so."

Lillis felt too weary to begin an argument, especially with Alexander of Gyer, who had evidently lost very few of them, if any, in his lifetime. Instead she asked him a question that had kept her awake for part of the previous night.

"Have you fathered any bastards, my lord?"

His look of shock was rather what she'd expected, but it passed quickly, and instead of shouting at her, he stated very calmly, "I believe I shall write the sisters of Tynedale and express my displeasure with the training you received there. How many men, I wonder, would not beat their wives for speaking to them in such a crude manner?"

Lillis found his words funny, and discomposed him by laughing. "Was it wrong of me to ask?" she questioned. "Forgive me, my lord. I was only curious, since you told me that Baldwins inherit certain familial features. I wondered how you would know this is so, unless you had children of your own already."

He frowned at her. "You are a very odd female," he said. "Your personality matches the uniqueness of your features, I think. Would you be upset were I to tell you that I had children outside of marriage?"

"Oh, no, my lord," she answered quickly. "Men are given to do such things, I understand, and children can be the greatest blessing of life. I should only be angered if you gave them no support, though I cannot believe even you would be that hard-hearted."

"Thank you," he said dryly, sitting beside her. "I have no children out of wedlock, or none that I know of, leastwise. I have always been careful about such things. A man who cannot keep from peopling the world with his bastards is an idiot for whom there is no excuse. I despise such men."

Lillis regarded her husband with some surprise, and not a little approval. "You are wise, my lord," she said softly, and when he looked at her she smiled. "Justin and Candis said that there is a pond in the garden."

Alexander nodded, and wondered if the throbbing in his chest foreboded some dire illness. "Yes, there is. We keep a supply of fish there for our meals. Would you like to see it?" Standing, he held out his hand to her.

"Yes, I should, thank you." She placed her hand in his.

"I'll show you the rest of the gardens first," he said as he led her forward, setting her hand on his arm and keeping it there.

"If it pleases you to do so."

"It does. You should see everything."

"Yes, I suppose I should. You may decide to never let me out again after this."

"On the contrary," he said. "I shall bring you out at least once a day for the remainder of your time here. Weather permitting, of course. I should have thought to do so earlier. It was lax of me not to know that you would enjoy being out of doors during the day." It was more than lax, he thought, it was purely unlike him. Never before had his usually competent brain been so useless and weak.

She glanced at him with surprise. "Your cousin will not like that," she said. "Do you not take her walking each afternoon?"

"Occasionally," he admitted. "When time permits."

"I have seen you in the gardens with her every day since I've come," Lillis protested. "Every day, my lord."

Now Alexander truly was surprised. So surprised that he couldn't think of what to say. She'd watched him, then, over the past few days, just as he'd watched her. The very idea made his heart beat that much more painfully.

Several moments of silence passed, and when Lillis realized he wasn't going to answer her, she asked tentatively, "If you will indeed take me walking in the afternoons, my lord—which I would much enjoy, I thank you—may the children and twins come with us? The children, especially, should be encouraged to play out of doors when they can. Do you not agree?"

The idea of spending the little free time he had with any of his siblings other than Willem was an idea that had never before entered Alexander's thoughts, but he said, "They may come if they wish."

The smile that lit her face almost made him forget to breathe. She was very easy to please, his wife. He found himself smiling back at her, and decided that he would lead her through the gardens very, very slowly.

"How beautiful it is. You are quite talented, my lady."

The man's voice made Lillis jump, coming as it did unexpectedly and from behind the chair in which she sat. She twisted to find John Baldwin standing next to her, nearly leaning against her chair and smiling pleasantly. She'd not heard him approach and didn't know how long he had been there. Once her initial shock left she felt rather irritated. She'd not yet had a chance to become acquainted with John Baldwin, though they'd been introduced at her wedding and had sat at the same table through several meals now, but she knew very well that it was exceedingly rude to sneak up on a person. Turning stiffly, she readdressed her needlework.

"Thank you, sir," she said. "I believe I have some skill in sewing."

"But you do, my dear Lady Gyer. I cannot remember when I have seen such perfect stitches. We will be most fortunate when you are able to grace the castle with one of your works." His voice was smooth and pleasing, like warm honey poured over bread. He moved to the chair beside her, which Alexander had vacated only half an hour earlier, having finished one of his short, regular visits to see how she fared.

"May I join you, my Lady Gyer?" he asked, seating himself before she could reply.

John Baldwin was a handsome man with red hair and a boyish face. He was forever smiling, Lillis thought, save for the few times she'd seen him arguing with Alexander. She didn't know what their arguments were about, though she thought they must involve Barbara. He was, after all, her brother.

"We've not yet had an opportunity to know each other, beyond introduction," he said, leaning forward slightly. "We are cousins by marriage now, and I should be greatly honored to improve my acquaintance with you, if you would allow such a thing, my lady."

"Of course," Lillis replied cautiously, wary of his solicitous manner, though he seemed most sincere. "Though our relationship will be a short one, my lord, as I will be leaving Gyer soon. But this you already know, I think."

He chuckled warmly. "Oh, yes, Cousin Alex was quite firm about that when he explained the necessity for your marriage. I believe you had already retired to your room when we had that particular family meeting, but, of course, you were in a great deal of confusion that night. The marriage was quite as distasteful to you as it was to Alex, was it not?"

The words fell like a hard slap, momentarily stunning Lillis, so that a moment passed before she managed to say, "Yes."

"The whole matter was distasteful," John went on with a disgusted shake of his head. "Never did I think Alex would be capable of doing such a thing—wedding an innocent woman by force, against her will, for the sake of a strip of land. I can only imagine how distressed you must have been, my dear lady, and how distressed you must still be. It is a very great sadness, and I am deeply sorry for what you've suffered."

"Thank you," Lillis murmured uncomfortably, all the happiness she'd known only an hour before when Alexander had sat beside her evaporating like dew under a hot sun. They had grown easy with each other these past two days, she and Alexander, since he had first taken her walking in the gardens, and now Lillis looked forward to those times during the day when he would seek her out and sit with her for a while, talking and laughing and telling her of the things he was working at. There had been no word from her father yet, and no sign of Edyth, but Alexander had promised that he would send some men to Wellewyn soon, if he still received no reply. Lillis rarely pressed him on the matter; she hated the discord that sprang up between them whenever her father was mentioned.

She had determined, instead, to make the best of her situation for the few remaining days she had at Gyer, and to make a friend of her handsome husband, instead of an enemy, and to enjoy his company whenever she could. Each afternoon, for the past two days, when he had finished his day's work, Alexander had come to take her walking just as he had promised, and each afternoon had passed as the most enjoyable of Lillis's life. Never before could she remember feeling so happy as she did when she walked with him, her hand upon his strong arm, and never would she forget the amity and pleasure of these few too-short days.

"My dear sister has suffered, as well," John Baldwin continued. "I never thought Alex would hurt her as he has. He always claimed to love her so well."

"I—I'm sure he has," Lillis said. "I'm sure he still does. He only did what he thought he must, and saw no other choice. She must understand that, surely."

"I do not know. This has been very hard on her. She has loved Alex forever, you see. Since she was a child. They were betrothed when they were very young and Barbara has spent her life expecting to be his wife. The disappointment has overwhelmed her."

"I am sorry," Lillis said sincerely. "I wish you would tell her how deeply I regret what has happened, and whatever part I may have played in it. I certainly never wished for the situation, and I am sorry she has suffered so.''

"Yes, I will tell her, my lady, and I thank you for your kindness. She'll be most grateful for your words. She has convinced herself of late that Alex has fallen in love with you and has stopped loving her, though Alex himself has repeatedly told her that this is not so. Your kind words will be most reassuring."

"Oh," Lillis said foolishly, not sure what to think. John's words seemed so normal, so perfectly expected, and yet for some reason they knifed at her heart.

"Yes." John sighed. "Sometimes I think Alex will grow weary with having to reassure her of how much he loves her, and of telling her that things will be as they once were between them when you have left Gyer. Barbara does her best to believe him, of course, but it is hard for her to wait until all of the matters have been settled, just as I know it is hard for Alex. And also for you, dear lady. I'm certain you will be very glad to finally be able to return to your own home and life."

"Yes," Lillis agreed softly, feeling as if she might cry. What did it matter to her if Alexander loved his cousin? She'd known all along that he did. She'd known all along that his invitation for her to remain at Gyer had only been a polite one, not something that he would ever truly desire.

"Hello, John, Lady Lillis," a familiar voice greeted. Lillis looked up to see Willem approaching and thought that she had never been so glad to see anyone in her life. He smiled and bowed over her hand. At John he cast a look of suspicious curiosity. "I've come to fetch you, my lady. Aunt Leta is going to give you a tour of Castle Gyer and then it will be time for the midday meal. I fear we shall have to desert you for now, John."

Lillis allowed Willem to pull her out of her chair, and she gratefully clung to his arm. It was very strange. Cousin John had been nothing but polite to her during their conversation, yet she somehow felt that Willem was rescuing her. Smiling, Willem covered her hands with his, patting them in a brotherly way.

John rose, as well, smiling lazily. "A tour of Castle Gyer, you say, Willem? Mayhap I shall go along to make certain the ladies come to no harm. I believe I'd enjoy seeing all of the chambers that are never used in this old place."

Perhaps Willem felt her hands squeezing nervously into his arm, or perhaps he simply felt the tension that developed in her at the thought of having to spend another minute with John Baldwin.

"That's all right, John," he replied steadily, still patting Lillis's hands. "I've already offered to escort the ladies and they shall be quite safe with both myself and Lady Gyer's two guards for protection." He nodded in the direction of Lillis's constant, silent shadows.

"Of course, Cousin." John made a slight bow. "Though I must regret being deprived of Lady Gyer's lovely company. Thank you for your kindness, my lady. Perhaps we shall be able to converse again at another time?"

Lillis nodded, flooded with relief. "Yes, certainly."

"Then I'll wish you a happy tour of Castle Gyer. I'll see you at the midday meal."

He bowed again and left, and Lillis released the breath she'd been holding. Willem looked at her with concern.

"Was John bothering you, my lady? Did he upset you? Shall I speak to Alex about him?"

"No! Goodness, no!" she replied quickly. "He was very polite. Indeed, he was."

Willem gazed at her searchingly and ran his fingers over her hands. "Lillis, you're trembling. He did upset you. What did he say to you?"

"Nothing, I promise you." She didn't want him to speak of it to Alexander. She didn't want to speak of any of these things again. "Do you think my guards would have simply stood by if he had done or said anything to upset me? Why, only yesterday one of the servants was a little rude to me and they physically put the man out of doors."

Willem didn't believe her. "John is a very vengeful man, Lillis, and it would be best if you kept your distance from him. He may seem innocent and harmless, but I can promise you he is not."

"He didn't seem dangerous to me, Willem, but I will do as you say and try to stay away from him. But please promise me that you won't say anything to Lord Gyer. I shouldn't like to cause any trouble when there is no reason."

Willem's eyes filled with disagreement, but he said, "I'll not speak to Alex this time, my lady, but if John should bother you again I'll go to him directly. He'll not allow our cousin to harass you, and neither will I."

"Thank you, Willem." Lillis smiled at her tall, handsome brother-in-law with real affection. "And thank you for coming to my rescue. You didn't really plan on making this tour of Castle Gyer, did you?"

He smiled in turn. "No, but I'm looking forward to it, I think. I can hardly imagine a better way to spend an afternoon than escorting such a beautiful lady through my home."

Lillis knew she was blushing. "I am hardly beautiful, Sir Willem, but you are kind to tell me such a pleasant lie."

Lillis wasn't aware of the intimate picture she and Willem presented as they walked side by side, their arms linked, his hand resting over hers, their two heads close together and smiles on their faces. They were laughing and talking, oblivious of the several other people in the great hall who watched their slow, relaxed progress, one of them being Alexander.

He was sitting by one of the fires with Barbara, having left Lillis and sought his cousin out in an effort to soothe her anger over his recent garden walks with Lillis. Alexander didn't enjoy seeing Barbara so unhappy, especially when he was the one responsible for it. So intent was he on his conversation with her that it was unlikely he would have even seen Lillis and Willem walking together had a servant not dropped a tray somewhere farther down the hall. The noise caused him to turn his head, but the sight of his wife and brother kept him distracted.

And more than distracted. He sat and watched as they made their way across the hall, so intimate and close, the expressions of laughter on their faces filling him with an inexplicable rage. He didn't hear the things Barbara chatted on about, he didn't know if she had even noticed he was no longer paying her any attention. All he could see was Lillis smiling at Willem.

Suddenly Lillis glanced up and saw him, and her smile died. Their eyes met and held across the wide, empty hall. Her gaze took in Barbara sitting beside him, and then she looked away. She and Willem were out of the hall in another moment and Alexander returned his attention to the beautiful redhead seated beside him. Barbara chatted on and on, but he didn't hear a word she said.

Chapter Eleven

The way Alexander kept looking at her made it difficult for Lillis to keep her mind on the story she was telling.

"So when the Trojans went to sleep that night the Greeks opened a secret door in the side of the horse and sneaked out."

He'd been looking at her all day long, and in the same intense, disquieting manner. During the midday meal, during their walk in the garden with his brothers and sister, during the evening meal, which they had only just finished, and now at the fireside as she sat doing her best to entertain the children and the twins with the story of the Trojan horse—he never stopped. Oh, he wasn't exactly obvious about it, at least not so that anyone save Lillis would notice, but he was doing it all the same. She found his eyes upon her whenever she worked up the nerve to glance at him, and the blazing look in them had her thoroughly unnerved.

"They destroyed the city and burned it down to the ground. All of the men in the city, including the male children, were killed, and all of the women were gathered up to be made into slaves."

What had she done to make him so angry? she wondered. His fierce expression made her shiver.

"As soon as the Greeks had rescued Helen they sailed for home, leaving naught but destruction behind them. And that was the end of the city of Troy."

The entire Baldwin family, along with a few of the other castlefolk, were gathered around her, listening to the tale, and their praise, once she finished, caused Lillis to flush. Willem, especially, was complimentary.

"I could listen to you all night long, my lady," he vowed, kissing her hand lightly. "The stories are as interesting to hear as the storyteller is to watch."

"I agree wholeheartedly, my lady," Cousin John added, gracing her with a bow. "It was most entertaining. Thank you very much."

"A wooden horse!" Hugh said from where he and Hugo sat on the floor by the fire. "Who would have ever thought of such a thing?"

"It was brilliant," Hugo agreed, as impressed as his twin.

"Brilliant, indeed," Alexander's voice said from out of the shadows in which he stood. Lillis glanced at him as he approached, her flush deepening. He held out a hand and she placed hers in it, looking at him with some confusion. His fingers closed possessively around hers.

"My lord?" she asked uncertainly.

"My lady," he replied, squeezing her hand. "My very talented, impressive lady wife." The words were curt, thoroughly cold. He released her, inclined his head mockingly, then turned and walked away.

She wasn't asleep when she heard the adjoining door to her chamber being opened, though many hours had passed and it was very late at night. She tucked the covers beneath her chin and waited. A few seconds went by, and then, as she'd known he would, Alexander pulled the bed curtains back.

He was fully dressed—she could see him well in the light of the fire that warmed the room.

"Good eve, lady wife," he said, leaning against one of the end posts.

"My lord."

"You have not found your rest yet?"

"As you see."

"Ah."

"And you, my lord? Do you have no desire to sleep this night?"

"Oh, yes, my lady, I do have the desire. I've not got the intention, however."

His eyes moved leisurely over her covered form, causing Lillis to shift restlessly.

"Did you wish to speak with me, then, my lord?"

"No." He shook his head. "I did not come to speak with you."

Lillis licked her dry lips and saw his eyes follow the movement. "Then, perhaps—"

"I've watched you these past many days," he said softly. "I've watched you since the moment we wed, and even before that, if I would be truthful." Slowly he pushed from his leaning position and moved toward her. When he sat beside her on the bed she tried to scoot away, but he set a hand on the other side of her, stopping her, and leaned over her. "Lie still, Lillis." Lifting his other hand, he touched her lips with his fingers, almost reverently. "You tremble," he whispered. "Are you afraid of me?"

Mute, she stared at him.

"I've watched you," he said again, his fingers moving to her cheek. "I've watched you with the children in the afternoons, telling them stories. Making them happy." One finger outlined the shell of her ear. "I've watched you with the twins, putting up with them, scolding them, making them behave. I've seen the way you speak to yourself when you work at your sewing and think no one watches. Oh, yes, Lillis, I have. I've stood and watched you for hours. I've watched the way your lips move as you concentrate, speaking silent words to yourself, and I've wondered what it is you say, if you're even aware of what you do." His fingers touched her lips again, caressed them gently. "Still you tremble. Do you think I mean you harm? Do you think I mean to rape you?"

"I do not know," she whispered.

"I could have you if I wished it," he admitted. "I am stronger than you are, and you've no candlestick to protect you now. I am the lord here, and you are my wife. No one would dare to enter and save you if you tried to fight me."

"You said you would not force me." The words came out like breaths. "You are a man of your word."

"Yes," he said with regret. "I am an honorable man. A man of my word."

"What do you want, my lord?"

"Can you not guess?" He spoke so softly that she shivered.

"Is it a game, then?"

Alexander lowered his head, his whole body, until his chest rested heavily upon her. The hand that touched her face slid deep into her hair, the arm that kept her imprisoned slid beneath the covers, under her back, embracing her. "Not a game, my wife. Not a game."

He was so near, Lillis felt his breath upon her as he spoke, and, frightened, she turned her face. He drew even nearer, and she shut her eyes when she felt his mouth beneath her ear, pressing there gently, murmuring. He kissed her ear, her cheek, stroked her hair away to expose her neck and kissed her there. He kissed her like that, so gently and tenderly, over and over, until Lillis felt she could no longer draw in enough air, until her body ached as if she had sickened, until she had no will left, but gave way and turned her face once more and offered her mouth to him.

He took it, making a sound of quiet exaltation. He was gentle and very skilled. Lillis had never realized that a kiss could last such a long time, or that a person's tongue had anything to do with it, or that it might feel so wonderful as it did. The hand beneath her back slid free, and he cupped her breast, causing her to gasp against his mouth.

"Alexander!" The voice that tried to scold sounded weak and breathless, instead.

Alexander, moving his hand on her gently, smiled, pleasure on his face. "My name," he murmured. "I like the sound of it on your lips." He bent and kissed her again, then lifted his head. "You have not known a man's kiss before this," he stated knowingly, with great approval.

"You are pleased, my lord?"

"I am most exceedingly pleased," he answered. "You were a good and honorable wife even before you were a wife, and you have done well since our marriage, though I doubted you until this moment. Continue to do well and I shall never have cause to be displeased with you."

His clear tone brought her own hazy thoughts to order. "I do not understand," she said. "What do you mean, Alexander?"

"I am not the husband of your choosing, but I am your husband nonetheless, and you shall accept me as such. I've said that you may take lovers, but I'll not be cuckolded by my own brother."

Lillis gaped at him, her passion-muddled mind taking longer than usual to understand what he said, but when understanding did strike, it was with all the force of a thunderbolt.

"You *wretch!*" She shoved at him, even tried to strike him. "You—you *filthy beast!*"

One flailing hand successfully slapped him hard across the face, making a good, satisfying thwack, and then Alexander captured both her wrists and pressed her into the mattress.

"Damn you, lady! Do you think me blind? Did you think I'd not care for the lovers' glances you exchanged with Willem this very day?"

Lillis felt sick and humiliated because she'd let herself think, while he kissed her, that he'd wanted to do it of his own free will. Now she saw the action for what it was; nothing more than a test of her ignorance—and innocence.

"I've done naught with Willem, save accept his kindness and thank God for it! Is it so shocking a thing that I should accept kindness where I can find it in this place?"

"*I* am your husband!" Alexander repeated angrily. "If you seek kindness while you are at Gyer then you will seek it from *me*. I'll not have my people—my family—whispering behind my back about my wife's secret trysts with my own brother!"

"I've done *naught* with Willem!" she repeated.

"Then make certain you never do," he warned. "Make sure of it, lady wife, else you'll live to regret it."

Lillis pushed at the hands imprisoning her, to no avail. He was too strong and too big to fight.

"When should I ever have a chance to do otherwise, when I am constantly guarded?" With furious disgust, she added, "You are a great fool."

"That I may be," he admitted, "but I am also your husband, and you will do as I say."

"I will do as you say," she said, "because you are my captor, because I've no choice but to obey you, just as I've not had a choice from the moment I knew you. How I wish to God that moment had never come!"

"No more so than I, madam. No more so than I." Releasing her, he stood from the bed and agitatedly ran his hands through his hair. "Damn! This was not what I'd planned. I didn't come here to argue. How is it that you make me so crazed?"

"If I do, it is certainly not apurpose! I did not invite you here, my lord."

Swearing again, Alexander moved toward the fire. For the space of a minute he stood before it, rubbing at the back of his neck with one hand. "Your maid Edyth arrived at Gyer only an hour past," he said grudgingly.

Lillis bolted upright, her coverings falling away. "Edyth!"

"I cannot tell why she came so late, or why your father kept her so long. She was full weary when she arrived, and I sent her to her chamber directly. You may see her in the morn, as soon as it pleases you."

Lillis slid from the bed and, careless of being clothed in nothing but her thin chemise, went to him.

"Alexander—" she set a hand upon his arm "—my father..."

Wearily he nodded. "Lady Edyth brought a missive from him. Jaward has consented to our marriage, and has signed the contract. The land is mine now. I will ride this night, this hour, to the place where the dam is, and my men and I shall begin tearing it down."

She let out a breath. "Oh, I'm so glad. How happy your people will be, my lord."

"Yes." He looked at her. "And you will be happy, will you not, my lady? You will leave Gyer?"

"Yes," she said quietly, "I will leave. And you will be glad when I have gone. Castle Gyer will be as it once was."

"Lillis—" he began, then stopped and shook his head as if telling himself something. "I do not know how long the tearing down will take. Perhaps a few days, perhaps a week. When I return, I would speak with you of—important matters."

"Of course, my lord," she agreed, thinking he meant settlements and legalities.

"I shall look forward to returning, then," he said.

"I will wish you Godspeed," she said, her hand still on his arm, "and good fortune."

"You are kind, lady, but I would rather have this than your blessing." Alexander gathered her in his arms and kissed her again, before Lillis could even think to protest. By the time he was done she felt weak and useless, a toy to be used as Alexander pleased. "Strange," he murmured, his hand making slow circles over the thin material covering her back, "but I shall miss you, lady wife."

The words undid her. Lillis put her arms around his neck, lifted up on her toes, pressed full against him and set her lips to his. Alexander made a deep, appreciative groaning sound, and when the kiss was finished, he smiled with satisfaction at her dreamy expression.

"When I return, my lady, we will have much to discuss." Slowly he released her. "Everything shall be settled between us."

Chapter Twelve

"**I** don't want to do this, John."

Barbara nervously sidled her horse closer to her brother's and looked all around as though she expected someone to spring out from behind one of the surrounding trees. "I wish to return to Gyer. Cannot one of your men serve to guard this road?"

"Now don't be foolish, darling," John chided, lifting one gloved hand in the air to bring his men to a halt. "Not a one of these fellows would be half as successful in delaying any travelers as you will be. A lone man on a forest road is hardly worth comment, but a lovely young maid...oh, that is another matter. You'll come to no harm, I assure you. Only do as I've said and all will be well. And, for mercy's sake, don't start wailing if someone does come along. They might think you a wounded animal and try to put you out of your misery."

Barbara's nervousness hit its peak. "Oh my! I don't want to be killed! Please don't make me do this, John!" When she saw that her brother would not change his mind, she cast helpless glances at several of his men. "Aaron, Miles, please!"

John dismounted and moved to pull Barbara from her steed. "It's no use, sweeting. You know my men will not go against my wishes. There." He set her down and patted her hand reassuringly. "You look most lovely, my dear. No man possessed of his senses could resist stopping to lend aid to such a beautiful, helpless young lady. Now don't look so frightened, love. You'll be perfectly safe, I vow. Look, I shall post two men within hearing. If anyone should happen along and behaves badly and you are unable to fend him off, you need only shout and they'll be here in a trice. And I shall be back for you in less than half an hour's time. Our task will take no longer than that."

"Oh, John! I wish you will cease doing these things! What would happen to us if Cousin Alex ever found out?"

John smiled at her and spoke indulgently, "You musn't worry about such things, sweeting. You know full well I'd never let harm come to you, especially at Cousin Alex's hands. Have I not always taken good care of you?"

"But, John—"

"Now you stay here and be a good girl and we shall be back before you know it."

"Oh, please, John! Please don't leave me here all alone!"

"You'll be fine," he said, mounting his horse once again. "Remember, now, Barbara. Let no one pass by you for the next half hour, no matter who it may be. You mustn't disappoint me in this, love, else I shall be quite, quite angry with you."

Barbara understood what that meant; John's anger was a most unpleasant thing. She fell silent and lowered her head.

John and his men rode away, leaving her alone and shaking in the middle of a seldom-traveled forest road. A light fog enveloped the area and every noise was magnified in her ears. The hooting of an owl made her jump, and she hugged her cloak so tightly that her fingers ached.

After several long, still minutes passed, Barbara made her way to the side of the road and sat, shaking so badly that even the ground beneath her seemed to tremble. "Dear God, let John come back soon," she whispered, comforted by the sound of her own voice, weak and warbling as it was.

More than half an hour passed before she heard the much-listened-for sound of horse hooves in the distance, though with some confusion she realized they were coming from the wrong direction. Slowly she stood, clutching her cloak and watching with heightened fear as several strange men on horseback came out of the mist like specters, nearing her at a trotting pace.

She froze with panic. So many men! She would never be able to fend them all off. A tiny hope in the back of her mind that John would suddenly appear and rescue her died as she looked into the face of their leader, who brought his men to a stop before her.

He was a large man and very dark, his long black hair falling past his shoulders like some kind of barbarian and his clear blue eyes intent upon her. He stared at her with some amazement before speaking.

"What do you do here, lady?" he demanded sharply.

"I—I—"

The handsome giant frowned at her and Barbara burst into tears, made worse by the memory of John's reprimand not to do so. She turned and ran headlong into the woods, heedless of her direction. She stumbled several times in her panic, picking herself up and throwing herself forward in terrified desperation until the black-haired man finally caught her. Barbara tried to scream, but his hand closed over her mouth, stopping her, and he carried her down to the cold, wet ground. Shutting her eyes, she waited for him to rape her, but he did nothing more than turn her in his arms, set her in his lap and hold her.

"There, now, my lady," he soothed, stroking her hair. "You musn't be afraid."

"P-p-please don't hurt me!"

"Of course I'll not hurt you," he said gently, holding her more closely as she sobbed against his shoulder. "I'll let no one harm you, and I shall not harm you."

"I was s-so af-fraid!" she wailed, gratefully accepting his comfort.

"You must not be, beautiful lady. There is nothing to fear." Pulling back a little, he looked at her. "What is your name?"

"I am B-Barbara," she murmured, sniffling and blinking her wet eyes.

"Barbara," he murmured. "Pretty. A pretty name for a very pretty lady." His eyes moved over her face and then her hair, which he touched reverently. "I've never seen hair of such a color, soft red and gold, like a sunset," he remarked with some awe. "I thought you an apparition at first. A beautiful witch come from out of the mist. But you are no witch, are you, Barbara?"

Barbara mutely shook her head, staring at him. He was the handsomest man she had ever seen, and so strong. His muscular body made her feel tiny and very safe. He lowered his head and kissed her, softly and lightly, lifting his head after a moment and smiling at her.

"What do you do here, Barbara? How have you come to be alone in my woods?"

Barbara smiled up at him dreamily, wishing he would kiss her again. "Your woods?"

As if reading her thoughts his mouth found hers once more, and he kissed her longer and more thoroughly. His arms slid around her waist to hug her tight, and Barbara tentatively set her own arms about his neck.

"Who do you belong to, little one?" he whispered a minute later, his breath warm against her cheek.

Happier than she could ever before recall being, so content in this stranger's arms, it took Barbara a moment to understand what he was asking, and in that moment she remembered who she was and that her brother might even now be watching them from some hiding place.

"My brother," she said fearfully, pulling away from him. "My brother!" she repeated, and struggled to loose herself. If John should see her thus he would be furious!

The dark giant refused to let her go. "If your brother, whoever he is, cannot take better care of such a beautiful sister, then I think I must lend him aid. There is no excuse for letting a lady roam unescorted in the middle of a forest. Any number of evils might befall you. Who is your brother, love? And how is it that he comes to leave you thus?"

"That is no concern of yours, sir. I don't even know who you are!"

"You do not know me?" he asked with some amusement. "But, do you not live in Dunsted?"

She looked at him blankly. He smiled and kissed her again. "I am your lord, dearling. Jason de Burgh." He leaned closer. "But I shall be more to you, sweet Barbara. Much more."

Barbara stared at him in shock. "More?"

He nodded meaningfully. "I've never seen a more beautiful woman in all my days, Barbara of the Forest. And since your absent brother cannot take care of you as he should I shall invoke my rights as your lord and take you under my own care. You shall come to live with me at Castle Dunsted." He put one large hand up against her cheek and caressed her gently. "The woman who was to have been mine has been stolen from me, but now that I have trapped such a pretty doe in my own forest, I do not think I shall mind overmuch. I will make you mine, lovely witch."

"Oh, my heavens!" With renewed strength she struggled up and away from him. Jason de Burgh stood, as well, setting his hands around her waist.

"Do not fear me, Barbara. I am a stranger to you, yet I vow I would never bring you harm."

"I do not think that you will, Jason de Burgh, but you don't understand. I must go now."

"Go?" he repeated, confused, and tried to hold her as she backed away. "No, you will not—"

"My lord!" one of his men shouted from nearby. "One of the crofter's huts is afire!"

Jason de Burgh swung around to see the man who approached them. "A fire! Where is it, Allyn?"

"Just down the road, my lord. The work of Gyer, no doubt."

"Damn!" de Burgh cursed. "Allyn, take this lady to the castle and make certain that she is held safe."

The man peered around his master. "What lady, my lord?"

Jason turned again, only to find that the lovely Barbara had disappeared. For a moment he thought of pursuing her, for she couldn't have gone far, but his need to attend to the fire held him back. He stared into the heavy mist that filled the forest, envisioning the little beauty who had so quickly enslaved him. Whether it was simple lust he felt, or something more, Jason didn't care. He would find her again, and then she would be his.

"No lady, Aliyn. She is gone."

The road that led to Castle Gyer from the very outskirts of the village proper all the way to the castle gates was lined with cheering people. Alexander and his men made their way through the throng, accepting with good grace the accolades that were shouted at them.

"You've given them a very good gift for Michaelmas," Willem, riding beside Alexander, shouted above the noise. "They are well pleased, I think."

Alexander laughed and nodded. "This is a welcome day in Gyer. It's good to see them so happy."

Minutes later they entered the great hall of Castle Gyer to be greeted with equal enthusiasm by the people in the household. Barbara threw herself at Alexander, kissing and hugging him and telling him how wonderful he was. Cousin John was there, as well, to embrace and congratulate them. Even the servants stood to one side, clapping and cheering noisily.

"Where is Lady Gyer?" Alexander asked above the din. "And the children and Aunt Leta?"

"I believe they are with Lady Gyer," John replied loudly. "Of late they spend a great deal of time with her in her chamber."

Since Lillis was the one person Alexander wanted to see more than anyone else, this news pleased him. He set Barbara aside and made his way through the crowd. When he reached the stairs he bounded up them two at a time.

He had dreamed often of his wife since leaving her three days before, and had envisioned over and again how sweet their reunion would be. They had come to an understanding on their last night together. He had demonstrated his desire for her and had said that they would discuss their future. Certainly she had understood what he'd meant. Now that the dam had been torn down and the Eel River was once again flowing, there was nothing to keep them from making their marriage of convenience a marriage of truth. He remembered vividly the ready manner in which she had returned his kisses on the night he'd left, and knew that she had wanted him as much as he'd wanted her. Tonight, he thought with a smile, this very night, they would continue what they'd begun, with no interruptions to stop them.

The guards outside Lillis's door stood aside to let him pass, and Alexander walked into the chamber without so much as knocking.

Everyone in the room looked at him in surprise, and he gazed back with equal amazement. The scene before him was visibly domestic. Aunt Leta and Edyth were seated near the fire, working on their embroidery. Candis and Justin sat on the floor near them, playing with what looked like dolls. Lillis and the twins were sitting by the bed, grouped together, their heads bent over lutes. It was clear that Lillis was teaching Hugh and Hugo how to play the instrument, an idea that pleased Alexander as much as it stunned him.

"Alex!" all but Lillis and Edyth cried, and suddenly he was covered with relatives. Candis and Justin each took possession of a leg while the twins shook his hands and Aunt Leta showered him with kisses. He laughed and hugged them in turn, looking over their heads to where Lillis and Edyth stood watching the family reunion. He smiled at Lillis and was disconcerted to see her frown and turn away.

"Did you not hear the commotion as we rode through the village?" Alexander asked. "The noise must have been loud enough to reach this window." He nodded toward an open alcove.

"We did hear something," Hugh admitted, "but we were playing the lute so it didn't sound like anything important. Did the town welcome you in?"

"Indeed they did. It was quite a sight to see! I'm sorry you missed it. I know how the two of you like a good scene."

Aunt Leta patted Alexander's cheek. "The people of Gyer are quite right to give you such a welcome, Alexander. You are a good boy and have settled our troubles with

Wellewyn peacefully. I'm very proud of you, just as your father and mother would be were they still alive.''

"I cannot accept all the praise," he said. "It took a great many men to tear the dam down and, of course, we couldn't have avoided war without my good lady wife." He looked at Lillis again and offered another smile. She glared back with open disgust.

"Edyth made us dolls, Alex!" Candis cried, tugging at his tunic to get his attention.

"Did she?" Alexander smiled at the children. "I shall like to see them, but perhaps now you will want to go downstairs and welcome Willem home. I wish to speak with Lady Gyer for a few minutes."

"Of course, Alexander," Aunt Leta said, taking the children by their hands. "We will all of us go downstairs and greet Willem, as is right. Come along, Hugh, Hugo."

The twins gathered up their lutes. "Wait until you hear us play, Alex," Hugh said. "Lillis taught us two whole songs!"

"Two whole songs!" Hugo chimed in. "And we never miss a note!"

Alexander shook his head in true amazement. "I'm impressed. Perhaps you will entertain us at the evening meal?"

The twins were nearly undone by this suggestion and left, discussing plans for how and what they would do to prepare for the evening.

"Lady Edyth," Alexander addressed that lady when the twins had gone, "will you leave us, please? I should like to speak with my wife alone."

Edyth planted herself firmly next to Lillis and looked as though she were about to be stubborn.

"Go ahead, Edyth," Lillis told her companion, staring at Alexander with eyes that held daggers. "I shall be quite all right and I, too, wish to speak alone with my *dear husband.*"

When they were alone Alexander waited expectantly. Perhaps she had been too shy to express herself before the others. Now that they were alone she would come to him and tell him how glad she was about the dam.

She did not move, however, but merely stood, glaring at him.

"You know about the dam, my lady?" he asked.

"Oh, yes. We saw the river flowing again just yesterday. I could see it from out my window."

He waited a moment, then, "Were you not pleased?"

She nodded slowly. "Most pleased. Indeed, my lord, was that not what you and I bartered the rest of our lives for? I should have been devastated had our sacrifice come to naught, but as it has I suppose the sacrifice was well worth it. No blood was shed, thank a merciful God."

Alexander was bewildered by the bitterness of her tone. He took a step toward her. "I must confess, I had expected to hear you sound happier about it. Is something amiss, Lillis? Did something happen to upset you while I was gone?"

She gave a short, contemptuous laugh. "Whatever could be amiss, Alexander of Gyer? You have all that you want, do you not? The dam that my father built has been torn down and the river is running again. You own the land upon which it was built and so have no fear of it being erected again, and you have avoided a bloody war. What more could you possibly want?"

"For you to be glad, as well," he replied, thinking, *for a much sweeter greeting.*

"But I am glad, my lord. Have I not already told you so? Now that everything you wanted has been accomplished, I may leave Gyer. Nothing, I assure you, could make me happier than that. All I wish to know from you is when I may leave."

Alexander was utterly confused. What had happened while he was gone? Had he only dreamed the kisses they had shared on the night he left; had he only imagined how sweet and giving she'd been in his arms? He felt suddenly lacking, and wished fervently that he had a better understanding of the female mind.

"You may not leave at all, as you very well know. I thought you had understood that."

She gaped at him with disbelief. "But I must go! You've no need to keep me any longer, and I refuse to stay! My father needs me and I must go to him!"

"You may not leave," he repeated stubbornly, growing angry. He didn't even like discussing the matter, and he certainly didn't intend to waste any time discussing Jaward. What he wanted to speak of was their future together. "Lillis," he said more gently, "I told you before I left that I had much to say to you regarding our future—"

"I don't care what settlements you wish to make on me!" she cried furiously. "I don't care whether you give me a fortune or make me a pauper! And I don't care what you do with the lands that come to you through my name. All I ask is that you let me go home, as you promised before we were wed."

"I will not let you go, Lillis."

"But why?" she demanded angrily. "You have all that you want!"

He spoke calmly, carefully. "I cannot let you go until I have the king's formal acceptance of our marriage. I've already told you that you may not leave until then, and I'll not discuss the matter with you until that day arrives."

"But my father is very ill! How can you keep me prisoner when he needs me so badly? You cannot be so cruel as that, my lord."

Alexander looked at her in surprise. "Jaward is ill? I didn't know. He made no mention of it in the missive he sent me." He saw that his words surprised her, as well. She eyed him with disbelief. "Lillis, I swear that I didn't know he was ill. Now, come, I am weary from riding half the day and I wish you would behave reasonably."

Her eyes narrowed. "You knew *nothing* of my father's illness? Do you swear it?"

"I did not know it. I give you my solemn vow that this is the truth, and you know I am a man of my word."

Her wary expression faded slightly, mixing with a look of chagrin. "If this is so, my lord, then I have behaved most foolishly these past several days, and must beg your pardon. Edyth told me of my father's collapse after you'd gone, and I assumed you knew of it and yet left Gyer without releasing me to go to him. I fear I was quite angry with you."

Alexander felt oddly relieved to know the source of her upset, to know how foolish it was, and he was rather amused, as well. Women were strange creatures. He recalled that Barbara, whenever she became overset, which was aggravatingly often, was quickly soothed by a few words of indulgence, accompanied by some small gift. What could he give Lillis, he wondered, that would have such a happy outcome? He vividly recalled her reaction to the brooch he'd given her after their wedding night.

"I'm sorry to have given you such a mean-spirited greeting, my lord," she said, offering him a small smile, then blushing and lowering her eyes. "I am truly glad that you've come home safe, and that you accomplished all you desired."

"I missed you, Lillis," he said without meaning to, but unable to stop the words once they started. She appeared startled when she looked him full in the face. "I told you I would," he added almost defensively.

"I missed you also, my lord," she whispered.

His heart gave a hard thump in his chest. "Even though you were angered at me?"

A moment passed, then she said, softly, "Even so."

He moved toward her. "By God," he muttered, grabbing her up in his arms. "I did more than miss you."

He kissed her hungrily, setting one hand at the back of her head to make her meet him, his fingers sinking into the silky strands there and loosening them. His other arm wrapped around her waist and hugged her tight to himself, to the body that wanted and needed her. Lillis answered in kind, with a tiny, glad whimper, opening her mouth beneath his and accepting his passion while her hands buried themselves in his hair. She protested only a little as his hands explored her curves, touched her slim waist and full breasts and slightly rounded hips.

"My wife," he murmured thickly against her mouth, "let me know you again. I must know you again. There will be no pain this time. I swear it. Let me prove it to you."

For a few short moments she let him kiss her with his deep, demanding need, and then, so unexpectedly that Alexander felt as though he'd had the wind knocked out of him, she tore away.

"No!" she cried in a terrible voice, setting both hands on her head and rushing all the way across the chamber, where she stood against one wall, facing it, visibly trembling.

Alexander stood where he was, watching her, his own body shuddering. He was too shocked to move for a moment, and by the time he was able to, she had forced herself under control and had turned to face him.

"I would ask you to go, my lord," she said, sounding badly shaken. "I think I—I think I must pack—my things and . . ." She began to weep and couldn't speak anymore.

As much as he wanted to touch her, Alexander didn't dare. "Pack?" he repeated helplessly.

She said nothing, but only stood there with her head bowed, weeping so that it tore at his heart. At last he understood what she meant.

"Lillis, did you think I would release you simply because your father is ill?"

Not looking at him, silent, she nodded. Alexander kept silent, too, giving her time to understand what the truth was, and time to gain control of herself. Such a proud woman was his wife; it was a terrible thing to watch her suffer humiliation.

"Please," she whispered at last. "Go."

He had never felt so helpless. So utterly, damnably helpless. "I could not jeopardize all that's been done, Lillis, you know I could not. And it might very well be false. The last I saw of Jaward he was perfectly hale. How am I to know whether he is truly ill, or whether it is some ruse? It is a risk I cannot take!"

Still weeping, she shook her head, and clenched her hands into fists.

"Go!" she shouted furiously. "Go, go, *go!*"

It was something borne within him, something inherited from centuries past that made him react as he did; something innate, which he could neither repulse nor deny. Like night changed into day, he became the Lord of Gyer.

"You'll make no such demands of me, madam!" he informed her coldly. "*I* am lord here! I am not commanded to either come or go! I am not made to do *anything!*"

Her hands, still fisted, fell to her sides, and she glared at him out of wet, angry eyes. "And *I* am your captive, *not* your slave! My father has fallen ill because of what you've done to me. He has suffered a complete collapse. Edyth only stayed with him so long because she feared he might die." Her blue eyes were hard and cold upon him, and when she next spoke, her voice was as ice. "I have given you much, Alexander of Gyer. Now, I would ask this of you, that you let me return to my father, who can cause you no more harm."

He wanted to shout at her again, but controlled himself and said, "I'll not release you, but as it means so much to you, I shall take you to visit him. On these terms—that you will not try to escape, and that you will return to Gyer afterward to await word from King Henry."

"When will you take me?"

"As soon as possible. I will rest tomorrow, having labored hard these past many days, but we can leave the next day if the weather permits. We will stay the day if you like, and if Jaward will countenance it."

She grew quiet and searched his eyes intently. "You will do this, Alexander of Gyer?"

"Give me your promise that you will return to Gyer with me, Lillis."

"Yes. I shall. I do so give it, my lord."

"Then we shall journey to Wellewyn on the day after tomorrow, if the weather permits."

She stared at him blankly.

"You do not believe me," he stated.

"I do not know how to do so," she replied.

She didn't trust him, Alexander realized with a shock. She had no faith in him or in his word, whatsoever. The feeling that moved through him was foreign. "I speak the truth," he insisted, much aggrieved.

Her expression was as stone, unmoving. "I have no way of knowing it," she said.

Fury surged in him, hot, deep, encompassing. *He was the Lord of Gyer.* His word was sacred. It had *never* been questioned.

"You will learn it," he seethed, beyond knowing what he spoke. "You will learn it, lady."

Lillis gazed at him without emotion, relaxed now. She gazed at him as if he were some kind of poor idiot, as if she pitied him. Alexander was only that much more enraged.

"I shall see you at the evening meal," he said curtly, moving toward the door.

"I'll not come for the evening meal," she declared. "I will eat in my chamber. Let your cousin play lady for you!"

"You will come down to table of your own free will," he said, "or I shall come and fetch you. Either way you will sit in your place as Lady Gyer. Believe me, madam wife, you will."

Chapter Thirteen

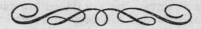

Lillis was asleep when the cold air that chilled her thinly clad body caused her to stir. Half-consciously she groped for the bed covers, her hand finding nothing but air until it finally came in contact with something warm. Her entire body was suddenly enveloped by the warmth, and Lillis was content to slide back into slumber. But then she became aware of movement, and realized, groggily, that she was being carried in someone's arms. Her mind came awake all at once, though her sleep-ridden body remained half-paralyzed. She was only able to make the weakest resistance to the arms that held her so tightly.

"Hush," Alexander whispered. "It's only me."

"Alexander?" she mumbled, straining against his arms. "What's happened?"

"All is well," he reassured her, stopping a moment to kick a door closed. "Don't be afraid."

She rubbed her eyes and looked around her, realizing that she was in his chamber. A hot fire lit the room and filled it with dancing shadows. "Why are we here? What's happened?"

"Hush, or you'll wake your guards."

It wasn't until he set her in the middle of his large bed and climbed in beside her that Lillis realized what was happening. She opened her mouth to scream, only to have it effectively stifled by Alexander's hand gently closing over her lips. He pulled her down against his body and, with his free hand, drew the covers up around them. Her back was against his chest; he held her more closely so that he could bring his mouth to her ear.

"This isn't what you think," he whispered, putting one giant leg over both of hers to keep her still. "I'm not about to rape you. I swear it. Do you believe me?"

Lillis shook her head violently and started to struggle, making ineffectual noises against his hand. Alexander merely tightened his grip on her waist until she thought he would break a rib or two, and continued to explain himself.

"You are my wife, and will sleep wherever I wish it. To-night you will share my bed, and you will learn to trust me, just as I promised you would. I am not going to rape you," he repeated. "Do you believe me?"

She neither nodded nor shook her head, but only tugged at the hand that covered her mouth.

"Lillis?" he prompted.

"Mmm!" she emitted furiously, still tugging. One foot kicked at him beneath the covers, making weak, harmless contact.

"I'll not release you unless you promise you'll not scream. It will do you no good even if you do, but 'twould be unpleasant, nonetheless. Do you so promise?"

She nodded vehemently, and when he at last removed his hand she gasped for air.

"Are you well, madam?" he asked with some concern, pushing up on one elbow to look at her.

She glared at him out of watering eyes. "What were you trying to do? Suffocate me?"

Lillis could see his blank look even in the dim light of the fire, his face was so close. "Forgive me," he apologized. "I didn't realize I held you so tight. I'm not used to having to hold a woman down in my bed. They've always stayed of their own free will before." He grinned at her in a very male way.

"I'm not most women!" she informed him hotly. "And I don't wish to stay in your bed! How dare you bring me here you—*animal!*"

He brought his face even closer and rubbed his hand against her stomach in a circular motion. "Animal, am I?

I'm your husband, madam, and have every right to bring you to my bed if I wish it." He kissed her quickly. "But for tonight I've promised not to touch you, and I'll not."

Lillis gazed at him warily, wondering at his strange, happy mood. They'd spent most of their time during the evening meal ignoring each other.

"You're touching me now." She said, and tried to turn away from him.

He held her tight and chuckled, the motion of his hand growing slower and more meaningful. "If you don't understand the difference between the kind of touching that you mean and the kind that I mean, I'd be most pleased to demonstrate."

"No, thank you. I wish to return to my own chamber, my lord, and I ask that you let me do so."

"No." He lay down and slid both arms around her, hugging her against himself. "You will stay with me tonight so that you may learn to trust me."

"I have no desire to learn any such thing," she hissed angrily. "I only want to be left alone until you let me leave this place. Have I not given enough in the past few days? Is the rest of my life too small a sacrifice for you?"

"You will learn to trust me," he repeated. "We are married and shall be for the rest of our lives. You will be the only wife I shall ever have, and I shall be your only husband. We shall have children together. I would have your friendship, and your trust."

"You want more of me than friendship and trust!" she cried.

"Yes," he admitted. "I'd have your passion, your need. I'd have you seek to join with me, as I seek to join with you. I'd have our beddings be times of joy and pleasure, rather than matters of civility and duty, as our wedding night was. It was as distasteful to me as it was to you, that night. I would have given anything to spare you that humiliation, to have taken you as gently as a bride deserves, but you know I had no choice. I did what I thought best, and finished the matter quickly. But next time—" he gently kissed the side of her neck "—next time it shall be as it should be, my lady wife. I shall give you sweet pleasure and great joy."

"You will make me your slave," she insisted. "You would have everything of me that you've not yet taken by force. My thoughts, my very soul. I shall be nothing more than your dog, slavering at your feet and begging for every crumb it pleases you to spare me."

"Is that what you fear of me?" he asked with disbelief, sounding strangely hurt. "Is that why you turned from me today?" With a groan he pressed his face against her hair. "It shall never be like that. I will take nothing more than you are willing to give, Lillis, and I will give whatever you ask of me. Is it too much to ask that there be such kindness between us? Must we live our lives as courteous strangers? Would you have our every coupling be mere ritual?"

"I don't know," she said miserably. "I don't know. Why do you speak to me of such things? We were wed out of circumstances, not out of friendship, not out of love. Why should our marriage be anything more than what it is?"

"Why should it not be?" he retorted.

Because you don't love me, she wanted to say, but instead closed her eyes and said wearily, "Please let me return to my own bed."

"No."

"What of Barbara? She would be unhappy to know that I'd spent a night in your bed."

She expected him to become angry, but was surprised to feel one of his hands moving up toward her face. He cupped her cheek and turned her head toward him, lifting his own to look down at her. "I do not care what Barbara thinks, Lillis," he told her softly, sincerely. "She is simply my cousin, now, and a very distant cousin at that. You are my wife."

Lillis turned to stare into the darkness. She said nothing.

"Lillis?" Alexander asked after a while, his hand caressing her bare arm.

"What?"

"What are your feelings for me?"

"What do you mean?" she asked with some surprise. He sounded so wistful.

"We've not known one another long, but do you care for me at all?"

"I don't know you very well," she replied, unable to speak the truth that she did, indeed, care for him, though the words were true enough in their own sense. She did not know him well.

He was thoughtful. "This is true," he finally agreed. "I will take you for a ride tomorrow, if the weather permits, and we will come to know each other better."

Lillis sucked her breath in at the thought of such freedom. "You would let me go outside of the village walls?"

He chuckled, sending vibrations down her entire body. "With my escort, yes. Would you not like to see some of Gyer?"

"I should like it very much."

"I'll have Cook pack some food for us," Alexander said with a yawn, "and we'll have our midday meal in a pleasant spot I know of by the river." She felt him smile against the top of her head. "It will be good to watch the river running again. I wish you could have seen it when the dam gave way and the river began to flow toward Gyer again. Your father was very clever in what he had done. He didn't actually build a dam. It was more like a diversion built right at the fork where the river splits into two. He had all the water flowing away from Gyer and toward Edington." He yawned again. "Very clever, indeed."

"I'm glad for you, Alexander," she said. "I'm glad everything turned out just as you wished." She stared at the shadows that danced around the room and tried to ignore the feeling of his body pressed against her.

"I'll not be able to sleep, Alexander," she whispered into the darkness.

"Neither will I."

Silence passed, then they spoke at the same time.

"Will you—?"

"Perhaps you might—?"

A half second of silence, and they both began to laugh.

"I thought," he said, chuckling, "that you might tell me something of your life at the convent."

"And I thought," she said, turning just enough to smile at him, "that you might tell me something about your life here at Gyer."

He looked at her with shock, as though what she suggested was an impossible feat. He began to shake his head, then stopped and gazed at her thoughtfully. "I suppose I could," he said, sounding very uncertain.

She turned her head back to the pillow and made herself more comfortable. What a strange thing it was, she thought, to lie in a bed beside him. As strange as it had been on their wedding night, and yet not at all unpleasant. "As I am not here of my own free will, sir, it seems only right that you should entertain me."

She felt him smiling against her hair again. "Very well, Lillis. Though the story will send you into sleep, most like."

"Never more than mine would you," she told him with heartfelt honesty, thinking how dull he would find the account of her life.

"We shall see," he said, and, pulling the covers up about them both more closely, began his tale.

Chapter Fourteen

Lillis stood in the great hall and peered through a crack in one of the window shutters, watching the never-ending downpour of rain. All of the castle windows had been tightly shuttered in order to keep the cold and wet out, and the dwelling had taken on a gloomy cast. Fires and candles were kept continuously burning in an effort to provide warmth and light, but it was not the same as sunlight.

She sighed. Would the weather never clear? Would she never be able to get home to Wellewyn to see her father? She thought of him constantly, wishing she could be with him, caring for him and making him well. How worried he must be! Alexander had been very kind on that first rainy morn when they had been supposed to travel to Wellewyn. The day before it, when they had ridden together and enjoyed their meal by the river, had been beautiful. There'd been no sign of rain then, but sometime during the night it had begun to pour, and Alexander had refused to take her anywhere in such inclement weather. But he'd commiserated with her quite sweetly, and had offered to send one of his men to deliver a missive to Wellewyn, if she wished to write one. It was the first time he had offered her a chance to communicate with her father, and Lillis had gratefully written the letter, spending more than three hours pouring all of her love and concern into it. Alexander had sent his sturdiest knight on his way within minutes of her handing it over to him. She'd felt guilty about sending the poor man into such bad weather, but her worry for her father had outweighed her guilt. The courier returned the next day with no reply. His only report was that her father had accepted the missive with shaking hands and had taken to his bed soon after reading it.

More than a week had passed since then; a week both confusing and wonderful. She saw little of Alexander during the days, as he steadfastly remained busy with the running of his estates, but he continued to stop work every hour or so to come and visit with her, though he was no longer content to simply sit wherever he found her. Instead, he would dismiss her guards and draw her away to someplace more private, where they would spend several minutes alone, walking up and down the halls, talking quietly. Sometimes he would hold her hand as they walked, and sometimes he would pull her into the shadows and kiss her. As confused as Lillis was by so much sudden affection from the husband she knew didn't love her, she found herself unwilling to make him stop. In truth, she looked forward to his visits. Indeed, she counted the hours between each one.

When it was time for the evening meal Alexander would put his work aside and devote himself to his family and to her. Once the meal was finished he would take her to a certain gaming table set in front of a fireplace in one corner of the great hall. There the rest of the family would follow and relax while she and Alexander played chess or backgammon. A servant would bring hot spiced wine for the women and tankards of ale for the men. Aunt Leta and Edyth would sit before the fire, working on their embroidery, either enjoying a comfortable gossip or entertaining the children. The twins, dutifully becoming proficient on the lute, would sit on the rushes in front of the flames, practicing their instruments. Willem would sit by Lillis, whispering advice to her about how to outmaneuver Alexander at chess and teasing his older brother whenever she beat him.

John and Barbara were there, as well, settling themselves by Edyth and Aunt Leta and conversing comfortably with everyone in general. Barbara worked on her embroidery and spent a great deal of time surreptitiously watching Alexander. Other times she would stare into the fire as though no one else were there. Lillis never missed the glances that Alexander spared his beautiful cousin, for he didn't realize how openly he looked at Barbara. The concern for her that was written on his face was as clear as a blue summer sky, and Lillis wondered why he didn't spend more time with the dainty creature than he did. He seemed always to be with Lillis, instead, and always he insisted that he wanted to win her trust.

He'd won more than that, Lillis thought, pushing from the window and walking back to where Edyth sat teaching the children some simple mathematics. The twins had refused to be taught but somehow always ended up hovering around in the background, learning in spite of themselves. She stopped and leaned against the coolness of the wall, watching as Hugh suddenly came alive. He knew the answer to a problem Edyth had posed and was very excited. Lillis smiled, remembering how good it felt to finally understand something you were trying to learn.

Her gaze wandered from Edyth and the children to the other end of the hall where Barbara and Aunt Leta sat with their women, gossiping and sewing, as they always seemed to do, especially now that the rain kept everyone indoors.

Her days with Alexander had been wonderful, but Lillis had come to live for the nights. She'd lain awake that first night after he had taken her to his bed, and after an hour or two he had quietly unbolted the adjoining door and come to get her again. He had come every night since then, carrying her to his bed and lying beside her, his arms holding her close. He told her each night that he wanted to make love to her but that he would wait until she wanted that, too, and then they would talk for a long while before falling asleep. He told her of his childhood, and about his parents, things that were difficult for him to speak of. Lillis, in turn, told him of her own childhood, of the the joys and sadnesses, telling Alexander things she had never told anyone else.

She had come to know him during those conversations, to understand him and to love him. How sad she had felt when he had told her of his father, a great, powerful man who'd never had much time for either his people or his family, save the twins, whom he'd notably favored and spoiled. Alexander always sounded so wistful and longing, telling her how he had loved his father but how hard it had been to admire the man. When he'd died, Alexander had felt lost and afraid. Gyer had had so many problems, its people held so many demands, and at the age of nineteen he was burdened with caring for all of them, as well as his family. His mother, whom he'd loved deeply, had died just after Candis had been born, and all the joy had gone out of his life for a long time.

"I suppose every boy thinks that his mother is the most beautiful woman in the world," he told her one night as they lay together, warm and comfortable, "but I think perhaps my mother really was. She was the kind of person who could light up a room whenever she entered it, like a living candle. She and my father fought a great deal, but they always made up in the end. I used to think, sometimes, that he didn't love her enough, or not as much as he should have, but he was always so relieved whenever they resolved a disagreement that I finally realized just how much he did love her. He couldn't stand to be kept away from her, even for one night, though sometimes they spent months and months apart."

"You still miss her, do you not?" Lillis murmured.

He nodded against the top of her head. "Not as much as I did at first, but I do miss her. After she died we went about living day to day, yet never really lived. Does that make sense? My father was hardly home after she died. He spent most of his time at court or at some of his other estates. He disdained Candis as though she were to blame for Mother's death. But she had nothing to do with it. My mother died of the chill, during wintertime. She suffered long and terribly before finally dying."

"I'm sorry, Alexander."

He squeezed her. "You've no need to be, my lady. It was difficult at the time, but we have lived through it. I think perhaps it was hardest on Willem and the twins. They were so young then, and needed her so much. Justin was only three and didn't really know what had happened. Candis has no memory of our mother at all. And I had Barbara to help me get through. She and John came to live with us just before my mother died. We were already betrothed then, though she was only a little girl. After my mother died Barbara spent a great deal of time with me, trying to cheer and comfort me." He chuckled at the memory. "She was such a tiny little girl and I was a nearly grown lad who had no use for her. I was just beginning to learn about women, you see, and here was this little girl following me around everywhere, trying to get my attention. She was persistent though, and I grew to cherish her. Everyone loved Barbara. She was such a sweet, beautiful child, and was my greatest delight in those days." He yawned and shortly fell asleep, but Lillis stayed awake for the remainder of the night, thinking on his words. She had never been happier, or more miserable.

"My lady." The sudden voice made Lillis jump in surprise. She turned to see John standing beside her and forced herself to smile. Where had he come from? The man never made any noise at all.

"What a fright you gave me, John. I wish you will cease doing that."

John grinned apologetically. "Forgive me, Lady Gyer. I didn't mean to startle you. I thought perhaps you looked far away. Do you think of your father? I know that he is ill. How you must worry for him! I'm a good listener if you would like to talk."

Lillis shook her head. "No, I thank you, sir. I should be getting back to Edyth. It isn't fair to make her do all the work with the children."

John's handsome face fell. "But how unkind, my lady! I've finally caught you alone and now you say that you will run away. Will you not spare your lonely cousin even a few moments of your time? We've not yet had a chance to get to know each other."

Lillis looked at his sincerely unhappy expression and wondered what she should do. She didn't wish to be rude to the man, yet she didn't wish to be alone with him, either. The last thing she wanted to hear at the moment were more veiled comments about how much Barbara and Alexander loved each other. He must have seen that she was trying to make up her mind, for he suddenly smiled most charmingly and held out one arm.

"Come, my lady. Walk with me to the solar and back, that's all I ask. Will you? Please?"

She couldn't refuse him now without appearing ill-mannered. With a sigh she set her hand on his arm. "Very well, sir, but only to the solar and back. It will be time for the midday meal soon and I must make certain that Candis and Justin are washed up before then. Even being kept indoors they somehow manage to get quite dirty!"

"From running around in the kitchen and getting into the ashes, no doubt." John patted her hand and led her down the length of the great hall. Her two guards followed at their normal polite distance. "I wanted to thank you for your kindness to Barbara, my lady, and for your understanding of her circumstances. She's been so much happier of late."

Lillis looked at him in surprise. "Has she? I must admit that I had not thought so. She seems very sad to me a great deal of the time. Indeed, I had thought to speak with her to see whether she is feeling well."

"Oh, she is quite well, I assure you, my Lady Gyer, though you are kind to worry over her. It's only the stress of the situation, and the waiting. I fear she's not happy with Alex for spending so much time with you, though of course she understands completely that he must do so in order to keep up the pretense of your marriage in front of the others."

Lillis felt a surge of anger and looked at him sharply. "Does she? I must tell you, John, that my husband has told me he has no plans to keep Barbara with him once I have left Gyer. He has assured me that he intends to find a suitable husband for her."

John smiled at her indulgently. "Yes, I imagine he would tell you such a thing. Alex can play the tyrant whenever it pleases him to do so, but more often than not he makes an effort to spare the feelings of others, at least as best he can. I must admit, however, that I have begun to wonder whether you might not be right, my lady. After all, I had thought you were to be allowed to go free once the king's approval of your marriage came, and since you are still at Gyer it may very well be that Alex does indeed intend to set Barbara aside." He shook his head. "If that is so, then this game he is playing with my sister is quite cruel."

"But I am going to be set free when the king's approval comes," Lillis told him. "Alexander promised that I may go home as soon as it arrives."

"Hmm," John intoned thoughtfully. "Is it the weather, then, that has kept you at Gyer?"

Lillis laughed. "What? No! It has kept us from making a visit to see my father, but that is all. And if it were up to me we would have gone to Wellewyn in spite of this rain, but Alexander refuses to take me until it stops. I'm still his prisoner, you see, until the king legally recognizes our marriage, and as you said, he can be tyrannical when he wishes to be. If the king's approval had come, I assure you, nothing would have kept me from leaving for home. Not even this wretched weather."

John stopped walking and turned to look at her. "But, if that is the case, then why—? My lady, did you not know?"

"What?"

"About the king's approval. It arrived two days ago, brought by one of the king's own regents. Didn't Cousin Alex tell you?"

Lillis was shocked. "No! He didn't. The king's approval arrived? Two days ago?" She could feel the hot flush that swept across her cheeks. "Then that means...that I'm free!" She was elated. "Are you sure of this, John Baldwin?"

"Yes, quite sure. I promise you it is true. But I think perhaps it was a mistake for me to speak of it. Alex obviously didn't wish you to know, and I fear I may have brought his wrath upon myself by telling you. I beg you'll not tell him that it was I who gave you this information."

"How foolish!" she chided. "Of course he meant for me to know, he was just—" she cast about for a plausible reason "—he was simply waiting for the weather to clear, that's all. He didn't realize that I would wish to leave right away."

Although how he couldn't know was a mystery to Lillis. She thought she'd made her desire to go home as soon as she possibly could quite clear to him. Dear Lord! The impact kept hitting her anew. She was free again! She could come and go as she pleased, she could move freely and make her own decisions—she could walk without having to constantly look over her shoulder to see whether her guards were following her.

John squeezed her hands and pleaded with her. "Please, Lady Lillis, you must promise me that you'll not tell Alex I told you of this. He would kill me."

"He'll do no such thing! He would have told me himself, I tell you."

"Promise me, my lady." He squeezed her hands even harder.

His fear of Alexander seemed very real, though Lillis couldn't bring herself to believe there was any reason for it. But she didn't have all day to argue the matter with him. She was going to go home!

"Very well, John. I so promise. Now release me, please."

He did, and Lillis didn't even spare a moment to bid him goodbye. She picked up her skirts and headed for the stairs, so intent on reaching her chamber that she never saw the thoroughly satisfied smile that settled on John's face as he watched her go.

Chapter Fifteen

The knock at the door made Lillis pause in her frantic packing.

"Enter!" she called out, glancing over one shoulder before neatly folding the last of her needlework.

Alexander walked into the room, smiling, looking very handsome to her loving eyes. He shut and bolted the door before strolling toward her.

"You wished to see me, madam? Urgently?"

Lillis turned and met his smile with her own. Alexander didn't quit moving until he had pulled her into his arms.

"Dare I think it was for personal reasons?" he whispered against her mouth, kissing her. "I was most hopeful when I received your summons."

The room was cool, but Alexander was warm, and his mouth even warmer as it moved over her own. His hands, sliding to her hips, pulled her intimately against him, almost making Lillis forget the reason she had summoned him.

"Alexander," she murmured, her arms moving around his neck.

"Mmm...sweet Lillis." One big hand moved up to cradle the back of her head while the other splayed over her buttocks, holding her firm.

The evidence of his desire brought Lillis to her senses.

"Alex—ander," she managed, mumbling around his seeking tongue.

"Hmm?"

She tried in vain to pull away, and when she couldn't she laughed. He lifted his head and gazed at her, grinning.

"Lady wife, are you laughing at me?"

"No! I'm laughing at me." She pushed at his strong arms. "Please, my lord, this is most pleasant, but we must talk." She had much to tell him, after all.

He groaned. "Lillis, sweet wife, I'm not in a talkative mood." His mouth dropped to nuzzle the soft skin beneath her ear. "Let me have you in the bed." She grew pleasantly pliant in his arms, and his mouth traveled down her throat. "We'll spend the rest of this rainy day warm beneath the sheets." She tilted her head to allow him greater access to her bare skin. "The things I want to do to you, Lillis! I want to touch you everywhere with my hands, with my mouth." He backed her toward the bed. "You know it must happen sooner than later. Let it happen now."

His seductive tone made Lillis shiver. "But we can't— Alexander, we can't."

Alexander smiled, hearing the indecision in her voice, sensing his victory. "We can, Lillis. We will."

"We can't. No, Alexander, stop. I'm packing."

At last Alexander lifted his head.

"You're what?"

She laughed and pushed at his shoulders.

"I'm packing, you ridiculous man, while you're trying to seduce me. Now let go of me, please. I don't want to waste another moment before getting started."

He freed her at once, his amorous mood flown.

"What in the name of God are you talking about, Lillis?"

She reached up and kissed him quickly. "What do you think? And why didn't you tell me you'd received the king's approval for our marriage?" She moved to where her bags lay half-packed on the bed. "I know you don't wish to let me travel in such inclement weather, Alexander, but there is nothing, not even the worst of weather, that could keep from going to my father now that I'm free to do so. I wish you had told me yesterday so that Edyth and I could have gotten a much earlier start." She picked up the needlework she'd just finished folding and carefully placed it inside one bag. "Edyth is in her chamber packing, as well. We'll be ready to leave within the hour, if you think you can arrange an escort for us that quickly. Oh, but please don't leave yet, for there is something I should like to tell you as soon as I'm finished with this."

Alexander stared at his wife, stunned. He'd thought he would have more time. Only a little more—that was all he needed to finish what he'd started. She was so close to giving in to him, he was sure of it, and once she did, it wouldn't matter that the king's approval had arrived. Nothing would matter, once she gave way.

Her nimble hands kept working, folding and packing, folding and packing.

"Stop, Lillis."

She stopped only long enough to glance at him. "I'm sorry, my lord. What did you say?"

"I said stop. Stop what you're doing."

"Stop?" she repeated, glancing at him again with an indulgent smile. "Alexander, I told you, I wish to get started at once and there is much to do. I don't have time to stop." She turned her back on him and started packing again.

Alexander, filled with a rage beyond his comprehension, didn't spare a moment to think of what he was doing. He closed the distance between them, grabbed what she was so carefully folding and flung it across the room.

"Alexander—!"

He took her by both shoulders and shook her. "Damn you, Lillis! I said stop it!"

She stared at him wide-eyed. "What in God's name is the matter with you? How dare you do such a thing? That was my best surcoat!"

"I don't care if it was King Henry's night rail!" he roared furiously. "Who told you about the king's approval arriving? Was it Willem? God, I thought I could trust him! He swore to me he wouldn't say a word to you!"

Dumbly Lillis shook her head. "It wasn't Willem. He didn't say anything to me." John's words about Alexander being angry surfaced in her mind, and along with the memory came an uncomfortable suspicion. "Does it matter how I found out, Alexander? Were you not—"

"Yes, it matters! I want to know now, Lillis. Who told you? Was it the twins? Did they break into my working chamber and go through my things? If they did, I swear by God I'll break both their wretched necks!"

"Alexander!" Distressed, Lillis tried to push from him. "It wasn't the twins! And it doesn't matter! Were you not going to tell me yourself? It doesn't matter how I came to hear of it."

Alexander's face registered shock, and he abruptly released her. "Of course I was going to tell you," he muttered, running both hands tensely through his hair. "But I was going to tell you in my own time, and in my own way. You might as well admit who it was. I'll only find out later, regardless."

Lillis stared at his rigid back in amazement. "Well, then, if you'll only find out later, there is no need for me to tell you. Perhaps I broke into your private chamber and had a look through your things and found out for myself. Are you going to break my neck now?"

He was pacing, looking like a caged animal. His tension unnerved her. "Of course I'm not going to break your neck," he replied angrily, not looking at her. "You'd never do such a thing. It isn't in your nature."

"I'm relieved to hear that you think so, my lord. Now if you will please excuse me, I wish to finish my packing." She turned to the bed and began folding her things again. A large hand grasping her shoulder pulled her back.

"I told you to stop that, Lillis."

A warning rang in Lillis's head as she gazed at her husband. He was as serious now as he'd been on the day when he'd told her of their impending marriage.

"Oh, God's mercy, Alexander, please—"

He took both her hands in his and drew her closer to the bed.

"Sit, Lillis. I need to speak with you."

She sat. Alexander settled himself beside her, still holding her hands.

"Lillis," he began slowly, "I know that I am not the husband of your choice. How could I be? I'm dull and plodding, only good at managing my people and my lands."

She shook her head in denial, but Alexander pressed on. "Please, Lillis—don't. It's no more than the truth, and I know full well I'm nothing like Ywain Giraut, or any of a hundred other men who would have thrown themselves willingly at your feet. I have never pretended to be a romantic or courtly man."

"But, that is not so, Alexander."

"It is. Listen to me, Lillis. I'm not good at explaining myself. It's not something I've had to do very often, and not something I intend to do much in future. I'm too used to making my wishes known and having them obeyed without question. That's what comes from being in a position of responsibility such as the one I'm in." He searched her face for understanding. "These past few days, I've been trying to reveal myself to you, but I've clearly not done well with it." He shifted uncomfortably and lowered his eyes to where their joined hands lay on his knees. "I've been courting you," he admitted, embarrassed. "I know I've been clumsy going about it, but damnation, Lillis, I've never had to be romantic with a woman before! Barbara was chosen for me by my parents, and all the other women I've ever known have—they have always come to me of their own free will. You're the first I've ever had to work at." He lifted his eyes again. "What I'm trying to say, Lillis, is that I don't want you to leave Gyer. I want you to stay here as my wife." He squeezed her hands tightly. "I want you to be my wife in truth."

Hope surged in Lillis's heart. This was just what she had meant to say to him, that she wished to return to Gyer, as he'd said she might, and be his lady. She'd been ready to agree to whatever conditions he might make, as long as he'd promise never to humiliate her with his cousin, but she had never let herself hope that he might truly want her to stay. "Alexander," she whispered, "are you trying to tell me that you love me?"

He looked first surprised, then bewildered, then a little irate, all in a moment's time. "These are serious matters I speak of, Lillis. Would you have us turn aside to such as that?"

Stunned, she tried to pull her hands from his grasp.

"Lillis!" He held her tight. "Does it mean so much? I shall honor you as my wife in every way! You shall never want for anything. Your happiness will be of all importance to me. Is that not more than enough?"

She wrenched her hands free. "I thank you, my Lord Gyer," she said stiffly, picking up a silk undergarment to fold it, "but I fear I must decline your kind offer. If you will arrange for an escort for Edyth and myself I would be most grateful."

He stood and reached for her. "Lillis—"

"Don't touch me!" she shouted, moving away from him and trying to stop the tears that overwhelmed her.

"Lillis!"

"I love you!" she sobbed, horrified at herself and humiliated beyond belief. "I love you, and you love Barbara, and I don't want to be honored and cared for! I want to go home to my father! My father loves me! My father needs me! If I have to stay at Gyer another day I shall lose my sanity!"

Her tears blurred her vision so badly that Lillis didn't see Alexander's arms as they roughly grabbed her, pulling her into himself.

"Lillis," he soothed, holding her tight and thinking to himself, *victory*. She was his now, unassailably, and the realization made him feel as if his whole being had been lit afire. "Do you love me? In truth? My God, you are the most wonderful woman alive." Nothing had ever made him feel like this before. "Sweet, lovely Lillis," he murmured, lowering his head to kiss her.

"Stop—" She pushed at him feebly.

"No. I'll not stop. Not this time. I'm a damned fool, and I've not been able to tell you just how much I care for you. I'm going to show you, instead."

His warm mouth moved over her face, absorbing her tears, until Lillis leaned away from him. "I'm going home to Wellewyn," she insisted.

Alexander's mouth followed her, kissing her chin, her neck, everywhere that her leaning away exposed to him. His hands moved to unfasten her clothing.

"Gyer is your home, and always will be. You are mine, now."

Her surcoat fell away easily, but when Lillis felt him pulling the silk undergarments from her body she pushed at him again. "No, Alexander, don't."

"You love me," he reminded, kissing her naked shoulder, pulling her undergarments down until she was bared to the waist. "Show me." His big hands moved up to cup and caress her breasts.

"No," she protested weakly.

"Yes." He lifted her to the bed and stripped the rest of her clothes from her. He undressed himself quickly and lay naked beside her, pulling her into his arms.

"This will not be as the first time," he murmured, kissing her, looking into her wide blue eyes. His hands moved over her warm skin with gentle patience. "This time we shall know one another as fully as possible." He pressed one muscular leg between both of hers, nestling his thigh against the center of her. "With as much pleasure as possible."

Before Lillis could protest again, he stole her ability to do so. With the skill and experience of many years, he touched her, moving his hands over her body knowingly, bending her to his will.

"Tell me you love me," he whispered.

She wouldn't. She shook her head in denial.

"Tell me, Lillis." His mouth moved gently over her breasts. "Tell me. Now."

Her hands clenched and she spoke the truth. "I do love you, Alexander."

"Tell me again, Lillis. Tell me that you want me as much as I've wanted you these past many days."

She writhed beneath his touch. "Please, Alexander—"

"Tell me."

"I want you. It is truth, Alexander. Please—don't—"

"Wife." He kissed her deeply. "My wife. Mine." He said the words over and over as he joined their bodies.

"Lillis," he moaned without thought. None of his memories remotely compared with the pleasure he knew now. He grasped her face with both hands and made her look at him as he moved in her.

"This, my wife, this is how I care for you. We are one. *One.*"

One, yes, she understood him, and knew at last what he'd meant when he'd spoken of joy and pleasure. They were one, and their joy and pleasure were one. It was pure and fine and wondrous.

He rolled to his side when it was all over, pulling Lillis along with him, holding her tight, reveling in the pliancy of her body. Alexander had never considered himself one to gloat, but he couldn't keep from grinning. She was sure to be angry for a little while over her defeat, but he would be a generous winner. He would shower her with so much gratitude and affection in the days to come that she would quickly forget everything about Wellewyn, including her devil of a father.

Lillis's arms came up around his shoulders, hugging him, and Alexander drifted off into the most contented sleep he had ever known.

He reached for Lillis when he woke some time later, only to find emptiness. It was dark in the room, night having fallen, but he could see very well by the light provided by the glowing fireplace.

She was sitting across the room, staring thoughtfully at her hands and looking very much as she had on that first day when he had first spoken with her in his private chamber—when he had first told her that she was his prisoner. What an eternity ago that seemed to him now. At Lillis's feet, carefully arranged, were her bags, all packed.

Very slowly, he sat. "Lillis."

Startled, her gaze jerked toward him.

"What do you do there? Take off your clothes and come back to bed."

Her eyes rested upon him solemnly. "You are awake, my lord. I've been waiting for you to be so."

"Come back to bed," he repeated. "I want you again."

"No. We must speak first. I want to know when you intend to let me leave Gyer. I am a free woman now, and I wish to return to my home. You promised me that I could when the king's approval of our marriage arrived."

The rage that stung Alexander surprised him. It was the same rage he'd felt when he'd first seen her packing, when he'd first understood that she meant to leave him.

"I seem to be even worse at expressing myself than I realized," he said. "Let me be perfectly blunt then. You aren't leaving Gyer, Lillis. You are staying here as my wife, and as Lady Gyer."

Her breasts rose and fell rapidly with the sudden shortness of her breath, and her hands trembled.

"Alexander," she whispered, "I want to go home to Wellewyn. My father needs me. You made me a promise. You said I could trust you."

"And so you can," he said. "Always. But you've given yourself to me, Lillis. By your own words you've done so, and now you are mine. You are my wife complete, in every way. I'll not let you return to Wellewyn now."

She shook her head. "I'm only your prisoner. Still your prisoner, my lord."

"You're my wife," he insisted with growing aggravation. "And if you'll only behave yourself you will be treated exactly as any other wife would be. I promise you shall."

"Your promises, my lord, leave much to be desired. And what of my father? He has waited more than patiently for me to be returned to him. If you don't allow me to leave at once you'll have broken the contract you made with him."

"Don't speak to me of your father, my lady," Alexander suggested. "If I hadn't come to care for you I would have returned you to him forthwith. But I do care for you. You are precious to me, more than I can tell. You are *mine* now, and I would never give a possession I valued to a devil such as Jaward of Wellewyn."

"How can you speak to me so? My father is not a devil! I love him! If I were as precious to you as you claim you would never say such things in my hearing! If I meant anything to you at all you would let me go to him at once! Can you not understand how I long to see him?"

"I never said you wouldn't see him. We will travel to Wellewyn, just as I promised, as soon as the weather clears. It shouldn't be more than a day or two."

"A day or two!" she shouted. "My father is ill! He needs me now!"

"I don't give one good damn what your father needs!" Alexander returned just as hotly. "I'm only taking you to see the bastard because I know how much it means to you. In future I'll keep you so far away from him that you'll forget what he looks like!"

Lillis shot out of her chair. "I'll not have it, Alexander of Gyer. I *will not!* I'll not stay here and be some kind of plaything for you!"

Alexander tossed the covers aside, intending to go and fetch her. "You said you love me, Lillis. I don't want you for a plaything. I want you for my wife!"

"What of Barbara?" Lillis asked, her eyes widening as she watched his bare legs swing over the side of the bed. Her question made him stop and look at her.

"What of her?"

"You love her, do you not?"

"Why must you always speak of Barbara?" he demanded. "What I feel for my cousin has nothing to do with us. How many times must I tell you that?"

"Not one more time, sir," she assured him. "I understand you perfectly."

"Good! Then quit this foolishness and come to bed before I fetch you back."

She defiantly crossed her arms over her breasts. "No."

"Lillis—" Alexander warned.

"What happened between us this afternoon was a mistake. It won't happen again," she promised.

"What happened between us this afternoon was pure heaven," he corrected, standing and starting toward her.

"And I'll not spend time courting you anew in order to have you again. You are my wife, Lillis."

Lillis moved behind the chair to fend him off. "As you don't love me, my lord, I would hardly dignify the lust we shared this day as anything so grand."

"Damn you, Lillis—" Alexander started, only to be interrupted by a furious pounding at the door. "Damnation!" he swore again.

"Alex, are you in there?" Willem shouted.

"What is it?" Alexander shouted in return, his tone indicating that whatever it was, it had better be good.

"It's Barbara! She's taken a horse from the stables and was able to get past the guards at the gate. I've sent men after her but we haven't been able to find her yet."

"She's gone out riding in this weather?" Uncaring of his nakedness, Alexander strode to the door and flung it open. Willem stood in the hallway, dripping wet. "At this time of night? Why in the name of all that is holy would she do such an empty-headed thing?"

"I don't know, Alex," Willem replied rather breathlessly, worry written all over his face. He took in Alex's bare body with shocked curiosity, then peered around his brother's large frame to stare at Lillis. "She was crying when she left, that's all I know. The guards in the stable said she was hysterical when she went there demanding that a horse be saddled. They tried to reason with her but she only became more upset. They did as she asked in an effort to calm her, but they never meant to let her go. One of the men sent a message asking that I come at once, but by the time I got there Barbara had already mounted the steed and ridden out into the rain. She was at a full gallop, they said, heading in the direction of Dunsted."

"Dunsted! How long ago was this?"

"Little more than half an hour past. I gathered ten men and we searched the immediate area, but we couldn't find a trace of her. This damned rain covers every track at once."

Alexander frowned grimly. "I want fifty men mounted and ready to ride in ten minutes. Make certain there are plenty of wax torches. They may not do any good in this weather but they'll be all the light we'll have. Go! I'll be there in a moment." He strode from Lillis's chamber without looking at her. "Fyodor!" She heard him bellowing for his squire. The door to his own chamber slammed loudly.

Lillis stood where she was, staring out the open door at her two guards, who stood in the hallway, looking back at her. Everything happened so quickly! One moment Alexander had been there, declaring his concern for her, and the next he was out the door and on his way to rescue his beloved Barbara.

She went to the door and closed it, then leaned back and wearily shut her eyes.

The chamber's adjoining door suddenly flew open, and Alexander stormed in, his squire right behind him, still in the process of fitting the chain mail hauberk over his master's large body.

"This isn't over," he told her, stalking toward Lillis and grasping her hands. She tried to pull away, but he wouldn't allow it. "Lillis! Don't make yourself miserable over this. There's no merit in it, I vow. You've said that you love me, wife. Have faith in me."

She kept her eyes turned from his. "Let me go, Alexander. If you care for me at all, let me go. Only then will I have faith in you."

"You are my wife—"

"I'm *not* your wife, Alexander of Gyer. I'm your prisoner."

His mouth was set in a grim line. "If that is the way you will have it," he said, "then so be it." He pulled her mouth forcibly toward his. His kiss was gentle but insistent, yet Lillis refused to participate. When he let her go she turned her face away. Alexander left without another word.

Chapter Sixteen

"Lillis, I tell you I didn't know my people were planning this celebration. I had no idea they wished to have a fair on Michaelmas, and I had nothing to do with it. Why must you behave as though I've committed some crime?"

Alexander felt as though he were beating his head against a rock. Lillis sat gazing out the window, totally implacable, refusing to even look at him.

"Kidnapping is a crime, my lord," she stated very calmly.

"Damnation! I did not kidnap you! You know very well Hugh and Hugo did that without my knowledge and that I punished them severely for it!"

Lillis shrugged.

Alexander ran a hand across his eyes in exasperation. Lord, he was weary of this! It didn't seem to make any difference what he said, or how many times he tried to explain the matter, she refused to listen or to even try to understand him.

When he'd returned to her three nights before, after chasing Barbara down, he'd been ready to settle matters between them. He'd been wet to the bone and weary and emotionally drained, as well, for the wretched state they'd found Barbara in had horrified him. His delicate little cousin had been struggling through the mud and rain on the road to Dunsted, half-crazed with hysteria and obviously confused about which direction Gyer was. Her horse had taken fright at a bolt of lightning and had thrown her onto the muddy road, stranding her in the darkness. Alexander hadn't taken any time to ask her what in God's name she'd meant by leaving Gyer in the first place, he'd simply had John take his sister up on his steed and they had all returned to the castle as quickly as they could. He still didn't know why Barbara had behaved as she had, for she had steadfastly refused to explain herself or even to speak of that night.

When he'd walked into Lillis's chamber, fully expecting to finish the conversation they'd started earlier, it had been to find her already abed. He'd taken that as an encouraging sign and had lost no time in undressing and joining her there, wanting nothing more than to hold her warm body against his own chilled one and find his rest. But she'd been stiff and unyielding when he'd taken her in his arms, and had actually tried to get up, insisting that she would rather sleep on the floor than share a bed with him. He hadn't let her do such a foolish thing, of course, and had forcibly held her down, but in the end he'd given way, and had gone to sleep alone in his own bed for the first time in more than a week. He'd been too exhausted to argue and too certain of his ability to win her over once he had a chance to explain himself, but that had been three days ago and Lillis was as unyielding now as she had been then.

"It doesn't have to be this way, Lillis," he said patiently. "The only one who makes a prisoner of you is yourself. I've told you time and again you may be as free as you please once you've agreed to behave yourself."

"And I have told you time and again, sir, that I wish to return to Wellewyn to see my father."

"I don't know why you should be so difficult about this!" he exploded. "I thought you would have been happy to remain at Gyer rather than live out your life in that ruin your father calls home."

"You are possessed of the bad habit, sir, of assuming a great many things. Had you asked me, Lord Gyer, you would know exactly how I feel about the prospect of living at Wellewyn, but as you haven't I do not think you've any right to be surprised that my feelings aren't what you expected them to be."

Alexander made a gesture of impatience. "Your sense of such things is too fine, my lady. Before my brothers intervened, you were happily willing to marry Jason de Burgh without ever having even set eyes on the man *or* his home."

The sudden rush of sound that came from Lillis was as furious as the tone of her voice. "Jason de Burgh at least had the decency to *ask* for my hand in marriage, and I was given the chance of accepting or rejecting him. You, my lord, have only ever *told* me what I will or will not do. It is quite obvious that my wishes and feelings mean less than nothing to you."

Alexander was fully insulted. "Madam, that is damned untrue. If I didn't have a care for your feelings I would have sent you to your father without a thought of the wretched future you'd have with him, instead of wanting to keep you at Gyer as my wife and lady. God's feet, Lillis," he said angrily, "you said that you love me!"

She stiffened. "I have asked you, Alexander of Gyer, not to use my own words as argument against me. It isn't fair. Besides, it matters not whether I love you or no. You don't love me, and love not matched is as a bow with no arrows, utterly useless. But I do not wish to discuss that topic with you any further. We have strayed far from our subject, sir. You promised me long ago that on the first day on which we had fair weather you would take me to Wellewyn to visit with my father. The sky is clear today, and I fully expect you to fulfill your promise."

"And I have told you, my lady, that my people have planned a fair for today, to celebrate Michaelmas and the running of the Eel River, and that I must, as the Lord of Gyer, attend. We cannot go to Wellewyn today. We'll go tomorrow."

Still staring out the window, Lillis seemed to struggle with herself, then at last she spoke, slowly and carefully, "Alexander, please let me go to Wellewyn today. You know that my father is ill, that he is so very worried about me. I've tried to be patient, but it's been more than two full years since I've seen him. I cannot be patient any longer. Please, Alexander. If you'll not take me, at least let Willem do so.

He has already said that he would. I promise you, I swear to you, that I shall return to Gyer this eve.''

The softening in her tone affected Alexander deeply, and as angry with him as she was he knew it cost her a great deal to speak to him so pleadingly. It was the closest she would ever come to begging, and he wished he could give her what she so sweetly requested. But he couldn't avoid attending the fair that his people had so quickly put together; as Lord of Gyer it was his duty to attend. And he'd be damned if he'd let his lovesick brother take Lillis all the way to Wellewyn. And, in truth, she was being exceedingly foolish. It made little difference whether she saw Jaward today or tomorrow; she would see him all the same.

Thinking to soften his refusal, and hoping to soften her anger, as well, he carefully approached her, placing his hands upon her shoulders. Lowering his head, he kissed the side of her neck.

"I'm sorry, darling," he murmured, squeezing her shoulders lightly. "We'll leave first thing in the morn. I promise it.''

She was taut beneath his hands but said nothing, and Alexander took her silence as a sign of encouragement.

"I'll tell you what," he said more happily, moving his fingers to caress the soft skin at the sides of her neck. "Put on your prettiest surcoat and come to the fair. We'll have a good time, I vow, and my people will be glad to have their lady attend. There will be contests and dancing and all manner of entertainment. It will help to take your mind off your father, and the day will have passed before you've realized it.''

She shook her head. "Thank you, my lord. I shall stay here and await tomorrow's morn.''

Alexander sighed. "Don't be foolish, Lillis. Why should you suffer because of your father? Come to the fair and enjoy yourself. You'll be the most beautiful woman there by far, and I want to show you off.''

Lillis shot out of the chair in which she sat and gripped the window's ledge.

"I am not some fine acquisition to be put on display for your pleasure, my lord. I am your prisoner. Nothing more and nothing less. If you want a willing female to play lady beside you, I suggest you take your cousin Barbara to your precious fair. She, at least, is desirous of your company."

Alexander had had enough.

"You are quite right, madam. Barbara is desirous of my presence, a fact she has made perfectly clear these past few days while another female in this household has done naught but give me her back and the sharp edge of her tongue. I've no doubt that Barbara will be a far preferable companion than my shrewish wife." He strode to the door and flung it open. "I will bid you a good day. May you have the joy of your own exceedingly unpleasant company. I, for one, intend to enjoy myself to the full. I can only thank God that my lovely cousin possesses a disposition so much sweeter than yours."

He left, slamming the door. Lillis dropped her head into her hands and burst into tears.

Barbara had realized long since that Alexander had left her, if not physically, then at least in his thoughts. She watched him surreptitiously as he paced near the trestle table at which she sat. All day he had been preoccupied and short-tempered, so that she wondered whether he had enjoyed himself or any of the entertainments at all. He had performed his duties as lord readily enough; none of his people could complain about that. He'd handed out awards at various contests with enough pomp and ceremony to delight one and all, and he'd been duly complimentary to the many musicians and performers who had plied their skills during the day, and of course, he had taken his place among the dancers when the sun had finally begun to set, dancing with as much vigor and skill as any one else present. And through it all he had dragged her along with an almost desperate sort of determination, until Barbara had begun to feel rather like a prize put on display, there for show and little more. How different it was from the days when Alexander had treated her with a gentle, almost reverent, deference. Strangely, though, Barbara believed she preferred it this way.

She watched Alexander as he hovered at the edge of the crowd of swirling dancers. He kept pacing and glancing at the castle over and over again until she thought he would go mad with his agitation. Suddenly he stilled, turning toward the dancers and letting his gaze wander carefully over them. Aunt Leta and Edyth of Cantfield were taking turns dancing with Candis and Justin and his eyes lingered on them momentarily. Willem had blushingly given way to dancing with some of the village maidens who had pleaded with him tirelessly to do so, and the twins had long since disappeared into the nearby woods with a pair of giggling girls. Finally he set his eyes on Barbara herself, and she instantly appeared to be thoroughly enchanted with the dancers. He stared at her for an uncomfortable moment, then he turned on his heel and was gone, striding purposefully toward Castle Gyer.

Barbara was glad to see him go—relieved, almost. She needed a moment of freedom; she needed to rest. She had rarely ever needed to do so before, when she had played out John's parts for her, but things had changed since that cold, foggy day in the forest of Dunsted. Everything had changed since then. Careful not to attract the notice of Alexander's guards, she quietly rose from the table, then slipped away unseen. There was a large tent behind the table at which she had been sitting and she stole into its shadow, edging her way along until she was safely hidden behind it.

She took a deep breath. John had signaled to her earlier that he was leaving with some of his men. It was a perfect time. Alexander and the people of Gyer would be too busy with their fair to notice that he had gone. Barbara had no doubt that tomorrow she would hear of some destruction that had been done to either Gyer or Dunsted.

She stood behind the tent, hugging the back of it and looking all about, then sneaked into the coppice of trees nearby. There were not many trees, but enough so that she felt safe from watchful eyes. A giggle, followed by a moan, made her aware of the several lovers who were lying nearby.

She picked up her skirts and ran deeper into the woods until she was certain she would be completely alone. Only then did she let down her mask. She sank gratefully onto the cool ground and put her hands up to massage her weary eyes.

Suddenly, without warning, a large, strong hand closed around her mouth, and another equally large and strong arm grasped about her waist, picking her up.

She tried to scream and struggle, but the noise was silenced by the hand and her motion was stifled, as well. Oh, God! she thought in a panic, envisioning the terrible thing that was about to happen to her and begging for some kind of miracle. The arms holding her turned her about roughly, bringing Barbara face-to-face with a hooded man whose angry visage looked extremely familiar.

"Greetings, Lady Barbara." He pulled back his hood to let his long, black hair fall free. "I've been hoping—nay, praying—for the pleasure of meeting you again."

"Jason," she whispered in disbelief. "Jason!" She threw her arms around his neck and hugged him with all her might.

He pushed her away. "You remember me. I thought you would."

He was angry—very, very angry. Barbara knew he had every right to be, yet she begged, clutching him, "Jason, please let me explain."

He shoved at her until she fell to the ground. "Explain! I've not come to hear your explanations!" He knelt, grabbed Barbara by both shoulders and pulled her up until their faces were level. She could see the pain in his eyes as he spoke. "I came because I couldn't believe what my men told me. I *wouldn't* believe that you were Alexander of Gyer's cousin. I searched the forests for you for three days after the fire—the fire you helped to make possible. A man died in that fire, one of *my* men, yet I spent every damned day for three days after looking for *you!*" He shook her, hard. "My God! What a fool I was!"

"Jason, forgive me," she whispered, reaching out a hand, wanting to still his pain.

"Don't." His expression held clear revulsion. "Don't touch me. Your touch sickens me." He seethed with anger and hurt, half pulling her toward him and half pushing her away. "You're worse than a whore. You're *his* whore. Do you think I haven't watched you giving yourself to Alexander of Gyer all day long? You're not even his wife and still you give yourself to him. You shame the woman who was to have been mine. Did you think I hadn't known?" He looked at her with disbelief when she shook her head. "Lillis of Wellewyn was to be my wife when Alexander of Gyer married her by force. Now she sits locked away in that castle, the Lady of Gyer, while you flaunt yourself with her husband like the veriest of lemans." He finally pushed her back to the ground, then stood.

Barbara's voice trembled badly when she spoke. "Jason, please give me a chance to explain." She knelt before him in the dirt, her hands stretched toward him pleadingly. "I think I love you. Nay, I know that I do. I have been able to think of naught but you since that day we met. Please give me a chance."

"You love me?!" He put his hands on his hips and barked with laughter. "You *love* me?!" he repeated incredulously. "Do you think me a complete fool, woman? Do you think you can sway me from my wrath by mere words? I should slit your throat for what you've done! The only reason I won't is that I'm loath to touch such a filthy whore."

Tears rolled down her face. "You have every right to be angry with me, Jason," she sobbed, "even though I had no choice in what I did that day. You cannot think I meant to cause a man to die, though even if you do I still shall not blame you. You may go ahead and kill me and I will not care. I will love you even as you carry out the deed. I love you, Jason. I beg that you will believe me."

He stood his ground, staring into her wet, miserable face. "And why should I believe anything you say, Barbara of Gyer? I have seen you with your lord this day. You throw yourself at him freely, yet you ask me to believe that you love me? I've let you trick me once already. I would be an idiot to do so again."

"No!" Barbara cried, dragging herself along the ground until she could hug his legs. "I do not have a choice in what I do. I don't love Alexander of Gyer, and yet I must make him think that I do. I love you, Jason. I tried to come to you three nights ago. I stole a horse and tried to come to you, but I was stopped by my Lord Gyer. Please believe me, Jason. I did try to come to you."

He reached down and dragged her up off the ground. "Cease your sniveling! You tried to come to me, did you? It's a good thing you were stopped then, for I surely would have killed you the moment I set eyes on you." He pointed in the direction of the fair. "Go back to your lover before I do kill you. The very sight of you disgusts me."

"Jason!" she cried, catching him by the arm as he turned to walk away. "Please take me with you! I beg you to take me!" She clung to him when he tried to disengage her. "I'll be your servant. I shall be your slave. I will spend my life trying to make up to you the wrong I have done. But please, Jason, don't leave me here to live without you."

He practically had to break her fingers to get her to let go of him. "You only try to hold me so that I'll be captured by your lover's men," he said. "You know he would kill me without a thought if he found me alone and unguarded on his lands, and no doubt you would further incense him by declaring I'd set hands on you. No!" He pushed her away. "I'll not lose my life for such a one as you!"

His words stunned her. Barbara hadn't realized how much danger he was in, simply being at Gyer. "Go, then!" She backed up until she came against a tree. "I don't know how to prove to you that what I say is true, but I'll not have you put your life in danger. Leave! Now! I will stop anyone who comes until you have had a chance to get far enough away. I swear by God that I shall." She grasped the trunk of the tree with both hands put behind her, and watched him with tears and longing as he turned and made his way through the forest.

Jason only got a few yards before the sounds of her quiet sobs stopped him. He clenched his fists to his sides and silently declared himself to be a fool three times over.

"Damn!" he muttered, striding back to where Barbara stood, crying her heart out. He grabbed her to him, yanked her head back by her hair and put his mouth over hers for a hard, passionate kiss. Her arms were just coming around his shoulders when he set her away. Before she could even open her eyes, he had already run into the shadows.

She stood where she was for a long time, crying, terribly aware that even the forest had hidden eyes that might be watching her at that very moment. It would not go well for her if John came to hear of what had just transpired between herself and Jason de Burgh, though she didn't care so much what happened to her. If it had only been her life she held sway over she would have been ready to receive whatever punishment her brother might give, but there were other lives to consider. Lillis's and Alexander's lives, and possibly even others. John had never been too clear about the details of his plans, but Barbara had some idea of all the people who might thwart his chances of success.

She stood there, staring at where Jason had disappeared, aching with love for him. He had every right to hate her—there was nothing about her at all that he could ever admire. Yet she was determined to prove that she could be worth something. Yes, she was going to prove to him how much she loved him, that she could be worthy of him, and she knew exactly how she was going to do it.

It took several moments, but finally Barbara was able to calm her body's trembling. She wiped her face and took several deep breaths. Alexander's men would be looking for her soon; she had to return to the fair. Another deep breath, a shake of her hair, one last check to make certain that her surcoat was brushed clean and set straight, then she picked up her skirts and made her way back toward the light and noise of the fair, her back perfectly straight and a beautiful smile set upon her face.

Chapter Seventeen

By the time Lillis awakened it was too late. Alexander had already slid into the bed. She tried to struggle away from him, but he caught her in a gentle grasp and held her tight.

"No!" she insisted with a groggy sort of fury, and struck out at him with both fists.

He grabbed her wrists and held them over her head, using his naked body to subdue her.

"Calm yourself, wife," he murmured, lying on her heavily to keep her still. "I have something to say to you and I'm not going away until I've finished. You may as well keep quiet and listen to me."

"You've said more than enough to me these past many days!" she said furiously. "I am weary to tears with listening to you! Why can't you leave me in peace?"

"I can't. And you are going to listen to me, else I'll not go away. And you know very well what's going to happen if I don't go away." He grinned at her lecherously.

She glared up at him, enraged at her inability to push him away. "Why did you come here? I can hear the music from the fair still playing outside my window. Never tell me your beloved Barbara grew so weary from dancing that she could no longer entertain you with her *sweet disposition.*"

His eyebrows rose. "No, my cousin's sweet and gentle nature is perfectly intact, I thank you. If I didn't know better, good lady wife, I'd think you jealous."

Lillis gasped and struggled beneath him. "You wretched beast! If that's all you came to say to me, then please leave!

I'm sure the sweet and perfect Barbara impatiently awaits your return.''

Alexander easily kept her in his grasp. "That isn't what I came to say, and I left Barbara at the fair without any intention whatsoever of returning to her."

His words stilled Lillis, and she looked at him warily. Alexander offered her another smile, more wan this time, and his eyes roamed over her features, taking them in as though to memorize her forever.

"I have spent the entire day," he said quietly, "trying to keep from thinking of you. I wanted to be angry, to remember the words we said to one another this morn, to convince myself that you have treated me unkindly, but I couldn't. All I could do, Lillis, was think of how beautiful you are, and of how you make me laugh so easily, and of how good you feel when in my arms. I tried to enjoy Barbara's company, but I wanted you. She is all that a man could ever want in a woman—sweet and beautiful and attentive. She once used to make me feel like the finest man on earth. Yet I didn't want to be with her this day, not for even one of the moments that I was. I wanted to be with you, Lillis. Regardless of your anger and fury, I wanted to be with you. Is that not strange?"

They stared at each other in perfect silence, searching one another's eyes.

"Is that love, Lillis?" he whispered. "Is it?"

"I do not know."

"I don't know, either," he returned just as softly. "I think it is love. I truly think it is, but I don't know. I've never known love, or what I've always thought it must be, not even with Barbara, and I'm afraid of mistaking such strong feelings. But is it enough, Lillis? Whatever it is, is it enough?"

Lillis could see the pain in his eyes, the pleading. "Alexander," she murmured, her anger dissipating into a gentle sadness, "I don't know what it is, and I cannot promise that it will be enough tomorrow, but for tonight, it is enough."

The pain left his eyes, replaced by a sudden fire.

"For tonight then," he whispered fiercely, "and we will let the morrow take care of itself." He lowered his mouth and Lillis met him eagerly, opening to him.

But the morning brought no resolutions.

Alexander had spent the night making love to his wife with sweet desperation, yet when the sun dawned he felt chilled at the prospect of having to take her to Wellewyn. He didn't want to do it and he certainly wasn't looking forward to seeing Jaward again. When he climbed out of her bed to return to his own chamber he purposefully put away the tender emotions that Lillis had wrought in him.

Lillis, sensing Alexander's withdrawal, likewise wrapped herself anew in her anger. Nothing had changed between them. He was taking her to Wellewyn, at last, but then he was going to force her back to Gyer, and when she returned she would become his prisoner again. There would be no more looking forward to someday being able to go home. She would be captive forever.

They ate their early meal in silence. Alexander had asked Willem to accompany them on the ride to Wellewyn, but Hugh and Hugo surprised him by rising early, as well. Since it was much too early for the rest of the castlefolk to be up and around, only the four of them sat at the long table, while all of Alexander's knights filled the trestle tables below, eating their meal in preparation of the long ride ahead.

"Alex," Hugh broke the heavy silence, "Hugo and I want to go to Wellewyn with you and Lillis."

Alexander didn't even spare him a glance. "No."

"We have our own horses," Hugo said, "and we are ready to go."

"No," said Alexander, his attention on his breakfast.

Hugh slammed his eating dagger into the wooden table with as much force and anger as a fifteen-year-old boy could, and he stood before the surprised glances of those present. "Damn you, Alex! Hugo and I want to go to Wellewyn with Lillis and that's all there is to it. If you don't allow us to go with her we'll follow all the same."

Lillis stared at Hugh in amazement. His eyes blazed with commitment as he stared down his elder brother.

She could feel her husband rising beside her and turned to look up at him. He towered above her, and his expression was one of outrage, but she was never to know what he had planned to say to his younger brother, for they were interrupted by one of Alexander's knights.

"My Lord Gyer," the man announced, "the Lord of Dunsted approaches. Sir Jason de Burgh."

Every eye at the table turned to look at the man then. Willem exchanged glances with Alexander and stood. They made their way from the dais, toward the front doors of the great hall and out into the courtyard, followed by several of Alexander's men.

Lillis found herself flanked by Hugh and Hugo.

"Don't be afraid, Lillis," Hugh told her. "We'll not let de Burgh harm you."

"That's right," Hugo said. "We'll keep you safe."

She almost laughed. "I have nothing to fear from Jason de Burgh," she said, standing. "Come, let's go watch from one of the windows."

But the moment they stepped off the dais the castle doors opened once more.

Alexander entered first, followed by five strangers and Willem. Her husband looked very grim, Lillis thought, watching him with curiosity as his gaze searched the hall. When his eyes fell upon her his expression grew even grimmer. He moved toward her with one hand outstretched, and Lillis put her own hand out to let him draw her forward.

"This is my wife, Lillis Baldwin, the Lady of Gyer," he said as the group of men stopped before her. Lillis nodded and received polite acknowledgments in return. "My lady," Alexander continued in a tone of pure displeasure, "I make known to you Jason de Burgh, the Lord of Dunsted."

A very handsome man with long, black hair bowed slightly, his blue eyes intense against the darkness of his skin and hair. He was large and muscular, the sort of strong, handsome man women dreamed of at night. This, then, was the man who would have been her husband.

He stepped closer to Lillis. "Now this is cruelty, indeed, Alexander Baldwin," he said, taking one of Lillis's hands and bringing it to his lips to gracefully kiss her fingers. "You have dealt me many a wrong in the past, but this is certainly the worst, to have deprived me of such a beautiful wife." He smiled at Lillis. "Our children would have had blue eyes, my lady," he remarked, his expression leaving no doubt as to what he was thinking. "It's a pity we shall never know what color their hair would have been."

Having never been spoken to so intimately by a total stranger, his words shocked Lillis, so that she could only stare at him, but Alexander reached up and snatched her hand from Jason de Burgh's grip.

"Stop molesting my wife and speak what you've come to, de Burgh." He pulled Lillis against his side. "You're not welcome in my home."

De Burgh nodded, his expression growing solemn as he turned his full attention to Lillis. "I regret to make your acquaintance under such circumstances, my lady, for I fear I bring you bad tidings." He glanced at the many people who stood watching and listening, then looked at Alexander. "Perhaps we should find a place more private?"

The words made Lillis's heart fall into her feet. The news must be bad, indeed, if Jason de Burgh wanted to speak to her privately. She felt weak, suddenly; her whole body trembled and she turned into Alexander's embrace. His response, the way he held her as though he expected her to collapse, told her what the news was before the words were even said. "No," she whispered. "Say what you have to say now. Say it quickly."

"Lillis," Alexander said gently, his voice sounding loud in her ears, "perhaps we should go to my private chamber."

"No!" she shouted. "It's about my father. Is it not?"

Jason de Burgh stared at her helplessly.

"Is it not?" Lillis demanded, fighting the hysteria that threatened to overtake her.

He nodded, and his gaze fell. "He was—found murdered in his bed last night. One of his vassals rode to

Dunsted to tell me. He would have come to you directly, my lady, but he feared being made a prisoner at Gyer.''

''Murdered!'' Lillis pressed her face against Alexander's chest. ''Murdered! Oh, my God! Father!''

Alexander held her tight. ''My love, let me take you to our chamber.''

But she shook her head and pushed from his arms. The way she looked at him made Alexander shiver. *''You,''* she sobbed. ''You did it! Murderer!''

''Lillis, love—'' He reached for her even as she backed away.

She wasn't able to say any more. She stared at Alexander with an expression of horror, her face gone white as death. She shook her head at his outstretched hand and then, for the first time in her life, Lillis fainted.

Alexander was surprised to find Jason de Burgh and his men still in the great hall when he came down the stairs a half hour later. He had carried Lillis to her chamber and stayed as long as his aunt and her maid would allow; once they'd gotten her into the bed, they'd made him leave, insisting that she shouldn't be subjected to the sight of him when she finally came awake. If he hadn't been feeling so much guilt and worry he'd never have obeyed, but he did feel those things, deeply, and hadn't known any way to defend himself against Aunt Leta's and Lady Edyth's anger.

''Why are you still here?'' he demanded of de Burgh, who stood by one of the fires, broodingly contemplating the place where Barbara and the other castle ladies sat across the way.

''I would speak with you,'' he replied, offering Alexander an expressionless face. ''There is, I believe, the matter of a bride we must discuss. I had a missive from one of the king's regents, saying that, in exchange for the king's agreement of your marriage to the bride who should have been mine, you have agreed to give me one of your marriageable cousins as wife.''

''This is truth,'' Alexander admitted. ''I did make this agreement.''

"And?"

"And what?"

"When may I expect the delivery of my bride?"

Alexander made a dismissive gesture. "I haven't the time to consider the matter now, not when my wife's abovestairs as she is. Now be on your way. Only make certain you don't kill any cattle as you leave Gyer," he added angrily. "My people are still reeling from your last such visit."

Jason de Burgh flushed. "I've heard before this accusation that you speak. Neither I nor my people had anything to do with the killing of that cattle. I don't know who did such a foul deed, but it had naught to do with anyone from Dunsted. We're too busy fending off your attacks to make any of our own."

"Ha!" Alexander laughed. "My people wouldn't lower themselves to trespass on that muck and mire you call land. You speak of being kept busy, but you know naught of such things. I could teach you all about it! Between you and Jaward I've barely had a moment's peace these past six months, and only God knows how my people have suffered!"

The expression on Jason's face was one of full confusion. His gaze fell time and again on Barbara as he spoke his next words. "I suppose you will deny having anything to do with that fire in Dunsted some weeks past? The one set at a crofter's hut? The one that killed a man?"

"What lies are these?" Alexander demanded. "I had naught to do with any such thing!"

"I have several of your banners in my possession that prove your guilt," Jason insisted, folding his arms stubbornly across his chest. "They were left at the site of the fire for bragging purposes, I suppose."

Alexander was equally stubborn. "And I have several banners of yours from the cattle killing."

"I had nothing to do with that!"

"And I had nothing to do with your crofter's hut burning."

They stared at each other.

"Someone is playing us for fools, de Burgh," Alexander finally stated.

"Aye, Baldwin," Jason nodded, looking at Barbara again. "Someone, indeed, is playing us as fools. What are we to do about it?"

Alexander shook his head. "I know not, but I'll spare no time thinking on the matter now. Give me time to take care of my wife and then we'll talk. Perhaps I've misjudged you." He rubbed the back of his neck wearily. "Perhaps I've misjudged many things. Let me help my wife deal with her loss, then we'll settle matters between our people."

"I'll give you some time," Jason agreed. "You may have my arm on it."

The two men shook solemnly, and Jason's men prepared to leave.

"That woman there," Jason said, nodding in Barbara's direction. "The redheaded girl. She is your cousin, is she not?"

"The lady Barbara is my cousin," Alexander replied warily, "though a very distant one. We share a great-great-grandfather."

"But she is still your cousin," Jason stated, "no matter how distant. It *is* one of your cousins I'm to be given as wife, is it not?"

Alexander's eyes narrowed. "It is, but—"

"And she is marriageable, for she was once your betrothed, is this not so?"

"De Burgh—" Alexander warned.

"Good," Jason said, slapping his gloves in his hand. "She's the one I want, then. I shall send a missive to the king at once, making the request. Tell your cousin I'll come to court her as soon as you've sent me formal permission." He smiled at Alexander's angry countenance and added, pleasantly, "Good day, Baldwin."

Chapter Eighteen

It was a quiet time of the day, late afternoon and close to being dark, almost time for the evening meal. Lillis stood by one of her chamber windows, carefully folding her needlework, her eyes gazing outside at the hard-pouring rain.

"It will be raining still tomorrow, most like," Alexander said quietly from where he stood beside the fire, watching his wife. "You should at least wait until the weather has cleared."

"No," she answered softly. "We will go tomorrow."

"As it pleases you."

"Yes." Lillis lowered her head. "Thank you, my lord." She turned, keeping her eyes from him, and went to place the needlework in the bag she was packing.

"Are you certain you'll not have Lady Edyth go with you? Will you not be lonely for her?"

"Oh, I think I will," she admitted, swallowing against the painful lump in her throat, "but the children need her so much more than I do. I couldn't take her from them." She pressed her trembling lips together briefly, and her voice wavered when she spoke again. "You would never find another tutor to replace her, I think."

"No. I do not think I could."

There was silence for a moment while Lillis continued to fold her belongings.

"There will be no women to give you company at Wellewyn," Alexander said at last, "other than the cook and serving maid you allowed me to hire. I wish you will let me send suitable companions for you."

"No." She shook her head, still turned from him. "I've told you already, Alexander, that there is no need for you to do more than you already have. Your kindness to the people of Wellewyn has been great, especially in light of all the misery they suffered at my father's hands, and I am so very thankful. I could not ask more of you."

He made a sound of irritation. "I've done what I am now responsible to do as the Lord of Wellewyn, and it is little thus far—not half of what I mean to do in the future."

"You are modest, my lord, especially when you know very well that you've kept the people of Wellewyn from starvation and death. You've sent food and supplies to help them through the coming winter, and have been more than generous in sending carpenters and masons and land managers to make repairs to their dwellings, and to the land. They will think you a god come from the heavens, after having lived under my father."

"Well I'm glad if I've pleased you," he grumbled. "I only wish you would let me send a few servants with you. Only a few—"

"No, Alexander," she said more firmly, moving to her open clothing chest and kneeling before it, drawing clothes from it. "I am used to caring for myself and others. Being at Gyer has spoiled me, I think, and I must keep myself from growing overcontent and lazy. And I'll have the twins for company, and Willem."

"Willem," Alexander muttered angrily, pacing before the fire and rubbing the back of his neck. "Yes, you'll have Willem." He'd sent Willem to Wellewyn several days before to act as chamberlain there. It had seemed, at the time, a good way of getting him away from Lillis, who had more and more turned to Willem for comfort and companionship, but now, when a month of her grief and silences had finally driven Alexander to set her free, he regretted the decision. Now she and Willem would be alone together, save for the twins, who had surprised one and all by announcing their determination to accompany Lillis to Wellewyn and live with her there.

"Alexander."

Her voice broke into his unhappy thoughts, and Alexander turned to find Lillis looking at him, for the first time since he'd come to watch her packing. She looked so sad that he wanted to take her into his arms and hold her and beg her to put an end to this madness that he couldn't understand. He'd never felt so lost and confused in all his life as he'd begun to feel when he'd finally told her last night that she could go. There was nothing for him to grasp on to, or to understand, in any of this. She loved him. She'd told him so, and Lillis was no liar. She loved him, yet she was packing all of her belongings, and she was leaving him.

"Alexander," she said again, and tears dropped onto her cheeks. "I'm deeply sorry for what I said—that day. For my terrible behavior."

"Lillis—"

"I didn't mean it," she said, her hands making a gesture of helplessness, "and I'm sorry if I hurt you. I would never hurt you apurpose, ever."

In all the days that had passed since she'd learned of her father's death, she'd not spoken so many open words to him. She'd hardly spoken to him at all, or to anyone else for that matter, not even to Edyth, but had grieved alone. Her pain had been one of the hardest things Alexander had ever known; accepting that he must let her go had been the hardest.

"You were in great pain," he told her, clenching his hands behind his back to keep from reaching for her. "I knew that then, and I know it now. I never held it against you."

She wiped her cheeks and lowered her eyes. "You are kind, my lord. Thank you."

"Don't speak of thanks to me," he murmured desperately. "I cannot bear it. I cannot bear your tears, Lillis, or your sadness. I love you."

She set her face in her hands and began to sob. Alexander was across the room and holding her before he even thought to do it.

"I love you," he said again. "Don't leave me, I—God, Lillis!" He enfolded her with desperation, stricken by the fear that she would never return to him. "Can you not forgive me? Only tell me what I must do to make matters right and I will. I swear by God I shall."

She shook her head against his chest. "It will always be there between us, if I don't find a way to accept it. There were so many things I wanted to tell my father—that I loved him when no one else did—so many ways I wanted to help him. But he's gone. *Gone.*" She sounded as if she were trying to convince herself, rather than him. "I need a little time, Alexander. If you tell me to stay I will, but it will always be between us, no matter how I might wish it otherwise."

"I know," he said, and it was true. Her eyes had once been filled with love and desire; now there was only pain and distrust, and sometimes, accusation. She'd accepted all of his apologies, yet the look in her eyes had not been banished, and he'd finally realized that it never would be, unless he let her go. "I've brought this down upon my own head," he said. "My foolishness was great, and so should my punishment be. Believe me, Lillis, when I say that I wish to God I'd taken you to see your father. I doubt I will ever regret anything more in all my days."

She lifted a hand to touch his cheek. "Let us speak no more of wrongdoing. You know I have forgiven you, and that I love you, Alexander. And if there has been any foolishness it is mine, from my foolish heart, which refuses to obey me and makes me go. I will learn to master it at Wellewyn, perhaps. I will try, my lord, and when it is obedient I will return to you, if you still wish it."

"I shall always wish it," he vowed, bending to kiss her. "I shall pray each day for your return."

"As I shall, my lord."

He kissed her once more, then asked, "Will you send for me, Lillis? If the time comes that your heart has opened to me once more, will you send for me?"

She smiled tremulously. "Yes, Alexander. I'll send for you. I will."

He let out a breath. "Then I shall wait for your summons, and I will come."

Several hours later, after the evening meal had been finished, Lillis stood once more by her chamber window, contemplating the ceaseless rain and thinking of what lay ahead in the coming days.

The sound of the door opening made her turn, and she saw the last person she either expected or wanted to see on this, her last night at Gyer—Barbara, pale and breathless—standing against the now closed door.

"Wonderful," Lillis muttered under her breath.

Barbara had made a point of keeping her distance during the past few days, and Lillis had been glad of it. Yet now the beautiful, redheaded creature stood against her chamber door, one hand over her heaving chest, looking like a pursued criminal.

"I don't have much time," she said, pushing from the door and coming toward Lillis. "I wanted to come to you sooner but I couldn't."

Lillis crossed her arms over her breasts. "What sort of nonsense is this, Barbara Baldwin? I must tell you that I'm not in the mood for such playacting."

"It's not playacting!" Barbara insisted, moving closer. "You know John is forever watching me and all that I do. I couldn't let him know I'd come to see you, and I only now just managed to sneak away unseen." She looked around the room and lowered her voice. "You must believe me, Lady Gyer. I've not enough time to say what I must and explain everything else."

Something in the girl's demeanor made Lillis believe her, and it was true that John Baldwin guarded his sister closely, especially since that night when she'd run away. "Very well. I'll listen to what you have to say, but you must calm yourself, Barbara. I'll let no harm come to you."

"You are kind, my lady," Barbara said gratefully, following Lillis to the chairs set before the fire. "Kinder than I deserve, I know. But I hope to make amends for my wretched behavior."

Lillis sat in one chair and expected Barbara to do likewise, but, surprisingly, the girl knelt on the floor beside her.
"First I must show you something," she said, looking
around again as she pulled a leather pouch from beneath her
surcoat. She shoved the pouch into Lillis's hands.

"Open it, please, my lady."

The pouch was tied with drawstrings and Lillis unknot-
ted and separated them, then opened the pouch and put her
hand inside. She drew out a small ceramic oval on which was
painted the portrait of a beautiful, white-blond lady who
smiled back at Lillis with stunning blue eyes. Lillis's hands
began to tremble.

"This is my mother," she whispered in disbelief.
"Where—how did you come to have this?"

Barbara bent to look at the portrait as well, smiling as she
did. "Yes, it is your mother. She was very beautiful, was she
not? My own mother looked very much the same, though
her hair was red, like mine." She turned her great green eyes
upon Lillis. "They were sisters, you know, or rather, you
probably did not know." She nodded at Lillis's dumb expression. "Yes, it is true. Our mothers were sisters and we
are first cousins. I know that you look upon this portrait
and see your mother, but I have always looked and seen my
Aunt Eleanor."

"You—*you* are my cousin?" Lillis repeated. "My mother
was your—?"

Barbara nodded again. "You never knew of your mother's family, did you? John and I didn't know about you for
a long time either, until our mother died and our father told
us. It is strange to be kept from part of your family when
you are a child, is it not? I'm not quite certain as to why we
never knew one another, though I suspect it had something
to do with your father." Barbara looked regretful. "When
my Aunt Eleanor married him she disgraced her family
name and was cast aside as one dead by her father, who is
our grandfather. He's a rather harsh man," she said, adding, at Lillis's expression, "Oh, yes, he is much alive, and
as mean as ever. I was scared to death of him when I was a
child. It was because of him that my father agreed not to

allow my mother to have any contact with her sister. It was terribly hard on my mother because the two sisters had been very close. She never spoke to John or me of our Aunt Eleanor, but father said she pined for her until her death. When she died he felt guilty for keeping the sisters apart, and for giving my mother such sadness, so he told John and me about our Aunt Eleanor and gave me this little portrait. It is a sad story, is it not? If you and I had known each other as children we might have grown to be great friends, instead of rivals."

Barbara couldn't have shocked Lillis more if she had hit her across the head with a club. She stared at the girl, open-mouthed, for a long, silent moment. She wanted to disbelieve her. She wanted to say that Barbara lied, that she had made up with the whole ridiculous tale, but she couldn't. Somewhere in the depths of herself, Lillis knew that what Barbara said was true. Her heart told her to cry and hug Barbara closely in a fit of familial joy; her mind got the better of her. "Tell me everything, Barbara. There is more to this than our merely being related. Why did you bring me this now? Why did you wait so long to tell me? And what of John? He never spoke a word of this to me, or to Alexander, either."

Barbara shook her head. "There isn't enough time to explain, my lady. John would kill me if he knew I'd told you—he never wanted anyone to know the truth. I cannot tell you why. Please, please don't ask me to do so, and please don't tell Alex. I would never have told you myself, save that I felt you should know before you left Gyer, and because I wanted to make amends for my behavior. Promise me, please, that you'll speak of this to no one."

"I cannot like it," Lillis told her. "Alexander should know."

Barbara looked like she might faint. "Oh, sweet mercy! If you tell him John will be furious! *Furious*. You don't know how terrible that can be."

"Come now," Lillis said soothingly. "Surely you know that Alexander would never allow him to bring you harm."

"It won't matter," Barbara insisted, panicked. "It won't matter at all. John will never, ever forgive me. Oh, I wish I'd not told you. I thought I could trust you, but I can't, and now my life will be miserable."

She was about to burst into tears, Lillis realized, and that was the one thing Lillis couldn't bear any more of. She gave way.

"Very well, Barbara, I'll say nothing for now. You have my promise on that. But one day soon, when you feel a little braver, you must speak with Alexander and tell him the truth."

Barbara looked thoroughly relieved, and brightened. "Oh, I shall, my lady. I promise you that I shall. One day soon. I promise."

"Good."

"There is something more I must tell you," Barbara said. "Something you will find very hard to believe, but which is true, nonetheless. But you must promise me beforehand that you'll not tell anyone about it, either."

"Barbara," Lillis said irately, "you sorely try my patience."

"But it's so very important," Barbara answered with a tiny pout. "Please, my lady, give me your promise. You'll not regret it."

Lillis sighed wearily. "Very well. You have my promise."

Barbara smiled with delight. "What I wished to tell you is this. You have more of a family than you think. The twins—Hugh and Hugo—as hard as this may be to believe, though it is quite true—the twins are your half brothers. I thought you should know. I'd want to know if I were you."

Lillis stared at her, then said, slowly, shaking her head, "You're mad. I really think I must call for Alexander—"

"No, it is quite, quite true, I assure you," Barbara insisted. "There is a document to prove that it is so and I have seen it. I cannot tell you how it came to be, but I promise it is true. You mustn't tell Hugh and Hugo, however, for I think they would be crushed to know that Jaward of Wellewyn was their father, especially now that he is dead. Don't you agree?"

For the second time in her life Lillis felt like swooning. Everything that Barbara said had a distinctly amazing quality to it, and she was hard put to decide whether she should believe the girl or not. It could be true, but it was just as likely that it was not.

As if reading her mind, Barbara responded, "You must believe me! I realize that I ask a great deal of you, but you must trust me nonetheless. All of those things that I said and did to you, especially that time when I threatened to kill you, well—I can only hope you'll understand how I felt at the time. It was horrible to be cast aside after so many years of thinking I would be Lady Gyer." Barbara's eyes grew wide and she nodded. "It was very hard on me, yes, it was."

"You told the children I was a *witch*," Lillis accused.

"Well, goodness," Barbara returned, much offended, "I was only teasing. Am I not allowed to have any fun at all?"

"Why should I believe the things you tell me?" Lillis asked tightly. "You and your brother have lied to me time and again. And you've every reason to want to be rid of me so that you can have Alexander all to yourself again."

Barbara shook her head. "No! I don't love Cousin Alex. Not the way that I love—I mean—" she faltered "—not that way that I love someone else."

Lillis eyed Barbara suspiciously. "Who?"

Barbara flushed and bowed her head. "Jason de Burgh," she answered. "I'm in love with Jason de Burgh, and please don't ask me how it happened, for I don't have time to explain that to you, either." She lifted her head and met Lillis's steady gaze. "And I'm not doing all of this only out of the kindness of my heart. That much, I must admit. There is something I would ask in return."

"What is it?

Barbara drew something else out from beneath her surcoat, a sealed missive, and set it upon Lillis's knees. "This is for Jason," Barbara whispered. "It is very important, but I've no way to get it to him without John discovering it."

"John doesn't know of your feelings for the Lord of Dunsted?" Lillis asked with a faint smile.

"Oh, no," she answered quickly. "He would be most angry with me if he did know. He still hopes, you know, that Alex and I might somehow—someday—" She flushed.

"It's all right, Barbara," Lillis said gently, feeling a sudden pity for the girl. "I think I understand. John has taken care of you for many years, and had plans for you that were suddenly disrupted. From what I have known of him, and from what you now say, a great deal has become clear to me. In truth, I'm glad, for if you do not love Alexander, I do."

Barbara gazed at her with luminous eyes. "It is not that I've never been fond of Cousin Alex, for I always have been, but I love Jason—oh, it's so hard to explain how it is. I love him so much, yet it hurts so deeply."

Lillis smiled. "Yes, it does, doesn't it?"

"Will you help me then, my lady? Will you send this missive to him when you are safely away from Gyer? Will you?"

"I will," Lillis promised. "Don't worry over the matter."

Barbara was relieved. She released Lillis's hand and said, "Thank you, Cousin. Perhaps, someday, when you've returned to Gyer, we will become friends. For now trusting must suffice. You must give me back your mother's portrait." She extended one delicate white hand to receive the requested item.

Lillis clutched the portrait tightly. "May I not keep it? I've never had anything of my mother's before. Let me have it, I beg you."

Barbara shook her head and insistently extended her hand. "When you are gone from here, and if I do not have the portrait in my possession, John will know I told you the truth, and I cannot take the chance of that. On that same someday when we may be able to become friends, perhaps we will be able to make a trade. My mother and yours exchanged their portraits on the day they were separated. Somewhere in Castle Wellewyn, if your father didn't destroy it, there is a portrait like this one but of my mother. Try to find it for me, Lillis. I'll return this to you even if you don't, but it would mean the world to me to have a remembrance of my mother, much as this would mean to you.''

Reluctantly Lillis handed the portrait to Barbara, and Barbara dropped it back inside the leather pouch, drew and tied the strings together, then pushed it inside her surcoat.

Chapter Nineteen

With one hand pressed against the small of her back and the other pushing against the snow-covered ground, Lillis slowly raised herself to a standing position. She was amazed at how such a simple thing as kneeling beside her parents' graves for only a few minutes could make her body ache so much, but then her body seemed to ache continually these days. Sometimes she attributed it to the cold winter weather combined with living in the drafty ruins of Castle Wellewyn, at other times she wondered if perhaps the cause weren't something altogether different.

She had come to visit her parents' graves earlier than usual today. There was still a great deal to do before Alexander arrived to partake of the meal she'd invited him to, and Lillis wanted everything to be perfect.

Lost in thought, she stood there for a few minutes, contemplating the fresh flowers she had just placed on her parents' graves. She remembered how the inner bailey had once looked, when she'd been a child. It had been wildly overgrown with weeds and so unwelcoming that she'd never dared brave it even to visit her mother's grave. How very different it was now, all made over into a lovely, charming garden and strictly maintained by two gardeners. It had been Alexander's gift to her, a surprise, set in motion during the days he'd been at Wellewyn, arranging for her father's burial and searching for the one who'd murdered him and caring for the people of Wellewyn. He had hired the gardeners and instructed them to make this place beautiful, for her pleasure, and to keep it beautiful in every season. Lillis had never known such happiness as she did in this little garden, or such peace. Even in the cold winter weather she enjoyed it.

It was cold for November, colder than usual, though the snow, thankfully, had not fallen for the past two days. Lillis shivered and wrapped her cloak more tightly about herself.

"Hello, Lillis."

The familiar voice both surprised and frightened her. She turned quickly.

"Alexander." She took a couple of steps toward him, then stopped. "You came early."

He looked thinner than she remembered, perhaps a bit tired. There were circles under his eyes and his face was pale, yet he had never looked more handsome. He was beautifully dressed in warm winter clothes made of a rich burgundy color that caused his dark hair and green eyes to stand out vividly. He had clearly dressed to honor her.

"Yes," he said, gazing at her with something like a cautious frown. "I could wait no longer. Is it all right, Lillis?"

"Yes. I'm glad. I've missed you." Slowly she moved closer, until she stood directly in front of him. He held himself perfectly still, and his eyes searched hers. "If I kiss you in greeting, Alexander," she whispered, "you'll not think me ready to return to Gyer, will you?"

He shook his head. "No," he tried to say, his mouth forming the word though no sound came out.

Lillis moved into his arms with the greatest relief she'd ever known and, starved for the touch and taste of him, raised her mouth to meet his. Their hands, urgent and demanding, found their way beneath the warmth of each other's cloaks to hold one another tightly. She reveled in the feeling of his strong, hard body against her own and beneath her seeking hands. To hold him now, to be held by him, felt wonderful and right. His mouth on hers was passionate yet gentle at the same time, and Lillis kissed him with all the longing and loneliness that the past month had wrought in her.

"I've missed you," Alexander said when he could. "It has seemed more like ten years rather than one month. There were times when I thought I would lose my resolve and mount the nearest horse and come storming all the way to Wellewyn just to have a glimpse of you." He pulled away a little and looked down at her. "I've been more lonely for you than I could ever put into words. Do you think—is there any chance that you might come home to me soon?"

"Let's not speak of it tonight, Alexander," she said. "I've been lonely for you, also, but I'm not yet ready to return to Gyer. If you can be patient for only a little while longer then I promise that when I do return I will never leave you again."

He made a groaning sound but kissed her. "I'll be patient for as long as you ask me to be. For now I can only thank God that I hold you in my arms again. Even this has been worth a month of misery."

She took Alexander's hand. "I know it's cold, my lord, but will you walk in the garden with me? You must see the wonderful present you've given me. Indeed, I've never had a present so fine. It's much smaller than your own gardens at Gyer, but it is very beautiful, and I do love it so."

Alexander tucked her hand warmly through his arm, covering it with his. They began to walk together, slowly and comfortably, the snow crunching beneath their feet. "Any garden you're in is the best place in the world to me, Lillis," Alexander said. "Better than heaven, even. I'm glad if it has given you pleasure."

"Oh, it has, my lord. Such pleasure. I think of you when I'm here. When I'm lonely, I feel closer to you. Is it not beautiful?" she asked. "Even with the snow?"

"Not half as beautiful as its mistress," he said.

She laughed. "I wish the children could see it. The twins spend a great deal of time having snow wars here. Sometimes Willem and I have to run for our lives."

Alexander tried to share her smile, but he wondered, in spite of himself, whether she ever walked through this garden with Willem as she now walked with him.

"Speaking of my wicked brothers, where are they? And where is Willem? I must admit I did expect something more of a welcome than the one I received when I arrived at the castle doors. The poor woman who opened them took one look at me and nearly swooned. I had to direct two of my men to carry her to a chair and try to revive her."

"Oh, dear," said Lillis rather guiltily. "I'm sorry, Alexander. That must have been Tildy. She's the new cook who took Agnes's place when she broke her arm last week. I would have met you at the door myself, but I expected you'd arrive later, though I am so glad you came when you did. As to Willem and the twins—well—I asked them if they wouldn't mind taking themselves off for the day." She blushed deeply. "I wanted you all to myself, my lord, and now you know the truth of me—I am exceedingly selfish, I fear."

Alexander didn't respond for a minute. He caressed her fingers with his own, playing with them in the same, unthinking manner she'd seen him do with Barbara. "I'm glad," he finally stated, slowly and quietly. "It will be good to have you all to myself after missing you for such a long time. And," he added, looking at her, "we do have much to discuss."

"Yes," Lillis agreed, swallowing, her whole body tingling from the warm, lazy tone of his voice.

"Where did Willem and the boys take themselves off to?"

"Willem went to Winslow to see about finding an artisan who can make new grindstones for the miller. One of the old ones is cracked and does a very poor job of grinding. He should be back on the morrow." She fell silent after this.

"And the twins?" Alexander prompted.

"The twins? Well, the twins have...the twins have—" She stopped walking and turned to him. "I cannot lie to you, Alexander, much as I wish I could. The twins have taken advantage of your absence at Gyer to go there and steal some of their birds and bring them back to Wellewyn. I'm so sorry. I tried to stop them, but they wouldn't listen to me."

Alexander gazed into his wife's beautiful, chagrined face and tried very hard not to laugh. She was such an innocent, and obviously didn't have the least knowledge that Hugh and Hugo had been making several regular early-morning raids on Gyer since the day they'd left a month before. Where did she think all of that good wine had come from? And all of those wax candles and heavy woolen blankets and imported spices? But he knew she would be unhappy to know the truth, and so he kept the secret. Besides, the twins were doing him a great favor—their thievery provided for Lillis as Alexander, himself, wanted to do and would have done, if Lillis had only allowed it.

He leaned down and lightly kissed her nose, then her mouth, and said, "That sounds like something Hugh and Hugo would do. But it's all right. You shouldn't feel guilty for them. The birds are theirs, and they should be able to have them if they wish. I know your father's mews are empty and have been for some time. Indeed, I shall be glad to know that Hugh and Hugo will be able to bring home a great deal of game with those birds and thus fill your larder. I would have sent you some birds myself save I feared you might be angry and send them back."

She looked unhappy in spite of his efforts. "You've already done so much, my lord," she said. "You have lost a fortune and more on Wellewyn, and it is all my father's fault. Can you not understand how deep my regret is? I could never add to that."

Alexander framed her face with his hands and stroked her cheeks with his thumbs. "You are my wife," he whispered, and gently kissed one side of her mouth. "I love you." He turned her face and kissed the other side. "It is my honor to care for you. For you, for your happiness, I would spend every groat and half groat that I possess." He kissed her fully then, and gave in to the passion that had simmered in him for so many lonely days. He knew he was crushing her, hoped he was not hurting her, and would have laid her right down onto the snow if some small leftover sense of reason hadn't told him that it would be too uncomfortable for her.

Lillis finally tore her mouth away, though she didn't push from him. Instead she pressed her face against his shoulder and held him somewhat more tightly. Alexander felt her breath hot on his neck and as rapid and uncontrolled as his own.

"Lillis," he said hoarsely, "I'll not be able to keep my hands off you. Perhaps I should go away."

She shook her head against him. "No. I don't want you to leave and I don't want you to feel as if you must keep from touching me. I am your wife, Alexander, and that is what I want to be. Not your prisoner and not your chattel and not your toy." She lifted her head and looked at him. "I didn't leave you because of the way that you loved me, but because of the way you treated me." There were tears in her eyes, which she wiped away quickly. She smiled weakly and took hold of his hand. "But come, my lord, let us not speak of these things now. Come inside and I shall set you before the fire and bring you some wine. I want to hear about everyone at Gyer, especially Edyth and Aunt Leta and the children."

Alexander didn't resist as she tugged him toward the castle. In a very short while he found himself seated in a somewhat feeble chair in front of the only working fireplace in the hall of Castle Wellewyn. Lillis disappeared behind a screen to fetch wine, and Alexander looked around the shabby chamber with a feeling of faint disgust.

He'd been at Castle Wellewyn enough times to be familiar with it, yet he never ceased to be amazed at the fact that people actually lived here. The stables at Gyer were more livable than Castle Wellewyn, which could not actually be called a castle by true definition. It was better named a keep, or even a manor house; Alexander could have easily fit ten or more Castle Wellewyns inside Castle Gyer.

He was gratified with the reconstruction work that had been done by the men he'd sent. He could see what areas had been repaired and rebuilt, such as the roof and the corner of one wall that he remembered as falling down. All of the window shutters had been replaced to keep the wind from whistling inside; Castle Wellewyn had no glass windows as Castle Gyer did. His men had done a good job thus far; at least the castle was safe from the snow and wind and rain. If they could only get the other two fireplaces in the room working, the place might actually be warm.

There was something else new about Castle Wellewyn. It was, for the first time in Alexander's memory, spotlessly clean. Lillis had been responsible for that, he knew, and he wished again that she would let him send servants to help her. The cleaning of the place must have been a laborious task. There were fresh rushes on the floor, the cobwebs and dirt had been washed from the walls, the black soot that had once covered the fireplace was gone, and even the screen partitions looked like they'd been scrubbed. Lillis had hung some of her beautiful needleworks on the walls, and on the one table that sat in the middle of the room there was a beautiful vase.

"Here I am, my lord," Lillis said brightly as she came around the screen bearing two plain pewter goblets in one hand and a mismatched wine decanter in the other. A horde of cats followed in her wake, meowing loudly and running around her swinging skirts. "I took a moment to check on your men and make certain that Tildy's keeping them comfortable in the kitchen. You must have thought I'd run away." She smiled and handed him the goblets.

Alexander held them out for her to fill.

"No, I didn't think that," he said, watching as she carefully poured the red wine that he knew had come from his own cellars. "I was admiring the many changes you've made here. It is a different dwelling, I vow, and most comfortable."

Lillis's cheeks flushed with pleasure, and Alexander's heart responded to this added beauty in her with a typical rapid thumping.

"Do you think so, my lord?" she asked hopefully.

Alexander swallowed and nodded. "Yes."

She put the decanter down and looked at him with shining eyes, unwittingly causing Alexander's heart to pump even more erratically. "I'm glad to hear you say so," she admitted. "I had hoped you would notice. Of course, most of the improvement is due to the work your men have done."

Lillis sat in the chair next to his, and Alexander handed her one of the goblets. He thought that this was heaven having Lillis beside him, at ease with him once more. "That is less than true, my love, but I'm glad if they've contributed some small part."

"They've done no less than make the dwelling habitable, sir, and you know that very well. I had forgotten in what disrepair my father kept it, but now it is quite worthy. One day, perhaps," she added with sudden shyness, "you will see fit to make one of our sons lord here, and he will be grateful, indeed, to have had his home so well kept for him."

"Lillis," said Alexander, taking her hand and bringing it to his mouth, "there are so many things I would say to you this night—" A bright orange kitten rudely leapt into his lap, interrupting him with its loud, demanding squeals. "Damnation!" he muttered, glaring at the small and shaggy creature.

Lillis giggled, and Alexander didn't have the heart to throw the thing off his lap. Seeing that their bold companion had not been tossed aside, several of the other cats decided to brave the ascent to Alexander's lap. Lillis began to laugh fully and Alexander was forced to stand in order to end the siege. Complaining, the cats and kittens scurried away.

"Where did they all come from?" he demanded. "I remember seeing cats when I came here before, but this is madness! You actually let them inside?"

Lillis had to wipe her eyes before she could answer laughingly, "Yes, I let them inside. I love cats. When I was a little girl I used to beg my father to let me bring home one of the village cats, but he always said no. He hated cats with a passion. He said they made him sneeze. But when I turned five he gave me a kitten for my birthday." Her expression softened and she smiled in memory. "She was the sweetest little gray-and-white creature and I loved her so much. Of course, once she grew she was pregnant every few months and soon the castle was filled with all manner of cats and kittens. My poor father! He hated each and every one of them and sneezed constantly, but he couldn't bear to hurt my feelings by getting rid of them so he put up with the misery." She sobered and grew thoughtful. "I was surprised to find there were still cats here when I returned. I thought surely he would get rid of them when he sent me to Tynedale, but I suppose he had grown used to them." She fell silent.

"Perhaps they reminded him of you," Alexander suggested, and the thought surprised him, for he'd never before considered Jaward capable of any tender feelings, not even toward his own daughter.

"Perhaps," she said, then added with a smile, "Would you like to play a game of chess before we eat, my lord? Do you remember how we used to play in the evenings at Gyer?"

"How could I forget? You were beginning to beat me too often."

"Only with Willem's help," she said, standing to fetch the one gaming table that Wellewyn possessed. "But he's not here tonight so we will be well matched. And it is the strangest thing. I don't recall there being a set of playing pieces at Wellewyn, for I can never remember my father playing, but the twins found it somewhere." She set the table between them and went to bring the pieces. When she returned with a red velvet bag, she said, "It is remarkably like the sets at Gyer, don't you think?" She dumped the pieces out.

Very remarkably, Alexander thought. Indeed, he might have said that they were *exactly* like the sets at Gyer, but he didn't. If Lillis was happy, he was happy. The twins could steal everything he owned in order to attain that goal.

They commenced a friendly game, and Alexander knew a contentment he hadn't felt since Lillis had left him. It seeped into him, into his very bones, so that he was thoroughly relaxed and happy. There seemed to be no better place in the world than the place he was, sitting before a warm fire in Castle Wellewyn, sipping wine and playing chess with his beautiful wife. Her face, across from his, animated with frustration and delight during the game, made him feel crazed with love.

They laughed loudly while they played, and talked in low voices, and laughed loudly again. Alexander dutifully told her about the children and Edyth and Aunt Leta, and readily answered all of her questions about everything from his plans for new crops to how the brothers at the monastery were doing. Lillis, in turn, told Alexander about the improvements being made at Wellewyn and of the growing satisfaction among the people there. She related how the twins had made themselves popular amongst the villagers with their cheery natures and willingness to help in the repairs being done. Willem, she said, had proved to be a capable manager, and had won the trust of the people of Wellewyn with his ability to quickly and fairly settle disputes, and with his ready availability to one and all, equally.

The cats and kittens grew braver after an hour or so and slowly crept back, one by one, to sit beside them. Before he realized what had happened, Alexander found that his lap was filled with warm, sleeping, purring cats, and when he looked he saw that Lillis was in the same situation. She must have seen him looking, for she smiled at him in such a grateful way that, though he wanted to, he didn't push the creatures off. He would do anything to please her, and with a jolt realized that perhaps he and Jaward had had more in common than he'd have ever thought.

Chapter Twenty

"Madam," said Alexander, setting his eating dagger down and patting his full stomach with satisfaction, "that was indeed a fine meal, just as you promised it would be. I give you my compliments."

"Thank you very much, sir," Lillis accepted grandly. "For our Lord Gyer we spared nothing, though I know our simple fare can't compare to that served at Gyer. More wine, my lord?"

Alexander extended his cup. "A little. I'll not drink too much more, however, else I'll never be able to stay atop my horse all the way back to Gyer."

Lillis smiled and poured the wine.

"Alexander," she said more seriously after a moment, "I wish to ask you something about Hugh and Hugo. Have you ever noticed anything different about them? Different from the rest of your siblings, I mean."

"Of course!" Alexander exclaimed, laughing. "Have not you? They're different from *anyone* I've ever met, much less my other brothers and sister. Why? Do you have reason to believe that my parents stole them from gypsies or some such? I assure you they didn't, though God alone knows I've thought the same thing at least a thousand times during my life. Over and over, after they've performed some particularly heinous misdeed, I've looked at them and said, 'They cannot be my brothers. They *cannot* be.' But, of course—" he shrugged and smiled "—they are."

Lillis smiled weakly in return, wondering whether she should say anything about what Barbara had told her. She'd thought much on the matter over the past few weeks, especially because the twins were constantly underfoot, forcing her to think of it. Could they truly be her half brothers? The idea seemed unbelievable, and yet, she must admit, they did resemble her father. She knew she was *trying* to see the resemblance, yet even so she couldn't dismiss the similarities that were there. What she couldn't understand was how they were her half brothers, if indeed they were, and how they had come to live at Gyer instead of Wellewyn.

"Do they resemble your mother's side of the family, then?" she queried.

"Yes, though they get their dark hair from our father. All of us do in that way, save Candis, who escaped with a little of my mother's red coloring. My mother had green eyes, which is where the twins and I got ours and where I suppose Candis got her hazel eyes from. My father was quite dark all over, much like Willem and Justin. Dark hair and dark eyes. He used to frighten me near to death when I was a child, all dark and omnipotent as he was." Alexander pulled a grape off a bunch that rested in a nearby bowl and popped it into his mouth. "I used to think he was the very devil," he added, smiling.

The very devil, thought Lillis. *Her* father had had green eyes and his hair had been quite dark until age had turned it white.

"That must have been a difficult delivery for your mother. Bearing twins, I mean."

"Oh, it was," Alexander agreed. "I shall never, in all my life, forget it. I was ten years of age and my father was away from home, as he generally was. Matters hadn't stood well between them during the months of Mother's pregnancy. He left, I think, to avoid being there for the birth, to punish her for some reason or other." He reached out and took hold of one of Lillis's hands, holding it with both of his on the tabletop.

"I remember my mother screaming with so much pain and crying like a little child. Willem was only eight then, and it was very hard on him. He had a hiding place beneath one of the tapestries in the great hall and I found him there, all trembling and crying. I tried to comfort him, though to little avail. We sat together for a long time, listening to the screams. It was odd," he said with a shake of his head, "but Aunt Leta wasn't at Gyer, either. I don't know why, but she wasn't.

"My poor mother! She had no one to stand by her. There were her ladies-in-waiting and the servants, of course, but no family. The screams were terrible. I could hardly stand them. And Willem! Willem cried and cried. I remember being so angry with my father. So angry that I hated him."

He fell silent and their eyes met. Lillis squeezed his hand and nodded sympathetically. Alexander continued.

"Finally I felt as though I could bear it no longer. I left Willem beneath the tapestry and went to my mother's chamber—the chamber that is yours now. The women who were there told me to leave, but I wouldn't. I went to my mother's side, and she reached out a hand and took mine, squeezing it so hard I thought it would break. I remember that she calmed a little and told me she loved me. Nothing short of death could have taken me from her side after that. I sat through the whole ordeal and held her hand. She could have wrung it off my arm and I wouldn't have cared." He smiled and brought Lillis's hand to his lips to kiss it. "She nearly did, too," he said.

"No one knew there were two babies, of course. They were all entangled when they came out, so that to this day we've never known which one came first. Perhaps they were inseparable, even in the womb. My poor mother! She was so weak and weary from the birthing, yet she wouldn't rest until she held her babies."

Alexander's eyes were distant, seeing anew of what he spoke.

"I have always hoped and dreamed that she looked at me when I was born the way she looked at the twins that day. She held them both at the same time, kissing them in turns. Her face was so beautiful, so filled with light—she looked like an angel to me. She let me name the twins. Did you know that? I was sitting there and watching her hold them and she looked at me and said, 'These are your very own brothers to care for, Alexander. Would you like to name them?' And of course I did. Hugh and Hugo seemed appropriate at the time, though I don't remember why. If the twins hate their names I suppose they can blame my ten-year-old ignorance." He laughed, and Lillis smiled.

"Mother liked the names," he continued. "At least, she said she did. She might have been only trying to humor me, or perhaps she was too weary to argue. I've always believed she liked the names, anyway. She let me hold them then, before she went to sleep. They were so tiny! Much smaller than other babies I've seen, and more like puppies than human babies. My mother told me to bring Willem up and let him hold the babies, too, and to tell him that she loved him and would see him when she'd rested. Willem was always her favorite, you know. She said he needed her the most."

He grew thoughtful. "Mother said one last thing to me before she went to sleep. She said, 'Promise me that you'll always take care of Hugh and Hugo, and promise me that you will always love them. They haven't anyone else to love them.'" Alexander shook his head at the memory.

"Of course, she was half crazed with exhaustion and didn't know what she said, but I made her my solemn vow nonetheless and then she closed her eyes and went to sleep. I was left sitting with the two babies, wondering what to do. Even then Hugh and Hugo seemed to sense a good opportunity for mischief. The moment Mother was soundly asleep they began to wail." He laughed. "I handed them to their nurses in a hurry! And then I kissed Mother and went to seek Willem out. Poor Willem! He'd cried so much that he'd fallen asleep beneath the tapestry and—Lillis, you're not crying, are you?"

She was, and Alexander set his arm about her waist, pulling her close. "My darling! I never meant to make you cry."

"What—what did your father do?" she asked tearfully.

"What did my father do?"

"Yes, when he returned to Gyer? What did he do?"

"He came home the next day," he replied, bewildered. "He loved them, of course. I've told you before that he ever favored them above the rest of us, and spoiled them. He and my mother made up whatever argument they were having and Aunt Leta came back to Gyer soon after and she loved the twins, as well. Who couldn't have loved them? They were the handsomest babies you ever set eyes on."

"Oh!" cried Lillis. "Oh, thank God!"

Alexander was thoroughly confused. He kissed the top of her head and asked, "Because everyone loved them, or because they were so handsome?"

"Both!" she wailed.

He forced her face up so that he could kiss the salty tears off her cheeks. "Lillis, I cannot bear to see you crying. Please stop."

He kissed her mouth, long and tenderly, until she stopped her tears and put her arms around his neck. He pressed his face into her hair and hugged her with all of his strength. "I want to have you in bed, Lillis. I will have you, unless you tell me to go away."

Her voice was a whisper when she replied, "I was going to sing to you first."

"First?"

"We haven't any minstrels here, as Gyer does. I was going to play the lute and sing to you first."

Alexander's usually agile mind was having difficulty understanding what these words meant. He said again, more hopefully, "First?"

Lillis stood and took his hand to lead him back toward the warmth of the fire. Halfway there Alexander stopped, tugged her back into his arms and kissed her again.

"Thank you for the wonderful meal, my lady. I enjoyed it greatly. I enjoyed your company even more."

"You are most welcome, my lord," Lillis replied. "I only hope that your men enjoyed their meals, as well. You don't think they will grow inpatient waiting for you?"

He understood exactly what she was asking. "My men will not intrude upon us unless they are ready to be dismissed from my service. Of that I give you my solemn vow. But what of your serving maid?''

Lillis blushed under the tender scrutiny of his gaze. ''I warned her that you might be quite, quite late in leaving this eve. She is well prepared to keep your men supplied with food and drink.''

''Ah, but you are a most wise and wonderful woman,'' Alexander murmured. He touched her cheek with his fingertips and kissed her softly. ''You had best play for me now, my lady,'' he suggested, ''for I intend to love you long and fully before I leave this place, and I'd not want either my men or your Tildy to suffer for it.''

In all of her life Lillis didn't think she had ever played or sung worse than she did that night. She seemed to have entirely forgotten how to play the lute; her hands refused to behave properly and her voice wavered every time she met her husband's meaningful gaze. She couldn't remember how the song she had practiced was either played or sung, and she forgot nearly all of the words. The only thing she could think of as she struggled through the ordeal, strangely, was the slow and tender way in which Alexander had made love to her at Gyer, of the way his hands and mouth felt as they moved over her skin. Somehow she got through it, though, for suddenly she found that she had stopped playing and singing and was simply sitting quietly, staring at her husband.

Slowly Alexander moved toward her. He took the lute from her hands and placed it on the floor, then he slid his arms around her waist and drew her close.

''That was nicely done,'' he whispered, his breath warm on her face. ''I thank you, my lady.''

She stared at him.

''Where is your chamber?'' he asked, picking her up in his arms.

She wrapped her arms around his neck. ''The first chamber at the top of the stairs,'' she replied somewhat breathlessly, anticipating what was to come.

Alexander stopped midway to the stairs. He looked at her and asked, ''Your father's chamber?''

She nodded again and smiled. Alexander shook his head and frowned.

"Is there nowhere else?"

"Nowhere else?"

"Some other place where we might—?"

Lillis was confused. "No!" she said. "My chamber is very nice. I've cleaned and refurnished it. It looks not at all as it did when it was my father's. And I've kept the fire well fed all day so that the chamber would be warm."

Alexander stood where he was, looking miserably uncertain. Lillis chuckled and stroked his cheek with a gentle hand. "I've had a new bed put in there," she whispered, "and I had my father's old one taken out and burned."

Alexander didn't need to hear another word. He bounded up the stairs with Lillis in his arms, pushed into the chamber with energetic zeal and kicked the door shut behind him with a resounding slam.

Many hours later, Alexander lay warm and comfortable in his wife's new bed, holding her limp, damp body against his own and feeling more sated and happy than he had in a long while. Lillis snuggled closer and made a little yawning sound. Alexander picked up one of her hands and brought it to his mouth. He kissed each finger, then drew her little finger inside his mouth, sucking on it lightly. Lillis laughed and pulled her hand away.

"Stop that," she said, then chided, "you are a very hungry man, my lord."

"Hmm. I am full for the moment, good lady wife. And for another half hour or so." Alexander yawned sleepily, trying not to think about the fact that he would have to leave Lillis soon. His men must have begun to wonder what had happened to him. It was dark outside now, and the ride back to Gyer would seem long and tedious, indeed. "If anyone had ever told me that I'd spend some of the happiest hours of my life in Jaward of Wellewyn's bedchamber, I'd have told them they were mad."

"But it is not his chamber any longer," Lillis reminded him. "It is very different, is it not? I couldn't have stayed here if I'd not changed it completely."

They were quiet for a while. Alexander thought perhaps Lillis had fallen asleep. He stroked her hair out of her face and kissed her forehead. With a slow hand he rubbed her smooth back.

"Lillis?"

"Hmm?"

"When will you return to me?"

She didn't answer right away. She turned her head on his shoulder, then hugged him a little. "Soon, Alexander. I shall come back to you soon."

"I need you," he said quietly.

"It will not be long, Alexander. I promise that it shall not be. The time I've spent here at Wellewyn has been good, for I've never before known such freedom and peace. There is no one to tell me what I must or must not do—no disapproving nuns, no ever-present guards, no unbending husbands." She gave him a teasing grin, but Alexander only looked grim.

"There'll be no more of that when you return to Gyer," he vowed. "You know I speak the truth. Everything will be exactly as it should be."

"Yes," she said. "Shall we become as dull and tiresome as other married people, my lord?"

"Duller. And much more tiresome. Perhaps you were not aware of the fact, my lady, but you've had the misfortune to be wed to the dullest, most tiresome man in England."

"Nonsense," she scoffed. "I've never met a man less dull or tiresome, or one more handsome either, and if you do have an inclination toward work and management rather than wasteful living, my lord, there is always your family to make up the difference. The twins, you must admit, are most lively, and Barbara's behavior could seldom be called dull, though it could often be thought most wearying."

"You've no need to worry over Barbara," he said, "for she'll not be at Gyer long. I've agreed to let Jason de Burgh court her."

"Have you?" she said, much surprised. "That's wonderful!"

"Yes, and she seems happy enough, though John has expressed displeasure over the possibility of their union. I'll not say I'm happy about the match, either, but I want you home again, Lillis, and if de Burgh makes an acceptable offer, and I believe that he will, I will accept and they shall be wed as soon as possible."

Lillis touched his face with the tips of her fingers, caressing so softly that he shivered. "That is good, husband, for I'll not share your affections with any other woman, whether you have ever loved her in truth, or no. And Barbara will be happy with the Lord of Dunsted. Indeed, I have cause to think she will be quite, quite happy."

"Not as happy as I'll be when my wife has come home again," Alexander declared. "I miss her so greatly that I would be content to sit by her dwelling door both night and day, if she would only let me."

Lillis laughed. "That might be rather cold for you in the snow, sir."

"Snow, rain, hail, wind, lightning and thunder or scorching heat, I wouldn't mind at all. I would be the happiest man alive to be so near her."

She sighed. "You do pay the prettiest compliments I have ever heard in my life, Lord Gyer, false as they may be. I must admit I do like to hear them."

Alexander closed his eyes and smiled. "They're not false," he insisted, yawning. "God's mercy, I'm tired. I wish I didn't have to ride home this night."

"You may stay if you like."

"I wish I could, but it would be unkind to make my men wait for me all night. Already they must be wanting to get home to their own warm beds."

Lillis set her hand against his chest, as if she would keep him from going. "I shall miss you, my lord."

"Shall you?"

"Yes. Very much."

Alexander rolled until Lillis was beneath him.

"And I shall miss you," he whispered, kissing her. "Let us join ourselves once more, then, to make the parting less painful. I will take the memory to Gyer and recall it often to keep myself sane, otherwise, when you return to me you shall find yourself wed to a raving madman."

Chapter Twenty-One

"Oh, my dear, how different it looks," Edyth exclaimed three days later, standing in the hall at Castle Wellewyn. "I never could have imagined that it might be so comfortable."

"Indeed," Aunt Leta agreed more sternly, striding forward to receive a proper kiss in greeting from Lillis. "It seems you have made quite an improvement from the way it was when Jaward lived here. At least, compared to the way Alexander told me Castle Wellewyn used to be. Why, this looks quite livable. Of course," she added, eyeing Lillis with severity, "Alexander is the one to thank for the repairs and the supplying of the castle."

Lillis finished hugging Justin and Candis and replied graciously, "Yes, Aunt Leta, Lord Gyer has been most generous. We never could have gotten through such cold weather without everything he has done for us."

Aunt Leta lifted her nose into the air. "Quite right," she pronounced, and sat in the one good chair by the fire.

Lillis put her arms around Edyth and hugged her. "Oh, Edyth! It's so good to see you again. I've missed you so very much, though I'm glad that Justin and Candis had you with them." She looked at the children. "Have you been very good for Edyth?"

"Yes," they both replied, nodding.

"They're perfect angels!" Edyth added lovingly. "Is that not true, my darlings?"

The children smiled at Edyth with glowing faces, causing Lillis to chuckle. She knew for a fact that the children were not *quite* angels, but neither she nor anyone else would ever be able to convince Edyth they were anything else.

"Lillis!" Aunt Leta demanded impatiently. "Stop this nonsense and order one of your servants to bring me some hot wine. I nearly froze to death on the ride here and am in need of warming."

Lillis nodded obediently. "My pleasure, my lady, though I will fetch the wine myself. We have few servants at Wellewyn. Edyth, you sit in the chair next to Aunt Leta, and children, you settle yourselves on the pillows I've set in front of the fire. I'm afraid we also have few chairs." She left to fetch the wine.

She returned in a few minutes bearing a tray filled with the requested wine, as well as all manner of confections and sweet cakes. She set the tray on a low table and then settled herself on the floor next to the children.

"I made the cakes myself," she told the children, inviting them to take some, "and the wine is amazingly good. I don't know how we came to have such a supply of it." She handed first to Aunt Leta, then to Edyth, goblets filled with the warm, spiced liquid, then proceeded to fill one for herself. She had brought warm milk laced with honey and cinnamon for the children to drink, and gave them each a cup.

"I'm so glad you've come to visit," she said when everyone was served. "I've been lonely for all of you."

"We've missed you, too," Justin said, munching a piece of tansy cake. "Will you come home soon? We have some rabbits now."

"Alex gave them to us," Candis added, taking another piece of almond shortbread.

"I shall come home soon," Lillis replied. "Don't tell your brother, but I've been thinking to surprise him by coming home at Christmastide. Will he be pleased, do you think?"

"Oh, yes!" Candis cried. "Will you come on Christmas Eve, like the yule log?"

Lillis laughed. "Perhaps I shall. But you must promise not to tell Lord Gyer. I want it to be a surprise."

Both Candis and Justin solemnly gave their promise not to tell, and Lillis was satisfied. She smiled at Aunt Leta, who nodded at her with approval.

"This separation between you and Alexander is the most ridiculous thing I've heard of in all of my days," she declared. "If you ask me, Lillis Baldwin, you're a very foolish young lady. Why, my nephew is one of the finest, most forthright—"

"Yes, Aunt Leta," Lillis agreed quickly, putting a halt to the oncoming tirade. "You are quite right. Will you have more wine, my lady?"

"Hrmph!" replied Aunt Leta, irate at having had a perfectly good speech so thoroughly defused. "Where are Hugh and Hugo?" she demanded.

"The twins? Well, they *are* around somewhere," Lillis replied, looking about as if she expected to see them suddenly jump out from behind one of the many screens in the room. "I told them you were coming today, but they had something to do and I've not seen them since the morning meal. They'll be hungry soon and will come looking for something to eat."

"We passed Willem on the way here," Justin announced matter-of-factly.

"He was going to see Alex," Candis added.

"Yes, I know," Lillis told them, looking at Aunt Leta again. "I thought it rather strange, but he said he'd received a missive from Alexander this morn asking him to come to Gyer right away. Nothing is amiss, I hope."

"Nothing that I know of. Why, I didn't know Willem was going to Gyer until we met him on the road. It was quite a shock, I can tell you, to run into one's nephew when one was fully planning on visiting with that same nephew later in the day. He asked me outright what it was Alexander needed him for and I told him I didn't know. Alexander said not a word to me about sending for him, not even when he escorted us through the village gates. Barbara suggested that perhaps Willem was mistaken about the missive being from Alexander, but he insisted that it was."

"Barbara?" Lillis repeated, surprised.

"Barbara was coming with us today," Justin explained before Aunt Leta could. "But she began to feel sick and turned back."

"She had a headache," Aunt Leta corrected, then looked at Lillis directly. "I realize Barbara wasn't invited to come, but she did express the greatest desire to accompany us. She said she wished to know if you'd found something she had asked you to look for. I thought it odd at the time, but that was all she would admit, and she did beg so prettily. What else could I say, save that you would surely welcome her?"

"And so I would," Lillis said. "I regret that she was unable to finish the journey."

"Yes, the poor dear," Aunt Leta agreed. "All was well until just after we had left Willem and gone on our way, and then she began to suffer quite terribly. We were only halfway here and she thought it might be best if she returned to Gyer. I sent three of our escort back with her, of course, and I do hope she arrived in good time. Poor child. She's surely overwrought because of that horrible Lord of Dunsted. The man is thoroughly uncouth! I don't know how Alexander can countenance him courting a sweet creature such as Barbara. I saw him kissing her in the garden only a few days ago and he was terribly ruthless about it. Yes, it is quite true, I assure you! I was shocked beyond belief, certainly, but poor Barbara was evidently so shocked that she wasn't even able to fight the brute off! She was helpless in his grasp, and even had to hold on to him to keep from fainting onto the ground." Aunt Leta shuddered visibly. "You must thank God every day of your life that you didn't have to marry that horrible man, Lillis."

"I thank God that I married Alexander," Lillis said instead, then added with care, "Aunt Leta, there is a serious matter I wish to discuss with you, though perhaps you may not wish to do so in front of the children."

Candis and Justin were instantly affronted; Edyth soothed them with a few words.

Aunt Leta looked a little surprised. "What is it?"

Lillis set her goblet aside and dug around in one of her pockets until she found what she was looking for. "It has to do with this," she said, carefully placing the small porcelain oval on the table. Candis and Justin leaned forward to look at the picture painted on it. "I believe this is what Barbara spoke of when she wanted to know if I had found something here at Wellewyn. This—" she indicated the portrait "—was among my mother's possessions."

"It's Barbara!" Candis declared, turning a toothy grin up at Lillis.

"She looks very much like Barbara, love," Lillis replied gently, "but I believe that this is a portrait of her mother. Is that not true, Aunt Leta?"

The older woman had never looked so pale to Lillis before, nor so stricken. With a shaking hand, Aunt Leta gingerly took the portrait up to inspect it more carefully.

"Yes," she said at last, her eyes moist. "This is Madelyne. Madelyne Denys. Barbara's mother. And John's." She recovered herself a little and smiled at the children. "She was your cousin's—John Baldwin's—wife. Not the Cousin John who lives at Gyer, but his father, who was also named John. You never knew him, of course. John Baldwin was my cousin in the fourth degree, and this lady was his wife. Oh, it's rather complicated, I fear, as the relationship is so distant. We have always called John and Barbara cousins, though they are really very far removed. But you understand, do you not, children?"

The children nodded solemnly and looked again at the portrait Aunt Leta held out toward them.

"Well," Aunt Leta continued, "John Baldwin married Madelyne Denys of the Huntington Denys. The Huntingtons are a very noble line, descending from the Romans, you see. And they're a beautiful people, as well, all of them. Now, John Baldwin, your distant cousin, married this very beautiful lady that you see here, Madelyne Denys, and she soon after presented him with John and later with Barbara."

"Oh," the children replied, plainly confused.

Lillis chuckled and looked at Edyth. "Perhaps you could take Candis and Justin into the garden, Edyth. It's very lovely, and I'm sure they'll find it more interesting than this.

And,'' she added as Edyth and the children rose to leave, "you must say hello to my cats. They're in a special shed next to the kitchen and would enjoy a visit. There are some new kittens, too, though you must be very gentle with them.''

"Oh, kittens!" Candis cried with great enthusiasm.

"We'll be careful," promised Justin, taking Candis's hand and pulling her around the table into Edyth's waiting care. In only moments they were shuffled out of doors.

Lillis watched until they were gone, then she turned to face Aunt Leta.

"I want to know everything," she said.

Aunt Leta set her goblet down unsteadily. "I fear I don't understand you, Lady Gyer.''

"You understand me very well. My mother was Madelyne Denys's sister. My mother was Eleanor." Aunt Leta's sharp intake of breath made Lillis tremble deep within herself. "You must tell me everything."

Aunt Leta closed her eyes and shook her head resolutely.

"You must!" Lillis insisted, leaning forward and taking hold of the older woman's hand.

"No, I cannot! I made a solemn vow. I promised my brother that I would never, never—''

"That doesn't matter now! You must say what you know or risk the chance of someday facing your God with the knowledge that you kept the truth from those who should have known it. Don't you think I have a right to know what happened between my family and yours? And what of Alexander? And the twins? You claim to love your family and yet you keep the greatest truths from them. Your brother was to you, I suspect, as John Baldwin is to Barbara. You were always beneath his rule, were you not?" Lillis went on her knees before her. "I'm begging you, Leta Baldwin. Do you see? I'm pleading with you to tell me the truth."

She felt the fine trembling that coursed through Aunt Leta's body as it worked its way through the older woman's hands. She could feel Aunt Leta's tears as they began somewhere in her depths and made their way to her eyes. Lillis was patient. She stayed on her knees, clasping Aunt

Leta's hands firmly in her own until the tears and the trembling subsided.

"You are so much like your mother," Aunt Leta whispered at last. "When I first saw you on that dark night so long ago, when the twins brought you to Gyer, I thought for a moment that I was seeing Eleanor again. Or that perhaps her ghost had come to haunt me. It was terrible." She fell into tears again and Lillis kept still, holding her hands as tightly as she could.

"There are things," Aunt Leta murmured, "that would hurt many people if they were known. The children—my niece and nephews— would be devastated."

"No, that is not true," Lillis said firmly. "They might be hurt for a little while, but in the end they would be better off knowing than not knowing. And you know, as well, that it would be wrong to continue in your silence."

"But Candis and Justin are so young!" Aunt Leta protested. "They worship the memory of their mother and father, just as the twins do. It would be cruel to shatter what they hold so dear."

"Very well," Lillis conceded. "Perhaps the children should be a little older before they are told the truth, but Hugh and Hugo are nearly men now and have as much a right to know about themselves as I have a right to know about my parents. As to Alexander and Willem, it goes without saying that they are certainly old enough to know. Now, Aunt Leta, tell me everything."

Defeated, Aunt Leta closed her eyes and nodded. "Yes. If you will know the truth, I shall tell it to you. Indeed, I'll be relieved to speak of it after all these years. Give me more wine, girl, and I will tell you the tale."

Chapter Twenty-Two

"There was a time," Aunt Leta began, speaking each word with care, "many, many years ago, when your father and my brother were very good friends. In truth, they were the best of friends, for they were as close as brothers. In those days there was a good understanding between Gyer and Wellewyn. Dunsted, of course, was already a thorn in my father's side because of the issue of the land, but with Wellewyn we were on good terms, mostly because of the friendship between my brother and your father. My brother, whose Christian name was Charles, and Jaward were fostered together when they were boys, long before either of them had to take up the responsibility of their estates. Wellewyn was always quite poor, but that made little difference to Charles and Jaward. They had been friends since their earliest days and grew to be even closer during their years of fostering.

"There was a great deal of visiting between the two families then." Aunt Leta smiled in memory. "I remember celebrating many holidays with the Ryon family. One Christmas Eve in particular I remember. Jaward and Charles brought home a yule log that was more tree than anything else. My father had to put six of his strongest men to work just to fit it into the fireplace." She laughed and shook her head. "I never have been able to figure out how those two sixteen-year-old boys were able to drag home that enormous thing." She sighed, smiling. "Oh, well, those were such good times, back then."

"And Jaward," she said his name wistfully, "he was such a handsome young man. I was quite in love with him, I fear, strange as that may seem." Aunt Leta blushed and inspected her hands minutely. "Mayhap you'll not believe this, but I was thought by many to be more than a little beautiful when I was a girl, and he was—Jaward was—so often at Gyer—being such good friends with Charles. There was a time when I thought—" She stopped, shaking her head. "But that doesn't matter now. Nothing ever came of it. But he *did* kiss me in the gardens once," she added as an afterthought, finally looking at Lillis.

Lillis smiled and nodded at her encouragingly. "I'm sure he must have, Aunt Leta, and you are still a very beautiful woman. I've always thought so. You must have been quite lovely when you were a girl."

Aunt Leta lowered her eyes and smiled. "Well, I did have many suitors, and more than a few who were eligible. But Father died when I was sixteen years of age, and Charles never allowed any of the men who requested permission to court me to do so. By the time I was your age suitors stopped coming to ask. I think perhaps they realized naught would come of it." She seemed rather sad as she spoke. "But Charles was always very good to me, and he did need me so much, especially after Father died. I managed the household then, just as I do now. Even when he brought Elizabeth Caldwell home as his wife, I continued to manage everything."

"But, once he had a wife to care for him, why did your brother not let you marry?" Lillis asked.

Aunt Leta shrugged. "I don't know. I was only five and twenty when they wed, and I did think for a time that he might allow me to go to court and seek a husband, but he always turned the subject whenever I tried to speak with him about it. He said he needed me, and I imagine that was true. Elizabeth was a beautiful young woman from a very good family, but she was younger than I and not much interested in taking on the responsibilities of running such a large household. You mustn't think she was lazy, though," Aunt Leta stated quite firmly. "She was nothing of the sort. Eliz-

abeth was a wonderful person, full of life and happiness and
beauty. Everyone loved her. Especially Charles. Oh, they
were so much in love in those days. You should have seen
them together, behaving more like two silly children than a
married couple. Elizabeth became pregnant very quickly
and soon Alexander arrived, and then, two years later,
Willem was born. Charles was never an easy man to live
with, but during those years he did seem happier and
more content than I had ever known him to be.''

"And what of my father and mother during these years?"
Lillis asked.

"Your father continued to visit us often at Gyer. His own
parents had died shortly after Alexander was born and he
became the Lord of Wellewyn. He was a good lord in those
days, though Wellewyn continued poor, as always. But
Jaward did work very hard at trying to bring things about.
I remember whenever he came to spend a few days with us
at Gyer, he and Charles would speak of nothing but crops
and plantings and animal stock. Elizabeth and I used to
think we would go mad if we had to hear one more word
about soil drainage on those occasions," she said with a
laugh.

"Your father was a little jealous over Charles's marriage, I think. He got along well enough with Elizabeth, but
there were times when I thought perhaps he disliked having
to share his good friend with another, even though Charles
was as devoted to him as he ever had been. Your father was
Alexander's godfather, which I'm sure you never knew.
Alexander never knew it, either, of course. When Charles
and Jaward had their falling out Charles made certain that
Jaward's name was erased from the church records.

"Well, enough about that. Let me tell you of how your
father and mother met. When Charles and Elizabeth had
been married for nearly four years, and when Alexander was
close to three, we received news that one of our distant
cousins, John Baldwin, was to be married. Now, John had
been fostered together with Charles and Jaward, so your
father was a very close acquaintance of his. Naturally, he
was invited to the marriage celebration, as well, and it was

decided between Charles and Jaward that we should all travel to the event together. It was going to be a very important occasion, you see, because the bride was one of the Huntington Denys.

"We arrived in good time for the wedding, coming, as we did, four days before the actual ceremony was to be held. Our cousin received us just exactly as he should have, and with great honor, as my brother was the head of the Baldwin family. The evening of the day we arrived, John held a very fine feast in honor of his bride and her family, who had arrived the same day. I shall never forget how lovely it was. The whole next week was wonderful, of course, but that night was particularly nice. Not many of the wedding guests had arrived as of yet and there was plenty of food and wine. The entertainments John provided were splendid! And the bride was so beautiful! All of the Huntington family are perfectly beautiful, even the men. I must have fallen in love with every single one of them, I vow! But, as lovely as the bride was, and as handsome as the men were, and as fantastic as the feast and entertainments were, there was a single woman present who caused everything and everyone else to appear dim in contrast to her extraordinary beauty. She looked exactly like an angel."

"My mother," Lillis whispered.

Aunt Leta nodded. "Your mother. The most beautiful creature I have ever seen. I've not lied when I've said that you are very much like her, but there was something in her that set her apart from the mortal beauty that you possess. She was radiant, perfect in every feature. Her whiteness, like yours, stood out against the ordinary coloring of other people. All of the men at the celebration, of course, were fighting for her favors, but her father had set four very strong men to guard and accompany her wherever she went, and so she was quite protected. I don't know if she was her father's favorite, but I suspect she was. He is the Earl of Saint Vincent, her father, and he is also your grandfather. He's still alive from what I hear, and just as wretched as ever. I wonder if he would be glad to know that he has a granddaughter who is a replica of his own perfect daughter, even though he so humiliatingly set her aside."

"Set her aside?" Lillis repeated. "I have always wondered why I knew nothing of my mother's family. My father never spoke of them, and he grew angry if I asked. Why did my grandfather set my mother aside?"

"She was from the Huntington line, my dear, and she was a very beautiful woman. Can you not imagine how valuable such a daughter would be to a father who might wish to mate her with an equally valuable husband? Why, he could have allied himself with any of the richest and most powerful men in England through her. But she chose your father, girl. Your poor and thoroughly unimportant father. Do you not understand, Lillis? Eleanor chose Jaward for her husband and gave herself to him so that her father would have no choice but to let them marry."

Lillis stared at her in disbelief.

Aunt Leta nodded. "Yes, and I never was able to understand how she managed to get away from those guards of hers to do it. Nevertheless, she was quite thoroughly ruined after that, and they were quietly married in the family chapel two days after Cousin John and your Aunt Madelyne were."

"Oh, my!"

"It is quite true, my dear, though I can certainly understand your surprise. But you mustn't be disgusted, Lillis, for I truly believe that your parents loved each other just exactly as they should have. If only you could have seen the way Eleanor looked at your father on their wedding day! I don't believe I have ever seen a more loving and radiant expression in my whole life. And your father! He was like a man walking on clouds! Yes, Lillis, they did love each other. You must never have any doubts about that.

"The difficulty that troubled their marriage was that so many men were in love with your beautiful mother and couldn't let their desire for her go. One of those men was my brother, Charles. He loved Elizabeth deeply, with his heart, but from the moment he set eyes on your mother he could not desire any other woman with his body. That's a terrible thing to say of one's brother, I know, but it is God's own truth. Charles made no secret of his desire for Eleanor, and even poor Elizabeth knew of it. Of course, it was the end of his friendship with Jaward. For years they neither spoke to nor saw one another. It was a dreadfully unpleasant time, and Charles, especially, was very hard to live with. He and Elizabeth fought constantly and for two years Elizabeth kept to her own chamber, refusing to have anything to do with him. In time they came to an understanding and resumed their relationship as man and wife, but matters between them weren't easy. Elizabeth suffered two miscarriages during the next four years, and when Charles heard that Eleanor had been successfully delivered of a child he was angry and said some terrible things about Elizabeth's inability to give him any more children.

"Six years after your parents' marriage, both families unwittingly went to court at the same time. I didn't attend because it was my custom to stay home with Alexander and Willem whenever my brother and Elizabeth went away, so the facts of what happened in London came to me secondhand, though I'm certain they are true.

"It seems that, during their stay in London, Charles succeeded in seducing your mother. At least, he succeeded in getting her into a chamber alone. I never was certain about whether he raped her or whether she gave in to him willingly or whether anything actually occurred at all. What I do know is that Elizabeth walked into the chamber and found them together and became thoroughly enraged. Your father must not have been far away, for Jaward, and many others, too, came running at the sound of Elizabeth's screams, and there he found his wife and Charles together in what looked like very damning circumstances. Charles laughed at your father, quite openly, and loudly announced to one and all that he had finally enjoyed the object of his greatest desire. Your poor mother only stood there and cried. If she was innocent in what had happened she must not have been able defend herself. Jaward certainly gave her no opportunity to explain. He and Elizabeth left court almost at once to journey back to Gyer and

Wellewyn. Somewhere along the journey they—comforted each other."

"And the twins were conceived," Lillis said bluntly.

Aunt Leta nodded. "Yes, although no one knew they were twins at the time. But Charles and Elizabeth hadn't enjoyed their conjugal rights for some time, and Elizabeth insisted that Jaward was the father of her unborn child. She had him sign a paper stating that fact and gave it into the keeping of one of her more powerful relatives as proof against any future punishment Charles might mete out to her or the child. Her belief was that if my brother ever dared to abuse her or her children she would make the document public so that he would be shamed. My brother's pride was a terrible thing. He never could have borne others knowing he'd been cuckolded, even though he'd publicly humiliated your father in exactly that way."

The thought filled Lillis with rage, and with hatred for a man she'd never even known.

"What happened to my mother?" she whispered.

Aunt Leta took a long drink of wine, then clasped her shaking hands tightly together. She didn't look at Lillis.

"Eleanor finally made her way home after what had happened at court," she said quietly. "Charles didn't bring her. He would have, I think, if she had let him, but of course she wanted nothing to do with him.

"There was a very kind man who was at court at that time, Sir Terence Simonton, who had once been my most favored suitor. Terence had always been the finest of men. I believed him when he said he loved me, though Charles would never receive him when he tried to speak to him of courting me." She glanced at Lillis. "I would have married Terence if I could have. I truly would."

Lillis neither moved nor responded to Aunt Leta's words, but only stared at her.

"Well," said Aunt Leta, looking away again, "Terence brought your mother home. He was perfectly proper, of course, and made certain that several acceptable women from court accompanied them the entire way, and never once mentioned the disgraceful episode at court."

"What happened to my mother?" Lillis pressed.

Aunt Leta fell quiet for a moment, then at last continued. "Your father would not receive her," she said in a voice thick with emotion. "She tried to speak with him and your father would not accept her. I have been told that she pleaded and pleaded with him and that he would not look at her, or speak to her, or even acknowledge her presence. Perhaps there was more to it. I don't know. Now that your father has died, none of us will ever know what truly happened between them on that day." Uncontrolled tears escaped her eyes. She wiped them away and cleared her throat. "Finally she—your mother—gave up trying to reason with him and went up to your nursery. From what I have heard she stayed there with you for many hours, holding and singing to you."

Lillis hugged her arms around herself and let her own tears fall. Memories of her mother flooded her. Always her remembrances of her mother had been vague, seen as they were through the eyes of a three-year-old child, yet suddenly they seemed very clear, and she could almost see the beautiful blond woman who had often come to her nursery and taken her out of her bed to hold and rock her. Lillis remembered perfectly how much she had loved touching her mother's unbound hair, and how her mother would laugh when she would take fistfuls of the white strands and tug on them.

When Aunt Leta spoke again her voice sounded labored and thin. "Finally—finally she put you back into your bed and made her way to the roof. She threw herself off. She killed herself. Your father—"

Lillis felt the loss as though it had only just happened, as though her mother had only died that moment. She began to tremble, and felt overcome by her grief. She covered her face with both hands and sat on the rushes and wept.

Aunt Leta struggled to regain some semblance of her own composure. Gently she set her arms around Lillis's shaking body. "There, there, my dear," she soothed. "Your mother loved you. She loved you, Lillis. You mustn't cry."

Lillis shook her head violently. "If she loved me," she cried, "then why did she leave me?"

"I think," Aunt Leta replied softly, "that she couldn't live without your father's love. Your poor mother was such a sweet and delicate creature. She couldn't face the anger he had greeted her with. I'm not even certain she was able to understand it, having been so admired as she was for so much of her life. You mustn't hold it against her, my dear. She loved you as deeply as any mother could love her child, of that I'm sure. She never would have left you if she hadn't felt she'd had no choice. You must believe that, for it is quite true."

Lillis cried quietly for several minutes while Aunt Leta comfortingly patted her back. Finally she wiped her face and lifted her eyes. "What happened to my father?"

"Your father found her first. He was never the same after that. Not toward you, or toward his people, or toward anyone else. My honest belief, Lillis, is that he would have forgiven her if she had only waited a little longer. He loved her so very much. She was his whole life. Even though he was hurt, I think he would have gotten over it soon enough."

Lillis nodded and sniffed. "What happened after that?"

Aunt Leta sat back in her chair and sighed. "After Eleanor's death, your father became very withdrawn, and perhaps even a bit demented. Other than you and a few particular servants, he didn't wish to see any living person. He buried Eleanor almost immediately, for when her father heard of her death he demanded that his daughter's body be brought to her family. He wished to bury her in the family site, you see, with all of the other Denys and Huntingtons. Jaward wouldn't allow it. Nor would he allow her family to attend whatever sort of funeral there was. He told them, in no uncertain terms, that they were never to come near Wellewyn or ever try to make contact with you. Ever. He said he would rather kill you with his own hands than let them take you from him, and they must have believed him, for they did as he said.

"We only saw him once after Eleanor's death. He came to Gyer all alone one early evening about six months after she had died, and sat on his horse in the courtyard, demanding to speak with the Lord of Gyer. He refused to come inside the castle itself. I watched the commotion from one of the long windows in the great hall and I remember being shocked at Jaward's appearance. He was so changed! He looked like an old man, for his hair had turned nearly white and his face was most haggard. When Charles went outside to meet him, his expression filled with a hatred that made him look even more wretched.

"Charles had been quite angry over the months that had passed, as well, and was furious that Elizabeth was pregnant with Jaward's child.

"They shouted at each other for the longest time, my dear. It was the most dreadful scene, made even worse by the memory of the close friendship they had once shared. At last they made some sort of declaration of war, and then— it was the strangest thing—they fell silent and simply stared at each other, as if they were both completely shocked by what they'd done. Everyone who watched could plainly see that the matter was very painful for them. Your father began to weep, just like a little child, and after a moment Charles began to cry, too. I shall never forget it. Jaward sat on his horse and stared at Charles and cried, and Charles sat on the castle steps and stared at Jaward and cried. So often, Lillis, I've thought that what happened to them in that moment was the final blow that killed the last bit of humanity in both those men.

"Your father turned his horse around and left Gyer, and Charles stared after him and cried for nearly an hour. No one was brave enough to go near him at the time, so we let him sit there on the castle steps all by himself. I don't believe I ever saw my brother more miserable than he was at that time, and I certainly never had seen him cry either before or since. It was his firm belief, you see, that men did not weep for any reason. Why, he didn't even cry when Elizabeth died, and he was quite horribly hard on Willem when the poor boy wept so openly. But Charles cried over the loss of Jaward. Just before he died, my brother told me that losing your father's friendship was the worst thing that had ever happened to him. Worse than our parents' deaths, worse than your mother's death, even worse than Elizabeth's death. I begged him to let me send a messenger to Jaward to ask him to come, but he would not let me."

"You should have done it anyway!" Lillis declared angrily.

Aunt Leta nodded. "Yes," she admitted, "I should have, for I do believe it would have meant a great deal to both men to have reconciled their differences while they still had a chance to do so, but my brother wouldn't let me, and unless you can understand the kind of life I led under my brother's hand you cannot understand why I did not disobey him."

Lillis felt instantly ashamed. "Forgive me, my lady. I never should have spoken to you so rudely."

Aunt Leta smiled. "I'm not offended, child. You haven't said anything I've not thought a thousand times and more, myself. Do not distress yourself over the matter." She let out a long sigh and gazed at the fire. "I never saw your father again after that day. More than fifteen years. We heard about him from time to time. Occasionally a servant who had been at Wellewyn would come to Gyer and we would have news of him. He let most of his serving people go, for he wanted to be left alone, and he stopped managing Wellewyn altogether, allowing it to fall into the greatest ruin. You couldn't have understood these things when you were a child, of course, because your father kept you so very cloistered. You couldn't have known that the rest of the world lived any differently."

"No," Lillis admitted. "I remember being amazed at the things I saw when he sent me away to Tynedale. Even the convent was a revelation to me. Compared to Wellewyn it was quite luxurious."

"But why did he send you there?" asked Aunt Leta. "There was no need for it. He could have continued to keep you here at Wellewyn."

"He wanted me to have an education and wasn't able to afford a private tutor," she replied. "The sisters at Tyne-dale taught and trained me in return for my services there. Papa didn't have to pay them anything, you see. But I was very happy at Tynedale and my father did provide Edyth to accompany me, and having known her has been an invaluable gift in itself."

They fell quiet again, until at last Lillis said, "My poor mother. How terribly she must have suffered."

"Yes," agreed Aunt Leta quietly.

"And my poor father. Is it any wonder that he was so upset when Alexander forced me into marriage? Can you imagine what he must have gone through, knowing that the son of his worst enemy, the son of the man who had been partly to blame for his wife's death, had married his only child? It must have seemed to him as though your brother had somehow reached out from the grave and destroyed the last and only thing that held any value for him."

Aunt Leta's expression was steady. "What you say is true, Lillis, but you mustn't blame Alexander. He has never known about what passed between his father and yours, and he was still so young when their friendship ended that he has no memory of Jaward at all. You know as well as I that he's been unable to understand why your father hated him so greatly all of these years."

"I don't blame Alexander for any of it," Lillis said. "I loved my father, but I know very well that he was an angry, vengeful man. He gave Alexander no choice in what happened. Indeed, my father had only himself to blame for my forced marriage."

"That is quite true, Lillis," Aunt Leta agreed. "I'm glad to know you feel this way, for I am sure Alexander will appreciate your sentiments once he finally knows the truth."

"Alexander and I have closed the circle, have we not?" Lillis said. "We love each other and have united the two families. Our children will make the final seal. The wound will be healed now."

"We must pray it will be so."

"And Hugh and Hugo are my brothers," Lillis said with a shake of her head, smiling in disbelief. "My very own terrible, wonderful brothers. What an odd thing."

"Yes," said Aunt Leta once more, "though I fear the truth will devastate them. Charles Baldwin loved those boys. They were all he had left of Jaward, and all of the love he'd once felt for Jaward he gave to Jaward's sons. The twins were his pride and joy, and what they felt for him was, and still is, something close to worship. Do you know, I've often wondered why Jaward never tried to make a claim to them, for he certainly must have heard of their birth, and must have known he had two sons being raised at Gyer."

"I do not know," Lillis replied. "Perhaps he felt they were better there. Perhaps, in spite of his hatred for Charles Baldwin, he realized the man would raise them well. Perhaps he knew he didn't have enough love in himself to share with them, especially as he would always have associated them with the events surrounding my mother's death. Like much of the tale, it is something we'll never know." She ran the palms of her hands over her face, and smoothed back several loose strands of hair. "I shall go and fetch the children," she said, rising to her feet, "and we shall have our midday meal."

"That would be welcome, indeed," Aunt Leta said, wiping the last hints of her own tears away. "Our conversation has made me most hungry, I fear."

"Aunt Leta," Lillis said, smiling warmly at her, "you are a very kind lady, and I thank you for what you've told me this day. I know it was not easy, and for that I thank you all the more. I will forever be in your debt."

She left before the older woman could give a reply, and in a moment pushed open the door that led to the gardens. She stopped there, at the door, and took in the beauty of the world. How odd it was, she thought, that life could give one so much joy, as well as such great sorrow. Her mother and father were dead and gone. Their passings had been tragic, and their lives had been equally so. Gazing into the cold blue of the December sky, Lillis vowed that she would never allow such misery to alter her own life, or Alexander's, or their unborn child's—the child she was now certain she carried.

"All will be well, my little one," she promised in a soft, private whisper, setting one hand against the place where her child even now grew within her. "I will never leave you of my own free choice, neither you, nor your father again. All will be well."

Chapter Twenty-Three

A foot kicked him in the thigh, hard, and the sharpness of the pain radiated all the way into his chin.

"Come now, Alex," a blurred voice said from far away, "you cannot expect me to spend all night waiting for you to wake, can you? I've a great many matters to take care of and you, my Lord Gyer, are the least of them."

Another kick made Alexander groan. He tried to open his eyes, to bring his muddled thoughts into focus, to simply move. All he could do was groan again.

The voice laughed and came a little closer. "The great Lord of Gyer! Who would have thought he could be so easily turned into a weakling babe with the merest of strikes? My God, I don't know why I never thought to do it earlier! If I'd known it would be so easy I certainly would have. But come, Alex, for I'm losing patience and haven't the time to coddle you. Wake up, man, else I'll kill you without delay and put us both out of our misery."

Alexander gingerly cracked one eye open, then the other. He blinked once, twice, then finally managed to keep his lids open long enough to see. And what he saw was rather odd. There was nothing but gray everywhere. Gray. He blinked once more and looked again, then realized at last, that he was staring at a bare stone floor. A cold, bare, *hard* stone floor upon which his entire body was stretched out, face-down.

Thinking to turn himself over, he tried to move and found that he could not. He lay thoughtfully for a few seconds, and finally decided that his hands were tied rather tightly behind his back. As soon as his dull brain registered this fact true, Alexander was then able to make a full assessment of his situation. He was lying facedown on a cold, hard, bare floor and he was trussed up like a felled deer. Yes, that was exactly the way things were at the moment. It was strange, he thought calmly, that he wasn't yet wary of his predicament. Perhaps the painful throbbing on the left side of his head had something to do with that.

Another rough kick, this time catching him in the upper chest, sent Alexander thudding over onto his back and he lay there, helpless as an overturned turtle, blinking up into the dim light of the room.

Someone loomed over him; a familiar face grinned down at him.

"That is better, is it not, Alex?"

"Hello, John," Alexander replied thickly, his mind reeling. "What's this about?"

John tilted his head and gazed curiously at Alexander. "Still a bit groggy, are you? I suppose Miles did hit you rather harder than I had expected he would, though you certainly cannot blame the lad for being thorough. Perhaps I can help you regain your senses a little. I do so want you to understand every word I'm about to say to you. I've not worked so hard and waited so long for this moment to have you sleep through the whole of it." He waved one hand in the air and stepped back.

Alexander didn't have a chance to sort out the words John had said before a wave of cold water poured over him, catching him so thoroughly unawares that a great deal of the fluid splashed into his mouth and nostrils, causing him to choke and sputter. Before he came to any harm, however, two strong hands grasped his collar and yanked him into a sitting position, allowing him the chance to cough the water out. He was roughly propped up with a chair behind his back.

"That should hold him," a gravelly voice stated.

Alexander sat with his head hanging down, furiously working to calm the wet, choking coughs that gripped him.

As uncomfortable as the method was, John had certainly been right about the water clearing his head, and now Alexander strove to understand what kind of danger he was in, and why.

The last thing he could remember before waking here—wherever here was—was walking into his bedchamber after having completed a particularly arduous bout of training with his men, and calling for Fyodor to come and help him bathe and dress. And that was the last thing—the very last thing he could remember. Or was it? He shook his aching head and drew in a long, unsteady breath. What had happened to Fyodor? He hadn't been in the chamber or, at least, he hadn't answered Alexander's call. Someone else must have been there. Someone who had evidently been able to hit him on the head hard enough to cause him to lose his senses. Someone, or some ones, rather, who'd been strong enough to carry him out of his room and to... where? His breathing was slower now, calmer. He cautiously lifted his head.

The chamber was filthy and very dark. The only light came from the flame of a small candle placed on a nearby table, hardly bright enough to illuminate more than a few inches of the dusty, muggy atmosphere. Alexander's eyes moved over what he could see of the room. There was a great deal of clutter, though nothing truly distinguishable in the darkness. Two men stood out of the weak sphere of light so that Alexander couldn't tell who they were. They looked big from the outline of their shapes, and their stances were watchful and taut, their arms folded against their chests. John stood closer by, leaning against the table and looking happy and relaxed. His arms were also folded across his chest, though loosely, and he had one ankle crossed over the other in a posture of comfort. He was still grinning.

"Feeling better now, Cousin?" John asked politely.

Alexander growled at him. "What game is this, John Baldwin? You were supposed to be out hunting these past two days."

"Yes, that's true," John agreed pleasantly. "In fact, I'm still out hunting. There will be all manner of witnesses who will testify to having seen me and my men as far away as Chestershire this very hour and day."

Alexander didn't need to have this statement explained; the meaning was all too clear. "Witnesses, you say? So that's the way of it, is it?"

"Aye, Cousin, it is."

"I see. And where exactly are we? I suppose I have a right to know where my place of death is to be."

John laughed with delight. "You don't know where you are, Alex? I'm shocked, truly. Lillis would be wounded to know that you didn't remember this chamber."

Remembrance washed over Alexander just as the water had. "Ah," he said with a short nod, "my wife's room of initial imprisonment." He looked around the filthy place again and shuddered, disgusted to think that his beautiful wife had ever been kept here for so many hours. Another thought struck him. He turned to look at John again. "We're still at Gyer?"

"Yes," John replied simply.

"And you plan to kill me here, at Gyer? In this room?"

"Yes. That's right."

"I suppose I should have expected something like this from you, and been on my guard, though to be honest I always thought you little more than a spineless wart and incapable of such a deed. But let me ask, do you think it wise to kill me in my own home? Do you not fear being caught for the crime?"

"Not at all, Alex," replied John easily, lifting one hand to inspect his nails, "though I do appreciate your concern. But there's really nothing for you to worry over. It's going to be very neatly done, you see, and there will be no clues left to lead to me. In fact, my dear cousin, your death will be seen as a suicide rather than as a murder."

Alexander's eyebrows rose in interest. "Is that so, *dear* Cousin? I'm sorry to disappoint you, then, but I've no intention whatsoever of killing myself—not now or ever. And especially not in the near future."

John chuckled. "But of course you have, Alex. Everyone knows how terribly unhappy you've been since you and your lovely wife have parted ways. It's common knowledge that you've been drinking heavily night after night, and that you've been letting the estates run into mismanaged ruin. Why, all the castlefolk have been able to speak of little else save how depressed their lord is, and how quiet and withdrawn he has become. I, myself, shall have to come forward after your funeral and reluctantly tell of the many, many times when you privately expressed your misery to me, and of the countless times you told me that you would rather die than go on without your beloved Lillis. And Barbara will finally admit to the nights when, in your misery and loneliness, you drunkenly tried, and failed, to find relief in her open arms. Your failures added to your misery and feelings of your lack of manhood, of course."

"Of course," Alexander said angrily. "There's only one problem with your plan, lackwit."

"Oh, and what is that?"

"It's all false! That's what! There's not a person in all of Gyer who would believe such a ridiculous pack of lies! Those in the castle know that Lillis and I have reconciled our differences and are planning to end our separation, and no one has seen me either depressed or drunk or lazy, for I've been none of those things. If anything I've been working even harder in order to make Gyer ready for Lillis's return, and *that* is what they have seen. Letting Gyer run into ruin, indeed! I truly would have to be dead to ever let that happen." Alexander struggled against his bonds with frustration. "By God, John, if I could get out of these damned ropes I would break your face in six different places!"

"Yes, I do believe you would, Alex," John said pleasantly, "if you could get out of those damned ropes, which, of course, you cannot. Now, as to everything you say, I must agree that you are, in truth, correct. However, if there is one valuable lesson I've learned in my life it is that people are very, very easy to manage. A few rumors dropped here and a few words of doubt dropped there and very soon even our sweet Aunt Leta will be recalling instances of your deep and dreadful depression." He laughed and pushed away from the table, walking closer to where Alexander sat, helplessly bound. "Human nature, Cousin," he said with a shake of his head, "is a wonderful thing." He squatted down until their heads were almost level. "In fact, I do believe it would be quite true to say that people are easier to lead along than sheep. Do you not think so?"

"What I think," replied Alexander, glaring at him, "is that you are an idiot."

John grinned and leaned forward just enough so that he could take hold of one of Alexander's eyebrows and tug it painfully. He laughed when Alexander grimaced, and said, "I'd not test me too far, were I you, Cousin, especially not when you know full well that I've the power to make your death a long and painful one. Indeed, you should be grateful that I know how to compromise. I'd have preferred to make you suffer, but in the end I had to bow to the necessity that your death must be quick and, therefore, relatively painless. But only relatively. If I cannot give you physical pain, I can at least enjoy giving you mental pain."

"Indeed? I suppose you'll tell me why you want me dead, then?"

"Oh, yes, dear Cousin, I'm going to tell you. But would you not like to try and guess first?"

"What I would like to do is break every bone in your body," Alexander said, "but I'll play your guessing game, if only to amuse myself. You want to kill me because I set Barbara aside."

"No," John said. "It would have been easier if you had married Barbara, but I was already planning on killing you long before you set her aside."

"Well, it's good to know that I've been supporting a crazed murderer in my home these past many years," Alexander commented dryly. "Next you'll tell me that the lady I was betrothed to since I was a boy was also planning on murdering me."

"Barbara was helping me, true, but she didn't exactly know I was planning on killing you."

"She didn't *exactly* know?" Alexander repeated incredulously.

John shrugged. "You know what Barbara is. She probably understood well enough what my intentions were but didn't wish to dwell on them. Ignorance is bliss, you know."

"My God!" Alexander whispered, shocked. "My God!"

"Yes, I know," John commiserated, thoughtfully rubbing his chin. "Love is a blinding nuisance, is it not? And you were certainly blind when it came to Barbara. When I think of how easily she wrapped you around her childish finger I am truly amazed. The great Alexander Baldwin, Lord of Gyer, led about like an obedient dog by a tiny, silly little creature like Barbara. Human nature, I tell you, Alex. It is simply astounding!"

He stood. "But I've little time to waste in discussing such matters with you, Alex. I'm sorry, but you must understand how much I have to accomplish tonight. Shall I simply tell you why I'm going to kill you and then we can get on with it?"

Alexander didn't think he had ever heard such a cold statement in all of his life. "I suppose so," he muttered angrily, casting about for a way to get out of this ridiculous situation.

"I wish to be Lord of Gyer, of course. I'm surprised you hadn't thought of that. It's not a purely selfish desire on my part, for I do feel that I'm much more suited to such greatness than you are. You're really too common to be in such a powerful position, Alex. Too common and too... dull, I suppose you could say. The Lord of Gyer should be a man of cunning, a man of sharp wit and high intelligence."

"And you are that man?"

John smiled and graciously half bowed. "As you see. But that isn't the only reason I desire to inherit the position. Mostly I want to do it for Barbara, to see her happy and well cared for. My sister deserves the very finest things in life, as I am sure you will agree, or once would have agreed, and I shall be able to give them to her when I am master here."

"But you said that you meant to kill me even if I'd married Barbara," Alexander stated, tugging at his ropes again. "If we had married I would have given her everything I owned to make her happy. And while we were betrothed I gave her anything she asked for, from jewels to the finest gowns. Yet you still wanted me dead?''

''I was willing to have Barbara safely settled as the Lady of Gyer before your death, Alex, but you cannot think that I actually wished my beloved darling to be chained to a man like you for the rest of her life.'' A shudder physically passed through John. ''God's body! Just the thought of her having to put up with your advances used to make me ill. My poor, sweet girl! The way you used to drool all over her was sickening!''

Though Alexander was in an extremely vulnerable position and knew that he was possibly facing death, he still had the presence of mind to know when he was being insulted. ''What exactly is wrong with being married to a man like me?'' he demanded.

''Come, now, Alex,'' John chided, ''you would have to ask Lillis to have your answer, would you not? Even she had the good sense to leave you when she could. Now, please, stop trying to free yourself. You cannot escape, so you'd best keep your temper and save your strength. Suffice it to say, Cousin, that no man is worthy of my Barbara and, in fact, she will never marry, or not for long, if she does. She will stay with her loving brother and I shall take care of her, as only I know how to do. Perhaps, if I can find some suitable old man to match her with in the future I shall, but you may be certain that he will die, too, once she is assured of inheriting a great deal from him, and then she will come back to me.''

''You,'' Alexander said, ''are insane.''

''Perhaps,'' John agreed affably, ''but I'm not the one who is about to die, am I? Perhaps being insane isn't such a bad thing.''

''You are also a fool,'' Alexander added.

John expressed a mild interest in these words. ''How so?''

''You'll never become the Lord of Gyer simply by killing me. I do have brothers, you know. Four of them, to be exact. Do you not think people will become suspicious if you start killing them off one by one?''

John leaned against the table and sighed. He shook his head and looked at Alexander with what might have passed for pity. "We've come to this so soon, have we? It's just as well, since I really haven't much time to spend with you. The truth, Alex, is that you don't have four brothers. Well, you *do* have four brothers, but you *don't* have four brothers who could inherit your title and estate. You only have two. Actually, as of now you only have one."

An alarm went off in Alexander's head. Until that moment the threat of danger had only been against himself, but now John talked of harming his brothers, his family. Damn! He had to get out of here!

"What are you saying?" he demanded, his fingers twisting in the ropes.

"Before I explain about your brothers, let me explain about my original plan," John said. "I think it's important that you understand everything before you die because I want you to suffer as finely as possible." He smiled like a happy child with a new toy. "My original plan was for you and Barbara to marry and remain married for, oh, say three months or so before your death. I had intended for you to die on the battlefield, like a true knight of the realm. You and Willem both, I mean, for he had to go, as well, you understand, being next in line to the title. It was a very good plan, if I do say so, for even if your deaths had to be helped along a bit no one would have suspected foul play. You would have died as honorable warriors and all would have been well."

Alexander almost laughed. "You *are* ready for the mad asylum, John. How is it that Willem and I were to die on the battlefield when there is no war? Were you going to start one yourself, or were you . . . going to . . ." His voice died away with sudden realization. His eyes met John's, and when John began to laugh Alexander nearly went mad. He fought against his ropes until his arms were cut and bleeding. "Bastard!" he shouted. "You damned, demented, evil bastard! You were the one behind the trouble with Jaward, weren't you? *Weren't you?*"

John's face lit with real pleasure. "I must admit, Cousin Alex, seeing you like this is better than I ever anticipated. Of course I was the one behind it. Do you begin to appreciate my brilliance now? Manipulating Jaward into building that dam was the easiest thing I've ever done. He was ripe with hatred for you, or rather, for your father. He wanted to see Gyer go down in flames, he did, and enjoyed every single second of suffering that your people went through." He laughed. "A man after my own heart, he was. Whenever I brought him news of yet another field gone to rot he would actually smile, believe it or no, and there was a man whom it hurt to smile. Having his daughter marry Jason de Burgh was my idea, as well. I knew you would think they were going to join together against you, and that you would probably declare war on one or both of them. It was all going so perfectly, too, until the twins brought Lillis home." He gave a sigh.

"And ruined all your plans."

John nodded and looked momentarily displeased. "Those damned twins! I could have killed them for making such a ruin of my hard work, especially after you decided to marry Lillis. And Jaward! Lord! I've never seen a more degraded man in my life. I tried and tried to force him to hold firm against you, but he would not. The thought of his precious darling marrying you made him as weak and worthless as a newborn babe. I doubt anything has ever given me more satisfaction than killing that old man."

Alexander felt as though he were suddenly suffocating. "You killed Jaward?" he said with disbelief.

John nodded and rested his hands on the edge of the table. "Strangled him," he said. "It was quite pleasant, really. I should have liked to try it on you, save your neck is a good deal thicker than Jaward's was and it might take too much time. Still, you cannot imagine what a good feeling it is to have someone's neck in the power of your hands." He lifted his hands in front of himself to demonstrate on a nonexistent neck. He twisted them in a convincing squeezing motion. "It's warm and soft and pliable. Mmm. Most pleasant. Especially when you can feel the breath stop coming through. That's the best part." He dropped his hands back to the table. "Jaward didn't put up much of a fight, being such a weak old man, but it was quite satisfactory nonetheless."

Alexander thought for a dreadful moment that he was going to lose his midday meal. If John had truly killed Jaward then he was capable of doing anything—of killing anyone.

"You said I've only one brother left now who can inherit Gyer." His voice was a hoarse whisper.

"Yes, that's true," replied John, "though you only had two full brothers who could do so to begin with. The twins, Hugh and Hugo, are only your half brothers, you see, and as you were present at their birthing, I don't think I need explain that you are only related to them through your mother."

Alexander was struck dumb, not so much by this revelation as by what John was leading up to. His heart began to beat more rapidly and his breathing sounded labored even to his own ears. His cousin seemed to be waiting for some response, but Alexander could not give it. He stared at John out of wide eyes and shook his head slightly.

"Aren't you even going to accuse me of lying?" John asked with disappointment, like a spoiled child being denied a treat. "You didn't know this already, did you? I made certain I should be the one to tell you!"

If he had proceeded to peevishly stamp his feet Alexander wouldn't have been surprised. Since he was behaving like a child, perhaps it might be best to treat him as one. "I didn't know," he forced himself to say.

"Well, then, will you not demand to know who their real father is?"

Alexander shook his head mutely. He didn't believe that Hugh and Hugo weren't his full blood brothers, but what he thought didn't matter. John obviously believed that they were not, and if the twins weren't in John's way then only Willem and Justin were left to dispose of, and John had said that only one of them was left now—

John huffed and made an impatient gesture. "Aren't you going to at least have the decency to look shocked at discovering that your sainted mother was no better than the village whore? Oh, God! This is useless! If I didn't know that I had better arrows left to aim at your heart I would kill you now and have done with it. But since you don't seem to care about the status of your twin brothers, perhaps you'll be interested to know what I've done regarding your remaining brothers."

Dread seized Alexander so completely that he could barely think. He couldn't keep the panic from his voice when he asked, shakily, "What—what have you done?"

John laughed, pleased. "That's better. I can almost smell the fear in you now, Alex. So you want to know what I've done, do you? Well, I'll tell you what I've not done first and let you worry a little longer. I have *not* harmed Justin. Not yet, anyway. I haven't quite decided how much longer I shall let him live, especially since I shall be made his guardian and shall be able to control him until he comes of age. It wouldn't do to kill him off too quickly, of course, because people might become suspicious if that were to happen. No, I believe I'll wait and decide about Justin's fate in, say, four or five more years. It won't be necessary to harm Candis, so you needn't worry over her. She shows every promise of growing into a very beautiful lady one day, and so will be more valuable alive than dead. I'll wait until she's twelve, perhaps, and then sell her to the highest bidder." John smiled at the thought. "There are some men in England who will pay almost any price to obtain a beautiful young lady. Or perhaps, if I find her to my liking when she is a bit older, I'll keep her for my own private pleasures." He shrugged and scratched his chin. "But that is not your worry now, my lord."

Every single word that came out of John's mouth regarding his siblings sickened and enraged Alexander, but nothing could keep his mind from wanting to shout out the one question he wanted answered. "Willem," he whispered, the very word an agony to say.

John chuckled and leaned forward as though he hadn't clearly heard. "What was that, Lord Gyer? What did you say?"

Alexander felt hot and cold all at the same time. A shiver ran through his spine. "Willem," he managed more loudly.

"Ah, you are asking me about Willem," John returned pleasantly, moving forward so that he could squat in front of Alexander again. "You want to know what I have done to dear, kind Willem. Well, I shall tell you." He stuck his nose right in front of Alexander's. "I've killed him." He leaned back after making this pronouncement and laughed out loud, thoroughly pleased.

Great drops of sweat poured down Alexander's face, and his breath came in short, painful gasps. It wasn't true, he told himself. It could not be true. This whole hellish nightmare was not true. "You lie," he murmured, then again, more loudly, "You lie! Willem is not dead!"

John laughed so hard that he had to rest on his knees. He shook his head and laughed so that he couldn't speak. Finally, gasping for breath between spurts of glee, he wiped his wet eyes and looked back at Alexander. "Oh, this is good, Alex. Truly good." He wiped his eyes again. "This is what I've dreamed of for so very long. But you think that I am lying, do you? At last we have the insistence that I am lying.

Untying a small leather pouch from his belt, John said, "I've proof of what I say." He opened the pouch and dug his fingers inside, carefully drawing out something that Alexander could not quite see in the dimness of the room. John held it up and Alexander's sharp intake of breath made him giggle. "I thought you would recognize this," he said merrily, "which is why I took it. You gave Willem this seal of honor yourself, did you not? It's quite bloody at the moment and perhaps doesn't look exactly as it should, but that couldn't be helped. He always wore it over his heart, and I did place my arrow in just that spot. See, if you look closely you can see where the arrow nicked it." He leaned forward and pointed with one finger to the spot he mentioned, then grinned fully into Alexander's pained expression. "Good shot, don't you think? I had a devil of a time cutting the seal off with that arrow in the way."

"Oh, my God!" Alexander uttered, unable to stop the hot tears that stung his eyes. "Willem." He collapsed against the chair and almost wished that John would kill him. The proof John had shown him was inarguable. Alexander couldn't even say that his cousin had obtained the seal from some other source, for he'd only ever given that badge to one person, to Willem; there had never been another like it made. The thought that Willem was gone overwhelmed him. His head fell back and the tears streamed silently down his face. He sobbed imperceptibly. He was too stricken by his grief to more fully express it.

"Most satisfactory," he heard John's much hated voice say. "In truth, Alex, I shall carry this moment with me for the rest of my life and think of it often whenever I shall wish to lighten my mood. But enough." He sighed. "It has been delightful, but I'm afraid I must kill you now and get going. I still have Lillis to attend to, you know."

The sound of his beloved's name coming from such foul lips and being spoken with such obvious intent sent Alexander into a frenzy. "Lillis?" he shouted, and reflexively lunged at John, knocking him over just before he, himself, hit the floor.

John didn't seem offended by the limited attack, and quickly rose, brushing himself off and laughing. He stood over the place where Alexander lay struggling and watched him as though he were watching a very interesting bug.

Alexander, on the other hand, was experiencing feelings of horror and fury such as he had never known existed. "You filthy lunatic!" he raged, fighting the ropes with every ounce of strength in his body. "You do not dare to touch my wife! I will skin you alive if you so much as look in her direction! I will crush you like a flea beneath my palm! I will—"

John kicked him in the groin, twice, to silence him. The acute pain effectively quieted Alexander, as well as doubled him over, though it in no way lessened his wrath.

"Really, Alex, you are most amusing," said John, "but as I have repeatedly told you, I don't have any more time to spend with you. I realize you're worried about your lovely wife and I do wish I could stay a little longer and enjoy your misery, but it's a long ride to Wellewyn and I must be there as quickly as possible. I promise that Lillis won't be made to suffer any more than you will. That will give you some small comfort as you are dying, will it not?" He sighed. "I must admit, I had at first planned to keep her alive and make her my mistress. You may find this difficult to believe, but I truly do have the greatest affection for the lovely Lillis. Such a beautiful woman! And so much fire, as well. We would have made the most striking couple. But, unfortunately, I received the unhappy information just this morn that she is very likely carrying your brat, and as I cannot risk the chance of her birthing a more legitimate heir to your title I think I must forego my own pleasures and kill her." He looked toward his men. "Bring the poison, Miles. Aaron, hold him still, will you?"

In moments Alexander found himself tugged back into a sitting position. He struggled but couldn't move against the combination of the ropes and the now strong arms that held him. John knelt before him again and uncorked a small bottle that had been handed to him by one of his men.

"Damn, you, John—!"

A rough hand grasped a fistful of his hair and painfully jerked his head back.

John leaned closer and smiled as he swirled the contents of the bottle, mixing them. "This poison will work within a few minutes, Alex, and you shouldn't experience any pain from it. You will fall asleep, you see, and perhaps, when you awake, if you've been very good all your life, you shall be with Lillis and Willem again. That is something to pray for, is it not? Now, please don't be foolish and fight me, for I need get only a few drops down your throat to kill you, and surely you realize how perfectly helpless you are by now. You are going to die, Cousin, and so you must spend your last few minutes praying to God for mercy."

Alexander stared into John's smiling face and realized that he was right. He was going to die, there was nothing left for him to do but make one last plea. For Lillis he would do anything. He would beg. "Don't harm Lillis," he whispered. "I'm begging you, John, don't harm her."

John grinned and patted Alexander's cheek. "Begging, are you? What a sweet sound that is, Alex. Now, open wide and take this like a good boy."

Alexander turned his head sharply to avoid the bottle that John set to his lips. The hands that held him jerked him back.

"Oh, dear, you've decided to be difficult, have you? Well, it won't do you any good. Just a few drops will do the trick." John's fingers bit into Alexander's lips and he managed to wedge the bottle up against his cousin's clenched teeth. "There," he said, relieved as the fluid poured into Alexander's mouth, spilling equally on his neck and face and clothes. He patted Alexander's face again. "Goodbye, Alexander Baldwin," he said.

Alexander was so quickly and suddenly released that he fell facedown again. He turned his head and watched John as he corked the bottle again. Strangely, he felt almost calm.

"Don't kill Lillis," he said.

John ignored him and conferred with his men. "You know what to do. He should be dead in no more than five minutes. When he is, untie the ropes and place the bottle next to his body. Make certain to wipe the blood from his wrists, else people might wonder. Take the ropes with you and burn them right away. They're the only evidence that could be used against us."

"Do not kill Lillis!" Alexander shouted as loudly as he could.

"You needn't worry if he decides to shout until he goes," John told his men. "No one could possibly hear him up here. Make certain no one sees you leaving. Very well, then, I'm off." He picked up his gloves and his cloak and turned back to look at Alexander as he put them on.

"Goodbye, dear Cousin. Pleasant dreams." He turned on his heel and left the room, leaving Alexander alone with the two silent guardians.

Alexander closed his eyes and gave in to a feeling of complete helplessness. He was going to die and John was going to kill Lillis. It was too horrible to think of.

"God in heaven," he whispered, "save my wife and my family. Let me see my brother Willem when I next open my eyes, but don't let my wife be dead, as well. I loved her— love her. Please—"

He yawned and knew, with detachment, that he was dying. He was beginning to feel light-headed and weak, and his whole body started relaxing. As he fell asleep he held on to only one thought, one name, and then, when he could no longer hold on to her, he slipped into peaceful darkness.

Chapter Twenty-Four

"Barbara, sweet, just try to remember exactly what it was that you put in the bottle. Was it water? Or wine, or ale?"

"I am trying to remember, Jason, but I wish you would be a little more patient! I have had a *most* trying day, and you cannot be so mean as to expect me to remember everything that I did two days ago."

An impatient sigh, then, "Yes, my darling, I know you've been through a great deal these past few days, but if you will only try to think a *little* bit harder. Can you not remember what you put in the bottle? Try to rethink your steps on that day. You went into your brother's room and then—?"

"Oh, God! This is madness! If you don't remember what it was that you put into that bottle, Barbara, I'll strangle you!"

A loud bout of high-pitched tears and wailing followed this rather pointed statement.

"If all you're going to do is shout at her, Baldwin, then you can damned well go away! We don't need you bleeding all over the place, anyway, and I'll not allow Barbara to be upset after all she's suffered. And you might remember that you'd not now be alive were it not for Barbara." The harsh voice grew softer after that. "There, now, my love, don't cry. He didn't mean to shout at you."

"But he—he did!"

More wailing. Alexander groaned and made a useless effort to move.

"God's feet, Barbara! This is no time for such childishness! I only want you to remember whatever it was that you put into that damned bottle!"

"I think, Sir Willem," came an icy retort, "that it might be best if you kept your mouth shut. I'll take care of Barbara. Now, darling, you must calm yourself and try to remember exactly what it was that you put into that damned bottle—I mean, into that bottle. Think hard now."

"Well," said Barbara, sniffling delicately, "I went into John's chamber and got the box out of its hiding place. It's a locking box, you know, that he bought from a very interesting man in London some years back. It has the most clever device for opening and closing, and is made of the prettiest rosewood from Italy. Or is it Greece? Well, I do know that it is made of rosewood. Or is it cherry wood? It is red colored and very pretty—"

A patient voice interrupted her. "Yes, darling, I'm certain it is very pretty, but what did you do after you took it from its hiding place?"

"I opened it. Yes, that's just what I did. I put it on a table and I opened it and then I... hmm."

"What did you do after that, Barbara?"

"I took the bottle out—yes, that's right. There were several bottles in the box but I knew which one it was because the poison was the same color as—well, of course! That's what I put into the bottle!"

"What?"

"Why, Jason, how foolish of me. I don't know how I ever forgot. The poison was the color of ink, so I poured it out and then filled the bottle with ink."

"With—ink?"

"Yes." Barbara giggled. "Was that not clever of me?"

"You mean to say that my brother had *ink* poured down his throat?"

"Barbara must be right, Baldwin. That would explain why his mouth and tongue are black, and why there are so many dark stains on his clothes. We should have thought of it ourselves."

"But if it was only ink, why is he so still?"

"He's breathing, is he not?" came the terse reply. "It's the residue of the poison left in the bottle that's affected him, most like. Barbara didn't have time to wash the bottle out, after all, did you, my darling?"

Alexander felt a large, callused hand strike his face none too gently.

"Wake up, Lord Gyer! Wake up!"

Alexander tried to groan again and hoped that they could hear him. Happy as he was to know that he was alive, he wasn't in the mood to be slapped around.

"He moved! He made a sound."

"Willem's right, Jason! I think Cousin Alex *is* trying to move."

"Is he? I believe you're right, my love. Let's see if we can't wake him a little better." Three more rapid slaps did just that. If Alexander could have moved he would have gladly strangled the fiend who was hitting him.

"Give way, de Burgh. You don't want to knock him out all over again, do you?" A more gentle hand gripped one of his. "Alex? Alex, can you hear me? It's Willem. Open your eyes and let me know you're all right."

Alexander felt as though he'd drunk tree sap rather than ink, for his mouth was strangely gummy, but he groaned again and tried to move his tongue.

"Wil-lem," he breathed.

"Yes, that's right, Alex. It's Willem. Thank God! Thank God you're alive."

"Willem," Alexander repeated, and cracked his eyes open.

"He's waking now," stated Jason de Burgh, whose unwelcome face Alexander saw first as that man was leaning directly over him. De Burgh turned away and addressed someone behind him. "Fetch the leech and have someone go tell everyone below that the Lord of Gyer is alive and well. They can cease their mourning and wailing."

Barbara's bright face came into view, peering over the Lord of Dunsted's shoulder. She tilted her head and her gaze was uncertain as she looked at him.

"Cousin Alex doesn't look very well, does he?"

De Burgh smiled at her lovingly. "He'll be fine, dearest. He only needs a moment to gain his senses. You saved his life, as well as Willem's, do you know that? If you'd not switched the poison he would be long dead now."

Barbara blushed and lowered her lashes. "Are you very pleased with me, Jason?"

"Very," Jason replied, and kissed her.

This most affecting scene made Alexander groan again. He rolled his eyes around until he caught sight of Willem, who was gazing at him with tears rolling freely down his face. Alexander grinned and weakly pressed his brother's hand.

"Willem," he whispered, "you're alive."

Willem nodded mutely and continued to cry.

"Thank God. John told me he had killed you. He had proof. I believed him. I thought you were dead."

Willem wiped his face and beamed at Alexander. "Proof like this?" he asked, gingerly pointing to his left shoulder, which was open and torn and bloody.

"God's mercy! Willem!"

"It looks worse than it is," Willem assured him quickly. "He shot me through the shoulder and was certain I would die shortly. I should have thought so, too, had I shot a man in such a way. But, other than hurting like Hades, I don't think too much trouble was done. I can still move my arm, and de Burgh was able to pull the arrow out without too much agony, so I'm content. The bastard stole my seal, though."

Alexander smiled at him. "I will replace it if you like. I'll give you a hundred seals if you like. Dear God, Willem, I thought you were dead." He gripped Willem's hand more tightly. "Help me to sit, brother."

"Slowly, Alex, slowly. You're very weak."

"And you," Alexander said as he struggled into a sitting position, "look as pale as very death." He eyed Willem's still-bleeding wound. "You should be abed, Willem. You're lucky to be alive."

"I know, Alex. I know. I wouldn't be alive at all if it hadn't been for Barbara." He glanced toward where Barbara was being held in the arms of Jason de Burgh. "John left several of his men to make certain I didn't live long. They were going to run me through with a sword and finish me off, but before they could, de Burgh showed up with all of his men. Barbara was with them. She knew what John's plans were and tried to intervene."

"We did our best to reach Willem before John did," de Burgh added, "but our timing was off. When we did reach him, John had already left to try and murder you. As I said, it's a good thing Barbara took the precaution of switching the poison out of that bottle, else you'd be a dead man now, Alexander of Gyer."

Alexander met Barbara's timid gaze and shook his head. "I don't know why you finally turned on your brother, Barbara Baldwin, for I know now that you've been at his side throughout these past many years. You have deceived my family and me and have dealt with us falsely. I can only thank God I didn't marry you after all, but for all that I thank you for saving my brother's life and my own. If you have only done something about saving my wife, I will indeed be grateful."

Barbara reddened and turned her face against Jason's shoulder. "I did it for Jason," she whispered.

"Did you?" Alexander gained his feet with Willem's help. "And you love her, do you not, Lord Dunsted? You want her for your wife?"

"You know full well I do."

Alexander's strength was returning rapidly, and he pushed from Willem and stood on his own two feet. He gazed levelly at Jason de Burgh. "Ride to Wellewyn with me now and lend me aid against John Baldwin and I shall place Barbara's hand in yours five days from now. You shall have a wedding feast such as this side of Britain has never before known. Her dowry will be rich and I shall give you, as a wedding gift, that strip of land your people have so long disputed. What say you, de Burgh?''

Jason hugged the breath out of Barbara with one hand and extended his other to Alexander. ''I say yes, Lord Gyer. My men and I are ready to ride even now.''

Lillis leaned farther over the rooftop ledge and strained to see better the flames in the distance.

''I cannot imagine how that fire started,'' she murmured, drawing her cloak more firmly about her shoulders. It was a cold night, and heavily damp, as well; it seemed strange that a fire should have started on a night like this.

It had started four hours earlier, shortly after Aunt Leta and Edyth and the children had left for Gyer, and it had grown quite large now, consuming several of the barns and two nearby fields and threatening to destroy several of the tenant homes, as well. Lillis couldn't help but be reminded of the terrible fire that had occurred at Gyer when she'd been there, and she wished that Alexander were with her now to take charge of the situation. Every man under her roof had been called out to fight the flames save one, whom she had sent full speed to Gyer to request her husband's immediate aid. She hoped Alexander would arrive soon. All would be well once he arrived.

If Willem and the twins had been there, Lillis might have been more confident, but Willem was at Gyer with Alexander and the twins had disappeared. She hadn't seen them since they had finished their morning meal. They hadn't even made an appearance to see Aunt Leta and Edyth and the children, whom they'd known very well were coming for a visit. The unmannerly wretches!

She shivered again and sighed aloud, the warmth of her breath fogging in the cold air. ''I only hope no one will be harmed,'' she said aloud.

Footsteps on the roof caused her to turn her head, and though she could not see who approached her in the darkness she immediately recognized the voice that hailed her.

"Here you are, my lady," John greeted, strolling toward her with ease. "I've been looking everywhere in the castle for you and had begun to worry that you'd somehow slipped away. How fortunate that you should come to the very place where I meant to bring you myself."

Lillis was so surprised to find John Baldwin on her rooftop that for a moment she neither moved nor spoke. He walked right to her, took her hand in a grand gesture and lifted it to his lips, kissing it lightly. The warmth of his mouth on her cold skin brought her back to reality. She jerked her hand from his grasp and gaped at him.

"What are you doing here?" she demanded, still disbelieving that she was actually looking at him.

John smiled at her charmingly. "Come to see you, of course, my dear Lady Gyer. Why else should I come? Certainly not to see the twins." He laughed and moved closer. "But, come, Lillis, it's has been so long since we last saw each other, and you are even more beautiful than I have remembered. Come and let me kiss you."

Lillis's arms reflexively shot out to ward him off and she backed away. "You are not going to kiss me, John Baldwin," she stated firmly, trying to keep the panic out of her voice. "Why have you come here? What do you want?"

He sighed and fell still. "I wish you would not be so cruel to me, my darling, for you must know how very much I want you. But, if you insist that I speak plainly, I shall. I have already told you that I am here because I came to see you. What I want is to make love to you."

Lillis's eyes grew wide. "You've gone mad," she said.

He smiled. "That's not very complimentary to you, my darling."

"Stop this foolishness, John, else I'll scream at the top of my lungs and bring—hundreds—hundreds and hundreds of men running."

He gave a loud, unhappy groan. "Oh, you are not going to be difficult, are you, love? I had hoped you would be more reasonable than this. You'd best accept the fact that I am going to have you, Lillis, one way or another. You can relax and enjoy yourself or you can fight and force me to be unpleasant. I should prefer it that you choose to relax, but either way I will have my own pleasure. And you may scream if you wish. It will do you no good, as you very well know. Every man, woman and child in Wellewyn is busy fighting that fire over there—" he nodded in the direction of the luminous flames "—which my men started to provide a suitable distraction for my plans. No one will hear you, sweeting, and no one will come to rescue you." He began very slowly to approach her again, holding one hand out. "Come to me now, Lillis, and don't fight me. I've no wish to hurt you, and I can promise to give you much greater pleasure than you have ever known before if only you will let me."

Backing away, Lillis cast a glance over one shoulder, looking to the place on the roof where the stairs would lead her into the castle.

"You will never make it, darling," John warned. "You are welcome to try, of course, but you will not make it."

"Listen to me, John," Lillis said reasonably, inching her way toward the stairs, "this is madness. You know I'll not willingly let you rape me, and you also know that Alexander will kill you should he hear that you even approached me in such a lewd manner."

John laughed with disconcerting delight. "You cannot threaten me with your husband's punishments, love. I've no fear of him whatsoever."

"If you leave now, I will forget that you ever came," Lillis went on calmly. "I'll say nothing to Alexander, or to anyone. But you must leave now, John, and you must never, never try such a thing again. You must promise me you will not."

His smile made Lillis shiver with apprehension.

"I'll promise you nothing more than that I am going to possess you fully. You will never be able to tell Alexander anything. He is dead, sweetest heart. Long dead now."

She shook her head. "You're mad," she declared, quite calm. "You lie."

"I do not."

"You're a mad fool," she repeated, growing angry. "I'll believe nothing you say. Alexander is not dead."

"Sweet Lillis," John replied, moving to close the distance between them, "I don't care whether you believe me or no. Alexander died by my own hand only a few hours ago, but that has naught to do with what is about to happen between us."

Too late Lillis made her move toward the stairs, for John leapt and easily caught her.

"No!" she cried, fighting him.

"But yes, my darling," he returned, tumbling her onto the cold, hard rooftop. He straddled her with his legs and held her arms down with both of his hands. "There, that is much better," he said once she was fully beneath him.

Lillis pushed and shoved to no avail. He was not a big man, yet he was certainly stronger than she. "I warn you, John Baldwin, you will regret this."

"Will I? I think, rather, that I shall enjoy it. And you should enjoy it, too, dear lady, for it is the last time you shall ever enjoy a man."

He leaned forward and tried to kiss her, and Lillis, with a sense of total revulsion, managed to loosen one hand and slap him. Only momentarily stunned, John slapped her back, hard, and then sat up a little and grinned at her.

"I'm going to give you one last chance, Lillis, to behave yourself. If you do not, I shall beat you until you are insensible and then I will enjoy your body in peace. Do you understand me?"

Unfortunately she did, and all too well. Her mind desperately grasped for any way of escape.

"I—John, I will let you make love to me if you will take me down to my chamber. I will let you do whatever you wish, only don't rape me here on the rooftop. It is cold and uncomfortable and—please, John. I promise to behave.''

John chuckled and leaned closer so that he could look into her eyes. ''Oh, my darling, you are so clever. We would have had such a good time with each other had I been able to keep you.'' He kissed her mouth lightly, then smiled at her. ''But that is not to be, for you must die, I fear. After I have made love to you, sweet Lillis, I am going to throw you from the parapet. You see? I shall throw you from the same place that your mother threw herself off. Is that not cunning of me?''

Lillis wasn't exactly frightened upon hearing these words, nor did she feel any sense of foreboding. Her own life was of little concern to her, but she would not, could not allow her unborn child to be harmed in any way. ''I'll not let you kill me, John Baldwin,'' she stated.

''No?'' John asked, amused.

''No!'' she shouted, freeing her hand once more. There was little space between her and John and the rooftop, but Lillis made do with what she had. She drew her hand back, fisted it and launched it sharply toward John's nose. The impact was amazing. She could hear the crunch of his bones quite loudly, and when, in shock, he covered his face with his hands, Lillis shoved him from her body and rolled away.

Not looking back, she ran for the stairs. They loomed before her as though in a dream, close enough to see but too far to reach. Mere steps away from them John caught her, throwing her to the roof and turning her beneath him again. He was rough now, and his face, when she saw it, was a picture of rage and pain.

''This is what you are wanting now, my dear,'' he said.

Lillis had never been struck in the face by a man before, but John proceeded to strike her with both fists, pounding her cheeks and teeth and eyes and striking again and again and again until she was stupid from the pain and force.

She had no knowledge of when the pain ceased and the other started. Her brain reeled as though drunk, all her senses were dimmed. Only vaguely did she realize that John was kissing and fondling her. She could hear moaning but didn't particularly know whether it was her own pained voice or his excited one that she heard. When his hands began to pull her skirts up she weakly tried to keep them down, but John wouldn't be deterred, and soon her surcoat was bundled up around her waist.

"Oh, my love, that is so much better, is it not?" she heard him murmur against her face. He was kissing her, wetly, all over her mouth and face so that Lillis was almost grateful for her muddled state. "I'm going to make you feel good, Lillis. So very good. You're going to enjoy this, darling. You want me, do you not? I know you want me."

She was sick and disgusted and prayed desperately for salvation. Alexander would come soon. Someone would come. Soon. She begged God to make it so.

And then, suddenly, Lillis heard several different things all at once. There was a loud commotion on the rooftop and the sound of John swearing aloud. A sharp whistle came from the direction of the stairs and then, strangely enough, a bird's answering call. John swore again and started to climb off Lillis, but before he was fully off a large bird attacked him, and then there was all the furious confusion of wind and flapping wings and feathers.

Though it was quite dark, and though Lillis's eyes were swollen from John's fists, she could still see enough to understand what was happening. A bird was attacking John as ferociously as it would have attacked any prey, and John was shouting and swearing and fighting at it, his arms flailing and his body twisting to escape the creature's fury.

Lillis scooted away from the struggling pair and then quickly, stumblingly, ran toward what she hoped were the stairs. Before she had gained more than a few steps, however, two strong arms came about her waist, lifting her off the ground to stop her.

She struggled and gouged her captor's side with one elbow before she heard him whisper angrily, "Lillis!"

"Hugh!" she cried, turning and throwing her arms around him. "Thank God! Hugh!"

"Hush!" he whispered harshly. "And come with me. You were about to run right off the roof, you foolish female."

He led her toward the stairway, carefully avoiding that area of the rooftop where, in the darkness, John's struggles with the fierce bird loudly continued.

"Here we are, Hugo," Hugh announced quietly, bringing Lillis to a halt. "Light the torch now."

A spurt of flames lit the darkness and then a torch illuminated the area around them, blinding them at first with its brilliance.

"Look!" Hugh pointed. "There's John and Lady. She—she's driven him to the corner of the roof!"

John had indeed stumbled to the edge of the roof, fighting the wild bird unsteadily, stepping back and forth, clearly confused from the savagery of the attack. The falcon swooped down on him again, pecking his eyes with her sharp beak and scratching his face with her claws.

"You must call her off!" Lillis cried. "You must call her off now! Oh, merciful God! No! *No!*"

Even as she spoke, John lost his footing and tumbled headlong over the side of the ledge, his scream and the bird following him all the way down until there was silence.

Lillis screamed with horror and the twins stared in mute shock at the place where John had disappeared.

"Oh, my God!" Lillis sobbed. "He was a terrible man, but he didn't deserve to die like that!"

"Do—do you think he's dead?" Hugh asked.

"I hope so," Hugo replied with equal dismay. "There'll not be much left of him if he isn't. It would be better to be—dead."

"It's terrible! Terrible!" Lillis continued to cry.

Hugo put his arms around her. "He must have been mad," he soothed, patting her back gently. "Don't cry, Lillis. There's nothing we can do now. He's dead. God's toes! Cousin John is dead!" He said it as if he only just understood it.

Hugh collapsed on the stair's top step and put his head in his hands. "God's my life, what a night! If only we'd gotten here sooner."

"Where were you?" Lillis asked, pushing from Hugo's arms and looking from one brother to the next. "Why—you're both covered with blood! What in God's name happened?"

Hugh lifted his head and looked at her. Lillis could see more clearly the bruises and cuts on his face and the bloody gash on one side of his head.

"We were supposed to protect you," he told her. "Barbara sent us a message yesterday telling us to be on guard in case John should come to Wellewyn. She didn't explain anything else, but only said that we should be ready to protect you if he did come. We weren't quite certain what to do, and we didn't want to frighten you for naught, so we spent all of today watching for him."

"And trying to think of what we would do if there was any trouble," Hugo put in.

"Yes, we had no plan formed as to what we would do, exactly. We thought we would wait until he arrived and then think of something."

"But we weren't the only ones doing the watching." Hugo sighed and rubbed his chin, which was beginning to swell and turn blue. "John must have had some of his men staying here at Wellewyn to keep an eye on us, for right after the morning meal when we went to our lookout post we were leapt upon by four men."

"Big men," Hugh added, nodding. "They beat us senseless and then tied us up."

Lillis shuddered at the thought.

"They locked us in a shed," Hugo continued, sliding down the parapet wall until he was sitting on the rooftop. He leaned his head back and closed his tired eyes. "We had the Fiend's own time escaping, and when we finally did we came straight here to find you.

"There was no one below, so we came up to the rooftop and heard you talking to John and trying to fend him off.

We didn't know how to save you and we certainly didn't have much time to figure something out. Setting Lady on him was all we could think of. It's a damned good thing we got our birds from Gyer when we did."

"Better than you even know," Lillis said. "He was going to throw me off the roof after he had raped me, or so he said. You saved my life. I'm so proud of you both, and more grateful than I can ever tell you."

Hugh smiled grimly at her. "Of course we had to save you, Lillis. You cannot think we would have let anything happen to you. The trouble is, what are we going to do now? John may be taken care of, but Wellewyn is filled with his men. Most of them are at the fire, causing it to burn just as fast as everyone else tries to put it out, but soon they're going to come looking for their master and when they find him—"

"We must leave the castle at once," Hugo stated, "and somehow get Lillis to Gyer. Alex will know what to do when we get there."

"That's right," Hugh agreed, struggling to a standing position. "We'll have to sneak some horses from the stables, first, and then—"

The sounds of a loud, violent commotion taking place downstairs made him stop. They looked at one another and listened. There was a great deal of shouting and yelling and clattering. It sounded as though every piece of furniture were being crashed against the walls, and as though every door were being rammed open.

"But why are they destroying everything?" Lillis asked with both fear and concern. There wasn't much furniture at Wellewyn to begin with, and now, from the sounds of things, there wouldn't be any.

Hugo put up one hand to silence her. "Hush!" he whispered. "Listen!"

The voice that sounded over all the noise was a distant rumbling at first, growing louder and closer with each passing second until it turned into a thunderous peal.

"Lillis! Damnation! Where are you? *Lillis!*"

The three standing together on the rooftop of Castle Wellewyn cried out in unison, and bumped into one another in their rush to get down the stairs.

Chapter Twenty-Five

"Darling, you must keep still!"

"Well—ouch!— You're hurting me, Alexander! Ouch! Stop it!"

Alexander sighed and lifted the towel he was cleaning his wife's face with. She lay on the bed where he had placed her, glaring up at him through swollen eyes.

"Is this any way to treat your wife after she's been through such an ordeal? I've no need to be mauled any further this night. John did a perfectly thorough job of it already."

Alexander's expression darkened and he dipped the towel in a nearby bowl of water, squeezing it out afterward as though he were squeezing his dead cousin's neck. "Don't speak that man's name to me ever again, Lillis. The only reason I wish he was still alive is because I should like to have the pleasure of killing him with my bare hands."

Lillis winced when Alexander dabbed the tender area by her left eye. "You don't mean that, do you, Alexander? John—er—your cousin was certainly a bad man, but you'd not have killed him, would you?"

"Yes, I would. And not because of what he did to me, or even for what he did to Willem. He hurt you, Lillis, and any man who hurts you is going to die. Now hold still."

Lillis wisely didn't point out that he was hurting her at that very moment. He was still murderously upset, and she wasn't going to do or say anything to make matters worse.

He was with her and he was alive and well, and she was content.

"The twins were very brave," she whispered, pleased to see Alexander smile a little.

"Yes, they were, were they not?" He chuckled as he remembered the sight that greeted him when he'd reached the bottom of the stairway that led to the roof. One moment he was in a dead panic, searching frantically for his wife, the next he was nearly knocked down by three half-crazed figures who came flying down the stairs, all shouting at him at the same time. "Who would have ever thought that those two fiends would be able to pull off such a feat?" he said with pride. "I suppose I shall have to give them some kind of reward."

Lillis smiled. "Yes, I suppose you shall."

They fell silent, and Alexander began to look grim again as he continued his gentle ministrations. Lillis reached up a hand and tentatively touched his cheek.

"Tell me the truth, Alexander. There are no mirrors here. I am ugly to look at, am I not?"

Alexander shook his head. "That's foolishness, Lillis. You're the most beautiful woman in God's world."

"Not now. My nose must be three times its normal size, and my eyes probably look like those of a frog. You shall have to put a grain sack over my head just to sleep in the same bed with me."

Alexander laughed. "A sack indeed! Your wounds will heal very soon and then you will be more beautiful than before, and well you know it! But if you wish to be reassured, my love, I will gladly do so. And I'll speak the truth to you." He looked into her swollen eyes. "You could be completely bald and have one eye sticking out of the middle of your forehead and I would still love you as much as I ever did, and you would still be the most beautiful woman in the world. And," he added, "if there was only some spot left on your face that wasn't bruised or bleeding, I would kiss it."

Lillis smiled, though the movement made her lips bleed again. "Do you know, Alexander, that is the sweetest thing you've ever said to me? And I feel exactly the same way. I love you just as much as I ever did, even though half your face has turned black."

"Quit smiling or you'll never stop bleeding," he demanded, mopping her lips with the towel again.

She touched his stained chin with her fingertips. "How did you get all black like this, husband?"

"Ink. That's what Barbara used to switch the poison out of the bottle."

"Ink?" Lillis repeated incredulously. "Oh, Alexander, you didn't drink ink, did you?"

"I didn't have much choice," he rejoined grimly. "I can only hope it will wear off in a few days. I suppose I should scrub it with some terrible potion or other. Aunt Leta will probably have a recipe for something particularly vile that will take it off right away."

"I imagine she does," Lillis agreed.

Alexander put the towel down and carefully slid his hands beneath her back. He hugged her tenderly, and Lillis put her own arms around his shoulders and held him in return, savoring the warmth and feeling of him. A minute passed before she said, "Alexander, tell me what's wrong."

He turned his face into the hollow of her neck. "I almost lost you today. I thought I had lost my brother. I thought I was going to die."

"But you did not. None of those things happened."

"But I wasn't able to protect you, Lillis. You nearly died because you were so far away from me and because you wouldn't let me leave more of my men here. Can you imagine how I felt as I rode here this night? Every moment I cursed myself for leaving you here so open and vulnerable."

"You could have left a hundred men here and it wouldn't have made a difference. Every man in Wellewyn was attending the fire. It wouldn't have made a difference."

"It might have."

"No, it wouldn't have. And who is to say John wouldn't have tried to kill me at Gyer? He tried to kill you, and very nearly succeeded."

"That does little to reassure me, wife."

Lillis laughed and stroked his hair. "He's gone and cannot harm us now. We must be thankful to God for all the miracles that have been given us this day. And we must be thankful to Barbara, as well, for it could not have been easy to betray her brother in such a way, after being under his mastery for so many years. She must have been terrified of him to have done all that he made her do in order to further his plans. And yet, she loved him, I think. How will she take the news of his death, I wonder?"

Alexander nestled against the warmth of her body and felt comforted. "That's Jason de Burgh's concern, not mine. He's pacing the great hall wondering what he shall say to her on the morrow. They're going to be married in a few days' time and we'll be rid of Barbara. We're going to give them the finest wedding ever had in Gyer."

"Better than ours?" Lillis teased.

Alexander lifted his head and looked at her, hating anew the bruises that covered her face and wanting to kill John Baldwin all over again.

"Our wedding was less than wonderful, was it not, my love?" He yawned and sat up to take his boots off.

"It was—a wedding," Lillis said.

He laughed. "I suppose that's the most you could say about it. It was, indeed, a wedding." Lying down beside her, he took one of her hands and brought it up to his lips. "I love you, Lillis Ryon, and desire to make you my wife. Will you do me the honor of wedding with me?"

Lillis returned his gaze steadily. "We are already married, Alexander."

He shook his head. "A forced marriage, not a marriage of love. We shall wed again, all anew, and repeat our vows and mean them, with naught between us but love. No land, no relatives, no fighting."

"No captivity?"

"Definitely not. There will be no more guards, and no more locked doors. I want you to be my Lady Gyer in every way, with all the honor and respect and dignity that you deserve. Will you marry me, Lillis?"

Lillis gazed into Alexander's beautiful green eyes with real wonder. How very far they had come from that night when they'd first met, when she had been his prisoner, and he had been her captor.

"There is something I must tell you first, my lord, before I give my answer."

"What is it?"

Lillis reached a hand out to hold one of his; their fingers entwined and Alexander rubbed his thumb gently across her forefinger in a loving caress.

Shyly she said, "I'm with child."

Alexander smiled, beaming down at her. "I know."

"You—know?"

He nodded. "John told me."

"*John* told you?" Her voice was tinged with anger. "That man whose name I am never to speak again *told* you?!"

Alexander could feel his wife's body growing taut beneath him. Shifting his weight atop her a little to keep her down, he did his best to soothe her.

"Well, he didn't exactly tell me, for he wasn't entirely certain himself. He only said that you were very likely pregnant."

"How kind of him!" Lillis said between clenched teeth. "Did he not realize that it is a wife's privilege to inform her husband of her condition?"

"He was about to kill me, dear," her husband noted logically. "I'm sure he didn't care for common courtesies at that moment. But that doesn't matter now. I'm very pleased about the child, love."

Lillis only half heard what Alexander said. "I had meant to surprise you with the news," she told him. "I was going to tell you myself. That rotten, horrible, cruel—" She stopped and looked at him. "Did you say that you are pleased, Alexander?"

He smiled and kissed the tip of her swollen nose. "Very pleased," he said.

Her anger melted away under the tenderness and pride in his gaze.

"Our first child," she whispered.

"The first of many, I hope," he said, covering her belly with his hand. "I'd like to have a dozen children with you, Lillis. I wonder if this one will take after his mother?"

Lillis swallowed loudly. "Alexander, if it is a boy, I should like to name him Jaward, after my father."

Alexander stared at her in disbelief.

"You jest."

She shook her head. "No. I wish to name him Jaward, after my father."

"No," Alexander said angrily, sitting up and away from her. "Absolutely not!"

Lillis looked at him sternly. "I only said I wished to name him Jaward. It is a request, not a demand. Can we not discuss the matter?"

"No!" he shouted. "No son of mine will carry that—that man's name! Don't mention this matter to me again, Lillis. Ever. I shall have the naming of the child." He stood and strode angrily to the window, flinging open the shutters with force.

Disappointment shot keenly through Lillis as she watched her husband's straightened back. She wanted to rage at him, to scream her frustration, but instead she turned on her side, shut her eyes and tried not to cry. She couldn't really blame Alexander for feeling the way he did. There were still so many things he didn't understand, so many things he didn't know about what had happened between their two fathers. He didn't even know the truth about the twins yet! She would be patient. She would speak with him again in the morn and then perhaps—

The bed dipped and Lillis stopped thinking. In another moment she felt Alexander's arms sliding around her waist, pulling her gently up against his chest. He sighed and rested his cheek against the top of her head. "Forgive me. I fear it may take some time for me to cease being so angry with your father, and even more to stop behaving so foolishly. Forgive me."

The tenderness in his voice undid her, and the hot tears made her swollen eyes sting. "It's all right, Alexander. I understand how you feel about him."

He squeezed her. "We'll discuss the matter of the child's name together. I cannot promise that I will agree to Jaward, however."

"I only ask you to consider it," Lillis replied, wiping her tears away. "That's all."

"I'll consider it, I promise."

"Then I will marry you."

She felt him smile against the top of her head. "Will you? Because I'll consider the name?"

She laughed. "Because I love you, and because I believe that you'll try not to tyrannize me so much."

"I have never tyrannized you, madam."

"You are probably the greatest tyrant in all of Christendom, sir."

"You're confusing me with Aunt Leta, dearest."

"Perhaps you're right," Lillis agreed with a laugh.

He gently pressed her onto her back so that he could look into her eyes.

"I'm very happy, Lillis, and so very fortunate. I have you and soon will have our child. I shall thank God every day of my life for giving you to me."

"As I shall thank Him for leading me to you," she said, then added seriously, "Alexander, there are a great many things I must tell you about our families. Things that will not be easy to hear."

Alexander was intrigued. "Truly? I shall prepare myself to hear them, then. But let us wait until the morrow, love. For now I want only to think of you." He very gently kissed her lips. "Does that hurt?" he asked.

"A little," she replied, putting her arms around his neck. "But not terribly. I've missed you so much, Alexander, since that last night we were together. Will you make love to me?"

He grinned at her. "I don't know. Do you happen to have a grain sack handy?"

Lillis gasped and punched him in the side. "You beast!"

Alexander laughed aloud and hugged her. "Calm yourself, woman. You know I only jest."

"You had best prove it, then, my lord."

"Gladly," Alexander replied, and happily set out to do her bidding.

*   *   *   *   *

Bestselling Author

Jasmine Cresswell

May 1995 brings you face-to-face with her latest thrilling adventure

Desires & Deceptions

Will the real Claire Campbell please stand up?
Missing for over seven years, Claire's family has
only one year left to declare her legally dead and
claim her substantial fortune—that is, until a woman
appears on the scene alleging to be the missing
heiress. Will DNA testing solve the dilemma? Do
old family secrets still have the power to decide
who lives and dies, suffers or prospers, loves or
hates? Only Claire knows for sure.

Harlequin® Historical

Ruth Langan is at it again!

Don't miss this award-winning author's
return to Scotland
with her new prequel titles to

THE HIGHLAND SERIES

Look for #269 HIGHLAND HEAVEN, the sequel to THE HIGHLANDER,
coming from Harlequin Historicals in May 1995.

If you missed THE HIGHLANDER, you can still order it
from the address below.

Harlequin® Historical

WOMEN OF THE WEST

Exciting stories of the old West and the women whose dreams
and passions shaped a new land!

Join Harlequin Historicals every month as we bring you
these unforgettable tales.

May 1995 #270—**JUSTIN'S BRIDE**
Susan Macias w/a Susan Mallery

June 1995 #273—**SADDLE THE WIND**
Pat Tracy

July 1995 #277—**ADDIE'S LAMENT**
DeLoras Scott

August 1995 #279—**TRUSTING SARAH**
Cassandra Austin

September 1995 #286—**CECILIA AND THE STRANGER**
Liz Ireland

October 1995 #288—**SAINT OR SINNER**
Cheryl St.John

November 1995 #294—**LYDIA**
Elizabeth Lane

Don't miss any of our Women of the West!

HARLEQUIN®

PRESENTS
RELUCTANT BRIDEGROOMS

Two beautiful brides, two unforgettable romances...
two men running for their lives....

My Lady Love, by Paula Marshall, introduces
Charles, Viscount Halstead, who lost his memory
and found himself employed as a stableboy by the
untouchable Nell Tallboys, Countess Malplaquet.
But Nell didn't consider Charles untouchable—
not at all!

Darling Amazon, by Sylvia Andrew, is the story of
a spurious engagement between Julia Marchant
and Hugo, marquess of Rostherne—an engagement
that gets out of hand and just may lead Hugo to
the altar after all!

Enjoy two madcap Regency weddings this May,
wherever Harlequin books are sold.

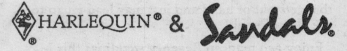

Fifty red-blooded, white-hot, true-blue hunks
from every State in the Union!

Look for MEN MADE IN AMERICA! Written by some
of our most popular authors, these stories feature some
of the strongest, sexiest men, each from a different state
in the union!

Two titles available every month at your favorite
retail outlet.

In April, look for:

FOR THE LOVE OF MIKE
by Candace Schuler (Texas)
THE DEVLIN DARE
by Cathy Thacker (Virginia)

In May, look for:

A TIME AND A SEASON
by Curtiss Ann Matlock (Oklahoma)
SPECIAL TOUCHES
by Sharon Brondos (Wyoming)

You won't be able to resist MEN MADE IN AMERICA!

HARLEQUIN®

Don't miss these Harlequin favorites by some of our most distinguished authors!
And now, you can receive a discount by ordering two or more titles!

HT #25607	PLAIN JANE'S MAN by Kristine Rolofson	$2.99 U.S./$3.50 CAN.	☐
HT #25616	THE BOUNTY HUNTER by Vicki Lewis Thompson	$2.99 U.S./$3.50 CAN.	☐
HP #11674	THE CRUELLEST LIE by Susan Napier	$2.99 U.S./$3.50 CAN.	☐
HP #11699	ISLAND ENCHANTMENT by Robyn Donald	$2.99 U.S./$3.50 CAN.	☐
HR #03268	THE BAD PENNY by Susan Fox	$2.99	☐
HR #03303	BABY MAKES THREE by Emma Goldrick	$2.99	☐
HS #70570	REUNITED by Evelyn A. Crowe	$3.50	☐
HS #70611	ALESSANDRA & THE ARCHANGEL by Judith Arnold	$3.50 U.S./$3.99 CAN.	☐
HI #22291	CRIMSON NIGHTMARE by Patricia Rosemoor	$2.99 U.S./$3.50 CAN.	☐
HAR #16549	THE WEDDING GAMBLE by Muriel Jensen	$3.50 U.S./$3.99 CAN.	☐
HAR #16558	QUINN'S WAY by Rebecca Flanders	$3.50 U.S./$3.99 CAN.	☐
HH #28802	COUNTERFEIT LAIRD by Erin Yorke	$3.99	☐
HH #28824	A WARRIOR'S WAY by Margaret Moore	$3.99 U.S./$4.50 CAN.	☐

(limited quantities available on certain titles)

	AMOUNT	$
DEDUCT:	**10% DISCOUNT FOR 2+ BOOKS**	$
ADD:	**POSTAGE & HANDLING**	$
	($1.00 for one book, 50¢ for each additional)	
	APPLICABLE TAXES*	$_____
	TOTAL PAYABLE	$_____
	(check or money order—please do not send cash)	

To order, complete this form and send it, along with a check or money order for the total above, payable to Harlequin Books, to: **In the U.S.:** 3010 Walden Avenue, P.O. Box 9047, Buffalo, NY 14269-9047; **In Canada:** P.O. Box 613, Fort Erie, Ontario, L2A 5X3.

Name: _____

Address: _____ City: _____

State/Prov.: _____ Zip/Postal Code: _____

*New York residents remit applicable sales taxes.
Canadian residents remit applicable GST and provincial taxes.

HBACK-AJ2